W9-DAN-606

THE NIGHT IS FOREVER

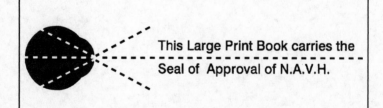

THE NIGHT IS FOREVER

HEATHER GRAHAM

THORNDIKE PRESS
A part of Gale, Cengage Learning

GALE
CENGAGE Learning·

Detroit • New York • San Francisco • New Haven, Conn • Waterville, Maine • London

GALE
CENGAGE Learning

LIBRARY OF CONGRESS CATALOGING-IN-PUBLICATION DATA

Graham, Heather.
  The Night is Forever / By Heather Graham. — Large Print edition.
    pages cm. — (Krewe of Hunters Series) (Thorndike Press Large Print Core)
    ISBN 978-1-4104-6142-1 (hardcover) — ISBN 1-4104-6142-4 (hardcover)
  1. Tennessee—Fiction. 2. Large type books. I. Title.
PS3557.R198N544 2013
813'.54—dc23   2013032196

Published in 2013 by arrangement with Harlequin Books S.A.

Dedicated with love to Al Perry —
for his patience — no matter what
we drag him into!

And especially for
Bryee-Annon Victoria Pozzessere,
my daughter, who first showed
me the wonders of Nashville
and Tennessee and introduced
me to something equally
wonderful — horse therapy.

Love you so much, baby!

PROLOGUE

There he was, Marcus Danby, dead in the ravine.

His eyes were open and he stared up at heaven. His limbs were twisted at odd angles, making him look like an image created by a mad artist.

"Marcus!" Olivia Gordon cried his name as she dismounted and swiftly scampered down the rocks to his side. Like an idiot, she hunkered down by him, touching him, speaking, praying that somehow he was still alive as he lay there.

But, of course, he wasn't. She studied his face — weathered, worn, beautiful with character — and silent tears slid down her cheeks.

"Marcus," she whispered, closing his eyes. Maybe it was the wrong thing to do — maybe the medical examiner needed to see him exactly as he'd been found. But she wasn't leaving him now and she couldn't bear to see his eyes open. He'd been staring up at the heavens, she thought. Staring up at the sky above him.

Ironically, the sky was exceptionally beautiful tonight. It was one of those twilights when the moon rose before the sun set completely, and as the sun continued its fall, sinking lower and lower into the horizon, a soft, opaque glow seemed to settle over the landscape. The hills here, just outside Nashville, Tennessee, appeared to be part of some kind of fairy-tale kingdom. Their rich shades of autumn — the gold, orange and crimson leaves on the trees — highlighted the emerald-green grasses. A slight coolness touched the air, making it clear and comfortable to breathe.

The sky and the landscape were what Marcus had seen as he died, Olivia reminded herself. It was why Marcus had loved this area so much, this place where he'd been born. Maybe there was something fitting in that, something poetic.

And yet . . . No question, Marcus had loved this countryside. He'd known it intimately. For that very reason, it seemed impossible that he'd fallen into this rocky ravine when he'd followed these same paths, on foot or on horseback, almost every day of his life.

Olivia heard Shiloh paw the ground. She looked up at her horse; he was obviously sensing her emotions, the change in her energy.

"Easy, boy, easy," Olivia said softly. "We have to wait here." Fresh tears stung her eyes and cascaded down her cheeks. She wanted to rise up and throw her arms around Shiloh's neck, feel the warmth of this living creature.

That, she knew, would be life-affirming.

Like all the animals at the Horse Farm — the therapy center Marcus Danby had founded and where Olivia worked — Shiloh was a rescue horse. Near starvation, he'd been found in the Florida Redlands. Animal activists from the state had arranged his transport to the Nashville area and there was something about him that had made him special to Olivia from the first time she'd seen him. He'd been a pile of bones, wild and terrified of people; he'd tried, more than once, to run her into a building to get her off his back. While the focus of the Horse Farm was teaching people to trust again — through their relationships with animals — Shiloh was, to Olivia, one of her best success stories.

Marcus had always told her that what she'd done with Shiloh was impressive, but what she managed with people was equally beautiful.

"Oh, Marcus, what did you do?" she whispered. He'd probably been missing long before any of them realized he was gone, because Marcus kept no set hours, didn't see patients and came and went as he chose. He'd founded the Horse Farm; it was his passion and his life. But while he loved to make sudden appearances and engage with patients, he did so in his own time and on his own terms. He'd been a wreck of a man himself — bipolar, an addict, homeless and an ex-con — when he'd found a horse on the small farm he'd, for some reason, been left through a family inheritance. Like Shiloh, the animal had been starved and beaten by a cruel master and was terrified. In earning the horse's trust and love, Marcus had learned to care about himself. He'd told Olivia once that he'd been so afraid something horrible would happen to the horse without him, he'd become determined to live.

In saving that horse, Marcus had saved himself. It wasn't that he hadn't grown up around animals; he had. His father had raised some of the finest racing horses in Tennessee. Maybe because he'd had money as a child, Marcus had known that happiness had nothing to do with wealth. When he inherited the family land, he had no interest in racehorses. He cared about people — damaged people. He'd been miraculously fixed by a horse and he went on to find out how to help others in the same way.

Olivia adored Marcus.

Had adored him, she told herself. No, she did adore him. All that he'd been and all that he'd taught her would stay with her forever.

He'd lived in a small house on the property, about a quarter mile from the stables, and the staff at the Horse Farm only knew he was gone because Sammy, his golden retriever — another rescue animal — had come to the stables, wet, tail between his legs, anxious. He'd been limping because he'd managed to gash his left leg quite badly.

Aaron Bentley, managing director of the Horse Farm, had tried to believe that Marcus had driven somewhere and Sammy had hurt himself trying to catch up with him.

But Marcus hadn't driven anywhere — not on his own, anyway. His old Ford pickup was still in the driveway. And Olivia knew Marcus would've died before allowing any harm to come to his beloved Sammy.

11

So they'd all become extremely worried. Aaron had called in the local authorities and they'd set up a search; Olivia had the backwoods acreage, while others had been assigned the pond area, the pastures and the adjoining farms, businesses and residences.

They had now been out searching for hours in their designated areas. She and Aaron, plus the other two therapists from the Horse Farm — Mason Garlano and Mariah Naughton. As well, the stable bosses, Drew Dicksen and Sydney Roux, had joined the search. And so had Deputy Sheriff Vine and his partner, Jimmy Callahan. Only Sandra Cheever — known as Mama Cheever — the house manager for the offices, had remained behind. There were miles of pastureland and forest out there — enough to keep them riding and searching for many more hours. But dusk seemed to be coming on fast.

Twilight. Twilight in these hills.

A dangerous time up here — if you didn't know your way.

But Marcus hadn't fallen in the twilight. He'd had his accident, if accident it was, in the brightness of day. . . .

He was cold now, stone cold. Olivia didn't have many skills in forensics, but she was certain that he'd been here for some time. He hadn't fallen in the dusk — a time when a tourist might become disoriented among the rolling hills, forested slopes and rocky dips.

This time of day frightened many people here. Kids told scary tales over campfires about the Civil War soldiers who continued to haunt the rugged terrain. Marcus had loved the legends; he'd once told her with a wink that the soldiers were his friends. In fact, he'd confided that Brigadier General Rufus Cunningham had been a big help when he'd decided to clean up — but he'd hoped his conversations with the long-dead man might cease once he was off the rum and heroin.

She was down in a ravine with a dead man who'd been a mentor to her, and it was getting dark. This wasn't the time to mourn him. Only a few minutes had ticked by since she'd found him. There was no point in wishing him alive. Death was unmistakable.

She dug into her pocket for her cell phone, praying it would work. Satellite communication here wasn't always the best.

But she called Aaron and he answered on the second ring. She got the words out, hard as they were, and told him she'd found

Marcus, explaining that he appeared to have fallen.

"CPR. Do artificial respiration," Aaron said urgently.

Olivia looked at Marcus. She had truly loved the man.

He was dead. He was cold; he was gone.

There was no way she was attempting artificial respiration.

"He's dead, Aaron."

"You can't be sure!"

"Aaron, I'm sure. I am not trying artificial respiration. Get the officers to this location. Please."

She hung up. And then she waited.

Full darkness was coming, and coming soon. She felt that she had to keep her hand on Marcus's shoulder, that she had to be there with him. She hated that he'd been alone when he died.

She hated that she was alone now and that the last mauve of twilight was turning to gray and would soon become black.

She always rode with a flashlight, but it was at the top of the ravine in the bag she'd attached to her saddle.

She looked up as Shiloh whinnied. The horse pranced nervously.

"Don't you leave me, boy!" she called to him. "It's all right —"

She broke off in midsentence.

She hadn't actually grown up here — not right here, about twenty miles west of Nashville off I-40 — but she'd grown up in the city. She'd often come out to her uncle's small ranch during her lifetime. She knew the legends of the area.

Many times, on foggy nights, she'd imagined that she'd seen *them* and seen *him.* In the mists that covered the hills, she'd seen the Rebel soldiers, cast from Nashville in 1862, trying to fight their way back, retreating in the darkness of night. She'd imagined the bloodstained battlefields; she'd heard the cries of wounded and dying soldiers.

She'd imagined seeing Brigadier General Rufus Cunningham, tall and straight and ever sorrowful at the death toll of the war as he watched his threadbare and beaten men ride by.

But she'd never seen him so damned clearly.

There, just above her, his white warhorse, Loki, stood feet from her own nervous Shiloh. The general stared down at her with sorrow and concern. He looked around as if he'd appointed himself her guardian.

For a moment, she almost felt there was something malignant nearby, some evil that crept toward her in the night. . . . Was that why the general was there? To protect her?

Then she felt as if a cold wind settled near her. She felt something . . . like a touch on her shoulder.

She turned.

There was Marcus Danby. Watching her.

She blinked; she looked down.

Marcus was dead on the ground before her.

Ghosts.

Her family was known for eccentricity, for seeing things, for knowing when it was going to rain, for a sense of foreboding when there was danger.

Her family!

Not *her*!

And she was looking up at a Civil War general and turning to see that the dead man before her was touching her shoulder from behind. . . .

She'd never thought of herself as a coward.

But she was!

"Liv," Marcus said. "Liv . . . I'm dead. Help me. I didn't slide back into drugs — I didn't! And it wasn't an accident. I was killed, Liv. It was murder. Help me!"

A strangled-sounding scream escaped her lips; she heard that much.

Then she keeled over on top of Marcus Danby's body in a dead faint.

1

The meeting Dustin Blake had been asked to attend was being held at the General Bixby Tavern, just off the I-95 South exit in northern Virginia.

Dustin knew it well. He'd often stopped there when he was a kid and his parents had taken him to D.C. — a place they'd both loved. Being historians, they would have lived at the Smithsonian if they could. At the time, he'd thought that the tavern's owners had hired an actor to portray General Bixby. Bixby had been kind to him and full of information.

Dustin remembered being humiliated and hurt, as only a kid could be, when he'd discovered that there was no actor and his parents were concerned about his invention of imaginary friends. Then, of course, he'd disturbed them both by knowing things only the general — or a much older person, and an expert on the Civil War — would know.

That had led to a number of sessions with a psychiatrist.

Dustin had then made the sage decision to agree that General Bixby was an imaginary friend. That had brought about deep thought on the part of his parents — and it had also brought about his sister. His extremely academic parents had worried that an only child might be given to such flights of fancy because he was lonely. So they'd set forth to add to their family.

That was all right. He loved his sister.

He pulled off the interstate and took an exit that led nowhere except Old Tavern Road. Soon he pulled his black SUV into the lot at the tavern and parked. For a moment, he sat and stared at the building.

What was now the General Bixby Tavern had actually been built during the American Revolution and been called the Wayfarer's Inn. During the Civil War, it had been renamed for the gallant Union general — the kind "imaginary friend" who had, while he was alive, braved heavy artillery to save both Union and Confederate soldiers. This was when a fire had broken out in the nearby forest. While many a leader might have sat atop his horse far from the carnage, Bixby had ridden right into the inferno. Wounded after dragging at least twenty injured men from the disaster, he'd been brought to the tavern where he'd died, pleading that the nation settle its differences and find peace.

He really was a fine old gentleman. Dustin knew that well.

He exited the car and headed up the old wooden steps to the broad porch that wrapped around the tavern. This many years later, the tavern was still basically in the wilderness — the closest town being Fredericksburg. Winter was approaching and there was a little coolness in the air, heightened by the thickness of the woods around them. Only its historic importance, and the plethora of "ghost hunters," kept it from falling into ruin.

When Dustin stepped inside the dim tavern, he blinked at the change of light. He wondered instantly if the meeting had been planned so he'd have a few seconds of disorientation — a time during which he might be observed and not observe in return.

As his eyes adjusted, he saw General Bixby seated at the bar. The general nodded gravely at Dustin, indicating a group across the room.

Dustin nodded in return, then moved toward the others. He saw David Caswell stand; he'd been sitting at a corner booth. Caswell wasn't alone. There were two other men with him. One was dark-haired with Native American ancestry apparent in a strong face. The other was light-skinned and light-haired. When they, too, stood to meet him, he saw that they were both tall and fit. And both were wearing casual suits. Not the usual feds — if that was what they were.

"Dustin!" David Caswell said. The pleasure of his greeting seemed sincere.

"Good to see you," Dustin greeted David, shaking his hand. He glanced at the other two men and waited.

"I'd like you to meet Jackson Crow and Malachi Gordon," David turned. "Jackson, Malachi, Special Agent Dustin Blake. When I first started with the police force in Savannah, Dustin and I were partners. He's the best — and rare in his abilities."

"Thank you for coming," Jackson said.

The men took their seats again. They studied him, and he returned their stare.

So the dark-haired man was the famous — or infamous — Jackson Crow.

"How do you like being with the feds, Mr. Blake?" Crow asked him.

"How do I like it? Just fine," Dustin said. And it *was* fine. He wasn't sure what he felt about being there today, however. There'd been a time when he'd wanted nothing more than to be assigned to one of Crow's "special" units. Now . . . he wasn't so sure.

In all honesty — and he didn't know if it was simply self-assurance or something less commendable — he'd expected to receive a good assignment when he'd graduated from the academy. Whatever that might be. And he'd gotten a good assignment. He worked with a group of four consultants sent on diverse cases when violent crime crossed state lines.

"You enjoy working with your team?" Crow asked. Was it just a polite question?

"Yeah, I do. My coworkers are good, savvy, personable and experienced. I work with one guy, Grant Shelby, who's six foot seven, nearly three hundred pounds of lean, mean muscle, with almost computer-powered intelligence. He's pretty good to have around in a hostile situation. And Cindy Greenstreet had the highest test scores in the past decade. I also work with Jerry Gunter — you might have heard the name. He used to be a mixed-martial-arts champ before entering the academy. He's pretty good to have around in a pinch, as well. If you've called me here, I'm sure you've read up on me, so you know that when I joined the bureau, I didn't start out as a kid but came in with a lot of experience, both in combat and law enforcement."

Crow nodded and Dustin realized that he'd known all this. Dustin's FBI unit was smart and tough — they'd been put together to get in and get the job done.

"Good assignment," Crow said with a nod.

"Yeah." As he'd told them, Dustin hadn't come into the academy as a fresh-faced twenty-something grad. Before he'd gone to college, he'd participated as a witness in a case involving a duo of oddly matched serial killers. From there, he'd gone into the military, and after the marines he'd gone into police work. He hadn't exactly entered the department immediately; there'd been a year when he'd been in total denial about himself and his "unusual" abilities — and about the heinous things men seemed willing to do to their fellows. He'd more or less walked into the wilderness. Actually, it hadn't been that dramatic. He'd taken a job as a forest ranger in the Everglades — except that he'd been led to bodies in giant oilcans and he'd realized it was time to move his efforts in the best possible direction. There were certain things a man couldn't escape — and his own nature was one of them.

22

So he'd decided to apply to the academy.

"You know all about me," Dustin said. "Why are we meeting?"

David looked at Jackson Crow and shrugged.

"What do you know about the Krewes?" This time, it was Malachi Gordon who spoke. Dustin knew his name; he was a recent graduate of the academy. He'd come into the bureau after working a case in Savannah.

Dustin leaned back. "I've read about what happened in Savannah," he told Malachi. "You know I worked with David so, of course, the beautiful city of Savannah is near and dear to my heart. In fact, I was somewhat surprised that my unit *wasn't* assigned to that case, but apparently, things were already being taken care of. And, to the best of my knowledge, that case has been cleared, the paperwork wrapped up and the feds are long gone from Savannah. Having worked there, I thought I might be of some help, but . . ."

He paused and grinned sheepishly at David. "It seems like you all did just fine without me."

"I'm sure you would've been an asset," Malachi murmured.

Dustin looked curiously at the other man.

"Thanks, but as I said — seems like you had it covered."

"That was then — and we did have it covered. However, although the Krewes are growing, there are never enough of us, and we're always looking for the right people," Crow told him. "Would you be interested in seeing how you work out with one of our units?"

Dustin smiled. That was straightforward. "I initially asked about applying to one of your units. They told me there was no application process. You formed your own units."

"That's true," Crow said. "And I wish I'd known about you earlier. David was talking to Malachi about you, and then Malachi talked to me. So, yes, I looked you up and pulled strings to get all the information I could on you. Thus far, each recruit has worked out. We're . . . careful in the people we approach. We have to be."

"Because you all have special talents, I take it?" Dustin asked. "And, of course, because all the other agents like to call the units ghost hunters and rib you all about it. But really, they're all envious of your record."

"Detective Caswell has told us that working with you was like —"

24

"Like working with me," Malachi Gordon cut in. "David and I were together in New Orleans," he explained.

"I see," Dustin said.

"Are you a candidate, Mr. Blake?" Crow asked him.

Dustin lowered his head, hiding a smile. He looked back at Crow. "Well, let me put it this way — if you haven't met him yet, I'd be glad to introduce you to General Bixby. He's sitting at the bar right now, next to the man in the jeans and Alice Cooper T-shirt."

That brought a grin to Crow's face. Dustin hadn't been sure the man was really capable of a smile.

"We haven't met formally, no, but we've been aware of his presence."

"I wasn't sure if I was being tested or not." Dustin leaned forward, resting his elbows on the table as he looked at Jackson Crow, then Dustin and finally the third man, Malachi Gordon.

"Why now?" he asked.

It was Gordon who answered him. "You're from Nashville," he said.

Dustin thought quickly. He was privy to law-enforcement reports daily. He hadn't heard anything about a kidnapping or murder in the city of Nashville.

"I am from Nashville," he said, frowning. "But I've been gone for a long time."

"You go back often enough, don't you?"

He did, except that he hadn't been there in a while. His academic parents were living in London. His little sister, Rayna, had grown up to be a country music singer. But she'd been on tour for the past year. He'd caught up with her — and his folks — for a few days in London earlier in the summer.

"Yes, but I haven't been back in about a year," he said.

"That's not too long," David said. "Have you ever heard of a man named Marcus Danby?" Malachi Gordon asked him.

"Marcus Danby." Dustin repeated slowly. The name was familiar. "Of course. Yes," he said. "He founded a therapy center. He brings in clients — patients — to work with horses. Or dogs, sometimes. He was the black sheep of a very elite family, wound up addicted to everything known to man. He did time, but he was the last living member of his family and inherited property. He also changed his ways. The Horse Farm is extremely well-respected."

"Danby is dead," Gordon said abruptly.

"I'm sorry to hear that. How did he die?"

"Fell into a ravine," Gordon told him. "He was buried two days ago but the autopsy report was just released. He had drugs in his system."

"That's a pity. The man must've been clean for at least twenty years," Dustin said. "What does this —"

"Some people close to him don't believe what they're hearing. We'd like you to investigate," Jackson Crow broke in.

"You don't believe it was a fall — or you don't believe he was on drugs?"

"Neither," Malachi replied.

"Are the police suspicious?" Dustin asked.

"No." Crow shook his head.

"Then I don't really understand —"

"Special Agent Blake, we often find ourselves slipping in when local law enforcement doesn't see an immediate problem," Crow said.

"I see."

Malachi Gordon told him, "We'd like you to go in as a patient."

"As a *patient.* You want me to go in as a patient and investigate an accident brought on by substance abuse when no one believes it might have been anything other than it appeared?"

"We have more than a suspicion that he was murdered," Malachi said bluntly.

Dustin stared at him. "How? Why? I'm in the bureau. I know how it works. We're usually called in when there's a suspicion that a serial killer is at large or when a killer is crossing state lines."

"Agent Blake," Jackson Crow began. "We move in on cases when we're afraid the truth may never be known because of unusual circumstances. We don't go barging in as a unit. We send one or two people and they assess the situation for us."

Dustin was surprised and, he had to admit, disappointed. This didn't sound like a case that was worthy of the Krewe.

The units had handled many truly unique cases. The sad demise of a man, even a black sheep who'd changed his own life and created a lifesaving enterprise — just didn't sound like the kind of puzzle that desperately needed to be solved.

He shook his head, baffled. "I need more than you're giving me. Yes, I'm interested in working with a unit. As you're well aware, a man can grow weary of finding excuses for knowing what he shouldn't because he's managed to have a conversation with someone who's dead. And can I go in easily? Yes. The Horse Farm is about twenty miles outside the city, but I'd have to go in as myself because I do have friends in the area. But, God knows, that could be easy. Enough people in law enforcement crack — that's a plausible reason. But I don't understand how this even came to your attention."

"My cousin called me, Blake," Malachi Gordon said. "She works at the Horse Farm and she's convinced that Marcus Danby was murdered."

Great. Someone's relative was upset.

Still . . .

It was an invitation to get a foot in the door with Jackson Crow and one of his Krewe units.

But if he was stepping in just because someone's relative couldn't accept the harsh fact that even the *strongest* person sometimes failed . . .

That wouldn't bode so well.

"Why?" he asked Malachi. "Why is your cousin convinced that Marcus Danby met with foul play?"

"Because, Special Agent Blake, Marcus Danby told her that he was murdered."

"I don't get this horse-assisted therapy," Joey Walters told Olivia as they walked around inside the pasture. "Unless," he said, flashing her a belligerent glance, "it's because our —" He hesitated a minute. She knew the word *folks* had been on his tongue. But he didn't have folks anymore. "— our *guardians* think we're as stupid as horses

29

and that they'll somehow fix us? The dumb leading the dumber?"

Olivia lowered her head, smiling, before she looked back at Joey. "Whatever makes you think horses are stupid?" she asked. She was glad to be working. They'd all taken a few days off for Marcus's funeral, but now they were back.

And she was *especially* glad to be working because her mind kept racing in denial regarding the autopsy reports.

"They're not smart — they'll eat themselves to death if you let them," Joey muttered.

"Horses have no hidden agenda," she said. "They have their boundaries, just as we have ours. And for your information, Mr. Walters, horse therapy works well for those who tend to intellectualize everything. You can't bully a horse. A horse can learn to trust you, but he or she requires *you* to be trustworthy, as well."

As if to emphasize her words, Trickster, the twenty-year-old mare she was using with Joey that afternoon, nudged him in the back.

"Hey!" Joey said. But he turned and looked at Trickster. The mare snorted and shook her head, looking back at Joey.

It was a simple exchange — very simple. But Olivia saw something in Joey's expression and the smile that touched his face. He might be telling her it was all a bunch of bull, but he already cared about Trickster and it was only their second time out.

"You weren't paying attention to her," Olivia said. "You brought her out here and then paid no attention to her. She wants to be noticed. She wants you to remember that you came to her."

"Technically, *you* brought her out here."

"Yes, but you brushed her and talked to her and started walking with her. She wants your attention."

"You taught me that we learn about *our* boundaries through horses, as well. Most of the time, a horse will want to be in control. Isn't that what you said? Not to let the horse push you around. She just shoved me!"

"Something else to learn, Joey," Olivia told him. "Trickster does care about you. She nudged you to get some affection back. You can maintain control — *and* give her affection. Life is like that, Joey. You can love people — but you can maintain your own thoughts and opinions, as well."

Joey's smile deepened. He stroked the horse's cream-colored neck, and Trickster clearly enjoyed his touch.

But then Joey stepped away. "I'll get attached to her — and then have to leave her, too," he said. "I'll be alone again, like after my parents died."

"Your parents would never have left you on purpose, Joey. And Trickster won't leave. You'll move on, but you can always come back and see her."

"Everybody leaves," he said sharply.

Joey had been sent to the Horse Farm because his parents were both killed in an automobile accident. At first, he'd been quiet, grieving, uncommunicative, his uncle had told them. Then he'd begun acting out. An athlete, he'd never been into drinking or drugs.

That had changed.

After his uncle had picked him up at a police station in Sarasota, their hometown, he'd begun to look for help. Joey was enrolled at Parsonage House about ten miles from the Horse Farm. The facility offered horse therapy to their "students."

"Joey, I'm sorry about your parents. It was tragic and unjust. But like I said, you have to realize that they didn't desert you, they loved you."

"It's not fair!"

"No. Life isn't fair," she said quietly. "We learn to cope with it the best we can." She paused and walked over to stroke Trickster's forelock. "Look at Trickster, for example.

She was a racehorse once upon a time, Joey. She was destined for greatness. Then a jockey whipped her into frenzy and she broke a leg — and she was worthless to the man who owned her. Instead of being grateful for the races she'd won and the money she'd made for him, his owner planned on having her euthanized. But —"

Her voice broke, which surprised her. She believed she'd accepted that Marcus was dead. She hadn't "seen" him since his death, and she and the rest of the employees at the Horse Farm were moving forward with the work Marcus had deemed so important.

"But?" Joey asked, puzzled.

"But Marcus heard about Trickster, and he bought her — offering her owner more money than the glue factory. He brought her out here, cared for her, and now she's beautiful, as you can see."

"They were going to make glue out of her?" Joey demanded, horrified.

"What matters is that she's here now. And she knows we love her. It took a while, because she was just thrown out in a pasture and allowed to starve, living in constant pain, before Marcus rescued her."

"But Marcus didn't stay with her," Joey pointed out.

"Marcus died, Joey. But he left her in the care of people who would continue to love her."

Joey took a deep breath and ripped out a strand of grass to chew on. He looked across the landscape and said, "I shouldn't have made life so miserable for my uncle, huh?"

"He was only miserable because he loves you. And I don't think he's miserable anymore because he knows you really do want to live a productive life. You just need to come to terms with what happened."

He shrugged. At sixteen, he was a tall boy, a good-looking kid in great physical condition. He turned to her with one of his rakish smiles. "You like me, huh?"

"Of course I like you," she told him.

His grin broadened. "I like you, too. But how I know you like me is that you've forgotten the time."

Olivia glanced quickly at her watch. His hour was up; it had been for the past ten minutes. He'd been a tough case to crack and she'd felt deeply for him. "Don't get ideas, kid," she said. "I'm your therapist."

"But you're cute, too."

"Great. Now let's head back."

"I can come and see Trickster when I'm older. Old enough to be a lot cooler in your eyes."

"Joey! Cut it out. You're just saying that to get a reaction out of me and you're not going to. I'm your therapist. And you're never going to be older than I am and we're never going to date."

"Wow. That life-not-being-fair thing is harsh!" he said. But he was still grinning. Then his grin faded. "They're talking about Marcus, you know. There's a rumor that he went back on drugs. That they found heroin in his system when they did the autopsy."

Olivia felt her back stiffen. "Marcus wasn't doing drugs," she said.

"So, it's a lie?"

She winced. It wasn't a lie. But it was something that, so far, wasn't common knowledge, even though the medical examiner had informed the staff at the Horse Farm. She'd assumed that unless an investigative reporter actually looked into Marcus's death, no one would know it was true. And yet, rumors were obviously running rampant.

"I heard there were drugs in his system," Joey said again.

"I knew Marcus, Joey. If there *were* drugs in his system, they weren't there because he voluntarily took them."

"You think he was tricked?" Joey asked.

"I don't know what to think yet."

"Wow. The plot thickens!" Joey said excitedly. "What if . . . wow. What if someone did drug him because they wanted him to die? Or what if he was pushed?"

"Joey, you're talking about someone who meant a lot to me."

"Oh, I'm sorry, Liv, really." Joey spoke with sincerity and she believed him. "It's just that . . . well, we don't have radios or TVs or the internet where I'm living right now. I'm embarrassed. I heard about this, and it was more interesting to think about that than . . . well, my own recovery, I guess," he finished lamely.

"It's okay. I'm not angry with you."

"Scary, though, huh? I mean, this place is here for therapy. Supposedly, working with animals saved Marcus Danby's life. If he wound up going back on drugs . . . well, it doesn't say much for therapy."

"No, it doesn't," Olivia agreed.

She looked toward the pastures at the Horse Farm. She hadn't seen Marcus again — or rather, hadn't seen his ghost. Had she *imagined* that she'd seen him? Did they — she and her cousin, Malachi — share a real gift? Or did they just imagine things, see them in their minds?

Uncertain, and unhappy with the official explanation, she'd called Malachi. But the

36

results of the autopsy had just arrived that morning. She needed to call him again. He'd promised her he'd try to arrange an investigation, but explained that he had to tread carefully; he couldn't come in officially unless invited. And because people knew he was her cousin, his arrival might give the appearance that the feds were intruding — or that she and the Horse Farm were receiving special treatment. But he'd said he'd figure something out.

Apparently, there was a government agent coming in as a client. A "burnout," someone had called him. Was he Malachi's answer to her request?

"Olivia?" Joey said.

"Yeah?" She tried to smile, realizing she'd been deep in thought and that he'd been watching her.

"I'm really, really sorry. I think this place is wonderful," Joey told her earnestly.

"Thanks, Joey."

"You all might have saved my life," he said. "It works if you work it. You're worth it, so work it!"

"Exactly," she said.

He nodded. She really did like the kid. Especially when he realized, as he occasionally did, that he *was* a kid.

"Tell Trickster we're going in," Olivia

instructed him.

Joey turned and stroked the horse's fore-head. "You are beautiful, Trickster," he whispered, then gazed up at Olivia. "Do I get to ride?" he asked.

"Next session," she said. "As you re-minded me, we're already over our hour. But next time, we'll definitely ride."

They returned to the Horse Farm. She watched as Joey brushed Trickster, brought her to her stall and fed her.

She didn't have the heart to go and wave goodbye to the others who were leaving.

In fact, she didn't even go back to the of-fice. Aaron and the rest of the staff would be worrying, trying to figure out how to handle it if the news got out about Marcus's autopsy. It was probably too late if a kid like Joey had already heard. Next step would be deciding how they were going to spin the information about his death.

When Joey left with his group, she quickly checked on the horses. She was the only one in the stables and assumed everyone else had either gone into the office for further anxious discussions — or hurried home. She headed straight to her car and left, driving the 4.5 miles to the little ranch house she'd visited so many times as a child. She'd purchased the place from her uncle

38

once she'd accepted the job at the Horse Farm.

Her home was old, dating from the 1830s. She loved the house, always had. A huge fireplace took up most of the parlor, the ladies' sitting room had been turned into a handsome kitchen with shiny new appliances and off the hallway was a computer/game/what-have-you room. There were two bedrooms upstairs, along with a sitting room, modern additions when they were built on in the late 1850s. They were all comfortable and charming. Her uncle told her that the house had always been in their family; a cousin, son, daughter, niece or nephew had taken it over every time. He'd given her a great price and held the mortgage himself. She'd paid it off last year on her twenty-sixth birthday.

As she stood at the door, she heard Sammy whining.

The dog could have stayed at the Horse Farm; God knew, there were enough rescue pets there! But Sammy had belonged to Marcus, and his leg was just beginning to heal. No one had objected when Olivia had said she was bringing him home.

She opened the door and there he was, tail wagging as he greeted her. Olivia didn't have to bend far to greet him in return.

Sammy was a big old dog who appeared to be a mix of many breeds. He had the coat of a golden retriever, the head of rottweiler and paws that might have belonged to a wolf. He had one blue eye and one half blue, half brown — it was a freckle on the eye, she'd been told.

He gazed up at her expectantly and sat back on his haunches. His hope and simple trust just about broke her heart. "He's not coming back, Sammy. I'm sorry."

Sammy barked in response. She wondered just what dogs did and didn't understand.

Olivia threw her keys on the buffet at the entrance and walked to the kitchen to give Sammy a treat. As he gobbled up the "tasty niblet of beef and pork," she promised him that she'd be back downstairs in a minute. He couldn't go running out into the yard because he was still recovering from the gash on his hind leg.

She dashed upstairs, stripping as she went. She breezed through her bedroom to the bath and stepped into the shower, adjusting the water temperature until it was as hot as it could get. She stood there, feeling it rush over her, for a long time.

She wished she could turn off her mind.

Leaning against the tile, she wondered

about Marcus. "You didn't!" she whispered aloud.

It was easy to believe that an addict had fallen back into drugs. It happened. Some relapsed and returned to therapy or recovered through their own determination and resolve.

But not Marcus! Marcus couldn't have relapsed.

She began to feel saturated by the heat and decided she was about to wrinkle for life. Turning the faucet off, she stepped out of the shower and reached for a towel, drying herself before slipping into her terry robe. Hurrying downstairs, she went back to the kitchen, ready to make a cup of tea. Rounding the stairs, she noticed that Sammy was quiet, just sitting there, staring at the front door.

"At last!"

Stunned and terrified, her heart pounding, she whirled toward the door. Her hand flew to her throat as she desperately wondered what weapon she might grab to defend herself.

But no one had come to attack her.

The speaker was Marcus Danby.

Or the ghost of Marcus Danby.

"Good Lord, woman! What were you doing up there? I mean, just how clean can someone be?" Marcus demanded. He moved toward her as he spoke. "Oh, come on! You saw me before. You see me quite well right now, just like you've always been able to see General Cunningham and Loki. You think I didn't know? Of course I do! You're like a ghost magnet, my dear girl. Close your mouth — your lower jaw's going to fall off. Please, Olivia," he said in a gentler voice. "I need your help. The Horse Farm needs your help."

2

Stepping off the plane and entering Nashville International Airport, Dustin heard the twangs and strains of a country music song. The sound made him smile. God, he loved Nashville. The city was unique in its mix of the up-and-coming and pride in its history. Music reigned supreme but without self-consciousness; it was ever-present like the air one breathed. People tended to be cordial. And, hell, what was *not* to like about an airport that had a coffee stand and the welcoming sound of good music the minute he arrived?

He paused for a minute, listening, feeling the buzz of activity around him. In the past decade he'd lived in a number of different places but there was nothing like Nashville and nothing like coming home.

He picked up the paperwork for his rental car, then walked out of the airport and over to the multistoried garage to pick up the

SUV he'd rented. A few minutes later, he was following the signs for I-40. Soon he was headed off the highway to a Tennessee state road, passing ranches, acreages with herds of grazing cows and pastures where horses kicked up their heels and ran or nibbled at the blue-green grass.

A little while later, he was on the dirt path that led to Willis House — the "retreat" where he had reservations. Willis House catered to those attending therapy at the Horse Farm and other nearby facilities. It wasn't a specialized facility, but advertisements for the inn stated that it was a "clean" environment in the "exquisite and serene" Tennessee hills. People didn't just come here because it was a "clean-living facility," though. They also chose it because the area was so beautiful, or because they were visiting family or friends who were in therapy nearby.

The gravel drive was huge; there was certainly no problem with parking out here. He slid between a big truck and a small one and noted that the other cars in the lot included a nice new Jag, a Volvo, a BMW and a sad-looking twenty-year-old van.

Willis House was . . . a house. There was a broad porch with rockers, and he noted an old-timer sitting in one of them, staring as he approached.

"Hello," Dustin said. The man wore denim overalls and a plaid flannel shirt. His face showed deep grooves of a life gone past.

The man nodded to him. "You the cop?" he asked.

"Agent, now," Dustin replied. He shifted his bag onto his shoulder and came forward to shake the old man's hand. "Dustin Blake, sir. How do you do?"

The man took his hand in a surprisingly strong grip. "Jeremy Myers — but they call me Coot. Welcome. You don't look like someone who needs much help."

"We all need help," Dustin said.

That brought a slight smile to Coot's lips. "Burned out on the job? Or did you go wacko and beat up on some piece of scum that deserved it? Young man, that's the thing today. No respect. Kids spit in teachers' faces and the poor teachers can't do a thing — less'n it gets called child abuse. So, you did your job *too* well?"

Dustin grinned. "Something like that."

"No need to explain to me. You'll have plenty of time to talk. Hell, all people 'round here want you to do is talk. Don't let me keep you, though. That bag must be heavy."

"Nice to meet you, Coot," Dustin said.

45

"Just open the door and go on in. The main house is open until sunset, and after that you'll need your key."

"Thanks." Dustin went in. It might have been any bed-and-breakfast in any rural section of the South. The entry led to a bright, cheerful parlor with the check-in desk being a bar, behind which was an equally bright and cheerful kitchen. He walked up and the young woman at the desk smiled.

"You must be Agent Blake," she said.

"I am."

"Hi, I'm Ellie Villiers. And you're wondering how I knew who you are. Well, we don't take in that many guests and we don't take anyone without a reservation," she explained. She was on a wheeled chair and she swung down to the end of the bar, where she plucked a set of keys off the wall. "We have you in the Andrew Jackson suite." She was a gamine of a young woman, tiny with short dark hair and a perky manner. She gave him a warm smile as she rolled back to him and leaned close. "It's not much of a suite, really. It's just a big room — a ballroom in the old days. But it has the only private bath in the house *and* a door to the back porch. We're careful who we give it to. Not that we have strict rules or regulations, but we do cater to those fighting their own demons, whether they come from a booze bottle, a pill bottle, stress, what have you." She smiled at him. "You sound pretty cool. I heard that the bosses at the bureau think you need some downtime, that's all."

"Talking about me, huh?" he teased.

She shrugged. "This is rural Tennessee, Agent Blake. All we've got to do around here is talk. Oh, that's not really true. There's a gorgeous stream and cliffs and historic trails. You'll love it out here. But wait — you're from Nashville, right?"

"Born in the heart of the city," he told her.

"Well, then you kind of know the area? I mean, you must have driven out of the city now and then. Of course, some people just get on the highway and keep going. They miss out on all this beauty, and so close to the city, too. Sad, although I guess that's just the way life is."

He laughed at her philosophy. "Sad, but true. And my first name is Dustin, okay?"

"Sure, thanks, Dustin. So the one key opens the main door in front. We try to remember to lock it at sunset. The other is to your room, which is just down the hall and to the left. There's a continental breakfast every morning from six to nine. It's right behind me in the dining room. If you need anything, give me a holler."

"I will, and thank you, Ellie." He started to turn away, but then paused. "Hey, are there any hack ranches around here?"

She seemed surprised by the question. "Why would you want to go to a hack ranch when you're going to the Horse Farm? They don't do trail rides, but you'll be working with horses, so — None of my business! Sorry, the question just surprised me."

"I used to come to this area when I was a kid. My folks are historians, so we did the Civil War trails around here, national parks, all that. In fact, we often did them on horseback, and I love to ride. I was just wondering . . ."

"There's a place — Hooper Ridge Stables. Just go back on that road and down a ways. You'll see a sign. There's not much else out here besides private property, the old chapel that's just outside the national park and . . . and a few therapy centers and lots and lots of cows. But it's too late tonight because they don't rent after five. When you want it, though, it's there. Still, once you're been to the Horse Farm . . ."

"I thought most of their animals were rescues," Dustin said.

"Oh, they are rescues. And if they're old or hurt, they don't do much, just get fawned over by the staff and the patients. Clients. Whatever. But when they're healthy, well, at the Horse Farm they become *really* healthy and they're beautifully trained." She swung the chair closer to the counter. "In fact, the owner — Marcus Danby — used to go by the local farms, and the owners all knew that if they had a broken-down horse or they brought in a wild one or a kicker, they could sell it to Marcus. Saved a lot of the poor bastards that way. I wonder what'll happen now that he's gone."

"Who'd he leave it to? Did Marcus have any family?"

Her eyes became very wide and she shook her head. "No. The only reason Marcus inherited the property was the fact that he was the very last member of his family. I mean, when he was a kid — way before I was born — he was a total black sheep. Then he straightened out, and I don't know if he made peace with his people, but . . . he was the last."

"So who inherits his property?" Dustin asked again.

Ellie shrugged dramatically. "I guess Aaron. Aaron's managed the place for him for a long time. He's a good guy. But who knows if he'll be as good as Marcus. Although . . ."

"Although?"

She couldn't have gotten any closer to him, not with the counter between them. But she tried.

"There's a rumor out that he died with drugs in his system," she said, dropping her voice. "Marcus, I mean, not Aaron. Can you imagine that? Founding a therapy center and then biting the dust because after *decades* you suddenly decide to shoot up again?" she asked, sounding incredulous. Gossip, he realized, was delicious to Ellie. But then, she probably searched for any excitement out here. He lowered his head and smiled. They weren't at the ends of the earth. Nashville was only twenty miles away. But he knew that people from the country usually stayed in the country.

"No matter how the man died, he apparently did a lot of good before his death," he said.

"He did. He helped so many people. . . ."

Dustin picked up his keys and finally turned to leave. "Thanks, Ellie."

"Oh! If you're hungry, the café down the road is open until nine or ten, depending on whether they have people in there. The food's actually really great. The best corn bread."

"Nothing like it."

"And the cheese grits are to die for."

"Another important factor," he agreed. "Thanks for the suggestion."

"Pleasure. Make yourself at home. Old Miss Patterson is in one of the bedrooms upstairs and Carolyn Martin's up there, too, along with Coot — you met him outside?" Dustin nodded. "He likes to come for the winter. He lives in the hills but he's a smart old bastard — knows he's too old to plow snow and manage up there once the cold hits. Oh, I forgot to mention. The living area here is for everyone and there's a room back of the dining area with games and stuff."

With a nod of thanks, he headed over to his room. Setting his bag down, he took out his computer and Wi-Fi connector. There was a lot he wanted to look up, background he hadn't gotten to yet. But neither had he stopped in the city to eat; it might not be a bad idea to check out the local diner and the clientele — especially since he was hungry.

First, though, he called Olivia Gordon, Malachi's cousin, to explain who he really was and what he was doing there. She evidently knew that an agent was coming in; she couldn't have missed that fact, since he was scheduled to start at the Horse Farm the following day.

She didn't answer. He'd try her again in the morning — or maybe he'd just show up. Either way, he didn't want to leave a message. Messages were recorded, and in his life, recordings could come back to bite you. But he also assumed that Malachi's cousin was an intelligent young woman. She knew he was coming, so she'd figure it out.

Examining his room, he discovered that he probably did have the best. His bathroom was nice and large with way more closet space than he needed, *and* his key worked on the back door, as well. It led to the rear porch area; if he ever needed to, he could exit without being seen.

He left his room, carefully locking the door behind him. He did it out of instinct, not because he suspected anyone wanted to go through his belongings. But you never knew.

He waved to Ellie as he left, and also waved at Coot, still rocking on the front porch, as he walked out to his car.

The café was even closer than he'd realized from Ellie's directions; it was just down the road. It was a true diner, converted from a pair of old connected freight cars. The tables were small but neat and clean, and his waitress, a heavyset woman named Delilah, was warm and friendly. The place was empty when he entered, but as she took his order — the daily special of pot roast, with a side of grits, okra and a serving of corn bread — the door opened and four young men walked in, followed by an older man. The boys were joking; the older man looked weary.

"The boys from Parsonage House," Delilah murmured to him, nodding.

"Parsonage House?" he asked politely.

"It's a center for wayward boys. At least that's what we used to call them. Addicts — and other kids who've gotten into some minor trouble. None of them are hardened criminals. The Parsonage runs a program for them, and they offer all kinds of therapy. Including horse therapy." She paused, wagging her head. "We have a famous facility for that, you know." When he murmured that he'd heard of it, she continued. "The Parsonage has a good success rate — although some people around here aren't so fond of having it in the neighborhood. But me, I like the boys. They come in every few nights, after their N.A. meeting at the old chapel," Delilah told him. "Some of them — well, quite a few of them, actually — make it. Some of them, though, they come back, and they come back — and then we hear they're up at the state prison or they've wrapped themselves around a tree off the highway. Drew, over there, he works for the Horse Farm. This is a sideline for him. Guess he likes the company of people now and then, seeing how most of the time he's with critters."

She walked away to fill his order. He picked up a copy of the free local paper, which was only six pages — mostly ads, a few columns of local news. The restaurant was small, and even if he wasn't interested in what was going on around him, he wouldn't have been able to avoid eavesdropping.

Two of the boys were cutting up, stealing another boy's baseball cap and tossing it back and forth.

"Stop. Give it back. We're in a restaurant," the older man said. He didn't yell, but he spoke sternly and they listened to him.

One of them complained teasingly, "Hey, Joey had a good day. He was out with Olivia Gordon for half the afternoon!"

"Yes, and you had your horse therapy session, too," the older man said.

"Yeah, yeah — but *I* had Aaron."

"Aaron's great with the horses — and with you kids," the older man said.

"Joey's happy he didn't get Aaron, right, Joey?" one of the boys joked.

Dustin could just see Joey. The kid was blushing.

"Joey's got a crush on his therapist!" another one teased.

"I don't have a crush on her — you guys have a crush on her!" Joey protested. "And it's dumb. She thinks we're all kids."

"You *are* all kids," the older man said.

"Hey, Drew," one of the boys said. "Did you ever try to date her?"

The older man laughed. "I've known Olivia Gordon since she was a kid, and no, Sean, we never dated. She was a Nashville girl, and we met when she came out here to visit her uncle."

"So? City girls didn't date country bumpkins?" Joey asked.

"No, Olivia was never like that," the man, Drew, said. He was smiling; it was evident that he liked Olivia Gordon, too. "She's always been nice to everyone, and she's very serious about her work. So don't go making life miserable for her, huh? She's . . ."

"She's what?" Joey demanded.

"She's just different," Drew said. "Special. And a really fine therapist, so you all behave like gentlemen when you're around her, y'hear?"

"Yes, sir," one of the boys who'd teased Joey said. "This whole thing, though . . .

It's all a little hypocritical, isn't it?"

"He's talking about old Danby going back on the juice," another boy said.

"Hey, that's nothing but a rumor," Drew said firmly. "Certainly at this point. I'm not even sure how it got started."

"But what if the rumor's real?" Joey asked.

"I don't believe it," Drew said. "I knew and worked with Marcus for years. But if he did go back to drugs, well . . . Hell, that's not what you want for yourselves. Found dead in a ditch. Anyway, he shouldn't be remembered for his relapse, if there was one. He should be remembered for everything he did right — for people *and* animals!"

Delilah stepped between Dustin's booth and that of the group. The boys ordered, and when they spoke again, they were subdued. In another few minutes, Delilah brought out Dustin's order. "Enjoy!" she said. She rolled her eyes toward the boys and Drew at the end of the dining car and hurried back around the counter.

The food was good, the corn bread as excellent as Ellie had told him it would be. But when he was done eating, Dustin stood and walked over to the group's table. "Hello," he said. "My name is Dustin Blake. My apologies, but I heard you speaking about the Horse Farm. My first day there is tomorrow. It sounds like you all think highly of the place."

Drew started to rise in greeting but Dustin urged him to keep his seat.

"The Horse Farm is a great facility," Drew responded. "I'm Andrew Dicksen, although I'm known as Drew. I'm one of the stable managers there, and these are a few young men who are working things out up there, too. Joey Walters, Matt Dougal, Sean Modine and Nick Stevens. I take them to their meetings a few nights a week and then we have a bite here — and maybe we'll see a movie. If they're polite, that is!"

The boys shook hands *very* politely, grinning all the while. They wanted to go to the movie, he was pretty sure. But they were quiet and respectful and they obviously paid heed to Andrew, even without bribery.

I hope these guys are the ones who make it, Dustin thought.

"It's great," Joey said. "The Horse Farm, I mean. It's the best of all the things we do."

"It's really cool when you get to actually ride horses," Sean added.

"It's cool even when you don't — especially if you get Liv." Nick made a strangled sound; Dustin realized that Joey had kicked him under the table.

"I hope I get to hang around long enough to get back there," Matt said. He was a lanky kid with long hair. He'd spoken last and almost to himself.

"Why wouldn't you go back?" Dustin asked him.

Matt flushed uncomfortably.

"Yes, why?" Drew echoed. "Is there a problem?"

Matt looked as if he wished he'd kept his words to himself. "Um, my dad may drag me back home and send me somewhere in Minnesota," he admitted unhappily. "He, um, said that if the people running the place couldn't stay clean, what chance is there for kids like us?"

This was followed by a brief silence.

"I'm sorry," Dustin said. "I heard about the tragic loss of the Horse Farm's founder."

Drew Dicksen nodded. "He was a good guy. A damned good man," he said quietly. "Whatever anyone says." He raised his head. "It's a wonderful place. I hope things work out. I believe they will," he said. "Anyway, Mr. Blake —"

"He's an agent. Agent Blake. FBI!" Sean said excitedly. He grimaced as he looked at Dustin. "Sorry. I heard Aaron adding your name to the roster. So, we were all talking about you. I mean, it's pretty exciting. We're at a place where the feds send their guys!"

"Thanks," Dustin murmured. "I guess."

"Hey, did you shoot somebody?" Sean asked. "Is that why you're here?"

Dustin shook his head. "Nothing like that," he said.

"So, why'd they send you?" Nick persisted.

"They figure we all need a break now and then. We see too much," Dustin explained

"Wow, cool. Who have you hunted down?" Matt asked.

"I'm here to *not* think about it for a while," Dustin told him.

The door swung open, and a woman of about thirty-five stepped into the coffee shop. She was in jeans and a blue denim shirt — attractive without being beautiful. She smiled at him and then at those sitting at the table. "Hi." She walked straight to Dustin and offered him a hearty handshake. "You must be Agent Blake."

"I am. Nice to meet you . . . ?"

"Mariah Naughton, and the pleasure is mine. Oh, I'm sorry, I must seem so rude. I work at the Horse Farm — I'm one of the therapists. We were notified that you were coming in tonight and that you'd be at the Horse Farm tomorrow morning. I believe

Aaron has you going out with a small group first."

"Is it with you?"

"No," she answered, "sad to say it's not me. You'll be going out with Olivia Gordon. Aaron likes to start people out with Liv — and in small groups. She's our most popular therapist. You'll see why. Hey, Drew, boys, how are you all doing?"

Sean laughed softly. "You're great, too, Mariah."

Mariah grinned good-naturedly at that. "I'm just not twenty-something and gorgeous, huh?"

"You're just fine," Matt said fervently. "We all —"

"Don't worry about it, Matt." Mariah laughed. "It's true that Liv has an exceptional gift with animals, so it's good for people to learn with her first. Now me, I'm the historian! My family's been here forever. We've lived here since the first frontiersman headed out to this part of Tennessee. In fact, I do tours every second Friday night and I lead these guys and a bunch of others on camping trips. We go out on horseback. I hope you'll be joining us."

"I'm sure I will. I'm a history buff, too."

"Yeah?" Mariah asked. "Then you should spend some time with Drew, as well. He's part of a reenactors' group," she said proudly. "They've even done reenactments for movies. They're really good."

Drew shrugged, looking slightly embarrassed. "I enjoy it. I particularly like the research end of it."

"Drew is *great* at making history fun," Sean said.

"Mariah does haunted history," Matt put in. "She's got lots of ghost stories to tell."

"It all sounds good," Dustin said. "I'll look forward to it."

"Glad you like the idea," Drew remarked. "But just to prepare you for tomorrow . . . With any kind of therapy, you have to be open to it. Although, honestly, half the time people aren't. And those people don't do well with the horses. Can't blame a horse for his reactions and he's probably not out to get you, right?" he asked, smiling.

"Yeah, the horses are way better than sitting there in psych group waiting for someone to talk." Sean brightened. "I like throwing things at the rock, though. That's fun."

"We make paper bombs and throw them at a big rock," Mariah explained. "Helps let out steam. Throw away anger, resentment, pain . . ."

"Well," Dustin said. "It's been a long day. Nice to meet you all and thanks for the information." Waving, he left the diner. He knew they'd be talking about him the second the door closed behind him.

Returning to the bed-and-breakfast, he realized he was more curious than ever about what was going on — and he realized, too, that he'd have to be very careful.

A hell of a lot of talking went on in this area.

Olivia sat on the couch in her parlor, an untouched cup of tea in her hands, while Marcus Danby was in the chair across from her. He looked as if he were alive. He wasn't, of course, but he was there — *almost* in the flesh. He appeared to move, to walk, to talk, to be her friend as he'd been in life.

Except, of course, that he was upset. With her?

She shouldn't be so frozen, she told herself. She'd seen ghosts before, *met* ghosts before! For God's sake, her cousin, Malachi, lived with a great old fellow, a Revolutionary War ghost.

And she'd seen the general on the Tennessee hills many times. Some in this area called it a gift, some called it a curse, and some thought those who claimed to have it were flat-out crazy. Therefore, most people learned at an early age to pretend that what was . . . wasn't. And when you knew that ghosts could make you appear crazy or even feel like you were crazy, you learned how to cope.

Malachi had kept her sane when they were kids. He'd convinced her that it had to be a secret they shared. And, of course, she sometimes had to be wary of the ghosts themselves. They stayed behind for a reason. It was best to know that reason before making friends.

She remembered one time when they were older, when he'd come out to her college graduation. He'd talked to her once they had some time alone, and she'd smiled because only Malachi had been able to make her laugh.

"I've got it," she'd told him with mock-seriousness. "The way to handle ghosts is by not acknowledging the dead. You keep walking as if you're in a hurry. You step over bodies along the way — ah, I've got it. Pretend you're a stereotypical New Yorker. You march forward with an agenda at all times, walking briskly, and for the love of God, you never make eye contact."

"Hey, some of my best friends are New Yorkers!" Malachi said, laughing.

Malachi had always had a sense of humor — and he'd always been tough. He'd gone into police work, and now he was with the FBI. She'd called him hysterically after the authorities had come to claim Marcus's body, and he'd been so helpful. He'd made her understand that the federal government had to be invited in when there wasn't a major crime that involved perpetrators crossing state lines, a kidnapping or circumstances in which local authorities had requested assistance.

Never once, however, had he suggested that she was making things up to save the Horse Farm, or that she was overwrought. He'd promised her that he would find a way to help her. "I'm not sure if I'm the right one to come out there at this point. Too many people are aware that I'm your cousin, and it'll immediately appear as if you're asking for outside help," he'd told her. "Good way to piss off the local cops."

She didn't care about appearances. She wished Malachi had come.

The most bizarre thing was that Marcus Danby — or the ghost of Marcus Danby — was speaking much more easily than she seemed capable of doing at the moment.

Olivia managed to take a sip of her tea. She stilled her shattered nerves, took a deep breath and spoke to him. "Marcus, there was an autopsy."

"I know. Ugh!" Marcus said, grimacing, a shiver racing visibly through his body. "Yes, no one's fault — accidental death and all that."

"And drugs were found in your system."

"That's just it, Liv. I swore, so many years ago, that I'd never touch drugs again as long as I lived. I wasn't tempted. I didn't hit what they call a trigger situation. I was a happy man."

"So?"

"Okay, here was my day. I got up, had my coffee. Came by the Horse Farm. I love this time of year — not cold yet, not hot like summer. Sammy was playful. I was going to go for a ride and then I decided on a walk so I could take him along. Suddenly, not far from the ravine, Sammy starts wagging his tail, then barking like crazy. He raced off toward the grove of trees west of the ravine and he didn't come back. So I called out to him and followed him, and the next thing I knew I was on the ground. I didn't feel pain. I was just . . . on the ground." He paused as if taking a deep breath.

He couldn't have been taking a breath. He wasn't alive. Olivia took another sip of her tea. She'd be heading into her kitchen for the brandy in a minute.

"You were on the ground," she said,

encouraging him to continue.

"I don't know if I was hit in the head, if . . . I just don't know. At first, there was nothing. And then . . . then I was on a high like you wouldn't believe, and I knew I was in trouble. I got up and started walking and then . . . I felt a shove at my back and I fell and you know the rest of it!"

"So you believe that someone intentionally drugged you?"

"Yes. Not to mention the part about killing me."

"I told the police you would never have intentionally relapsed, Marcus. I've sworn it, I've defended you, I . . . I called my cousin."

"Malachi?"

"He's an FBI agent, Marcus."

"And he's coming out here?"

"Ah, no. But he's working on something. After I talked to Malachi and he promised to get someone here, I found out that we have a federal agent showing up as a client tomorrow. I'm sure he's the help Malachi's sending."

"Why doesn't Malachi come himself? Why doesn't he tell you things directly?"

"He's with the government. Those guys are all paranoid, I think," Olivia muttered. "Anyway, it's complicated, Marcus. People in this area know that we're cousins. Some of them know Malachi. Like you. Sorry, I mean, you *knew* him —"

"It's all right. Go on."

"You can't just step on the toes of the local police. So Malachi's managed to get a big shot to believe that something's wrong here, and they're sending someone out. Under the guise of a client."

Marcus remained somber but he nodded and looked at her with hope in his eyes. "Thanks, Liv. You have to solve this. The Horse Farm is a one-of-a-kind place. We work with addicts, with autistic and Down syndrome kids, with burned-out adults, the severely depressed. . . . But you know all that. And you know that it was always my way to make amends and to help others live quality lives and . . . you love the Horse Farm, too," he finished.

"I'll do everything I can, Marcus," she promised. She closed her eyes for a minute.

When she opened them, Marcus was gone.

Great. In death, Marcus — always the most polite of men — had suddenly decided to be rude.

3

Dustin arrived at the Horse Farm. There was a massive sign on the narrow paved road that led to a long dirt drive, a sign announcing that he'd reached the Horse Farm.

It was an impressive place. Acres of rolling fields surrounded it, gorgeous hills crested in the background and rich forests stood beyond the pastures and meadows. When he got there, he saw that to the right of the drive were the massive stables, painted a cheerful bright red. To the left was the office and rec building; it, too, was large, but built ranch-style with only one story. Parking in the dusty drive out front, he headed for the office. Opening the door, he found old western furniture, walls covered with prints, paintings and newspaper clippings of horses, and overstuffed leather sofas. He saw a games room with people playing Ping-Pong and heard the whack, whack, whack of the ball going back and forth. A young woman breezed by him with a quick "Hello!" and hurried on to the back. "I'm challenging the winner!" she called.

A woman in her mid- or late thirties stepped aside to allow the young blonde to move past, to the games room. She shook her head but smiled tolerantly.

"Sorry, Mama Cheever!" the younger woman said.

"It's fine, Liz. Go save your spot." There was something both matronly and business-like about her. She wore western-style boots, jeans and a colorful cotton shirt. She'd seen Dustin arrive and was coming toward him. Her hair was pulled back in a severe bun. Maybe that was it. She had a long, sharp-featured face that rather resembled a giraffe's.

"Agent Blake?"

"Yes," he said.

"Sandra, Sandra Cheever. Or Mama Cheever, as you heard, which I still don't get. I don't cuddle patients, don't tuck them in — I don't even brew tea, for God's sake. But I do handle the paperwork and the scheduling around here. We have everything we need except your signature for the files. These days — especially working with animals — we have to get waivers. But your office took care of everything else."

"That's great. What do I do? Where do I start? I'm ready to sign."

Hands on her hips, she cast her head at an angle to study him.

"It's good to hear your enthusiasm," she told him. "I was afraid you'd be hostile to the situation — that it was a 'come here or lose your job' scenario."

"I'm from Nashville, but you know that. You probably know everything about me," Dustin said. "And I love horses. This sounded better than any other offer I've had, so yep. I'm enthusiastic."

"Excellent. Then I'll just bring you in to see Aaron. He's our managing director."

She lifted a hand to point at a door with a placard that read Aaron Bentley.

"Just tap and go on in," Sandra said, grimacing as they heard a loud squeal from the back. "I'm going to go supervise. They're good kids. When they're here, anyway. But . . . they can get a bit crazy."

Sandra hurried to the back. Dustin watched her go as he tapped on the door.

"Come in, it's open!"

Dustin stepped into the office. It was old-fashioned, to say the least. While the desk bore a laptop computer and a printer, an old blotter still sat on it, too, along with a memo tray piled high with papers. The room had two big leather-covered chairs in front of the desk and a worn couch to the rear. Windows looked out over one of the pastures.

The man standing behind the desk was about six feet tall, bearded and balding. His beard was neatly clipped; he seemed far better organized in his personal appearance than he did in his office management skills. Thin gold-rimmed glasses sat on his nose. He smiled seeing Dustin and walked around the desk, offering his hand.

"You must be Agent Blake. I'm sorry. One of us should have been out there to greet you."

"Oh, a nice woman named Sandra did greet me. And yes, I am. But please call me Dustin."

"We go by first names here, so that's great. I'm Aaron. Aaron Bentley. We're glad to have you here, Dustin. We've broken ground with many different groups, you know. About ten years ago, we started working with veterans — the physically wounded, and those who have wounded minds. We help children with disabilities, addicts of all ages, you name it — horse therapy can work wonders. But you're our first law enforcement official. Let's sit down for a moment."

Aaron returned to the swivel chair behind

his desk, while Dustin sank into one of the old leather armchairs. It was comfortable. As messy as the office might look, that apparent chaos actually contributed to a sense of ease.

"I spoke with your supervisor, a Mr. Jackson Crow," Aaron said, folding his hands in front of him. He didn't glance at papers or fiddle with anything on his desk. He gave his absolute attention to Dustin. "He said you were having nightmares and that he believes you're —"

"Burned out?" Dustin suggested.

"No. Experiencing one of those spells where you're having trouble weighing the good you're able to provide against the horrors you have to see. I admit, when I first got the call, I suspected you'd been involved in some dreadful situation where innocents had been killed. But he tells me you're one of his best agents and that he wants you to take some time off. He also said you don't do well with traditional psychiatrists or therapy and that he hopes this will work for you."

"Ah, did he tell you that?" Dustin murmured. He'd had a general idea of what Jackson Crow had planned on saying; he didn't know how close to home it might be.

"I smoked once, Aaron. Years ago. Cigarettes, I mean. I went to a hypnotist to stop. Thinking about water and staring at a bull's-eye on the wall did nothing for me. I merely wanted to kill the hypnotist."

"Well, this isn't like that, but . . . we do have group and individual therapy. We also do camping trips to the little brook a couple miles from here. You don't have to think about the water — you can walk right into it if you choose. Frankly, I'm not sure we'll be what you're looking for, but we're anxious to see if we can help men and women in your situation. If nothing else, a little R & R is always good for someone who is constantly under life-or-death tension."

"I'm glad to be here. You know I live in northern Virginia — D.C. area, really — and I love it. But Nashville and these hills — well, this is home."

"Good, good!" Aaron seemed genuinely pleased. "Now I should tell you that we're in the middle of a real shake-up. We've just lost our founder — Marcus Danby. It's a tough time for all of us. So . . . your people knew he was dead when they called. The fact that you wanted to go ahead, anyway, is a testament to Marcus. At any rate," he said briskly, "I put you in with a small group this morning. I understand you met one of the kids, Joey, last night. Young man, acting out. Terrible loss in his family. Anyway, I won't tell you any more. Come on out. I believe that Liv's at the stables and the troops are gathering."

As they went out the front door, another man was coming in. Aaron paused to introduce the two of them. "Dustin, meet Mason Garlano. You met Drew and Mariah Naughton last night, so once you've spent your first session with Liv, you'll know all of us except for Sydney Roux. He takes care of the horses and the stables with Drew."

Mason Garlano had sleek, curly dark hair and dark eyes. He was in his twenties, with a slightly exotic flair and unmistakable charm. He quickly shook Dustin's hand. "We're glad you're here — and hope you enjoy your visits."

Dustin thanked him and followed Aaron to the stables.

At first sight, Olivia Gordon was little short of spectacular. He understood immediately why the adolescents he'd met the night before were so crazy about her.

She resembled her cousin, Malachi, except that everything that made Malachi Gordon appear rough and rugged came out as pure beauty in Olivia. They had the same sable hair, a color that was rich and shiny. Hers was long, waving down her back.

Jeans and a blue denim shirt had never been worn so well.

When she turned to look at him, he saw that her eyes were a crystalline blue. They seemed to have a million different facets, all of them subtle shades of blue and green.

Her eyes widened when she met him. "So, uh, welcome. You're the FBI man?"

He grinned. "Yep." Did that mean she understood why he was there? He assumed so. "A pleasure to meet you. I believe I'm with your group now?" he asked.

She nodded, glancing at Aaron. "I hear you work in the D.C. area — or you're based there, anyway. Do you know my cousin? Malachi Gordon?"

"Yes, I do. You two have quite a resemblance."

"We're double-cousins. Our mothers were sisters and our fathers were brothers," she told him.

"Hmm. Well, that must explain it."

They gazed at each other, but were interrupted by a small body that raced past him — and threw his arms around Liv.

"Oh!" she gasped, and then laughed, hugging the intruder. "Brent, turn around now. I want you to meet a new member of our group. This is Dustin. Dustin, please meet Brent."

Brent had Down syndrome. He studied Dustin unabashedly and smiled, thrusting out his hand. "Pleased to meet you, Dustin." He enunciated his words carefully.

"Brent, pleased to meet you, too, buddy," Dustin said.

"I'm here, I'm here!" A woman came trotting out to the paddock.

"Hey, Patty," Olivia said.

"Am I late?" the woman asked. She looked at Olivia but then stared at Dustin. "Hi."

"You're not late," Olivia said. She introduced Dustin. The woman kept staring at him.

"Joey should be here any minute," Olivia said. "I'll be right back."

She made her way to the stables. "Hi, Patty," Brent said.

Patty smiled at him. "Hi, there, Brent." She looked at Dustin again. "So, you're really with the FBI?"

Dustin nodded.

"What have they got you in here for?" she asked him.

"I'm not even sure how to explain it," Dustin told her. She was still smiling as she studied him. He slanted his head. "What is it?"

"Sorry!" she said. "I'm in court-ordered therapy because of some . . . problems I had. I'm glad. I need my life back. I have a little girl and I want custody of her. At least shared custody. Her dad's half the reason I'm here — nope! *I'm* the reason I'm here. But now I get to say I was in with an FBI agent, and that makes it . . . I don't know. It makes it better somehow. I mean, people who do important things, people like you, can have problems just like me."

"Well, uh, good," Dustin said, a little helplessly.

"Especially after what happened to Marcus," she added.

He didn't get a chance to say any more. Joey was there. Dustin was glad to see that he seemed to have a special place in his heart for Brent and made a point of greeting him.

Olivia Gordon reappeared, leading a massive bay gelding with a glossy coat. He had to be about seventeen hands high.

"This is Cheyenne. He was bought as a three-year-old for a young rider. He was too much for her and the father sold him to a hack ranch. He was never handled properly and started throwing riders. One of the stable hands thought that whipping him would work and Cheyenne threw him into a field. He was then put in a paddock and basically ignored until —" she paused for just a second "— until Marcus Danby came upon him. We've had him about three months now and we're working with him today because we're working on boundaries. So, first, one by one, get to know him."

Dustin had to admit he wasn't sure how getting to know a horse was going to be therapeutic for an adolescent boy, a Down syndrome child and a woman in court-ordered rehab. Or how a difficult horse could help anyone with "boundaries." Or why the three of them seemed like a good combo.

But as their time together progressed, he realized that what Olivia was telling them was true. They each worked with the animal, leading him, stopping with him, leading him again. She taught them to respect the horse — but to maintain control. They were given a distance to cover; they weren't to stop because Cheyenne tried to bully them into walking over to the grass. Neither were they to jerk on his reins or in any way harm the horse.

It was interesting — even for Dustin — because the horse was a powerhouse of muscle. They were encouraged to speak to one another. And they were all encouraged to give the horse encouragement, to applaud his compliance. When Olivia ended the session, she released the gelding and he immediately bolted for the field. Cheyenne ran about for a few minutes. And then he ran back to them. He nudged Brent, and Brent laughed delightedly and returned the animal's affection.

"How did you get him to do that?" Patty asked Olivia.

"I didn't. He *chose* to come back," Olivia said. "Okay, we'll take Cheyenne to the stables now. Grooming time."

It was an intriguing exercise. Olivia supplied brushes and they decided among themselves who'd do the mane and tail and how they'd share this one-person task.

Then their two-hour session was over. Olivia told Brent to say hello to his mom for her, said goodbye to Patty and informed Joey that they'd be ready for his ride in half an hour. She turned to Dustin. He was struck again by the beauty of this slender woman who seemed to have so much confidence, such easy control.

She was obviously waiting for the others to walk away so she could speak to him privately. But they were talking and laughing among themselves.

He moved closer to her. "I'm here because of Malachi," he said quietly.

She glanced quickly around. "Someone

could have called me and told me that yes, it was being handled."

Her taut response gave him a start. He lowered his voice. "You could answer your phone," he told her. "Although one would've thought that if you'd called an agent for help and another agent showed up, you'd put two and two together. Then again, if you answered your phone, you might have spoken with both of us."

She looked away. "Yesterday wasn't a good day for us. We got the autopsy report in the morning."

"Yes, I know that, Ms. Gordon. Because the day before, I was about to head out on a serious case — kidnapping and murder in the Northwest. Instead, I'm here — where an addict might or might not have gone back to his old ways."

She flashed a glance at him, her eyes shimmering with hostility. "I'm sorry. I would think the murder of *any* human being was important and worth investigating. If we're not gruesome enough for you, I do apologize. But you *are* here to investigate. I —"

She paused, moving a step closer. She might work with horses in a stable, but she wore some kind of subtle perfume that made her smell like the whisper of flowers in the breeze.

"I have two individual sessions this afternoon. You're not one of them. Everyone starts off with a session like you just went through, to see if they feel this will be of benefit to them. That will allow you to fit in here, which is the point. So, now you can investigate. What are you going to do?"

He frowned at her, somewhat irritated that she'd gotten under his skin. All his life he'd walked a straight line. He felt he had sympathy for those left behind after a death, although he wasn't and never had been a counselor in any way. But he didn't let emotion invade his work. In his position, he couldn't. He'd wind up . . .

In therapy, he thought dryly.

"Well?" she asked. "What will you do this afternoon?"

He angled his head thoughtfully. "I'm going to play Ping-Pong. What time do you get off, Ms. Gordon?"

When Olivia finished with her last session, she discovered that Dustin Blake was still at the facility. He was playing doubles; he and Joey were partnered against Sean and Matt.

Officially, the Horse Farm was there for equine therapy. But any "guest" — as they officially called their patients or clients — was welcome on the grounds during open

hours, which usually ended at six. They'd
long ago noticed that their guests were
comfortable at the Horse Farm and, because
of that, many stayed long hours reading in
the back room or playing games.

Olivia wondered if perhaps he'd been
waiting for her. But she paused by the
reception area, pouring herself a cup of coffee and watching him. She'd managed to
call Malachi on her cell during her last ride,
and he'd managed to call her back. Yes, if
she'd answered her phone, she would have
learned that Blake was the agent who'd
been sent.

He was a curious choice, she thought. He
was hardly nondescript. The man stood at
about six foot four. He had the kind of lean,
hard muscle that might be seen on a basket-
ball player. His every movement hinted at
agility. His face was chiseled, his jaw square,
and he had flashing dark eyes that seemed
to view the world around him with a certain
amount of skepticism. No one could miss
him. Hardly the type to slip in and out of
anywhere unnoticed.

But then, he'd come here as what he was
— or mostly as what he was. Aaron was
practically giddy that the bureau had chosen
their facility as a place for the man to
unwind, chill out or vanquish his demons.

Nowhere in the paperwork had it been suggested that he was addicted to alcohol or other substances, but you didn't have to be an addict or suffering from a physical or congenital disadvantage to benefit from the Horse Farm. Marcus Danby had believed that the best therapy brought various kinds of people together. For instance, a stressed-out business exec could learn that patience and tolerance for an autistic or otherwise handicapped child was something that should come naturally. Equally, a young man like Brent could show true acceptance and affection to a drug addict or alcoholic who discovered that friends — real friends, or the ones who'd enabled their addictions — were afraid to be there for them anymore.

But while they'd had handsome high school and college football heroes, a number of pro athletes, musicians and some of the people who pulled major strings on Wall Street, they'd never had anyone quite like Dustin Blake.

He was the topic du jour.

Drew Dicksen stepped in from outside. He walked directly over to her and the table with the ever-present coffee service.

"Hey, how are you doing, kid?" he asked her.

He seemed to look at her with concern all

the time now.

"I'm doing all right. How about you?"

"Fine. Fine, thanks. So, you met the new guy."

"Yeah."

"How did it go?"

"Okay."

Drew leaned against the wall, pensively watching the back room. "I wonder why he's really here."

"Pardon?" she said, startled. Did people know?

He smiled and lowered his voice. "I mean, what did he do? The kids talk about it constantly. They think maybe he cornered a serial killer — and shot him down rather than arresting him. Or he freaked in the middle of a tense situation. They keep making up scenarios — and they're making me wonder, too." He laughed. "In fact, it's hard not to join in with their fantasies."

"I doubt that he freaked out, or that he's violent. If he was, I don't think he'd be here," Olivia said pragmatically.

"He's sure got a rapport with kids," Drew said.

"The kids adore you, too. More than that, they respect you."

"Most of the ones we get are good kids," he said. "Don't worry, I'm not jealous. My real job is basically pooper-scooper. And he's an FBI guy — where's the comparison?"

"Andrew! You and Sydney save animals, animals found in the worst possible conditions sometimes. You care for them, and you keep everything in this place running."

"Don't say that in front of Aaron!" he said with a laugh. "Me, I don't want to be an FBI man. I'm not at all fond of the concept of people shooting at me. Can't help but be curious, though. So how did he do today?"

"Fine. He worked well with others and seems to know horses."

"He *is* from Tennessee."

"Drew, not everyone from Tennessee rides horses," she reminded him.

"No kidding?"

Olivia rolled her eyes.

They heard a loud shrill of delight. "We won!" Joey cried happily.

"Rematch tomorrow!" Sean shouted back at him.

Sandra Cheever suddenly appeared, marching over to the boys. "Tomorrow being the key word. Out, young 'uns. We have to lock up."

"Aw . . ."

The kids began filing out for the night. They all said their goodbyes to Olivia and

Drew. Joey paused by the door. There was a sign-up sheet for the history/ghost tour and camping trip Mariah was planning to lead on Friday night.

Joey paused, turning around. Olivia thought he was talking to her at first when he asked, "Are you going?"

Then she realized that Dustin Blake was standing right behind her.

"What is it exactly?"

"Mariah Naughton. Remember, she was talking about it at the diner last night? We take the horses and ride out to sites that aren't part of the National Battlefield Parks. I mean, they can't own *everything,* and there was Civil War action all around here. She talks about Tennessee battles, the ghosts that remain, and then we go set up camp by the stream. It's really cool."

"Seriously, nothing here is really cool, man," Sean said, sticking his head back in and placing his hands on Joey's shoulders. "But it's the coolest thing we get while we're in purgatory."

"You're right. I do remember. Sounds great," Dustin said.

Olivia glanced at him, trying not to frown. *Ping-Pong and camping?* That was how an agent worked?

Joey scribbled on the sheet and turned

back to Dustin. "I put your name down, okay?"

"Thanks."

Aaron had come out of his office. Sandra — herding the boys out the door — was now behind Dustin.

"Guess I need to get out of here, too," Dustin said. "Thank you. I've heard about this place for years. It's fantastic. Good day for me."

"Glad to have you, Agent — Dustin," Aaron said.

As he walked out, Aaron turned to them. "Drew, can you get Sydney? And, Sandra, can you find Mariah and Mason? We need a little meeting."

Five minutes later, they were all seated on the couches and chairs in the entry room. Once everyone had settled in, Aaron said, "We have to decide how to handle this situation. First, just to let you know, Sandra and I have rescheduled all our sessions for tomorrow — the lawyer's coming in the morning." He cleared his throat. "I guess you're all aware that Marcus was the end of his line. I believe, since he and I discussed it many times, that the facility was left to me, but no one can be certain of anything until his attorney reads his final will and testament. I know, as well, that he left something from his life for every one of you. There are also clauses that protect the property and the livestock in the event of *my* death. So . . . that's one thing. The other is . . . we have to decide on spin."

"Spin?" Mariah asked.

Aaron exhaled. "Well, the information about the autopsy is out. Naturally, in today's age of instant information and social media, it was inevitable, and some people are going to make a big deal of it. We all know the autopsy revealed he was on drugs. The blood tests made that clear. I saw Marcus that morning — he was fine. In fact, he was in a great mood. What happened to make him relapse after all those years . . . I don't know. The thing is, it puts us in a bad light. What good does any of this therapy do if the man who founded the Horse Farm died while on drugs?"

"He didn't take drugs willingly," Olivia said firmly.

They were all silent, looking at her. She knew that pitying stare. They all believed she just couldn't accept it.

To her surprise, Sydney Roux, Drew's partner in looking after the stables, spoke up, too. He stood to do so; Sydney was an old Tennessean. His grandparents and their grandparents had grown up in the nearby hills. He was a gentleman to the nth degree. He fingered the baseball cap he'd removed when he entered the office as he said, "I can't believe it, either. I remember I was in my room above the stables one evening when he came by. I'd been drinking a beer and I tried to hide it. He told me, 'Sydney, I'm an addict. You're not. Don't go thinking you can't have that brew because I stopped by. I'm long past my trigger days.' And I believe that — just like Olivia believes it. Something happened. Someone tricked him."

"If only," Sandra murmured.

"How could we ever find out? How could we prove such a thing?" Mariah asked. "We had cops out here. They searched with us that day."

"They didn't find anything!" Olivia said, sitting up straight.

Aaron looked at her. "Right."

"Don't you see? They didn't find *anything*. They didn't find heroin, crack or anything else on him — *and they didn't find a needle in his possession*. Where were the drugs or the paraphernalia he would have needed?"

Sandra came and sat on the edge of the sofa by her. "Oh, Liv, the acreage here seems to go on forever and we're sur- rounded by forests. He could've left stuff

89

anywhere on the property and we might never find it. A hundred years from now, when they're digging the place up to build condos, they might come across a broken needle or something and wonder *what the hell?*"

"Someone else could have put it in him," Olivia said stubbornly.

Sandra looked helplessly at Aaron.

"I don't know what happened and I probably never will. And it doesn't matter. Marcus was one of the greatest men I've ever known," Aaron said. "The point is how do we handle this?"

"With honesty," Mariah said. "What other way is there?"

"We downplay it," Mason insisted. "We tell the truth. We're honest. But we say that it never happened before — and that *is* the truth. We say that Marcus had thirty years of clean living, and many people — and animals — benefited because of him. And that we're continuing on in that fine tradition of faith and belief."

"Mason," Mariah said. "That was wonderful! If you get tired of being a therapist, you can go into public relations."

Olivia nodded. "It really was a good statement."

"And it's the truth," Aaron agreed. "All

90

right, then. We just lie low. When asked, we say that we don't know what was going on in his mind at the end but that we loved him and he did a world of good. We'll say that we'll never forget him or what he gave to others. However, don't bring up the subject unless you're asked. So, everyone, have a good night."

"Wait, wait, wait," Olivia said, rising. "I think what we've talked about here is important. We also need to find out what happened." She looked around at all of them. "Do you honestly think Marcus just had a stash out in the woods? That he had it there for a long time — just in case the day came when he suddenly broke after *decades* of clean living? We need to pursue the truth."

"How?" Mariah asked. "We'd need an army to comb the property and the woods. There are just seven of us. The police have other things to do, and we're not asking clients — some of them *addicts* — to look for drug paraphernalia!"

"There's his house," Olivia said, turning to Aaron. "If his house was searched, we'd at least know he wasn't using there — or considering it."

Aaron left out a soft sigh. "I believe that, as of tomorrow, the house will be mine. You can search to your heart's content, Liv. And if any of us thinks of a forest hidey-hole, we can search that, too. Liv, I don't know what else to do!"

"I've been in his house," Sydney said. He worked the cap furiously in his hands. "I went to get his suit for the funeral home. I didn't search the place, but it's not big, and I sure as hell didn't see anything that would indicate Marcus had lost it. Of course, that was before they released the autopsy report."

"Maybe tomorrow night you and I can go back," Olivia suggested.

"Yeah," Sandra said. "Oh, Olivia, honey, I know how much you loved Marcus. But what can we possibly prove?"

"That he didn't fall back on drugs, Sandra! It could mean everything for the Horse Farm."

"You search his house tomorrow night if you want," Aaron said. "Olivia, you can do anything that'll make you feel better, and when you need our help, just say so."

She had the feeling that what he really meant was emotional help; still, it seemed that Aaron was on her side, and that mattered.

"Thanks," she told him.

"So the attorney is coming here at ten,"

Aaron said. "See you in the morning."

They all moved. Some of them would get into conversations about Marcus — or about Dustin, Olivia knew.

She didn't want to get into a conversation.

She drove home. Sammy greeted her and she stroked the dog's back and spoke to him for a minute before she looked around downstairs.

"Marcus?" she called.

There was no answer. She went up to her room and changed into comfortable sweats, then came back downstairs.

Marcus was there, in the kitchen. "Wish I could've put the teakettle on for you," he told her.

"That would have been nice." She put the kettle on and leaned against the stove. "Maybe in time," she said.

"In time!" he protested, then smiled at her. "That's almost Biblical. A time to reap, a time to sow — and a time to walk into the light. I want to walk into that light, Liv. I've seen it. It's beautiful. I should go there."

"Oh, Marcus." She wanted to give him a hug — but she couldn't hug a ghost. "Marcus, if the light is there . . . and it's what you want, then you should go into it. We'll get along here, I promise. I'll do everything

93

I can. Malachi sent an agent out to investigate." She paused. *Yeah, and he likes to play Ping-Pong and go camping!*

"Marcus, have faith. In me, I mean. You can go to the light."

"No, actually, I can't. Not yet. Not until I'm proven innocent. People do fall back into drugs. But the thing is — I didn't. So I just can't leave."

"Why not?"

"I don't know why not!" he said, aggrieved. "*You* figure out the meaning of life and death — I sure as hell don't know it!"

Before she could respond, Sammy suddenly stood up and barked. Right after that, there was a knock on her door.

Olivia stared at Marcus, wondering why she should feel so alarmed. "Why don't you answer that?" Marcus asked.

She nodded. "Fine. You stay put."

She squinted through the peephole. The man at her door was Dustin Blake.

Surprised, she opened the door.

"We're really not supposed to fraternize," she said. "Not when I'm your therapist."

"You're not really my therapist," he said. "And I'm not really in therapy. May I come in, please? I need to understand a lot more about what's going on around here. One of our computer whizzes back in D.C. got me

either. There isn't really any book of the dead. I've come across spirits who haven't learned to communicate, and I've come across those who might be any friend chatting with you before a fire. We don't know why. Then, there are some who are quick to appear before many people — and there are those who only appear after centuries and only because they believe they've found the person with whom they need to communicate."

She stared at him, wide-eyed. He stepped back. "Are we okay?" he asked.

"Yeah," she said thickly. "Want to hand me another tea bag?"

He did. She finished preparing the two cups of tea, picked up both of them and walked out to her parlor. She placed the cups on a coffee table and sat on the sofa, curling her legs beneath her. He sat across from her on one of the old carved wooden chairs. The place was nice, he thought. It was historic, but it had been treated lovingly and had aged well. It seemed to offer the best of the old and the new.

"What do you need from me?" she asked. Before he could answer, she asked, "How did you get here? Do you have a car out front? We're really not supposed to hang out with guests."

He leaned forward. "No car out there — I walked. I'm at Willis House and I have the room with the separate entrance. People saw me go into my room, but they didn't see me leave. Even if they find out I'm not there, they won't know where I am."

"You walked? Willis House is several miles from here."

"Yeah. Pretty country for walking. The temperature is great."

She reached for her cup and took a sip of tea.

"And no one saw me — unless, of course, they were hiding in your bushes. But if someone was messing around outside your house, I think Sammy would've known. I heard him bark before I came up the walk."

"Aaron told me today that he and the others would help me in any way they could," she said.

Dustin felt his brow furrowing and made an effort to ease it. "They know you're convinced that Marcus was murdered?"

"I — I didn't exactly announce that he was murdered. But I did deny that he'd gone back on drugs."

"Just to Aaron — or to everyone?"

She looked at him warily. "Well, to everyone. We had a meeting at the end of the day. Marcus's lawyer is going to be at the Horse

Farm tomorrow morning to discuss the will. We're all mentioned in it, apparently. From what we know, the Horse Farm itself goes to Aaron Bentley, but I believe Marcus had safeguards written in. I don't understand the legal ramifications of any of it. As far as we're aware at this point, we go on exactly as we've been doing. We're nonprofit, so it isn't as if anyone stands to get rich."

"Yes, I know."

"You know?"

He grinned. "Everyone has access to public records, Olivia. We have access to a little more than that." He was quiet for a minute and then said, "That's why it's hard to understand why someone would have done this."

"Do you think I'm in denial? Panicking?" Her tone was as stiff as her body.

"I didn't say that you were in denial or panicking."

"It's everyone's first thought, isn't it?"

"First thought, maybe. But calling Malachi was the right thing."

"You know Malachi?" she asked. "You've worked with him?"

"Yes, I've met Malachi. No, I haven't worked with him. This is my first assignment with the Krewe of Hunters."

"What?" She jumped up, sloshing tea, and

101

then set her mug on the coffee table as she stared at him. "What? Oh, I don't mean to be insulting, it's just that . . . I call for help, and my cousin sends a newbie?"

"I'm hardly a newbie, Olivia," he told her, trying not to lose his temper. She was looking at him as if he'd barely managed to graduate from high school. "I've been with the bureau. I've been a marine. I've been a cop. I think I'm up to the task."

"I — I — I said I was sorry," she said. "I'm not trying to offend you, but this isn't . . . Well, you can see how much good it's done to go to the police, to anyone —"

"And I told you that I believe you when you tell me you're speaking to a dead man!" He was letting his voice grow too hard. She didn't *mean* to offend. She wasn't *trying* to do so.

But it seemed that she didn't need to try.

She opened her mouth and closed it again, struggling for poise. He kept his own mouth shut, waiting. He was a professional, for God's sake. He would act like one.

"Okay," he said at last. "Cards on the table. I wasn't thrilled to have my first Krewe assignment be a situation in which we're not even officially invited and in which everyone I meet seems to think I'm a lawman run amok. Half of them assume I

102

shot up a pool of suspects and the others figure I went crazy. Still, that's part of the job. I said I believe you, and you need to do me the same courtesy. But you have to trust in me and keep me informed. And please don't worry so much about my credentials. According to Jackson Crow, I've been on his radar for a while now, and when this came up, it seemed the right time for him to call on me. I'm from Nashville. I know the city and I know this area. Malachi couldn't come himself — not with any real validity, or any real chance of blending in with the locals, if you will. Do you understand?"

She slowly sank back onto the couch.

"Yes," she said flatly. She still didn't look happy.

He shook his head and leaned forward. "There are laws, and this country has a constitution, Olivia. You're fighting for a friend. You hoped that Malachi could get the government barging in and demanding that it all be solved. It doesn't work that way. And that's why we're doing what we're doing."

"I said yes. My capacity for comprehension is actually pretty good."

He wasn't sure if she was trying to lighten up or if she was speaking seriously.

He leaned back again. "Okay, so tell me what happened with you."

"With me?"

"The day Marcus was killed."

"I'd had a few sessions and I'd just finished up with the last one when I heard a commotion going on. We knew something was wrong when Sammy came running to the Horse Farm, badly hurt. Marcus loved Sammy. And the dog was devoted to him. If Sammy was there, something had to be wrong with Marcus."

"You didn't let Sammy lead you back to him?"

"By then, the dog was exhausted. He'd lost too much blood. Physically, it would've been impossible for him to search. We did call the police, and two officers came out to help us look." She was quiet for a minute, pensive, remembering. "I — I've never blacked out in my life before, but . . . after I found Marcus, I blacked out. When I came to, Aaron was at my side, the police were already making notes and . . ."

"And?"

"And then Marcus's body was taken away."

"Why did you black out?"

She pursed her lips. "You're from this area, right?"

"I'm from Nashville. But naturally, growing up, I came out to the country plenty of times. Every school kid's done some of the battlefield tours. I've been hiking, camping, skiing . . . you name it." She was still quiet.

He smiled. "Ah."

"Ah?"

"You've seen the general," he said.

She sat straighter. "You know, then — you know about General Rufus Cunningham?"

"Everyone knows about him." He grinned. "Okay, not everyone, but most people who've lived around here. My grandfather belonged to a Civil War roundtable. You know — groups of men who may or may not do reenactments, but who are fascinated by the history of the Civil War. They love to argue strategy. Which side did the right thing when, what could have changed the tide of battle. I've been to a few. They're especially interesting here in Tennessee, because this state was so divided. Tennessee seceded from the Union, but the Union held Nashville early in the war, beginning in 1862. Pitched battles went on around Nashville, but the Confederates never regained the city. When they're all arguing policy and strategy at the roundtables, they occasionally agree on one thing. Like the fact that General Rufus Cunningham was one hell of an interesting and commendable man. He was out to win back the city, but he was also a humanitarian. When he was in charge, the wounded were helped, no matter what the color of their uniform. He'd take personal and physical risk when necessary."

She nodded. "It always seemed to me that his death was a terrible tragedy." She paused again. "Have you ever seen him?"

"Yes."

"You have?" She asked the question very carefully.

He nodded. "I was about sixteen. We were at the old Brentwood Campground. I've heard the acreage has been bought by a large corporation and is due for a major building operation, but back then it was a campground. It's only a few miles from here and borders the same stream that runs through Horse Farm acreage. I woke up in the middle of the night during that camping trip. I was restless. Didn't want to wake the other kid in my tent so I went outside. The general was standing by the stream, just staring at it, almost like he was keeping watch. He had a foot up on a rock. He was leaning on his knee with one arm and he held his horse's reins in the other hand. He looked at me. I looked back at him. He tipped his hat, and I waved."

"Did he disappear? Fade into the night?"

"No, he stayed there."

"So — then what?"

"I waved again and went back to bed."

"You weren't frightened?"

"No. Are you still frightened when you see the dead?"

"Actually, I haven't seen that many just wandering around. I've seen General Cunningham a few times. But half the world's seen General Cunningham, or at least a lot of people *believe* they've seen him, so . . . And I know my cousin's ghost. Zachary Albright. He's been around since the American Revolution, but he's . . . I don't know. That was easy. Malachi was there and Malachi and I are the only two in the family, as far as we know, who . . . talk to the dead."

"I don't think anyone would need to be afraid of General Cunningham. He hated the war, hated pain and suffering. I think he stays around to try and prevent it," Dustin said.

"Yeah. Maybe. And I'm not frightened of him."

"But . . . you were frightened of Marcus Danby?"

"It was the way it all happened," Olivia

explained. "First, I found Marcus down in the ravine. Then, I saw General Cunningham up on his horse. Next thing I knew, I was with the body of Marcus Danby when the spirit of Marcus Danby tapped me on the shoulder. Frightened? Stunned? Both. But I'm not *afraid* of Marcus. He's so . . . real."

"Well, in a way, he is real. He's just not flesh-and-blood real," Dustin said.

"Strange dilemma, isn't it?" she asked, and then gestured with one hand. "Anyway, I'm not prone to hysteria or passing out, but when I was holding Marcus, and Marcus was behind me at the same time, I passed out cold. Just like I told you. When I came to, there was no sign of Marcus's spirit or the general's."

"But then Marcus visited you here?" he asked. "Twice?"

"Yes. This was the second time. But as soon as I walked to the door to let you in, he disappeared."

"Does he know what happened to him?"

"He told me that Sammy ran ahead of him in the woods, barking. He went to find the dog — and after that, he doesn't know. So, whoever did this was waiting for him."

"Or happened to be there."

"You don't have heroin available to inject

into someone if you're not expecting to see that person," Olivia said.

"Unless you were in the woods doing heroin and didn't want to be found by Marcus Danby."

"Why hurt the dog?" Olivia asked.

"Maybe Sammy attacked the person."

"Sammy doesn't attack."

He smiled. "Glad to hear it. Or maybe not so glad. Olivia, if someone did intend to kill Marcus —"

"They more than intended it. They accomplished it," she said. "I'm not making any of this up!"

"I never suggested you were. What I'm saying is that you might have put yourself in danger."

That seemed to puzzle her. "Me? I have no power over anything."

"Most murderers don't want to get caught. Whoever killed Marcus has an agenda, which probably doesn't include prison. That means his killer *doesn't* want an investigation. This person wants Marcus's death accepted as an accident. Your house is out here — with pasture and forest around it. Do you have an alarm system?"

"I have locks on all the doors and windows," she told him.

"That's not an alarm system."

"You think someone would really break into my house to kill me?" she asked incredulously. "That would hardly be an accident."

"All kinds of accidents can happen in a home," he replied. "A fall down the stairs . . . a hair dryer being dropped in a tub or the sink. A slip on the floor. Trust me, 'accidents' can happen. Do you have a gun?"

"Yeah. I have a Revolutionary-era Brown Bess in a display box upstairs. And an 1853 Enfield rifle that my uncle found on this property. I'm afraid I have no ammunition for either of them — nor have I ever fired a gun."

"You should be able to protect yourself. I'll see that you have mace or pepper spray, at least," he said.

"I have Sammy."

"You just said Sammy's not an attack dog."

"But he'll bark his head off," she said. "He'll give me plenty of warning."

Dustin wasn't sure that a dog barking was going to be enough. There was property around all the houses here. Lots of woods, lots of distance. No matter how good emergency services might be, it took time to get to the scene of a crime.

It only took seconds to kill.

But for the time being, he let it go and stood up. She stood, as well. "I guess I should go back, just in case anyone's watching the activity around here. I'll be back tomorrow night to make sure you're armed to defend yourself. I'm going to text you my phone number. Get it into your home phone on speed dial and your cell phone's list of contacts."

She nodded. He was glad she wasn't fighting him.

"Is Malachi going to be able to come at all?" she asked.

"I think that's still up in the air," he told her. So much for her faith in him.

He didn't move for a moment, just looking at her. The woman was breathtaking and still, somehow, while she must have considerable strength of will given her work with people and animals, she had a touch of naiveté, too. She was slim and athletic, but well built. Her eyes were that haunting crystalline blue, touched with green. They compelled him to want to watch her; they also seemed to have a touch of vulnerability. Someone had died and, in her mind, he'd been definitely and irrefutably murdered. And Dustin didn't doubt that she'd spoken with a ghost. She saw things others couldn't.

111

Yet she didn't see her own danger.

He suddenly felt as if they weren't alone. It was a sensation he knew fairly well; he was being watched. Marcus Danby, he thought.

Marcus was nearby but wasn't planning to show himself at the moment.

Olivia didn't seem to be aware; she wasn't accustomed to waiting for that feeling that was like catching a glimpse of something out of the corner of one's eye.

"You can go out the back," she was saying. "If you cut through the forest it's dark, but there's a decent moon out tonight."

"That's fine. That's the way I came. My nocturnal vision's pretty good, and then there's this modern thing called a flashlight. I always have one with me," he told her, offering a smile.

She didn't smile in return. Instead, she looked at him gravely. "Be careful."

"I'm not the person anyone's going to be after," he said.

"Oh? Really? They all know you're an agent. What if the killer's afraid you'll be snooping around and then he wants you out of the picture?"

Maybe she wasn't so naive.

"But I'm also a big guy who works out, has had training — and carries a big gun," he said. "That does make me safer."

"Hmm. All right, I'll go along with that," she conceded.

"By tomorrow night I'll see that you at least have some mace. Friday night, we'll both do the camping trip."

"Camping and Ping-Pong," she said.

"Exactly. Ping-Pong is a great way to get to know the people who hang out at the Horse Farm. And camping will give me a glimpse of a lot more. If we're going to find out who did this to Marcus Danby, we need to find out why."

"Okay," she said. "That makes sense. Come on, I'll walk you out back."

Olivia led him through the kitchen, the dining room, something that now seemed to be a family room and, finally, out the back door. She was polite and agreeable.

"Make sure everything's locked down tight," he told her. "If someone's determined to get in, they'll figure out a way. But it's best to make it as hard for them as possible. That gives you more time to call the cops or come up with an escape route yourself."

"I will lock everything," she promised.

He had the feeling that the minute he was gone, she'd be on the phone calling Malachi and asking him if the agent he'd sent was really capable of getting anything done.

Olivia had never been afraid in her own house before. Now it was inhabited by a ghost who appeared out of nowhere whenever he chose. And on top of that, she was worried that someone might try to break in while she was asleep.

It was still early. She returned to the kitchen, ready to forage through the refrigerator for something to eat. Instead, she walked around downstairs and then upstairs, closing and locking windows. When she was done, she checked the front door again, followed by the back door — even though she'd just locked it behind Dustin Blake.

There was nothing else to lock.

She returned to the kitchen once more only to freeze, startled.

Marcus was back.

"Thank you very much. You made me look like an idiot," she said.

"I had to see who it was and make a judgment call," Marcus told her. "Besides, I'm pretty sure he knew I was here."

"Oh?"

"I've walked around the Horse Farm. I even waved my hands and tried to blow cold breath at people. They can't see me. But this guy — I think he may be the real deal."

"What are you talking about? He didn't tell me he saw you."

"I didn't say he *saw* me. I said he knew I was around. I didn't intend to be seen. Not yet."

"Why not?" Olivia demanded, annoyed with him.

"I had to be sure he's the one," Marcus said.

"The one *what?*"

"Who could really help. I mean, if they'd just sent you a facts guy, we'd be in trouble. But I think he does believe you, and I know he can see and feel and sense what's there — and what's not."

"You might have introduced yourself at the end, Marcus. And how will all these abilities actually make a difference? You weren't killed by a ghost — were you?"

"No," he said. "Someone flesh-and-blood killed me. But . . . now I'm sorry I asked for help. I want the killer caught and the truth exposed, but I hadn't — well, I hadn't recognized the danger I was putting you in."

Now Marcus was telling her she should be afraid, too!

"So," Marcus continued, "you have the agent here. He'll investigate, and you just need to keep quiet from now on. If they say

I fell back into drugs, let them say it."

"Isn't it too late?" she asked him. "They're already saying it. And move, please. You're blocking the refrigerator."

"I can't really block it," he said, but he moved aside.

She reached in and brought out a head of lettuce, shaking it at him. "And quit appearing and disappearing."

"All right. I'd, um, give you a hand if I could. Since I can't . . . I'm going to go prowl around the Horse Farm and see what I can learn."

Olivia set the lettuce on the cutting board and looked at him. She'd been about to warn him to be careful. She managed to refrain.

"Marcus, why do you think someone wanted you dead?"

"Let's see. I wasn't blackmailing anyone. I wasn't sleeping with anyone's wife. I wasn't dealing drugs and I hadn't robbed any banks. I'll be damned if I know, Liv."

"The property?"

"The Horse Farm is nonprofit, and while the management remains in the hands of Aaron Bentley, there's nothing to be gained by my death. Oh, well, there are specific bequests in the will, but nothing anyone would kill for. Anyway, I'm off."

"Are you coming back?" she asked him. "I'm so jumpy I actually wouldn't mind having you around."

"Keep everything locked up, like the fed told you."

"But will you be back?"

He smiled. "Of course I'll be back. I intend to watch out for you through the night."

Sammy whined and Marcus leaned down to pat his head. Olivia thought the dog couldn't possibly feel his hand.

And yet it was as if he did.

Then, just like Dustin Blake, he left through the back.

Except that Marcus didn't have to open the door.

Dustin walked back to Willis House and entered his room by the private door. He put through a call to Malachi and told him he'd been to see Olivia and they'd talked about Marcus Danby. "Do you have anything more on the situation, or on Danby?" Dustin asked.

"Nothing that would explain why anyone wanted the man dead. The property is really only worth anything with a functioning business, and the business only functions if the Horse Farm is successful. The land is valuable to an extent, but there are acreages of similar land if someone was looking to buy, and some of it's for sale. I don't think anyone's crawling out of the man's past — the Horse Farm isn't a rehab facility, it's a therapy center. On paper, there's nothing our people have been able to find. How is Olivia?"

"She's fine. I'm sure she's called you."

"Not since you've been there," Malachi said.

That was a surprise.

"She was asking about you coming out."

"I need to handle this delicately. If local law enforcement believes we're trying to home in on their territory, it could get dicey."

"Right. Well, as far as I know, law enforcement considers his death an open-and-shut case."

"What do you think?"

"I think your cousin has spoken to a ghost and that the ghost knows he was murdered," Dustin said flatly.

"Tread carefully."

"I intend to."

"And keep an eye on Liv for me, will you?"

"I'll do my best."

They rang off. Dustin figured that since he hadn't eaten, he might as well go to the

118

diner again. He just might pick up something more than dinner there.

The house was silent as he headed out. The other residents were either gone or in bed. He locked the door behind him, and as he did, he realized Coot was sitting in his usual rocker on the porch.

"Hey, there, Coot," he said.

"Howdy. Nice night." Dustin heard the sound of Coot's rocker moving back and forth.

"I thought I'd go to the café for a bite to eat. Do you want to join me?" Dustin asked.

He thought the old-timer would say no. To his surprise the rocker creaked and Coot stood up and walked over to him. "Sure. Be happy to go along. Thanks for the invite."

"I'd enjoy the company," Dustin said, guessing there was more to be learned from the old man.

"We gonna drive?"

Dustin nodded. It seemed like a simpler and safer alternative, with a possible killer skulking in the nearby woods.

Coot knew which car was his and waited patiently at the passenger door for Dustin to open it.

The drive was short. Coot didn't talk; he merely gazed out the window at the darkened landscape.

119

Delilah, who was waiting tables again, welcomed them both warmly. Her coffee was fresh, good and strong, and in a few minutes they ordered — the daily special, chicken potpie — and sat facing each other. The café's only occupants when they came in were a family foursome that appeared to be parents and a girl of twelve or so and a boy of maybe ten.

Delilah, of course, knew all about them. They were the Richardson family and they were driving to Nashville from Colorado; their daughter had won tickets to see the newest sensation on the Nashville charts.

Coot sipped his coffee and stared at Dustin while they waited for their meals.

"You don't look like you're in any trouble to me," he said.

"I'm not in trouble."

"Thought you law guys hated it when they want you to see shrinks or go through therapy."

"No, I was ready for a respite. That's about it," Dustin responded.

Coot shrugged and lowered his head, trying to hide a smile. Then he glanced up. "I know who you are," he said.

"You do?" Dustin smiled. "Dustin Blake. That's my name, sir. Special agent — that's what I do for a living."

"I heard about a boy they called Dustin about twenty years ago. I was a reporter in my day. In Nashville, I used to hang out with the cops — I handled the police beat. I'm pretty sure that boy was you. You would've been a kid, a few years older than the two at that table over there, when this all happened, but I remember your name. Hell, even the media has some decency. They didn't let out your name, and maybe I just heard your first name among friends. Anyway, you picked up some knowledge on the street — or in some other way — that helped them find a killer. Am I right?"

Dustin's coffee cup was halfway to his lips. He paused. It was so long ago. No one ever connected him with the Opry-Buff, as the killer had been labeled, or the police shoot-out that had taken him out.

"I am right," Coot said, nodding sagely. "So what are you doing here?"

"I'm enjoying the Horse Farm. Really."

"Sure. So, you seen the general?"

"Hasn't everyone?"

"Oh, everyone claims he sits on that war-horse of his up in the hills, ever watching out. But not many really *see* him."

"But you have?"

"Yep. I've seen him. I've had him tip his hat to me. When the mists are lying low over

121

the pastures and fields, some folks see him 'cause they want to. They see him in the cloud patterns, too, on a summer's day. But there are those who really see him. Like young Olivia."

Olivia, he thought, had to be in her mid- to late twenties. To Coot that was young.

"And, I reckon," Coot went on, "you."

"Who knows what we see and don't see?" Dustin said evasively.

"I've been thinking about Olivia, you know. She's one special person. The girl could've done just about anything, gone just about anywhere. But she's done some mighty good things instead. Sometimes she's got kids with autism so bad the parents are at wits' end, and she can calm 'em down for a few hours and get 'em grooming the horses, laughing in the field. She's great with the youth-in-rebellion types, too. I don't want anything happening to her."

Dustin felt a coldness in his gut. This old man — this old *observer* — was worried.

"She thinks someone killed Marcus Danby," Coot said.

"Well, she's upset. She doesn't want to believe he went back to his old ways."

Coot snorted. "You really figure that's what he did? I didn't take you for a fool, Special Agent Blake!"

Dustin was careful when he spoke. "So you think someone drugged Marcus Danby and threw him in the ravine?"

Coot narrowed his eyes. "Threw him, or gave him a shove. Yeah. I knew Marcus. A guy like that doesn't go twenty-odd years, then take a walk in the woods one day and decide he's gotta have a fix. Think about it, boy. It doesn't work like that."

"I've seen addicts go in and out of recovery."

"There was nothing — absolutely nothing — to make Marcus do that. It would be like me waking up and saying to myself, 'Hey, nice day, think I'll put a Smith & Wesson in my mouth and pull the trigger.' "

"Everyone else seems to have accepted it."

"They only see what's there. They aren't looking for more. Sometimes people have to look beyond the obvious to get the real picture. Hell, you know that."

"But who would have killed Marcus — and why?"

"Now, there's a dilemma," Coot agreed. "Aaron gets the place, or rather, the management of it and the pay that comes with being boss, even when you're nonprofit. That means things aren't going to change much, since Aaron's been in charge a long time. Marcus never liked being in charge.

He liked to be more like a . . . a shaman walking down from the mountain to impart his words of wisdom and go off on another nature walk. But someone had to be in charge and do the day-to-day work, and that someone was Aaron Bentley. Then, of course, there's Mama Cheever, as they call her. Sandra Cheever. Why she's Mama Cheever, I don't know. Nothing maternal about that woman. More of a drill sergeant type. Schedules are everything to her. She yells at the kids and gets obsessed about upkeep."

"Why would she want to kill Marcus?"

"He was sloppy? Well, he was. Came in and left his coffee cup wherever, tracked mud into the offices . . . Ruined her schedules a lot. He'd make an appearance and a whole class might run late."

"You think that would cause her to kill him?" Dustin asked skeptically.

"No . . . Just sayin'."

"What about the students? The clients."

"The 'guests,' you mean?" Coot said dryly. "No. The students come and go. None of 'em that I know of ever had a grudge against the place."

"Has any kid — or adult, for that matter — ever been kicked out?"

"Nope. Not a one. If there's problems

124

with a therapist, they just shift people around."

"How do you know so much about the place?" Dustin asked.

He grinned. " 'Cause Marcus was my friend. I'm an old horse-lover from way back. Found a few animals I got him to take. Animals that needed rescuing. There's a big old Lab-shepherd mix you'll see around the stables. I found him on the road and Marcus took him in."

"I'm sorry for your loss," Dustin told him.

"Thanks. I can see you mean that."

"So," Dustin pursued. "If not a student, who?"

Coot shook his head. Delilah was bringing their food. "You've heard that old saying?" he muttered. " 'Tell a woman, telegram'? Well, it was written for Delilah."

Delilah arrived at their table, and Coot smiled up at her. "Thank you, Delilah! Looks wonderful."

"Enjoy!"

She stood there a minute, but they both made a pretense of being fascinated with their chicken potpie.

"More coffee, gentlemen?" she asked.

"Yes, please," Dustin told her.

She refilled their coffee. Then the family of four apparently needed some directions, and Delilah was distracted.

"I'd say look at those closest to him," Coot said in a low voice. "Isn't that what you law types do in situations like this?"

"Usually, yes."

Coot nodded. "So at the Horse Farm you've got two more therapists. You've got Mason Garlano. The guy's great with animals, but too much of a narcissist to be as good with people. I think he's waiting to be in the right ice cream parlor at the right time and have some Hollywood type 'discover' him. He gets some modeling jobs on the side. Mariah Naughton is nice enough. A bit of an edge to her sometimes, as if she believed there'd be more in the world for her."

"Doesn't sound like they'd have anything against Marcus, though."

"No. Then you're down to the stable managers. Drew Dicksen and Sydney Roux. They're both decent types, far as I can tell. They run a tight ship there, not easy with the number of animals Marcus was always bringing in. His door was open to any abandoned creature, and I should know, since I brought him a bunch. He'd try to find homes for the cats and dogs, but most of 'em wound up staying at the farm. That meant lots of animals to feed. Lots of housekeeping. Lots of — literally — shit to shovel."

"So even if you resented him because of the workload or whatever, don't you think you'd find another line of work before killing a man?" Dustin asked.

"Yeah. There's the dilemma. Which one would have an agenda? Damned if I know."

A few minutes later they finished their meals. Coot was insistent that they split the check; he wasn't taking taxpayer money by letting Dustin pay, he said, but neither was he going to pay more taxes by buying Dustin's meal.

They rose to leave, setting their money on the table.

About to walk out, Dustin thanked Delilah, who was busy wiping tables, preparing to close for the night. He could honestly tell her the chicken potpie was excellent.

The house was quiet when they returned. But Coot didn't have any more to say. He started up the stairs to his own room.

"Nice to talk with you, young fellow," he told Dustin.

"Nice to talk with you, too, sir," Dustin said politely.

In his own room, he went on his computer to look into everyone's backgrounds.

Mariah, Marcus and Sydney Roux were

all from the area and had families that had been around these parts for over a hundred years. Mariah had already told him as much, at least where she was concerned.

Aaron Bentley was originally from Arkansas, Andrew Dicksen from Biloxi, Mississippi, Sandra Cheever from White Plains, New York, and Mason Garlano was from Austin, Texas.

He wondered if any of that would be significant. Probably not, he assumed — but you never knew.

Olivia had actually fallen asleep when the dog suddenly went crazy. She was dimly aware of a little woof by her side, then the patter of his nails as he raced down the stairs. At the front door, he started a frenzy of barking.

Nervously she jumped out of bed. She looked around the room and realized that Dustin Blake was right — she was virtually defenseless. She thought about the knives in her kitchen and decided they wouldn't do her much good. If there really was an assailant, he'd just turn her own knife on her. She wasn't a weakling by any means, but neither did she know about combat.

Her heart thudding, she threw on a robe,

then snatched her phone off the bedside table.

The screen told her it was 4:31 a.m.

As she started down the stairs, the barking seemed to come from the back of the house.

She reminded herself that the place was completely locked down.

But . . . if the person at her door had a gun, he could easily shoot out the locks. If so, wouldn't he already have done that? It wasn't as though she had neighbors who'd hear. She hesitated for a split second and then, instead of hitting 9-1-1, she called Dustin Blake's number.

She wasn't sure what she thought of him yet.

But at least he wouldn't think she was an alarmist.

He answered on the second ring.

"There's someone outside," she whispered. "Sammy's going crazy."

"I'm on my way. Stay back from the windows. Don't let yourself be seen. Don't open a door until you hear my voice!"

"Okay."

She hung up, wondering how long it would take him to get there. She stood at the top of the landing and saw the knob on the front door turn. Someone outside was obviously trying it.

Sammy's barking escalated and he threw himself at the heavy wooden door.

The doorknob stopped moving. Barely daring to breathe, she stared down at her cell and watched painfully as time seemed to stand still. Then she dropped the phone in her pocket and hurried to the kitchen, where she shoved the knives below the counter to make them harder to find and, without turning on a light, scrabbled around until she came up with her weapon of choice.

The waffle maker. The handle was just long enough for her to get a good grip and the body was hard. It would make a great weapon for a surprise attack-and-run should she need it.

5

Dustin's phone had rung at exactly 4:32 a.m.

It took him until 4:34 a.m. to throw on some clothes, his holster and gun, jacket and shoes and to sling his backpack over his shoulder. He was out the back door in ten seconds, in his car in another twenty and speeding down the road. Thankfully, walking distance to her place from Willis House was less than fifteen minutes at a brisk pace and driving there — even with the winding Tennessee country road — was about six minutes.

His eyes were on the house as he pulled into her driveway. But there was just one car there and no sign of anyone. Jerking to a halt, he leaped out of the car, still surveying his surroundings, and raced to the front door. He could hear the dog barking inside. "Olivia, it's Dustin."

The door flew open. "Sammy, it's all

good. It's Dustin, a friend."

She had evidently been waiting for him; she was wrapped in a long velvet robe. Her hair was mussed but she was as striking as a lingerie ad.

Her features were tense; her whole body was tense. She gripped the handle of a good-size waffle maker.

"You all right?" he asked.

She nodded. "But someone was here, Dustin. I saw the front door being tried. The knob was moving. And Sammy . . . well, Sammy knows when someone's there."

"But you're certain no one got in."

She shook her head. "Sammy would know."

"Stay here. I'm going to take a look around."

"Oh, no, no. I'm not staying alone," she said. "Sammy and I are coming with you."

She might be frightened, but there was determination in her eyes.

"Get the keys. If we're both going out, we'll lock the front," he said.

She picked up the keys sitting on the buffet near the front door and frowned. "What's that?" she asked, pointing at his backpack.

"Supplies," he said.

She arched her brows.

"You'll see."

She followed him out. A look at the front door yielded nothing, of course. Digging into the backpack, he came out with his fingerprinting kit, quickly dusted the door and searched for prints.

"Well?" she asked him.

"Smudges."

"What does that mean?"

"There should've been prints. Your prints and other prints, all on top of one another. I think someone had gloves on and made a point of smudging the surface, as well."

Resealing the container of fingerprint powder, he searched the porch. There'd been no dust on it and no snow, and there wasn't the faintest sign of a footprint. As he walked slowly down the porch steps, he continued to search, playing his flashlight over the dark grass and nearby shrubs.

He wondered if his movements were being observed.

He paused when he reached the ground.

Olivia Gordon plowed into his back, she was so close behind him. She still held the waffle iron in a death grip.

"Sorry," she murmured.

"It's all right."

And it was. He'd rather liked the feel of her — vividly warm, sweet-smelling, seductively shaped — crushed momentarily against him.

Suddenly aware of what he was doing — and feeling — he stepped forward. An expanse of clear rolling ground lay to the front, rear and sides of her house. The front yard stretched out to the road, and there was forest on either side of the cleared land. He could see trails, some more established than others, leading through the trees. He made a mental picture of the area; he already knew the way to Willis House through the woods. If he moved to the rear, he could take the trail that led over the hills to the pastureland and then on to more trees, more rolling hills and the Horse Farm. The stream that went through the area for several miles could probably be reached through the rear of the property, as well. Anyone who'd been here could have gone anywhere, in any direction. Her nearest neighbor was down the hill a few acres away; trees separated them.

He'd need an army to find someone out there.

He walked around the house with Olivia at his heels. Sammy trailed along, wagging his tail. The dog was a perfect monitor, and his actions certainly didn't signal that anyone else was present. Whoever had been there was definitely gone.

There was no indication that anyone had tried to break window locks, although he could well imagine the route someone might have taken to do so.

When he'd completed a circuit around the house, Dustin inspected the ground as best he could in the dark, with only his flashlight to provide illumination. He headed toward the trail that wound through the trees and led to Willis House, but there was no sign that someone had come through. It might not have meant much in any case, since there was national parkland that wove in and out around them. People could easily wander off government land and onto private property without ever knowing it.

At last, he stopped and turned to look at her.

"I'm sorry. There's no way for me to find anything now."

"That's okay," Olivia said. "Thank you for coming so quickly."

"It's what I do, ma'am," he said lightly.

She turned and walked back to the house. He followed her thoughtfully.

"We'll have coffee," she said. Then she stopped and looked back at him. "Well, I guess that was presumptuous. I'm going to make coffee. It's past five and I don't see any reason to go back to sleep. But, of course, you might want to. Anyway, Sammy and I are fine now. Really."

He could tell that she wasn't fine; she was afraid. But she was going to try hard not to show it.

"Coffee would be great, and you're right. It's morning. It'll be light soon. No sense going back to bed."

She unlocked the door and walked inside, flipping on lights. She paused for a minute, as if trying to sense something.

"He isn't here, is he?" Dustin asked.

"Marcus, you mean?"

"Right."

"The bastard said he was coming back. To watch over me. He didn't."

"In all seriousness — although I suppose he could warn you if there's trouble — I'm not sure what he could do. You made the right call. The pun's accidental, but it's still true."

"You're better than 9-1-1?"

"You tell me."

She didn't answer, but moved on into the kitchen. There were old attractively refurbished stable stools in front of the counter. Dustin sat on one of them, watching as she returned the waffle iron to a lower cabinet and set about making coffee.

"I don't understand," she mused. "Why

would someone come to my house like that? It would be hard to break in during the middle of the night and make it look as if I had a terrible accident."

"When someone with the right agenda wants in, they'll get in," Dustin said. "But no one tried to break a window or shoot up a door. My guess is that this was just a trial run, a way of testing the waters."

"So someone's out to get me — because of what I've been saying?" she asked.

Sammy whined and settled at his feet. Dustin leaned down for a moment to pat the dog. When he looked up, she was at the counter, waiting for him to face her, waiting for his reply.

"I would guess that's it, yes," he told her. "Here's the good thing. Whoever's doing this hasn't gotten to a point where they're desperate. This person is just . . . researching the situation right now."

"What should I do?"

"Tell everyone you're getting an alarm system."

"And then?"

"Get an alarm system."

"Oh!"

"Listen, no one else believes that Marcus met with foul play. Well, other people might suspect it, but the police found nothing that would lend to more of an investigation than the one that's been done. You can't blame them. They found you with a man who was already dead. Thankfully, he'd been dead for hours, or you *might've* ended up as a suspect. But they found a man who'd been an addict dead with heroin in his system. There was no one around and no sign that anyone had been. There were no obvious marks on his body, other than those attributed to the fall."

"There were also no needles or drug paraphernalia," she reminded him sharply.

"True, but no addict keeps his stash where it can easily be discovered."

The coffee gurgled its last and she poured them both cups.

"The attorney's coming to the Horse Farm today to explain the will and dole out the individual bequests Marcus left."

"Just go, listen, watch other people. And as soon as possible, call an alarm system company."

"You don't think that's kind of paranoid?"

"Paranoid is better than —" He broke off. He'd been about to say *dead*. "You've heard the old adage a thousand times. Better safe than sorry."

She smiled at that. She'd known what he'd been about to say. "Would you hang around down here for a few minutes while I go up and get ready for the day?"

"Of course."

She'd drunk half her coffee. Leaving it, she turned around and dashed up the stairs.

He was going to be sorry to see the beautiful robe go, he thought.

Restlessly, he walked the ground floor of the house, checking windows as he went. The place was sealed tight. He sat in the parlor, thinking about the psychology of what had happened. Whoever had done this wasn't a serial killer with a penchant for a certain physical type; this was a person or persons with an agenda.

Dustin knew he should be looking for someone who was after something that wasn't obvious. Or maybe Marcus's killer had been seeking revenge for some reason. But if revenge was the only agenda, why come after anyone else?

No, fear of discovery had to be the motive for targeting Olivia Gordon. What did she know that she didn't even realize she knew?

And how far was the killer willing to go to safeguard a secret?

Olivia came down the stairs, Sammy at her heels. It was barely seven and beginning to get light outside.

He rose. "I have an idea. Go to the café in

your car. I'll get my own car and follow you. You *are* allowed to dine with 'guests' if you happen to arrive at a restaurant at the same time?"

"Yes, we always run into people at the café and there's never been any kind of policy against sharing a meal. After all, we do the camping trips, Mariah runs her ghost tours . . . ? I'm sure that 'running into you' will be fine."

She seemed grateful for the suggestion.

He collected his backpack; she picked up a shoulder bag.

"All right, Olivia, I know I already mentioned this, but it's important. You need to make it known that you're hiring an alarm company."

"What reason would I give for suddenly doing that?"

"You say you heard noises — and that you're far away from anyone else. You're just feeling nervous, that's all."

"Okay," she said.

They headed out.

At the door, Sammy whined. "You need to protect the homefront," Olivia told him, then locked the door, checking it a couple of times.

She got in her car; he waited until she was safe inside, backing out onto the drive. Then he followed. As they approached the café, he slowed his car. He wanted her to be there for a few minutes before he joined her.

And yet, he wondered if whoever had attempted entry at her house had been there all the while, hidden somewhere in the trees.

Watching him watch Olivia.

Olivia was the first customer to arrive at the café that morning. Behind the counter, still setting up, Delilah looked at her with surprise. "Liv, honey! What are you doing here so early?"

"Oh, I couldn't sleep, so I got up and I didn't feel like my own company," Olivia explained.

Delilah nodded as if she understood. "I hear ya, honey. I know you people at the Horse Farm have to meet up with Marcus's attorney this morning. That's going to be hard for you."

"I'm okay, Delilah," Olivia said. And she was, although she felt angry with Marcus. Not the anger that typically came with grief, in which a person was angry about being abandoned by a loved one; she would have recognized such an emotion. No, she was angry with Marcus's spirit — a spirit who showed up to shock her and then disappeared just when he was needed. A ghost who didn't bother to return when he'd promised he would.

"I've just gotten this new-fangled machine in here." Delilah pointed at a shiny silver contraption. "Makes a perfect espresso every time, according to the box. You want to try one?"

"Hmm. I'd love a cup of regular coffee — with a shot of espresso," Olivia said.

"Hey, great idea. Maybe I should try one of those myself. I've been working long hours lately. My waitress — you remember that sweet young thing, Genie? — she took off for Nashville last week. Decided she was going to get a job in the city. Can't say as I blame her. I mean, folks out here like country and the city is close enough . . . but a young girl? She needed more. So, anyway, to make a long story short, I've been filling in mornings *and* nights. But I own the place and Steve back there has been my cook for the past twenty years. Reckon we'll make it till we get some help." Delilah grinned wickedly. Steve was her husband as well as her chief cook and bottle washer.

"If I hear of anyone looking for work, I'll send them your way," Olivia said. She pulled out her smartphone and started looking for area alarm companies.

"What ya doin', honey? Can I help?" Delilah asked.

"Oh, I'm going to get an alarm system installed," Olivia replied.

"Out here? We never have trouble out here. Of course, I've got my man and a shotgun if anyone's going to give me trouble!"

Olivia shook her head. "I don't have a man or a shotgun."

Delilah wagged a finger at her. "You should get yourself a man, Liv. Pretty little thing like you. Just 'cause that ornery Bill Preston decided to up and head on out of your life . . . And that was more than a year ago!"

Olivia sighed. She'd been in an almost-live-in relationship with a music promoter. After a trip to Austin, he'd discovered some great opportunities there. It had come time for her to weigh the importance of the relationship. She hadn't been in love. Not enough to leave.

"Bill's a good guy — we were just going different places, Delilah."

Delilah tsked at her, then selected a little pod for her new machine; her frown became a smile of pleasure when her espresso machine instantly began to steam up and pour out dark brown liquid. She prepared the coffee, added the espresso and set it before Olivia. "I should name this concoction after you!" she said proudly.

"Oh, I don't think it really needs a name," Olivia told her. "The chain coffee shops have it already, I'm afraid. They just call it coffee with a shot of espresso."

"Here's it going to be a 'Liv'!" Delilah insisted.

The door opened and Dustin made his entrance. "Morning, Delilah," he said. "Good morning, Olivia." He walked up to take a seat at the counter beside her.

"My, my, you folks are up early today," Delilah remarked. "Nice to see you, Agent Blake. Sorry — Dustin."

"Thanks."

"How about a 'Liv'?" Delilah offered.

"A Liv?" he asked with a question in his eyes as he smiled over at her.

The man had a good smile, Olivia thought. At the moment, it revealed charm and a touch of amusement. He really was a perfect man — lean, hard-muscled and fit. His skin was slightly bronzed, his eyes a striking deep green and his shock of neatly clipped hair defined the concept of auburn.

She hoped he couldn't read her thoughts. She felt her cheeks flush and spoke quickly to cover her embarrassment. "I happen to be the first person Delilah's ever served a

144

coffee with an espresso thrown in. She's going to call it a 'Liv' from now on."

"Oh," he said gravely, turning to Delilah. "Sounds wonderful. Looks wonderful. How does it taste?"

"It's excellent," Olivia assured him.

"Guess when you're up and at 'em this early, makes good sense," Delilah said. "So, did you find an alarm company, hon? I can't really help — we never needed an alarm around here, you know?"

"I found one." Olivia stood up. "Excuse me while I give them a call." She walked down to the end of the little diner. The office was open and she arranged for a technician to come out on Saturday. That was the earliest someone would be available.

It would have to do, she told herself. Two days. She returned to her chair.

"Any luck, honey?" Delilah asked.

"Yeah, I'm all set up."

Delilah turned to Dustin. "I said I couldn't advise her. I've got a shotgun — and a man." She nodded knowingly, then gestured at Olivia. "Can you imagine? This sweet young thing was with a fella who lit out for Austin!"

Olivia could feel Dustin's eyes on her.

She groaned. "Delilah, he's making a great living in Austin and I'm happy for him. I'm

145

perfectly fine on my own."

"Some people are fine, you know," Dustin said. There was amusement in his voice. But he seemed to sense her discomfort and changed the subject.

"I'd love to have a 'Liv,' too," he said. "And some of your pancakes, please."

Olivia decided on an omelet.

Whistling, Delilah conveyed their orders to Steve and set to work on Dustin's coffee. After glancing at Olivia and obviously trying not to grin, Dustin chatted casually, asking her how they went about choosing the right horses to work with people.

"Well, obviously, when Marcus brought in a rescue animal with bad kicking habits, or one that nipped, we kept working the horse ourselves."

"And could you retrain all of them so they could work with others?" he asked.

"Most of the time, rescues have been neglected but they can work well with people and enjoy human interaction. Every once in a while, though, we've gotten a horse that was so abused it could never be assigned to anyone who wasn't experienced with horses."

"And then?"

Olivia shrugged. "And then one of the staff would just keep working with the horse or sometimes use it for group trail rides. Occasionally, if a horse had been so abused that Marcus could never feel comfortable allowing anyone to ride it, the horse was just retired and allowed to stay in the paddocks for the duration of its natural life." She looked straight ahead for a moment. "Marcus made the Horse Farm a no-kill shelter."

"Nice," he said quietly.

The door opened, and Olivia twisted her head to see who had arrived.

It was Deputy Sheriff Frank Vine. He'd been on duty the day Marcus had disappeared. For a cop, Frank was an exceptionally gentle man. Fifty-something, with hair that was almost pure white and a laid-back manner, Frank could be tough, but he listened, weighing every situation carefully.

He'd even listened to her when she'd found Marcus. He'd soothed her and told her sadly that people didn't always live up to their own expectations or those of others. It didn't make them bad people. They just hadn't had the strength they'd needed.

"Morning, Frank," she said.

"Olivia, good morning. And how are you doing, young lady?" he asked, sliding onto the stool to her left. He beamed at Delilah and then leaned back, unabashedly studying Dustin. "Hello, sir."

"Frank Vine, Dustin Blake." Olivia made quick introductions. Dustin stood for a moment to shake Frank's hand. Delilah came over with a cup and the coffeepot. "Morning, Deputy Frank," she said. "Dustin here is one of your own. A federal officer of the law."

"Oh, yeah?" Frank looked at Dustin again. "Are you out here for any special reason?"

"I am. I'm attending the Horse Farm," Dustin said.

"Oh." Frank nodded but obviously remained curious.

"And I'm originally from Nashville."

"Ah." That seemed to make sense to Frank. "Our own Music City." His pride in Nashville was evident.

"No better place," Dustin agreed.

Frank nodded happily; Dustin had made a friend.

"I hear the Horse Farm had to do a lot of rescheduling this morning, because the lawyer's coming to discuss the terms of Marcus Danby's will," Frank said.

"It's a formality, but I guess it's necessary," Olivia put in.

"Deputy," Dustin began. "I'm curious. I believe the medical examiner concluded that Marcus Danby's death was accidental.

The result of a fall, possibly brought on by a mind-altering substance. Heroin. Where did Marcus inject?"

Frank's face turned a mottled red. "The usual," he murmured.

"Vein in the arm?" Dustin asked. "I guess at his point in his life — when he fell back into drugs — he wouldn't have collapsed veins, and the needle mark would've been easy for the medical pathologist to find."

"Right," Frank said. He looked over at Dustin. "He was a mighty fine man and the Horse Farm is a mighty fine place. We don't judge Marcus harshly, and we ask you not to do so, either. You're here for healing, I imagine, son, so let the healing begin. Now, Liv," Frank said, turning to her. "Today will make things all legal. Aaron takes over, and that's fitting. Aaron's been Marcus's right-hand man for over a decade now. But . . . I need you to do me a favor."

"What's that, Frank?"

"There's a big old yellow dog on the property. Marcus came back with him after a trip to Memphis. He was at some animal shelter over there and was running out of days," Frank said.

"Homer. He's some kind of Lab mix — probably about three or four years old. He's a great dog."

"I'd like to have him. Think you could make that happen for me? Marcus might've left him to you in his will. He liked the big old mutt almost as much as his Sammy."

"Frank, you know animals come to the farm not because we need more animals, but so they can survive. Whether Homer was left to me or Aaron or anyone else, I'm sure we'd all be delighted for you to have him."

"Thanks. The kids are all grown up now with kids of their own, and since last fall . . . Well, I figured that dog kind of took a hankering to me and I kind of took a hankering to him," Frank said.

Frank's wife had passed away the year before from cancer. Olivia patted his hand. "Homer would be privileged to live with you, Frank."

Frank nodded. Delilah brought plates of food for Dustin and Olivia and took Frank's order. Twenty minutes later, Frank had finished his corned beef hash and grits and headed off to work. Olivia looked at her watch and asked Delilah for her check. She glanced at Dustin, who'd grown thoughtful when Frank left.

While Delilah tallied their bills, Dustin said, "So that's the officer who won't believe you about Marcus? Seems like you two get on well enough."

"That's one of them. We have two sheriff's deputies who handle this area — Frank, and Jimmy Callahan. They're both decent guys. But . . . they feel sorry for those of us who wear rose-tinted glasses, as Jimmy phrased it. They're very kind when they try to make me understand what they see as the sad truth."

Delilah was on her way toward them, and Dustin fell silent. "See you in class, Agent Blake," Olivia said, rising to take her bill and put money on the counter. "Delilah, thank you. Delicious as usual."

"Bye, honey. See you soon," Delilah said.

The sun was bright now. Special agent Dustin Blake was still at the counter in the diner behind her as Olivia walked to her car, wondering if she'd simply imagined that someone had tried to gain entry to her house.

She drove the short distance to the Horse Farm. Pulling into the parking area in front of the office, she saw that Drew and Sydney had been up early, too; the horses were out in the pasture. A quick count assured her they were all there. Shebaan, an aging Tennessee Walker. Trickster, often used in therapy sessions. Beloved Battle-ax, an old Percheron mix who was as big as a house and gentle as the Easter bunny. Zeus, a Paint. Carina, a gentle palomino. Martin, an Arabian mix. Chapparal, a one-time champion barrel-racer. Pixie and Nixie, rescued mixes from the swamps of Georgia. Gargantua, some kind of Clydesdale mix Marcus had owned forever. Beryl, a sweet bay, and her own personal favorite, Shiloh.

"Hey, guys. Morning!" she called to the horses.

She entered the office. Drew and Sydney were there, talking with Aaron, who held one of the Horse Farm cats on his lap. Sandra Cheever was seated on the arm of the sofa, and Mason Garlano stood by the window, smoothing back his hair. She saw that the window was providing him with a reflection.

"Who are we missing?" Aaron asked, waving her in.

"Just Mariah," Sandra announced. "She gave me a call a minute ago. She's on her way." She glanced at Olivia. "Liv, you're looking a little . . . tired. You okay?"

"I'm fine, thanks. I didn't get much sleep, though. Had some kind of animal sniffing around the house last night."

Mason turned to her with a grin. "Some kind of animal? Olivia, you practically live in the woods. Or the country, anyway. There are *lots* of animals around you."

"I know. But it made me decide to get an alarm system installed."

"That's never a bad idea," Aaron said.

"Not really necessary around here, in my opinion," Sandra said. She smiled. "But whatever. If creeping animals are giving you . . . well, the creeps! . . . you should get an alarm system."

"Yep," Mason agreed. He gave Olivia his best sexy smile. "Pretty girl in the woods. You never know when a wolf will show up."

"We don't have any wolves around here," Aaron said.

"Ah, well, they also come on two feet, don't they?" Mason teased. He grinned at Olivia. She grinned back. He'd tried to get something going with her when he'd first started working there. She liked him — as a friend. She knew that while he could be an effective therapist, he was also self-involved. He knew it, too. But his ego didn't get in the way of his sense of humor, and they both saw the absurdity in many situations.

"They definitely come on two feet!" Sandra said, shaking her head. "Mason, would you bring me some more coffee?"

"Sure. Where's the attorney?" Mason asked, walking over to the coffee service to oblige her. "He's late."

153

"I think that's him driving in now," Aaron said. "So, everyone, get your coffee and get settled."

The attorney came in. Olivia had met him once before, just in passing. Aaron introduced him as Kevin Fairchild. He was a slim man, balding and out of place at the Horse Farm in a black business suit, white tailored shirt, striped tie and silver tiepin. But he was friendly, smiled easily and didn't seem to care if he got dust or animal hair on his suit.

Mariah followed him in a moment later, sweeping her hair into a ponytail as she walked. She slid next to Olivia on the sofa and rolled her eyes. "Can you believe it? I overslept."

"We're all here, so we'll get started," Aaron said. "Mr. Fairchild, if you will? I have a feeling you'll have to explain everything in layman's terms. For me, certainly. I tried to fill out my own living will once and it confused the hell out of me!"

They all smiled and laughed, a little nervously, Olivia thought, although there was no reason for anyone to be nervous. *Marcus's will should hold no surprises.*

"Well, ladies and gentlemen, let's begin. I'll explain the legalese as I go along and feel free to ask me questions."

Fairchild started to read, and Olivia's mind wandered as he went through legal phrase after legal phrase. It was more or less what she'd expected, although she'd never been to the "reading" of a will before. She found herself looking around at all her coworkers, trying to grasp the fact that one of them might have killed Marcus — and might want to kill her.

Aaron leaned against the counter, looking perplexed as he listened. Drew Dicksen appeared to be deep in thought. Sydney Roux dangled his key chain and stared out the window; from where he stood, he could see their horses in the field. Homer, the big yellow dog Deputy Frank Vine had asked her about, was running after a bird.

Mariah seemed to be dozing off.

Mason was worrying a fingernail.

Sandra Cheever was trying to look as if she was paying attention, but her eyes kept glazing over.

Olivia started as she suddenly heard her name. Fairchild was silent, as were the others; they all studied her curiously.

"I don't understand," Sandra said. "Aaron gets the place, but not really. And after him, Olivia gets it, and if she doesn't run it into the ground, she names her own successor?"

"Thanks for the vote of confidence,"

Olivia murmured to Sandra, except that she was surprised herself and realized Sandra hadn't meant to be offensive. She flashed her an apologetic smile.

"Don't worry, I'm not going anywhere," Aaron said.

"Better not!" Olivia told him.

"The Horse Farm is in a trust," Fairchild explained. "Aaron maintains the senior position and makes all the decisions. In the event of something happening to Aaron, Olivia will take over as senior operating official. Sometime in the next year, they're to name the others who'll follow in their places, and so on, down the line. It's very straightforward. Marcus had this will written so he could ensure that the Horse Farm would continue. The nonprofit will not be dissolved, and someone will always be there to see that it goes on doing the work he intended."

"What would happen in the event of a natural catastrophe, like a flood?" Mason asked. "We did have that major one a few years back!"

"Okay, if something catastrophic were to happen or if the Horse Farm fell into such severe financial hardship that it couldn't be maintained and your salaries couldn't be paid, the property would revert to the actual estate. The land would go up for sale, and any profits would be distributed to a number of other charities. Do you all understand?" Fairchild asked, looking around at them.

They all nodded.

"Now let me go on with the individual items he's left you."

Olivia listened but his words blurred. Marcus had left them things that were special to him. A saddle and a desk to Drew, collectible books to Mariah, a sterling tea set to Sandra and other personal property to others. She heard her name again and looked up.

"What?"

Once more, they were all staring at her. "Another house," Sandra said. "Nice."

"What?"

"He left *you* his house and the immediate property around it," Aaron told her with a smile. "You can now search it to your heart's content."

"You can tear it to pieces, if you choose," Fairchild said. "The house is yours, free and clear."

"The house," she murmured. It should have gone to Aaron. But Aaron didn't seem disturbed, didn't seem to care.

Was it an act?

You bastard, Marcus! Why didn't you warn me?

"And, of course, Shiloh," Fairchild added. "He felt that you and the horse shared something unique. You're free to keep Shiloh at the facility or build a barn at the house you've just inherited or on your own property. There's a lot of fine print here — but that's what it means."

She nodded, grateful for his explanation. She wasn't sure she needed another house — but she did love the horse!

"What about Homer?" she asked. "Yellow Dog as we sometimes call him."

"What about him?"

"Deputy Vine asked if he could have him," Olivia said.

Fairchild looked at his papers. "Rescue animals will continue to come and go from the facility as determined by those in charge. No animal will be put to death or set into the hands of those who would euthanize said animal or abuse it. Adoptions will be given due consideration by the entire staff and should continue with majority approval."

"I say Deputy Vine gets Homer." Aaron surveyed the room as he spoke. "Agreed?"

"Sure. One less mouth to feed at night — until one of us drags in another," Drew said.

"Agreed," Sydney chimed in.

"Hell, yeah!" Mariah said.

"Well, then, that's it," Fairchild told them. "My office is available to you. Anyone feeling any confusion is more than welcome to call me for clarification." He paused a little awkwardly. "Marcus was my client. I didn't know him that well. But he held each of you in high regard, I do know that. Naturally, none of us suspected he'd be leaving us quite so soon, but . . . you should be aware how valued and appreciated you all were in his eyes." He looked at each of them in turn and then at Aaron. "Well, then, I'll be on my way."

When he'd departed, Drew and Sydney stood, leaving to attend to their duties. Mason got to his feet, too, and was out the door before the women had even managed to rise.

When the door closed behind him, they were all silent. "Well," Aaron said brusquely, "that's it. We start up again right after lunch, so if you want a break, take it now. Thank you all for being here on time, and . . ." He sighed. "That's it," he repeated. "The will's been read, the die is cast, Marcus is gone. We carry on."

Looking over at Aaron, who stood near his office door, Olivia shivered.

Aaron frowned at her. "Olivia?"

"Sorry. I just got a strange feeling. Someone walking on my grave, or whatever that saying is."

"It's all right," Aaron said gently. "We all have to get back to normal. We have a legacy to live up to, but Marcus *is* gone."

She nodded.

Except that Marcus wasn't gone at all. He was leaning against the doorway of Aaron's office, arms crossed, grinning as he watched the proceedings.

He smiled at her and then seemed to fade into the wall.

Was he just letting her know he was around, watching?

Ever hopeful that he'd see or hear something that would help catch his killer?

6

"The one-eyed Persian is Oscar. The old ginger boy sound asleep in the hayloft in Trickster's stall is Orange Cat. You'll see about a dozen of them running around, going into and out of the office," Drew told Dustin. "Marcus was a sucker for just about anything that had a heartbeat, so you'll see cats, dogs and a few other pets an owner brought home and then tossed. Horses, needless to say. If you see a cat you like or a pup, just talk to Aaron. We're continuing with the policy of bring 'em in — and if you find a good home, let 'em go."

Dustin had just admired one of the massive cats keeping "rat guard" in the stables. Now he knew the feline's name was Orange Cat. Not imaginative, but certainly fitting.

"It's a wonderful policy," he said. Drew didn't seem to mind that Dustin was there and had been for about forty-five minutes. He'd helped bring some of the horses in

from pasture and brushed them down. Mariah had an individual therapy session coming up and Mason was taking out a new group.

He'd been scheduled for a ride with Olivia — but not alone. Apparently, because of the time lost that morning, Joey Walters was going to be with them. Which was fine; he liked Joey.

After breakfast at the café, Dustin had spent a few hours on his computer and done some fact-checking with the office back in Virginia. He'd read bios on everyone here over and over again. Nothing stood out. No history of mental illness, much less homicidal tendencies. Before coming to the Horse Farm, Sandra Cheever had worked for a medical office, arranging schedules and dealing with patients for a group of psychiatrists; she'd left only because Aaron had lured her away. She'd never received even a parking ticket. Mason Garlano had been working at a physical rehab center until he followed his girlfriend to Nashville. They had since broken up, but the girlfriend was alive and well and working as a sound technician for a studio in Nashville. Andrew Dicksen had moved to the Nashville area from Biloxi, Mississippi, with his family when he'd been ten. He'd done the rodeo

circuit until his thirtieth birthday when a fall from a bull had damaged his collarbone; he'd known Marcus, and Marcus had offered him the job. Aaron Bentley had been a college student studying toward a business degree and working at a hack ranch when he'd met Marcus, who'd hired him. That had been twenty years ago. Both Sydney Roux and Mariah Naughton were from the area, and had lived there all their lives. Sydney had been arrested once in college for protesting a military action. Not one of them had a history of violence, theft, drug abuse or any other ill-doing that might have raised a pale pink flag, never mind a red one.

And still, Dustin was convinced that Marcus had been murdered and by someone close, someone who knew him well. That meant — as he'd assumed earlier — that there had to have been a motive, a secret agenda, since no fight had broken out. He hadn't been killed in a fit of anger. His murder had been carefully calculated to look like an accidental death.

Official records were helpful, but they didn't say much that was personal about anyone. Dustin was grateful for social media; he looked up every form of internet page or link he could for each of his suspects. Apparently, Drew had yet to enter the media age. He had a Facebook page but never posted. Mariah, on the other hand, loved her page — and used it, of course, to promote the ghost tours she did twice a month. Sandra Cheever used hers to communicate with family in New York. Mason kept up with friends in Texas — and made social arrangements with his friends in Nashville. Sydney Roux posted a lot of pictures of the animals at the Horse Farm. He took good pictures and made it clear that the puppies and kittens who wound up there were available for adoption to good homes. Aaron only had a professional page that led back directly to the Horse Farm.

He found himself looking up Olivia's Facebook page, as well; she, too, liked to post pictures of the adoptable animals at the Horse Farm but she also mentioned social events and proudly posted beautiful pictures that showed off the grace and beauty of Tennessee.

He could spend his life on the computer, but it was nothing compared to actually spending time with people, face-to-face. He'd discovered he liked Drew; he really hoped the man wasn't hiding some kind of dark secret. One thing the academy had taught him was that you could never be too careful — it was dangerous to trust a friendly face. Some of the nation's most heinous serial killers had actually been charming when not slicing or strangling their victims.

"Did you ever meet Marcus?" Andrew asked him, hoisting a saddle onto Shiloh.

"No, I never did."

"But you're from the area?"

"From the city, originally," Dustin said.

"Nashville's the best city in the world, but I love these rolling hills out here," Drew told him. He shrugged. "I guess even though it's small in comparison to New York, Atlanta or Chicago, Nashville's actually pretty big. Folks could wander around for years and never meet one another. Out here, we do." He grinned. "And regardless of how long I've lived in the state, I'll never be a real homeboy to people who are from here — like Mariah or Sydney. They can trace their families back for generations. But Olivia used to come out here all the time with her parents, and I know she and Mariah never met." He shrugged. "A lot of life is an accident of timing, isn't it?"

"I guess so," Dustin said. "It's easy to go through life not knowing everyone — even in a small town, let alone a big city," he added wryly.

"That's true enough." Drew grinned. "Listen, thanks for the help."

"Not a problem. I love horses," Dustin said. "And cats — and dogs."

"Plenty around here," Andrew said. "In fact, you really would be a good candidate to take home a pup or a kitten."

"I wish I was. I'm never in one place long enough to be a good owner."

"Because of your work."

"I'm a field agent. That means going out in the field."

"Yeah, well, takes a good man to know when he can't have an animal, too. That's the problem, people picking up cute kittens or pups and not realizing the little critters are going to get big. So they dump them. Or the dog messes in the house. Or they get the pet and then have kids and forget they have the pet. But all the animals lucky enough to come here, well, they'll still be taken care of."

"No surprises in the will, huh?" Dustin asked.

Drew shook his head, adjusting the saddle on Shiloh. "Not really. Oh, yeah, there was one. Marcus left his home and the property it's on to Olivia."

"That was a surprise, then?"

"We thought it would go to Aaron. Aaron

loves this place and manages it really well. It would've been easy for him to live there, and go back and forth to the Horse Farm."

"Actually, couldn't he just live here if he chose? You and Sydney do, right?"

"Yeah, but . . . we're not management types. We keep our places pretty nice, but hey . . . this is a stable, and it smells like a stable. But . . ."

"I'm sure your living arrangements are fine," Dustin said. "So where does Aaron live now?"

"Oh, he rents a house down the road. He should've bought a house when the buying was good. Guess he figured maybe he didn't have to," Drew said with another shrug. "I doubt it's a problem. The Horse Farm being nonprofit doesn't mean he doesn't get a nice salary."

"What about you guys?" Dustin asked.

Andrew laughed. "I like my life just fine. I have a comfortable place to lay my head at night. I love my work. I enjoy working with kids. I wake up every morning to fresh air and beautiful country. No rush hour. Yeah, I'm pretty happy with my life."

"Good to hear," Dustin said.

He saw that Olivia was coming out of the office. He'd gotten a brief text from her, saying that she planned to stay at the office where there'd be several people around until her afternoon sessions.

But now she was headed his way. "Hi, Dustin. And thanks, Andrew." She patted Shiloh's neck. "I could have saddled him."

"I get restless with nothing to do," Andrew told her. "So, things have changed a bit. Are you going to keep Shiloh here? Or do you plan on building a barn?"

"I'm here most of the time, and you and Sydney are always here," she said. "I'm happier having him stabled where someone's on duty 24/7."

"That makes sense." Andrew looked at Dustin. "You never know with a horse. I had some friends who lost two of their horses a few years back. No one was home. Somehow a pasture gate was left open. The horses got onto the road and were hit by a semi and they had to be put down. You just never know."

"Have you seen Joey yet?" Olivia asked.

"On his way right now," Dustin said.

Joey had been let out of a van that had the words Parsonage House written in script on the side. Two other boys stepped out — Matt and Sean, Dustin saw. They headed into the office, while Joey walked toward them, smiling.

"We get to ride today, right?" he asked

Olivia. "Oh, hello, Dustin, Drew."

"We're still riding today," Olivia said. "Joey, I have you on Trickster, and Andrew, I see you've gotten Chapparal saddled. He'll be perfect for Dustin, unless he was saddled for someone else?"

"He's all yours. In fact, Dustin brought him in. He's been here helping me."

"Thanks." Olivia nodded. "Well, then, shall we?"

Ten minutes later, they were mounted and striking out beyond the pastures. The hills rose and fell until they reached a stretch of relatively flat land. Olivia said, "Okay, Joey, we'll run them for a minute here, but we're not racing. Remember that everything we've learned about trust and boundaries works when you're riding, too. Don't let Trickster take you. You're taking her."

Joey nodded, flushing with pleasure. Olivia glanced at him and Dustin nodded; she was going to head out first. He'd bring up the rear.

It wasn't a wild ride. It was a pleasant canter and then a brief gallop across the flat land. Olivia reined in first, waiting for the other two. Joey slipped sideways when Trickster reverted to a trot, but he gripped the horn of his western saddle for a mo-

ment, regaining his balance. He beamed at
Olivia.

"We're doing okay," he said.

Olivia smiled at him but her smile faded.
Dustin saw that she was gazing past Joey —
back up to the hill that rose between them
and the Horse Farm.

He followed her line of vision. The sun
was high; it seemed to cast shadows on the
mound.

But Dustin saw someone there.

There, but not *really* there.

The image of a tall rider sitting proudly
on a great steed gradually appeared. He
wore a plumed hat and the gray-caped
dress-coat of a Confederate general. Dustin
thought he lifted a hand, almost as if in
warning. Then the sun blazed brightly, coming from behind a white cloud, and the
general was gone.

"Hey, Liv, you're coming on the camping
trip tomorrow night, aren't you?" Joey said,
unaware.

"Pardon?" Olivia brought her attention
back to the boy.

"The camping trip. You're coming, right?"

"Uh, yes. I suppose so," Olivia said.

"And you're coming, too," Joey looked at
Dustin. "You said you would."

"Yes, sounds like fun. I used to go on

camping trips around here years ago," Dustin told him.

"Mariah's going to tell ghost stories," Joey said.

"She's good at talking about history, too," Olivia added a little sharply.

"Yes, but you can only have a ghost if you have the history of someone who lived," Joey said reasonably.

"Yes, of course, but . . . history is important, Joey," Olivia said. "There was a famous philosopher named George Santayana who explained why it's so important to understand history. His words are often quoted. 'Those who cannot remember the past are condemned to repeat it.' We need to learn from all the things that came before. It's a good thing that we remember the American Civil War — especially when we see politics get heated today. Tennessee was the last state to secede from the Union, and the people were split on their beliefs throughout the war. East Tennessee actually tried to secede from Tennessee when it left the Union, but troops were sent in. The state was truly divided. The east was for the North, the west for the South — and the middle of the state cast the deciding ballot. It was horribly sad and tragic here. Only the state of Virginia saw more battles. The

Battle of Shiloh was, at the time, the bloodiest in the nation's history. But we learned from the war, Joey."

"In many ways," Dustin murmured.

Joey turned to face him, "Yeah, I know," he said dryly. "My dad told me they still study Civil War strategy. Like today, you wouldn't fight the same — we have automatic weapons and bombs and drones and stuff. But the military today can still learn from the strategies they used back then."

"We also learned about compromise and holding a country together," Dustin said, hoping he didn't sound too much as though he was lecturing. "It's easy to be harsh now when we look at the past. Sometimes you have to wonder what the hell were they thinking, and you have to try to understand the context and the reasons — and the mistakes. That's history, and that's why it's important."

"And why we get ghosts!" Joey threw in cheerfully.

"But ghosts are good, too," Olivia said. "For instance, General Rufus Cunningham is a famous ghost around here, and he tells us a lot about humanity. He was a leader, but he didn't consider any of his men expendable. And he valued human life even when that life belonged to the enemy."

172

"Yeah, and he died. 'No good deed goes unpunished,' " Joey blurted out, grinning.

Olivia groaned. "Oh, I give up!"

"Kidding, just kidding!" Joey said. "I love the stories about the general. Are we going to ride? Or are we going to just sit here?"

"We'll take the forest trail to the curve, come back around and let them run again for a few minutes. It's beautiful riding through the trees," Olivia said.

She led the way. Trickster tried to stop for grass, but Olivia reminded Joey that the horse shouldn't be calling the shots; he could give Trickster an apple back at the stables. Joey regained control, grinning at her proudly as he did.

Olivia rode on, and the others followed. She reined in at a copse, and they paused behind her. A doe and her young fawn were nibbling on short grasses near the edge, barely visible beneath the canopy of the trees.

"Wow!" Joey whispered.

"Let's go around. Maybe they won't bolt," Olivia said.

They skirted the high pines, giving the doe and her fawn a wide berth. The doe looked up and stared at them. For a moment, her instinct and fear were visible. But she didn't move. She studied them, then went back to her nibbling. They guided their horses around her.

Dustin didn't see exactly what happened next. He heard something — a whizzing sound in the air.

Shiloh let out a snort of terror and reared up. Olivia calmed him quickly, and turned to look at Dustin and Joey.

"You okay?" she asked.

"Fine," Joey said. "What was that?"

"I don't know. The world's biggest bee, maybe." Olivia was in control, but Dustin saw that she was shaken. He heard rustling. It seemed to come from behind them.

He turned Chapparal. The horse could whirl around on a dime — good thing for him at the moment. The trail was narrow here, but led back to the trees. The doe and her fawn were no longer there; they'd obviously been spooked. He kept moving, inspecting the trail on the other side. He didn't see anything, but when he dismounted, he discovered that the ground had been disturbed and a number of low-hanging branches were broken. He continued to follow the trail, leaving Olivia and Joey behind. He heard Joey call out and paused, wanting to take his investigation all the way to the road — but afraid to leave the two of them alone in the forest where something had, apparently, flown through the air with the speed of a bullet.

Had it been a bullet?

And had Olivia been a target?

Frustrated, he rode back to where Olivia and Joey waited for him.

"Nothing," he said with a shrug.

"Weird!" Joey said. "A small bird. That's what it looked like from here. A dive-bombing bird."

"You saw it?" Dustin asked.

"Well, not exactly. I just *heard* something. . . . And I thought I saw something whiz by close to Liv and Shiloh — a really fast bird, like I said — but I don't know for sure. Maybe —"

"We've got to head back," Olivia broke in. "I have another session this afternoon."

"Not riding?" Dustin realized his tone was sharper than he'd intended.

"No, just in the pasture. A group session."

"We get to stay until five," Joey said. "Double with me against Sean and Matt at Ping-Pong?" he asked Dustin.

"Okay. I'll hang around," Dustin said, looking at Olivia. She showed no reaction, and he couldn't decide whether he was disappointed or relieved.

As they rode back, Dustin kept watch on everything around them, still uneasy about the flying object that had whizzed by them all.

It hadn't been the world's biggest bee.

Or a dive-bombing bird.

But neither, he thought, had it been a bullet. So what the hell . . . ?

True to her word, she allowed Joey and the horses their time to run. Then they returned to the stables. As good "guests," he and Joey took care of their mounts. Joey was happy to give Trickster the promised apple. Dustin enjoyed watching him with the horse as he assured Trickster that it was *much* better to have an apple at the end of a ride than munch on lousy grass during it.

He was still at the stables when Olivia went out with her next group; he wanted to keep an eye on her. But since she was surrounded by several people, he determined that she was going to be all right.

If something was going to "happen" to her it wouldn't be here — in front of others.

Joey was waiting impatiently for him to play Ping-Pong. He decided he might as well oblige now.

Matt and Sean were there, too, eager to take them on. Dustin played the game, paying heed to what was going on around him, as well. Sandra Cheever swept by, telling them all, in her usual curt tones, to play

176

fair, and marched into Aaron's office.

He thought he heard the two of them arguing.

When he and Joey took the game by a single point, he went to get coffee, trying to listen to what was being said in Aaron's office.

Sandra was speaking heatedly. Aaron was arguing with her in a soft, restrained voice.

"Boy, and they're supposed to be teaching *us* to get along!" Matt said sarcastically, coming up beside him.

Dustin grimaced. "Have they been at it all afternoon?"

"No." Matt frowned. "I don't think they were here. In fact, I know they weren't. Aaron showed up about an hour ago and said hello to all of us. That was odd, 'cause usually there's someone in the office all the time — when it's open, I mean. Hey, rematch?"

"Sure, just give me a minute," Dustin told him. "I'll meet you in the games room."

Matt nodded and sauntered off, and Dustin moved closer to the door. "It's wrong. It's just wrong!" Sandra Cheever was saying.

"Look, it is what it is," he heard Aaron reply.

"Not necessarily," Sandra said. "You're

going to have to take steps."

He didn't get a chance to hear any more. Mariah Naughton came breezing in. "Hey, there, Secret Agent Man. I'm thrilled you guys are coming on the camping trip. Liv sometimes comes along, and I love it when she does. I guarantee that you'll have a good time."

"I hear you tell great ghost stories."

She waved a hand. "Oh, well, the area's full of them. I don't tell anything new. You know all about the general, I take it, since you're from around here."

"I'm certainly familiar with him."

"Nashville has great ghost stories, too!" she said enthusiastically.

He nodded in response and she grinned. "Well, I hope we're giving you the rest and relaxation you were looking for."

"Definitely. I'm falling in love with horses all over again."

"Well, that's great, but . . . you have to fall in love with yourself again, too. That's part of it."

"I'm on my way to finding out what I need," he assured her.

The door to the office flew open. Sandra Cheever burst out, looking somewhat flustered. Seeing the two of them, she regained her composure quickly. "You're finished with your sessions for the day?" she asked Mariah.

"Yes, all done."

"Well, good." Sandra turned to Dustin. "As soon as Olivia comes in, we'll close the office."

"Where's Mason?" Mariah asked.

"He had some business in Nashville this afternoon." Sandra shook her head. "I'm ready to go home! This has been a long day and I'm exhausted."

She turned abruptly and left them. A minute later, Olivia came in. Before she could speak, Aaron hurried out of his office. "Hey, Liv. I've got the keys to Marcus's house, if you want them. You don't have to take them today, but I was thinking you might want to get those locks changed. Who knows how many keys Marcus might've had made to give to friends — or strangers! — who needed a place to stay."

"Thanks, Aaron. I will take them. I — I . . . think I'll go by and just take a look at the place," Olivia said.

While she was with Aaron, Dustin sent a text to the office in Virginia, asking for Marcus's address and directions to his house. He didn't want to head out with Olivia.

But he'd be damned if he'd let her go to

179

that house alone. The Ping-Pong rematch would have to wait.

Marcus Danby's small ranch house really had no historic significance. It was little more than an extended log cabin with only one floor.

The front door opened into a small hall-way; immediately to the right was the kitchen and beyond that a spacious living-dining area. Marcus had furnished it with quilted throws and handcrafted furniture. There was Native American art on the walls and various sculptures; he'd loved dream catchers and there were a number of them scattered about.

Olivia stepped into the living room, switched on a light and looked around. "Marcus?" she said aloud.

There was no answer.

A fine layer of dust was beginning to form on the furniture and objects. Other than that, it was just as Marcus had left it. Or so it appeared. Olivia glanced at the hall that led to the three small bedrooms. One he'd kept as a guest room, one was an office and one was his own.

She walked into the living room and sat on one of the sofas. A quilt — hand-stitched by the grandmother of one of their guests who'd proven to be a success story — was draped over a sofa. The sofa had also been handcrafted by another former guest who'd started a furniture-making business. Marcus had always helped out, not just with his talks and the Horse Farm, but also by supporting those who were trying to make a new life for themselves.

She looked at the coffee table, carved from the trunk of an old tree. There were a number of colored pages on it — drawings done by some of the boys who'd stayed at Parsonage House.

"So, you're being a jerk as a ghost, but you were one hell of a good guy, Marcus," she said. She studied the drawings. She knew the boys were sometimes asked to draw what they saw as the demons of their pasts, and sometimes they were asked to draw what they saw as their futures.

She picked up one that Joey had done. It was actually a good drawing. He'd portrayed a gaping black hole with demon eyes and razor-sharp teeth reaching into a sunlit room where he sat at a desk. Emptiness. Joey feared the emptiness of his life, she thought.

Hearing a sound behind her, Olivia started, jumping to her feet and whirling around in one motion.

It was Dustin. He still wore his casual tweed jacket over a denim shirt and the jeans he'd been wearing earlier.

Somehow, she'd known that he'd come. He would come because Malachi had sent him here and because protecting her was part of his job description.

She was glad he was there. He seemed to fill a room — an area, even in the midst of a forest or pasture — with confidence, with strength, like an invulnerable bastion.

"What the hell are you doing?" he asked her, clearly irritated.

So much for being glad to see him.

"I'm looking around Marcus's house," she said. "My house," she added.

"You didn't even lock the door!" he admonished.

She flushed. She hadn't thought to lock the door; she wasn't accustomed to being worried about her every move.

"I knew you were coming," she told him.

"You didn't know who else might be coming," he said, still aggravated. He started walking into the house.

To her amusement, he suddenly tripped. A corner of the rug stretched out on the hardwood floor had curled back.

Straightening, he swore softly.

"He has no right to be rude to you!"

Olivia heard.

Turning around, she saw that the ghost of Marcus Danby had decided to join them.

"Rude!" Dustin snapped. "What the hell? I'm trying to keep her from getting killed, and you don't seem to be helping a whole lot!"

Olivia turned again to look at Dustin, who was staring at Marcus.

"You see him," she breathed.

"Of course I see him. And hear him. And, Mr. Danby, under the circumstances, it's about time you stuck around to meet me," Dustin said. "I need to know everything about you and everything you did on the day you were killed. Your memory might be the only thing that can keep Olivia alive."

Marcus, startled — and offended — made his ghostly way across the room to stand in front of Dustin. "You — you're FBI. *You* have to find the truth of this. *I'm* not the one putting Olivia in danger."

"You put her in danger the minute you dragged her into this!" Dustin snapped.

"Hey, someone killed me! It's not just Olivia's life that's at stake. The Horse Farm itself is."

"So, you'd get her killed, as well?"

"She could hear me. I had to tell someone the truth."

"Excuse me," she began.

But neither seemed to hear her.

"You need to be worried about her safety before anything else," Dustin was saying.

"And you have to find my killer," Marcus countered. "That'll keep her out of danger."

"But you obviously have the information we need."

"No. You're the one with all the advantages. You're the one —"

"Yeah?"

"You're the one who's . . . alive."

7

Marcus's final statement apparently won the argument. Within minutes, he and Olivia were seated on the sofa, while Dustin was in a wing-back chair across the coffee table from them.

Olivia and Dustin had coffee — black. Marcus had told them the coffee was fine, but since he'd been dead for a while now, the milk probably wasn't so good. Olivia should throw it out.

Marcus went over the day of his death with Dustin; Dustin asked for details but Marcus really couldn't tell them anything they didn't already know. Dustin pressed him, anyway.

"Okay, you heard the dog from the woods and you went to find him. That's the last you remember?" Dustin asked.

"Yes, I just said that," Marcus replied in an exasperated tone.

"Which woods? Where were you *exactly*?"

"I don't know *exactly*. . . . There's a riding trail — the only real *trail.* You'll see little paths here and there, but if you were on horseback, you'd have to take the trail. That's where I was."

"And it was daylight, correct?"

"Yes. Although it was a little overcast. The canopy of the pines and the other trees can create this green darkness that's almost surreal. When we have fog, it's like being in a fantasyland," Marcus said.

Dustin ignored his lyrical description. "How far had you gone in?" he asked briskly.

"A hundred yards or so? I'd reached the copse."

"And then?"

"Then I don't remember."

"Did you feel a pain in your head? A prick in your arm? Anything that would explain how you lost consciousness?"

"No . . . Yes! Maybe. I thought I'd been stung by a bee . . . or gotten a spider bite. Something like that. Something you don't even pay attention to," Marcus said.

"The medical examiner has released the information that there were drugs in your system. We have to figure out how they got there," Dustin said.

"Well, there's nothing in this house, I can

assure you of that," Marcus responded indignantly.

Dustin looked at Olivia. "And tomorrow, at work, you should say that you searched all over the house and you didn't find anything — but that you're resigned to the fact that Marcus must have suffered a relapse and hidden his stash in the forest somewhere," he said.

"What?" Marcus demanded indignantly.

"Someone tried to get into Olivia's home last night, Marcus," Dustin told him.

"Oh. Oh, no!" Marcus said, giving Olivia an anguished look.

"I thought you were coming back," she reminded him.

"Yeah, I meant to, but . . ."

"But what?"

"I made some discoveries."

"Like what?" Dustin asked.

"I never knew Aaron and Sandra were sleeping together," Marcus said.

"You were *spying* on them?" Olivia shook her head in disgust.

"Not the way you think. I . . . went to the Horse Farm and Aaron was still there. I went —" He paused. There was an air of sadness about him that seemed palpable. "I went out to see the horses. Big Orange Cat was hanging around in Zeus's stall, and I swear that animal could feel me there, feel me pet him. That's a great cat, Agent — if you're thinking of adopting."

"He's a great mouser, too, Marcus. Good in the stables," Olivia pointed out.

"But he's special. Ah, hell, they're all special." Marcus sighed.

"Marcus," Dustin said, steering him back. "When you were at the stables last night, did you see Sydney or Drew?"

"No, but they were in their apartments," Marcus answered.

"Both apartments are upstairs. Sydney's is above the stable office and Drew's is over the tack room," Olivia clarified for Dustin's benefit.

"How did you know they were in their rooms? Did you go up?" Dustin asked.

"I could hear Drew playing an old Beatles album. Sydney was watching that reality show about people who own wildly expensive collectibles and don't even know it," Marcus said.

"But you didn't actually *see* either of them."

"No, because when I was in the stables, I heard noise over at the main office, so I went there."

"And did you see Aaron and Sandra?"

"Yes. I'm not sure where Sandra came

from. She might have stayed there after closing. Maybe she was just doing paperwork in the peace and quiet and fell asleep on one of the sofas. I've seen Sandra stay over to do paperwork and reports occasionally. Aaron drove in."

"Sandra said she was going straight home," Dustin said.

Marcus shrugged in response.

"What time?" Olivia asked him.

He looked at her curiously. "Time . . ." he repeated slowly.

"Yes, what time was it?"

"I don't really know. It's really not much of a concept to me anymore."

"Does that explain why you didn't come back to my house last night?"

Marcus seemed stricken by the reminder. "I am so sorry."

"You really can't help her, Marcus," Dustin said.

"I beg your pardon? I can warn her —"

"Yes, but, you're right. The responsibility falls to me. As you pointed out, I'm the one who's living."

Olivia wanted to pat Marcus's leg and remembered that she couldn't. "A warning is always helpful, Marcus. And I would've appreciated one last night," she muttered under her breath.

Dustin leaned forward. "Marcus, when you walked into the woods, do you remember hearing anything?"

"I walked in because the dog was yelping — crying. I knew Sammy was hurt," Marcus explained. "Did I hear anything else? Yes, actually. Something like a . . . flying sound. A buzzing? Sort of like a mosquito next to your ear. But then I . . ."

"But then you lost consciousness," Dustin finished.

Marcus nodded in a dazed way. "You're really not safe, are you, Liv? I *have* put you in danger."

"She's my responsibility now," Dustin said.

"Stop it!" Olivia exploded. "I'm not anyone's responsibility. I'm an adult. We're all here to discover the truth behind Marcus's death, not to treat me like . . . like an infant."

Both men stared at her.

"Do you want to get killed?" Marcus asked fiercely.

"No, of course not!"

"Hmm, let's see. He's a trained FBI agent and you're not. I say you need to let him take responsibility," Marcus told her.

She threw up her hands. "Can we not make it sound so . . . pathetic?"

They both looked at her again and then at each other. Dustin resumed his questioning. "Okay, Marcus, this is important. You believe — but you're not certain — that Sydney and Drew were in their rooms last night?"

"Yes."

"You don't know where Sandra Cheever was, but Aaron drove back to the Horse Farm. *And* you believe they're having an affair?"

"Yes. Discreet, of course. But . . ."

"It would explain today," Dustin murmured.

"What about today?" Olivia asked.

"I think they were arguing. This was before Sandra left — she said she was going straight home, by the way — then you came in. I didn't have a chance to find out what the argument was about, though. My, uh, eavesdropping was interrupted by Mariah, who started talking about the camping trip tomorrow night."

Marcus nodded. "The camping trip. If you're together, then Liv will be safe. But what about tonight? Someone could come looking for her here — or at her own house."

"I thought about that. I figured we'd go into Nashville. There's a small chain motel on the outskirts. Actually," he said, glancing at Olivia, "I was going to suggest a break. We could go in for dinner and get a couple of rooms at the motel. Olivia can leave her car at her place in case anyone's watching. It's more plausible that I might be in the city, since people know I have a sister who lives there. She's not in town at the moment, but no one knows *that*."

"Sounds good," Marcus said approvingly.

"Wait a minute." Olivia decided she had to put a stop to the way they were assuming control — or at least get them to acknowledge her rights in this situation. "I truly appreciate all the *responsibility* you two feel you need to take, but I'd prefer to be involved in these decisions," Olivia told them.

"Okay. Olivia, I would like us to have dinner in Nashville. Would that be all right? And in the interests of keeping you alive — without me sleeping in your living room, which will certainly elicit an eternal round of gossip — would you like to stay in that lovely little motel off I-40?"

"Yes, that sounds lovely, thank you," she said primly. "I just need to be kept in the loop, okay?"

Loop? The two of them were talking to a ghost.

Yet, even as she spoke, she saw that Marcus seemed to be fading.

"Be safe, kiddies," Marcus said, his voice growing as faint as his image. "I can't seem to stay around that long. . . . Still getting the hang of this. . . ."

He was gone. They were talking to an empty space on the sofa.

For a moment, Olivia felt awkward. She was so intensely aware of being there alone with Dustin. There was something about him, a quality that made him the focus in any room. And it was attractive and seductive.

She cleared her throat, trying to concentrate. "You're really afraid for me to stay by myself?"

"Aren't you?"

"Yes," she admitted.

"You'll need a few things. Just pack an overnight bag. We'll go to your house, so you can deal with the dog and collect your things. I'll follow you and keep watch from a safe distance."

"What about you? Don't you need to pack a bag?"

"I have extra clothes in the rental car."

"So, we're going to dinner?" she asked. "Shouldn't we be doing . . . something to solve this?"

"Tomorrow I intend to search the woods

until I find what flew by you."

"You think that someone's —"

"I think someone's afraid of you. I think you're in danger. You have to make sure you're always with a group of people — or with me."

"That's not going to be easy."

"We'll take it day by day," he said. "I'll let Malachi and Jackson know that we have to get some members of the Krewe units out here. In fact, I'll call Malachi while I wait for you."

She smiled. "So where are we going for dinner?"

"A place my sister loves. F. Scott's."

"But you said your sister's not in Nashville right now."

"True. She's in London on tour."

"Tour? What does she do?"

"She's a country music singer."

Olivia stared at him, bemused. "Really? That's fascinating."

"I might be prejudiced, but she's pretty good."

"What's her name?"

"Rayna Blake."

"Wow! Rayna Blake's your sister?"

"You've heard of her?"

"I saw her as the opening act for the Band Perry. She's *extremely* talented."

She kept smiling.

"What?" he asked.

"Oh, I don't know. Country music star, federal agent. Your parents must be very interesting people!"

"Oh, they are," he assured her. "Historians. Very interesting."

"Too bad she's not here doing a concert. I'm sure you could get really good tickets."

"We'd have to go to London for that — which is where my parents happen to be. And . . ."

"No London." Olivia laughed. "Way too complicated. Just Nashville," she said. "Wanna do a ghost tour?"

"Really?"

She shrugged. "We'll be in a group."

"Sure. Why not?"

He stood and she did the same. She felt strange, awkward, yet somehow exhilarated and even a little frightened. That fear wasn't about the threat of death or attack, but the thought of an evening with him. . . . She quickly turned and headed for the door. None of this was real, she told herself.

Only, Marcus's death had been real.

Dustin parked down on the road while Olivia drove up to her house. Although she lived in an area where every home had acreage around it — whether that was owned by the household, pasture belonging to nearby farmers or land owned by the park service — the front of her house was clearly visible from the road. No large bushes provided hiding.

The hiding places lay to the sides and the rear, where forests flourished.

In this section of the countryside, "neighbors" were far away.

He watched, trying not to smile as she came out. He'd given her a small bag of dirt to scatter on the front porch. He wanted to know if anyone tried to drop in on her that night.

She was actually pretty good at being unobtrusive as she spread the dirt around. He didn't think anyone was watching the house at that time. He kept a careful eye on the front; he doubted that anyone hiding in the woods would be able to see exactly what she was doing.

He didn't believe they were dealing with a master criminal, although he was equally certain the killer wasn't stupid.

She hurried down the dirt-and-stone drive to the street where he was parked and slid into the car. She carried a large backpack rather than a suitcase, and he found himself pleased that she'd evidently realized a backpack might go anywhere while a suitcase would advertise the fact that she was going away.

"*Is* this the right thing to do?" she asked anxiously, fastening her seat belt. "I mean, shouldn't we be doing more to pursue the killer?"

"I can't burst into homes and demand that people let me interrogate them," he said. "At the moment, we're doing what's most important."

"What's that?"

"Making sure the killer doesn't strike again." He drove in silence as they headed for the highway.

"You do know exactly where you're going," she murmured.

He lifted one shoulder in a shrug. "I've told you — I really am from Nashville."

"That was convenient for us all."

He couldn't quite tell what the tone of her voice meant so he didn't respond. It was already growing late so he drove straight to the restaurant. F. Scott's was a casual place where some dressed up and some dressed down and the music and food were good. Their table was in a corner by the wall; when they were seated, it seemed intimate. He couldn't help marveling again that she could look like her cousin — and be so beautiful.

"Why are you staring at me?"

He grinned. "Honestly? I was finding it incredible that you could look so much like Malachi — but be so attractive."

"Malachi is very handsome!" she said, defending her cousin. "And thank you. I think."

"Sorry," he murmured. "I think."

The waitress arrived. Olivia ordered a Jack Daniel's on the rocks; he opted for the same. They both decided on steak and their order was in.

She sipped her drink when it was served but still looked restless. "I just wish we could be doing something more."

"We actually are," he told her.

"We are? How?"

"Back in the offices, they're sifting through backgrounds and finding out everything that they can about everyone involved with the Horse Farm."

"But you've done that, haven't you?"

"We just keep going deeper and deeper," he said. "Trying different approaches and looking for new connections."

"And does that help?" she asked. She rubbed the condensation on her glass. "I guess I'm afraid we'll never get to the truth."

He was surprised when he found himself

reaching across the table to take her hand. "We will. That's what the Krewe units do."

She nodded.

And she didn't pull away.

"This is all new to me," she said. "Malachi was working for himself and the next thing I know he's at the academy. I researched the Krewe of Hunters and read between the lines. I asked him a lot of questions. I was stunned to discover that he's really happy. He's engaged to a coworker and . . . and then when this happened and I called him . . ."

"You ended up with me."

She didn't reply; their food arrived. When the waitress left, Olivia cut a piece of meat and asked, "How did you come to be part of . . . this? How did you find the Krewe?"

"They found me. Actually, Malachi was partnered in New Orleans with a detective who joined the force in Savannah. And I worked with the same guy, David Caswell, in Savannah. He'd suggested me before your situation came up, and since I do know Nashville and vicinity, it seemed like a good time and place to start."

"Oh."

"I know what I'm doing," he told her. "I'd wanted to get in with the Krewe — but you don't just apply for it. And guess what, Ms.

Gordon? I have seniority over your cousin. He got roped into the academy through the Krewe. I was already an agent when I got recruited." He stopped talking. He didn't need to defend himself.

She smiled. "I didn't say anything. I'm just glad someone believed me. Except that I knew Malachi would." She inhaled a shaky breath. "How . . . how did you find out? Are you one of those people who sees them —" She broke off, and lowered her voice. "Who often sees ghosts?"

He nodded. "Often enough. It started when I was a kid. I used to talk to an old fellow who haunts a tavern — the place where I first met your cousin, by the way — and my parents thought I had an imaginary friend. I think, prior to that, I was intended to be an only child. No, I think I was a surprise myself. But I do know I made them decide to have another."

"You must have been a wonderful kid."

"Nope. I scared them. Anytime Rayna starts getting uppity with me, I remind her that she might not have existed if it weren't for my 'imaginary' friends."

"She gets uppity?"

"Occasionally." He shook his head. "But not usually. She's a good kid. And she's the perfect product of Nashville. She loves music. In fact, she's like a kid herself when she sees others perform."

"Aha! It's parental and sibling issues that plague you! We can work on that at the Horse Farm," she said solemnly, but a small smile curved her lips.

He grinned, sitting back. "My parents are great people, too. They're major-league academics and spend their lives pursuing interesting places and knowledge, even in retirement. They don't see ghosts or believe in them. Ghosts aren't scientifically verifiable, in their opinion. What about you? What's your history with ghosts?"

She hesitated. "I've tried to avoid seeing them — or else I tell myself that I *don't* see them. But of course Malachi always knew and when I needed someone to talk to about a ghost or . . . when I was scared, I talked to him." She smiled. "You may already know this, but Malachi has a live-in ghost who's friendly, charming and interesting. I've always seen General Cunningham, but I guess I usually pretend I don't. None of this is easy."

He shook his head. "No, it's not. So, tell me about the jerk who left you. Did that have to do with you seeing ghosts?"

"Ouch!" she said, straightening. "He's not a jerk. No, it had nothing to do with ghosts.

He never suspected I saw anything . . . unusual. He's in music, like your sister. A producer. He had fabulous opportunities in Austin. He asked me to come with him, but I knew our relationship wasn't really going anywhere. We were . . . comfortable together. That's all we were by then. So, what about you? Did the love of your life slap you down in public for being too inquisitive?"

He laughed, setting down his fork. "No. No love of my life. In high school, I became involved with the police because I'd seen a ghost. Naturally, I didn't tell them that." He hesitated and then shrugged. Her life had been laid bare for him; no reason not to tell the truth. "I was dating the high school prom queen, the puppy love of my young life, when I met Sarah Sharman. She's dead, by the way, and she was dead when I 'met' her.

"She was standing outside the alley where I'd wait for my sister. I'd pick her up after her private music class. So I talked with this young woman who seemed very sad. After I'd seen her a few times, I guess I wound up having an adolescent crush on her. I said I wanted to take her out somewhere, make her happy. She said, 'Oh, Dustin, don't you understand? I can't go anywhere. I just stay here, and I watch and I wait and I try to help.' Turns out this killer was kidnapping women and taking them to a derelict meat plant, and what he was doing before they died is . . . not dinner conversation. Anyway, she gave me some details that I passed on to the police, and they caught him before he could kill the next girl. I claimed I'd overheard a conversation in an alley. It all turned into a big deal, and I tried to hide from it. In the midst of talking to the police and the whole thing, I missed some school, missed some games . . . and my high school queen ended up with the quarterback."

"That was your last affair?" she asked dubiously. "If *affair*'s the right word."

He grinned. "The last one that broke my heart, anyway. I was seeing someone in Savannah for a while. But I was restless, and I wanted to go to the academy. So I guess I'm the jerk. I felt I had to leave. We split up."

"And that was it?"

"Well, there were a few brief interludes. We never exchanged numbers."

"Ohh," she said.

"What does that mean?"

"It means . . . oh."

"You don't approve."

"I don't think it's any of my business."

"You've never wanted to have a wild, fantastic night with no obligations?"

"Sounds . . . meaningless."

He laughed. "Well, it is meaningless. That's the point."

"I guess it's not me."

"You're never lonely? You'd never like a night where you were with someone, no commitment? Or where you just go out?"

She shrugged. "I — I'm boring, I guess. I don't just go out. We don't have that many places to just go out."

"You never come to the city?"

"We do. Sometimes we all go to the Ryman Center for a concert, or come in to see a movie or . . . we go bowling."

"Bowling is fun."

"Bowling *is* fun!"

"Hey! I'm agreeing with you. So, let me get this straight. The guy you weren't really in love with went to Austin. And you decided to remain unattached. Single and celibate?"

"No. Not that it's your concern, but I haven't decided anything."

"Ah."

"Ah, what?"

"Online dating!" he said. "That's the answer."

She laughed, shaking her head. "No, but

don't knock it. I do have friends who've found the loves of their lives through online dating."

"I always wonder what happens when everything looks perfect but you meet someone and you just don't gel."

"Then you part ways. Maybe *you* should try online dating."

"And what do I put? 'Must love ghosts and be willing to spend long evenings waiting for them to appear'?"

She smiled at that and smoothed her napkin on the table. "Speaking of ghosts . . . We've got ten minutes to make the downtown ghost tour."

"You really want to do it?"

"I really do."

"Then let's get going."

He was afraid she'd argue over the check, but he insisted and she acquiesced. A few minutes later, he was finding parking downtown at the meeting spot, and they joined the group and listened to the stories. Dustin was astonished to realize what a good time he was having with her. They heard a few stories that might have occurred anywhere, like the one about the waitress who haunted a particular bar, serving up ale when people weren't expecting it. Apparently she was still waiting for her soldier to return from the war. They heard about the four thousand Native Americans who died as U.S. policy forced them from their homes to reservations west of the Tennessee border. They went by the Ryman Auditorium — originally the Union Gospel Tabernacle and still undisputed mother church of country music. Dustin teased her that he could've given her a much better tour — an insider's tour — if his sister had been home.

When they came to the capitol building, the guide went into a coughing fit and kept excusing himself. Olivia hurried to a nearby bar to get him some water. Dustin was actually feeling so comfortable and relaxed that he offered to tell the story. The distressed guide raised his eyebrows; Dustin launched in. Olivia, running back with a bottle of water, looked at him curiously.

He bowed to her and began his speech.

"When Tennessee first became a state, the capital was Knoxville — Nashville was the frontier back then, little more than a wilderness. But by 1806, Nashville was starting to thrive. Yeah . . . a lot of outlying areas were still wilderness, but she was now becoming a great city. An important city. So Nashville was voted as the capital but the seat of government was just a small building. In 1845, Architect William Strickland was hired to construct the new capitol building. He fought constantly with Samuel Morgan during the many years it took to get the building completed. Morgan, called the 'Merchant Prince of Nashville,' had been appointed by the Capitol Commission to oversee construction. The two men *did not* get into a duel or murder each other, but alas, they both died, William Strickland in 1854, Morgan some years later, in 1880. The capitol building wasn't complete at Strickland's death, but he would be interred in a vault within its walls. This honor went to only one other man — Samuel Morgan. Today, people believe, you can still hear the two of them, arguing eternally over the most minute details of construction."

By then the guide had recovered. He asked if Dustin would mind if he took over again, and Dustin stepped back beside Olivia. Not thinking, he placed an arm around her shoulders. She laughed at the guide's antics and didn't seem to notice.

When the tour was over, he drove back to the small chain motel, where they checked into adjoining rooms under his name alone.

He bade Olivia good-night and went to his own room. He'd slipped his Glock into the top drawer of his bedside table and had stripped down to his briefs when there was a knock at the adjoining door.

He rose and walked over, opening it partially.

Olivia stood there in a sheer black gown with red trim. It might have been the most seductive garment he'd ever seen — on the most seductive body.

"Hi," she said.

"Hi." His voice was too deep, too gruff.

"I . . . was thinking about those one-night no-obligation flings you talked about."

He felt as if he'd suddenly become paralyzed, and then he felt as if someone had set him on fire. He lowered his head, fighting the fierce longing that ripped through him.

"I'm sorry," she murmured. "I apologize. I can tell that . . ." She started to step back, to close her side of the door. He stopped her, his hand firmly on the door she would have closed.

"Don't you see?" he asked her, his tone harsh. "I *do* know your number — and it would mean something."

She didn't fight him. She didn't run in embarrassment.

She met his eyes. "Yes, yes, it would. Thank you. Thank you for rejecting me. I think."

"I'd never really reject you," he whispered.

She looked down and then back up at him, a trace of amusement in her eyes. "That's very sweet. Thank you again. And good night."

Olivia shut the door, and he allowed her to do so. He went to bed, knowing he should have been seeking a killer in his mind even as he fell asleep. He should have been thinking about clues, about putting together small pieces of information in some logical order.

Instead . . .

He dreamed of what the night might have been.

8

No way out of it. Olivia was almost certain that the morning would be incredibly awkward. She wasn't sure why she'd done what she'd done; maybe it was the way they'd laughed together or how much they'd shared. Maybe it was simply that she'd been impressed with the man from the moment she'd seen him. Maybe it was the fact that she'd given too much of herself and her life to the Horse Farm.

It was a wonderful place. No, they weren't a cure-all or a fix for everything that befell humanity. They didn't cause autism to vanish; they didn't make Down syndrome disappear. They couldn't automatically make an addict see the light. But they did help people learn about trust, self-worth and their ability to control themselves, their own lives, within the world around them. Most important, perhaps, to believe that they could love themselves. All this because of

Marcus Danby.

All of it could be ruined. And here she was, upset about being rejected when she'd made her first sexually aggressive move ever. An action she still didn't entirely understand . . .

But what a nice rejection.

For a moment, mortification seized her. Did men talk? Would he call Malachi and say, "That cousin of yours is really something. She tried to hop into my bed last night."

She didn't think so — oh, not that men didn't talk! She just didn't think Dustin would be so callous.

She'd just finished brushing her hair when there was a tap on the connecting door. She opened it. Dustin was dressed and ready to go. "I figure you have to be at work," he said.

"I do. But I have to go by the house first to take care of Sammy."

"Of course. Sorry. I was planning on stopping at your place first, anyway. I want to see if we have footprints on your porch." He grimaced. "You can tell I don't have a pet."

"You *should* have a pet," she told him. "You'd be a good pet owner."

"Pets deserve more than I can give," he

211

said. He glanced at his watch. "Let's grab some coffee in the lobby and drive to your house. After that, once you get your own car, I'm still going to follow you."

"Sounds good."

She picked up her backpack and they walked to the lobby, where the motel offered coffee and Danishes. They each filled cups and quickly chose some food.

To her relief, their time together wasn't awkward at all. He was completely natural. Still fun, still quick to smile, even quicker to tease her.

But when he pulled into her driveway, he sat there for a few seconds, looking over at her. It was going to get awkward then, she just knew it.

"I don't even know how to say what I want to say, what I want you to know. I can't tell you how much I would have loved to have been with you last night. You're . . . spellbinding. That's the only word I can think of. You must have some idea how attractive you are. More than attractive — beautiful, inside and out. And I admire what you do. But . . . I wouldn't want just one night. I'd want a lot more. And we both know what it's like when people leave — or when you have to go."

She gazed down at her hands and then

raised her eyes to meet his. "When I said thank you, I meant it. You were really decent about the . . . situation. You were honest — and kind. You're a good person." To her, there was no higher praise.

"No, no, I'm not. I spent years being bitter and wondering why I was a freak. Then I spent more years patting myself on the back for being a freak — but for dealing with it so well. I finally figured out that my . . . unusual skills could be of some service in the right line of . . . Good? Decent? I don't know. I'm kind of hard and brash and not always socially adept. I'm constantly looking over my shoulder. But I do care about you, and —"

"I have a dog who must really need to go out by now," she said.

He smiled, lowering his head. "Yeah. But first . . ."

She didn't know what to expect when he opened the compartment between the seats. What he produced was a can that looked like it might contain hair spray.

"Pepper spray," he told her. "Better than nothing."

"How does it work?"

"Flip this tab. That's it — no safety or anything. Flip the tab. Keep it on you at all times, okay?"

"That's going to be a little tough."

"Why?"

"I don't carry things when I'm working. I leave my purse in the office, and I shove my phone in a jeans pocket."

He sighed with exasperation. "I was afraid of that," he said. "Keep the pepper spray with you, in your bag, so you have it while you're in your car, or going to and from your car — whenever you're out. I've got something else that'll do during the day. This is the best I can manage unless you want to go to a shooting range, and that can't be done for a while."

"What is it?"

He reached into the console compartment again. The next thing he took out looked like lipstick.

"This one, you do have to pull the cap. It's also pepper spray. It works just like a tiny perfume bottle. The spray is small but you can at least aim for the eyes and blind someone temporarily."

She took it from him. "This will fit in my pocket," she said. She'd bent close to listen to him and could feel the energy of his body, which seemed to radiate to hers. They looked at each other. She'd already been rejected once, but . . .

She leaned in even closer and kissed him

swiftly. Felt his lips, and the vibrant aura of assurance about him. Something threatened to spring to life and she instantly pulled away — not giving him another chance to reject her. Then she opened her door to get out of the car.

Oddly, she was hurting more than she had last evening. But, of course, he was right. If they got involved, where could they go with it?

"Wait up," Dustin said, exiting the car and running behind her. He stepped in front, blocking her as they reached the porch. "Someone's been here," he said.

She glanced around him at the porch. The dirt she'd left yesterday had been disturbed. He moved ahead of her gingerly, hunkering down to study the prints in the dirt. She bent down to look. "There's not enough to get a clear impression. But I'd say a man in boots — probably a size twelve or thirteen."

"That could be Aaron, Mason, Sydney or Drew," Olivia said. "Or half the men in the area. It's horse country, farm country — cow country, too. Everyone wears boots."

He nodded. "But who gained the most from Marcus's death?"

"Well," she replied unhappily, "Aaron."

He stood up and smiled grimly at her. "That means Aaron might have been here.

On the other hand, the fact that he benefited from the will doesn't prove anything. So . . . it could equally be someone else. And whoever it was may well have come here to hurt you."

"So we haven't got anywhere?"

"No. But it's a good thing you're getting an alarm put in tomorrow," he said.

"I have to let Sammy out and feed him."

He stepped aside, and she started to open the door, inserting the key. She gave him a questioning look before she turned it, despite Sammy's frantic barking.

He raised his voice. "We already know that whoever came here wears gloves," he said. "This person wouldn't have known if you were here or at Marcus's house, but prob-ably tried both."

"So, if someone asks where I was last night, what do I say?" Olivia asked.

"My guess is that no one will ask because no one's going to admit he was hunting you down." Dustin shrugged. "Or if someone does ask — and there is, of course, a slight chance that your visitor was legitimate — you can say you were going back and forth between the two places. That's not even a lie. You were at both houses last night."

Olivia opened the door. Sammy greeted her as if she'd been gone an eternity. "Hey, boy! It was just overnight," she murmured.

Either Sammy didn't know it was Dustin's idea they not spend the previous night there or he was so happy to see anyone human that he leaped up on Dustin in a frenzied greeting. "Down, boy, down, and I'll scratch ya good, I promise." Dustin kept his promise, and Sammy barked happily, then headed for the door.

"Does he need a leash?"

"No, not really, but —" Olivia broke off, remembering that the dog had recently been injured. "One of us should be out with him. He'll just run around and then head to his spot at the side of the house."

"I've got him," Dustin said. Olivia set her bag down. She hurried into the kitchen to refill the dog's food and water, then changed her mind. Sammy was coming to work with her. The camping trip was tonight, and she'd leave him at the Farm with Sydney.

She ran upstairs and packed fresh clothes, then exchanged the regular shoes she'd been wearing for her boots. When she hurried down, Dustin and Sammy were back inside. "He's coming with us today," she told Dustin.

"Okay." They went out again, Dustin starting for his car, and Olivia for hers. He made an abrupt turn.

"What's your schedule today?" he asked.

"Two groups in the morning. A couple of hours with a patient — but only in the pasture — this afternoon. A group meeting with Mariah and the kids coming on the camping trip at five. And then we all head out." She hesitated. "Are you going to be around during the day?"

"I have some business to deal with, so I'll need a few hours this morning. Nothing's going to happen to you while you're with the groups. I should be back by about noon. First, though, I'm going to see that you get there safely, and please keep that pepper spray handy."

She waved, and Sammy jumped into the car. "You can hang around the horses but you have to behave, okay, Sammy?"

Sammy gave a pleased whine, obviously grateful that he wasn't being left home again.

He could call it professional interest. Or curiosity. Either way, Dustin wasn't really worried about getting into the morgue.

And, in fact, it wasn't difficult. He flashed his badge. The handsome middle-aged woman at the reception desk accepted his credentials without question and told him she'd page Dr. Wilson. A moment later, he came out and shook Dustin's hand.

Dustin told the most plausible story he could, which was — in the midst of his lie — the truth.

"I'm attending the Horse Farm, doing a few sessions there. It's a vacation with some therapy thrown in. I've been on some rough cases lately," he told Wilson.

Wilson shook his head. "I worked L.A. for a while and wound up doing autopsies on some of the victims of a serial killer — a sexual sadist. I can see where you guys might need a break now and then." Wilson seemed trustworthy and solid. He was probably in his late fifties, lean, with white hair that was thinning and tufted on top. "Come on into my office," he invited.

When Dustin was seated in front of him, he asked, "What can I do for you, Agent Blake?"

"I'll get right to the point. I'm interested in Marcus Danby. I've become aware of some, shall we say, dubious circumstances concerning the way he died. What can you tell me?"

"Mr. Danby was buried four days after his death, you know."

"Four days? It was about eight, wasn't it, before you let the police have the results of the autopsy?"

Wilson nodded. "I was holding off. Not stalling, mind you, but holding off. I was waiting on a few of the tests I had done because, frankly, I didn't want the truth out there. Trust me — every move I made was within the law. But I have to say, it broke my heart to release that report. I sent a nephew out to do some sessions at the Horse Farm. Changed his life. Well, I guess the whole rehab thing I got him into had a lot to do with it, but the Horse Farm gave him a new direction. He's still working with horses. He bought into a hack ranch in the area. Anyway, I had a lot of respect for Marcus Danby."

"So how did he take the drugs?" Dustin asked.

"It was easy to find. Needle mark right in the crook of his arm."

"But there was no drug paraphernalia found near him. And it appeared to be a first-time event for Marcus? I heard that he'd been clean for decades."

The medical examiner nodded again. "No collapsed veins, nothing to indicate he'd relapsed at any point before. Just the one needle mark."

"And no needles anywhere around him."

"I work on the human body, Agent Blake. The police are responsible for finding evidence. I can only tell you that Marcus Danby did receive a lethal dose of heroin that caused his heart to fail."

"No alcohol in his system, or some kind of pain relaxer or antianxiety pill that might have made him want to go further?" Dustin noted that Dr. Wilson had said "received" rather than "shot up" or any other term.

"Nothing. Just heroin."

Dustin leaned forward. "Do you really believe the man killed himself — accidentally or otherwise?"

"I just look at facts, Agent Blake," Wilson said.

"Well, thank you for your time. I really have no official standing here, you know," Dustin told him, getting to his feet.

"No problem." Wilson rose, too, and Dustin turned to leave.

"Odd, though," Wilson said in a low voice. Dustin immediately turned back. "Suppose a man who'd been clean for over twenty years suddenly decided he couldn't take the pressure anymore, that he had to feel the high one more time . . . Suppose that happened. He was off by himself. He could've had a stash in the woods. But . . . if it were me, I would've shot up between the toes, done it somewhere hard to find. That way — if I wasn't planning on killing myself, and I don't think Marcus was — it would be much harder for anyone to see." He paused. "Addicts know about these things, these little tricks."

Dustin studied the medical examiner for a moment. "Thanks again for your time," he said. "This has been very informative."

"Don't mention it. I don't even remember that you were here."

Matt Dougal, Sean Modine, Nick Stevens, Joey Walters and Brent Lockwood were scheduled to be in Olivia's early group that morning. They'd be staying all day, helping out at the stables and joining Mariah's tour and campout that night. Olivia was gratified to be working with everyone in this group.

When the boys from Parsonage House had first started doing group with Brent, they'd giggled behind the young man's back, making fun of his Down syndrome. Brent had quickly proven how adept he could be with horses; he'd shown them nothing but unconditional acceptance and had beaten the heck out of them in a game of Pictionary following a session.

They'd learned a lot from working with Brent. She believed Brent had learned to be himself, discovering that he could have fun with others — and his parents had learned that they didn't need to be everywhere with him, protecting him.

As Brent had once told the boys, "I know you'll like me or you won't. But if you don't accept me the way I am, well, I may have Down syndrome, but that means *you're* the ones who have a mental handicap."

Olivia remembered the day he'd said that. Sean had grinned and given him a punch on the shoulder. "I guess we have to like you 'cause we're cool dudes — and so are you."

Arriving at the office, Olivia went to her desk in the long room behind Aaron's office, where the therapists kept their notes and records. Mason was at his desk, working away at his computer. "Hey," he said, not looking up.

"Hi, Mason." She set her purse under her desk and opened her own computer. She needed to finish some notes on Matt. She didn't intend to embellish anything, but she wanted his father to know how well he'd been doing in his interactions with others at the Horse Farm. He'd been a withdrawn, sullen kid at first.

She'd just started when Mason got up and walked around to her desk, perching on the edge.

"So where were you last night?"

"Pardon?"

"Checking out the new digs? Personally, I like the house you already have better. So, what do you think you'll do with Marcus's place?"

"Mason, I haven't even begun to think about it."

"I don't think everyone's happy the house went to you," he said, grinning.

"We're therapists, Mason. We're not supposed to be gossips!"

"Yeah, yeah." His grin was even wider now. "We're human." He glanced around, then bent low to whisper to her. "I think Aaron was planning to go and talk to you about the house last night."

"Aaron can talk to me about the house anytime he wants. I was just as stunned as everyone else, and I'm not surprised he feels the same way."

"He wants to talk in private." Mason raised one shoulder in a careless shrug. "Actually, Aaron seemed okay about it. But guess who might just have it in for you?"

"Mason! Stop it."

"Sandra," he told her, leaning closer still. "I was eavesdropping. Well, I really couldn't help it. They didn't know I was still here. She said it was too bad *you* hadn't taken up drugs and OD'd."

He straightened suddenly. They'd both heard footsteps. But then Mason seemed to relax; it was just Mariah. "I'm so excited," she said. "Everyone's coming tonight! Except for Sydney — he says we never should leave the whole place entirely deserted. It was one thing for Marcus's funeral, but that was only for a few hours and we were close by. So —" she counted off the names on her fingers "— it'll be Brent, Sean, Matt, Nick, Joey, Drew, you guys, plus Aaron *and* Sandra. Oh, Liv, pitch in with me on the stories, will you?"

"Sure, if you want," Olivia said.

Mariah shrugged. "Oh — I forgot. And the cool FBI agent. He seems to have a thing for you, Olivia."

"I'm just his therapist!"

Mariah nudged Mason and they both laughed.

"Therapists are human, Olivia. I already told you that. Right, Mariah? Hey, you think every therapist out there lives a perfect life? Come on, you won't be this guy's therapist forever."

"Are you telling me you haven't even thought about sleeping with him?" Mariah asked.

Olivia frowned but didn't respond.

"Don't worry, I've learned to live with

rejection. I know you're not sleeping with *me.* But, seriously, you want to turn into some old maid? You've got to sleep with someone," Mason said.

Olivia groaned and let her forehead fall onto her desk. "Please, guys, could we have a little decorum here?"

Mariah punched Mason again. "Yeah, get up. Mama Cheever's on the way. I could tell the click, click, click of that woman's boots anywhere."

The two of them stood quickly, going to their separate desks. Olivia returned her attention to her notes. Sandra poked her head in. "The boys are here, Olivia. Sydney has them stashing their gear for the day. They'll be ready as soon as you are."

"Just finishing a report on Matt, for his dad."

Sandra frowned. "You'll let me see it before you send it?"

"If you wish."

"We need to be very careful these days, you know."

"Yes, I know. I'm being very objective here, Sandra — not exaggerating Matt's accomplishments, but not minimizing the truth, either."

"People will believe in us or not, Sandra," Mariah said. "We can't sugarcoat everything and we can't constantly be vigilant about what we say. We just have to move forward. And the rest of us . . . well, we weren't addicts so we can't fall back."

"Some people think that former addicts are the best therapists. They know where their charges are coming from," Mason put in.

Sandra sighed. "We're here to help *everyone* who comes to us deal with their personal issues through equine therapy. Not all our guests are addicts! Brent's not, for God's sake! We're much more than you're implying we are." She turned briskly to Olivia. "I'd like to see the report. Aaron wants me to approve everything before it goes out."

Olivia punched a key on her computer. She smiled sweetly. "On its way to you now, Sandra."

As she walked toward the front door, she realized that the floor was dirty. She paused, looking down. It appeared to be the same fine dirt she'd dusted on her porch before leaving with Dustin the night before.

She bent down to touch it. As she did, Aaron came out of his office. He beamed at her. "Morning, sunshine."

She straightened. "Good morning, Aaron."

"I have to talk to you later, if that's okay."

"Of course. Anything in particular?"

"I want to rent Marcus's house from you."

"Okay."

"Okay, you'll talk? Or, okay, you'll rent me the house?"

"Both. I didn't expect to get the house, Aaron. You know that."

"It's okay, Liv. Marcus really loved you."

"And you, Aaron."

"He left me everything I need," Aaron told her.

As she began to leave, she was certain that she heard someone snicker behind her back.

When she turned around, Sandra was watching her, arms crossed. When she noticed Olivia's scrutiny, she acted as though she'd been waiting for Aaron, immediately asking him a question about schedules.

Olivia hurried over to the stables and the paddocks. She could see that the boys were already there, talking with Drew, who held Trickster, ready to go out.

Brent turned and saw her. "Livia!" he cried, coming toward her. The other boys looked her way and smiled, too, calling out to her.

"Trickster! We're taking Trickster today!" Brent said, giving her a hug.

As she walked to join the group, Sean was telling Matt, "I told you it was Bruce Willis in that old movie."

"I wasn't sure," Drew told the boys apologetically. "I can look it up on the computer while you guys are on your ride."

"If Brent says so, then I believe it," Matt said. He ruffled Brent's hair. "He's our resident expert."

Brent grinned at Olivia happily. He was shorter than the other boys, but he was on a good diet and in darned good shape.

"I'm a resident expert!" he told Olivia.

"So you are," Olivia said, smiling at the other boys.

She remembered why she loved what she did so much.

From the morgue Dustin drove out to the Horse Farm, but he didn't pull into the drive.

He passed the farm and parked along the side of the road. He was on adjoining land that bordered the trails; he assumed it belonged to a local farmer — he saw dairy cows behind fences, grazing and letting out a chorus of moos now and then.

He walked around the far side of the fence, heading into the forest.

Walking trails were plentiful and they were

actually something of a maze. But once he reached the first riding trail, the path was cleaner and broader. He moved quickly, listening and watching all the while.

It was a good brisk walk but eventually he reached the copse where they'd seen the deer and her fawn the day before. He searched through the trees, which was way more than a one-man job, but he wanted to get in at least a cursory inspection.

That wasn't the real reason he had come.

He was convinced that he wasn't going to find a stash of drugs or drug paraphernalia.

There were no hollows in any of the trees he searched. He walked on, determined, looking harder.

Something had whizzed through the trees.

Joey had heard it. Olivia's horse had reared.

What?

It sure as hell hadn't been a bee. Or a bird.

It was hard to remember exactly where they'd been, hard to imagine the exact trajectory. He calculated and recalculated. In the end he moved deeper into the woods, through the trees themselves, ignoring the trails.

Still nothing.

Tired, frustrated, he leaned against one of the trees.

And then he saw it.

It was tiny, so tiny it was barely visible. The little bit of feathering was what had caught his attention. When he went to retrieve it — carefully, using his handkerchief — the feathers detached and all he drew from the tree was the tiny point of something that looked like a needle.

He studied the point, wrapped it and, trying not to move his feet, hunkered down.

It took forever, sifting through the leaves and bracken on the forest floor. Then he found it — a delicate cluster of feathers.

Though small, they would have helped direct the tiny needlelike object.

It was a dart. It had been aimed at Olivia — or her horse.

He began to leave, but hesitated, pulling out his knife to cut away the section of bark it had struck. He got out the handkerchief and very carefully rewrapped all the tiny pieces of his find.

Then he started back through the forest.

So a dart had come whistling through the woods.

It was too small to be deadly . . . unless a toxin of some kind had been placed on the tip. He hurried back to his car and checked his watch. Still early; Olivia would be with her group.

He drove back to the morgue. He would've preferred to send the specimen to the Krewe lab, but he didn't want to take the time. And sometimes a man had to go on gut instinct.

Wilson was surprised to see him again but listened earnestly. He promised results on lab tests as soon as humanly possible.

To his extreme bad luck, he ran into Deputy Sheriff Frank Vine as he was leaving.

"Agent Blake," Vine said, eyes narrowing as he studied him.

"Hello, Deputy."

"What kind of therapy are you having at the morgue?"

"Oh, I just stopped by to ask about Marcus — how he'd injected the heroin."

"You think we don't know what we're doing out here?" Vine demanded.

"I never suggested such a thing. You didn't really give me an answer when I asked, that's all."

"Well, you've got your answer now. And you have no jurisdiction out here. We really do know what we're doing, Agent Blake."

"Yes, sir," Dustin said.

Vine stared at him, obviously still irritated. He walked past Dustin, stopped and came back, wagging a finger at him. "You stay out of our business, Blake. You're not here to police my officers. I'll call your superiors, do you understand?"

"Yes, sir," Dustin said again. "I'm on my way." He smiled and strolled out to his car.

He prayed that his gut had been right and Wilson wouldn't betray him.

Then he drove as quickly as he could — watching the speed limit — to the Horse Farm.

God knew he didn't want Vine arresting *him* for a traffic violation!

9

By five-thirty that evening, they were ready to start out on their camping trip.

Olivia was, naturally, taking Shiloh and she was glad to see that Drew had chosen Chapparal for Dustin. The two seemed well-suited to each other. Dustin was obviously familiar with horses and had riding experience.

The horses were all in use except for Martin, and he'd remain behind with Sydney. If for any reason someone needed to be reached quickly during the night, Sydney knew where they'd be and had Martin to get to them.

Mariah led the way on Pixie as they rode out, not starting her spiel yet, since they were riding single file on the forest trail.

They moved deep into the trees. Eventually they came to a clearing in the forest and Mariah reined in, allowing them all to break and dismount for a few minutes. She directed them to a little path that led deeper into the thickness of the woods, an area where the dying sunlight now brought about an eerie green darkness. Everyone had a penlight, while Drew, Aaron, Mason and Sandra carried lanterns.

Mariah said, "In a few minutes, we're going to visit one of our small Confederate graveyards. You have to remember that when you go to a national cemetery, you won't find any Confederates, unless they were pardoned and joined the Union army after the war. Confederate dead have their own cemeteries, or else they were returned to their hometowns. And certainly many soldiers — North and South — remain in unmarked graves on the fields where they died. While it was incredibly important for both God-fearing men of the North *and* South to retrieve their dead, it wasn't always possible. They died on bloody fields that had to be abandoned, or they were beyond recognition by the time they were found.

"A side note of interest — what we celebrate now as Memorial Day was begun by Confederate women who decorated the graves of their loved ones. Many places lay claim to having the first true 'Decoration Day,' but most historians agree that the widows and other grieving women of the

South began what became our national holiday before the end of the Civil War — or, as we were sometimes taught to call it, the War of Northern Aggression." Mariah grinned. "No one get mad at me for getting my history wrong tonight, huh? Remember, Tennessee was always a divided state and we're all darned glad we're one Union now!" Mariah stopped speaking, reaching for the water bottle attached to her saddle. She looked at Olivia. "Want to take it for a minute?"

"Sure," Olivia said. "Mariah was preparing you for the first step in the 'ghost' tour part of this. We'll tell more stories when we've made camp. But right now, we're in a little graveyard begun by locals who found their own boys, and other dead soldiers, left behind after the Battle of Nashville. In some instances, those who lived in this area stumbled upon the dead and did their best to bury them in accordance with whatever identification they found on the bodies — you know, sometimes they got them back to their states or buried them here with others from their homes or regiments, Feds or Rebs. Sometimes the dead they found were their own. Some of them were brought out here for burial.

"During the Civil War, the forest was different from the way it looks now. There'd been a farmhouse just up the ridge, and this had been land that belonged to a George C. Turner. George and one of his sons were killed in the battle, and when Mrs. Evelyn Turner discovered the bodies — and those of others — she got the local preacher and a stone carver to create a little cemetery. Actually, Evelyn Turner herself wound up in this little burial ground. It's said that on a misty evening she can be seen walking through the trees, searching for more dead, determined that they be given a Christian burial. She's buried just down that path with her husband and her son — and our area's most famous ghost, General Rufus Cunningham. So we'll take a walk down the path, pay our respects and then go on to the campsite. Once we're there, we'll set up our tents and start a fire, cook our dinner — and settle in for some good stories."

She glanced back at Mariah, a question in her eyes.

"You want to lead them through with Mason? Drew, Aaron and I can watch the horses," Mariah said.

"Let's go, then," Olivia urged. She noticed that Brent looked frightened.

"You don't have to come," she told him. "You can stay with Mariah and the guys and watch the horses."

Brent shook his head. "I — I want to go."

Dustin walked over and slipped an arm around his shoulders. "I'm a little scared, too," he said. "We'll go together."

Olivia smiled at Dustin. "Well, then, we forge ahead."

She accepted a lantern from Mariah and started through the pine- and leaf-covered trail. The others followed. They entered a small graveyard. Perhaps twenty stones remained, some broken, most at an angle, all shrouded with lichen. The break in the trees allowed the last light of the day to seep through, but it cast an aura of something mysterious, perhaps sacred, over the stones.

"Here!" Sean called. "Here, right here! I found Evelyn Turner's grave — and her son's grave and . . . here's the dad!"

The other boys rushed over. Holding the lantern high, Olivia saw that Dustin — Brent close at his side — had come upon the most famous grave, the one with the largest stone and flowers strewn upon it.

"General Rufus Cunningham," Dustin read aloud. He went down on his knees to study the writing on the stone. " 'Hero of the Battle of Nashville. To save lives, he gave his own.' "

Sean let out a creepy sound. "He's here! I

can feel him. Can you feel him? He's here with us!"

"Where? Where?" Brent asked, alarmed.

"It's all right, Brent," Dustin said. "If his spirit's still around, he doesn't mean us any harm. He was an exceptional man who wanted the best for everyone."

"Don't mock the dead!" Joey snapped at Sean.

"Oh, come on, Joey," Sean said. "Have some fun!"

Olivia hadn't seen the general among them; Malachi had told her once that it didn't really make sense for a spirit like Rufus Cunningham to hang around his grave. Malachi believed he still watched over the living. But just as she opened her mouth to speak again, she saw him.

He was on foot.

Maybe ghost horses couldn't make it through the dense growth of trees and brush that now surrounded the little burial ground.

But the general *was* among them. He wore his uniform, passing by the others, pausing to give Sean a stern pat on the back of his head.

Sean jumped a mile high.

Matt burst into laughter. "Scared?" he demanded.

"Who did that? Stop it — that wasn't funny!" Sean yelled.

"Neither is disrespect for the dead," Dustin said quietly.

"I'm sorry, I'm sorry! Can we go now? I'm starving," Sean muttered.

"Everyone okay with that?" Olivia asked.

"One minute. Can I take just one minute?" Brent looked up at her.

She nodded. Brent went down on his knees and bowed his head, hands folded in prayer.

One by one, the other boys joined him. Olivia held the lantern and watched, deeply touched.

When they started back, Matt asked her, "How come we can read some of those stones so clearly?"

"Because volunteers come out now and then and see that the headstones are kept clean," Olivia told him. "Some of the graves were known, and some weren't after time took its toll, so the carving was scrubbed on all of them."

"But everyone knew the general, right? And they knew about Mr. and Mrs. Turner and their son."

"Right," Olivia assured them.

When she reached the end of the trail and the boys had gone on ahead of her, she looked back. She could see the general; he stood in a military position, watching as they left.

She smiled. He was still keeping guard over the land. But then her smile faded. She'd seen him when Marcus died. What had he been trying to tell her? Had he come upon Marcus too late?

"Liv? You ready?" Mariah called.

"Coming."

Brent was riding Battle-ax, a truly big boy, although gentle. She went to give him a boost up but Dustin was already with him, helping him onto the horse.

As they rode, she noted that although Dustin was keeping an eye on Brent, he was staying close to her.

He was also watching everyone riding with them — and the forest around them, as well.

Soon, they reached the open ground that led to the stream and the bluff that forded it, where they usually camped. The rocks created an overhang that had been useful whenever they were surprised by rain. Tonight, however, promised to be beautiful.

They pitched the tents, the work going well, everyone helping. Sean now seemed subdued; he looked over his shoulder frequently — and kept close to the others. Aaron sent the boys to gather wood for the fire. They used the camping area often and had a fire site ready. It was on clean, swept soil and surrounded by rocks to prevent the fire from spreading.

Within forty minutes of their arrival, the tents were pitched and the fire was blazing. Aaron quickly had coffee going, while Mariah and Mason set up the grill. They'd brought hot dogs and beans and the makings for s'mores. Everyone seemed hungry, and it wasn't until they'd eaten and had gorged themselves on the s'mores that Joey asked Mariah when she was going to get to the ghost stories.

"Ah, well, now!" Mariah smiled at him and gestured grandly. "Now that the moon is high, and the mist will soon gather and rise on the moor!"

"Is this a moor?" Joey asked.

"No, not really. It's a field in the foothills, but close enough," Mason said.

"Remember, I don't just tell ghost stories. A ghost story doesn't amount to anything unless you know why the ghost stayed behind," Mariah said. "And that means knowing the history."

"So you're going to tell us about General Rufus Cunningham, right?" Joey asked excitedly.

"With a little help from my friends," Mariah said. "Liv, you want to start?"

"Okay, if you'd like," Olivia said. She looked around at all the boys, and forced herself not to smile. Brent was sitting on Dustin's left side.

Sean was on his right — sitting even closer than Brent.

"The best stories always come with truth and time," she began. "And to understand what brought about a ghost, you first have to understand some history, just like Mariah said. As I'm sure you already know, Tennessee was the last state to join the Confederacy. That happened on June 24, 1861. As soon as Tennessee seceded, it was like Nashville had a target painted on her. Because the city was a major shipping center and had a major port on the Cumberland River, both sides saw Nashville as extremely important. Battles couldn't be fought without supplies, without a way to keep soldiers clothed and fed. And, of course, Nashville was also the capital of Tennessee. It was important for the Union to take a capital, because that affected morale. One thing we learn in therapy of any kind is that morale can dictate what happens. We can create self-fulfilling prophesies — believe there's no choice but to fail and you will. Believe you can make it and you will."

Joey cleared his throat. "Uh, Olivia, the South did lose the war."

"Yeah, didn't you hear?" Matt asked her, giggling.

"Okay, it doesn't always work." She smiled. "Hard and bitter as that defeat must have been for the Confederates, time has shown us that we're better and stronger as one country. To many people living in the nineteenth century, the main focus was states' rights, and, okay, that *was* connected to slavery — and the economy. But one of Lincoln's great triumphs was that slavery was abolished. Today, we can look back and wonder how any human being believed he could own another human being." She paused to let the boys think about that.

A moment later she continued. "But, as I said, it was important for the Union to hold the city. Protecting Nashville was Fort Donelson, which fell on February 16, 1862. As soon as the fort fell, Union troops came in and the federal occupation of Nashville began. And Nashville became the first Confederate capital to fall to the federal government. Again, something that was actually good for some — the Unionists — and not so good for others — the ardent secessionists. Remember, we were divided on the matter of secession. The state government moved to Memphis at that time. But the Union sent in a military governor. Anyone know who that was? I'll give you a hint. A future president."

"Andrew Johnson!" Matt called out.

"Gold star for that boy," Olivia said. "Okay, so there was a Union Army of Tennessee and a Confederate Army of Tennessee. On December 2, 1864, the Confederate Army of Tennessee came to face off against the Union Army south of the city. On December 15, the Union Army arrived and started the Battle of Nashville. While the Confederates fought hard, they were badly defeated and had to retreat."

"And that's where we get our famous ghost!" Mariah said, beaming.

Matt set his flashlight beneath his chin so the beam would give him an eerie look. "General Rufus Cunningham!" he moaned.

"Hey, stop it!" Sean said. "Remember — we respect the dead."

"Exactly!" Mariah then took over the story. "General Rufus Cunningham had a daughter and she was married to one of the Union lieutenants with the troops occupying Nashville."

"Wow, the girl was kind of a traitor, wasn't she? Ooh — maybe she hated her dad!"

Sean suggested.

"No, no! It was very sad," Olivia said. "The whole war was tragically sad. Many of the men — the foot soldiers and ranking officers — were good friends or relatives of the soldiers they fought. Cunningham's daughter was named Eliza. She married Nathan Randall in 1858, and she met him because her father had been his commanding officer at the time. Many of the men went to West Point or other military academies together. Many of them had fought together in Mexico. The thing is, General Rufus Cunningham loved his son-in-law. But even if he *hadn't* loved him, he would have tried to save him. He'd ordered that any man who'd been injured — whether wearing blue or gray — was to be given medical attention."

"So," Mariah continued, taking up the story, "Nathan Randall was injured. Seeing him — although he was already in retreat with his troops — General Cunningham stopped. In saving his son-in-law, he was caught in the crossfire between the advancing Union and the retreating Confederates. He died not far from where we're camping tonight and he's buried in the tiny Confederate Cemetery we just visited, where you saw his grave."

"And," Joey added, "it's said that General Rufus Cunningham still rides these hills, watching out for those who are in danger, trying to save lives."

"Yeah, well, he failed with Marcus, huh?" Matt said. His words were followed by silence.

"I'm sure he would have helped if he could," Olivia said.

Brent rose and sat next to Matt. The tough guy smiled at the Down syndrome boy and placed an arm around his shoulders.

"Hey, there's a romantic story, too," Olivia quickly offered. "The beautiful stream we can hear trickling. Know how that was formed?"

"Someone's tears?" Joey asked.

"You bet," she replied. "There was a beautiful maiden called Little Deer. She was in love with a warrior named Soaring Eagle. This was during a terrible time in our history when we were land grabbers — and we forced all the eastern Native Americans west, toward Arkansas. The two of them were torn apart because Soaring Eagle was with a peace delegation sent to argue out terms. He should've have been back before Little Deer was forced to leave. But the army was determined to get this done. There was a horrible mistake in communications. Soaring Eagle was only trying to reach Little Deer, but he was shot down because an army lieutenant thought he was trying to create an uprising. Little Deer heard the shot from miles away. She cried this stream that runs from the river down to the hills and plains. Sometimes at night you can hear the two of them calling to each other."

"And," Aaron said, rising, "sometimes at night, people go to bed. I say we call it a day and we'll get an early start tomorrow. Then we'll argue with the black rock!"

Dustin glanced over at Olivia. She wished she didn't feel herself tense every time he looked at her now. Or that, in the middle of a group of people, she could tell him she didn't give a damn what happened in the future, she'd like one night with him. Just one . . .

"The black rock is a natural boulder stuck out here, and it's black because it's aged," she explained. "Okay, maybe it's more of a dirty gray. The kids tell it everything they're angry about — and throw water balloons at it. Believe it or not, it actually seems to help."

"And it soothes the old soul," Mason said. He stood, yawning. "I do have to say it feels great to be out here, huh?"

"Yes, and may I remind you all . . . bathroom visits demand clothing of some kind," Mariah said sternly. "Boys' bushes to the left — girls' to the right!"

"Who wants to help rinse off the plates and pots and pans?" Olivia asked. "You can grab your toothbrushes and we'll get water for face washing at the same time."

Joey, Matt and Brent said they'd come with her.

Sean no longer seemed willing to be by himself and refused to leave a crowd.

The boys helped her with the dishes. When they returned to the camp, everyone was settling in. Brent, Sean and Joey were in a large tent with Dustin, whose sleeping bag was closest to the entrance — closest to where she was, in the second tent with Mariah and Sandra. Aaron, Matt, Nick and Drew were in the third.

"You think this was too soon?" Mariah asked worriedly as she lay on her cot. "I mean, too soon for one of these trips — after Marcus died?"

Sandra, ready to turn down their lantern, sighed. "Mariah, we have to go on as usual. You're just telling stories that you grew up with. It's fine."

"I guess," Mariah murmured. "What do

you think? Did they all like the little cemetery?"

"They seemed to," she said.

"No one 'saw' the general?" Mariah asked.

"Oh, we all see him one way or another, don't we?" Olivia said.

"No," Mariah told her. "I never have. I wish I *could* see him. I *should* see him. You can trace my family back in this area for two hundred years! You'd think he'd appear to me."

"He's an image in people's minds!" Sandra said impatiently. "Let's get some sleep!"

The tent went dark. The night was lit by an almost-full moon and the remnants of the fire in the clearing. Olivia lay still, listening to chirping of insects around them. There were coyotes in the hills, but they'd never bothered them, not here at the campground. The cows were sometimes in danger — the Horse Farm dogs occasionally came back with a piece of beef that hadn't been processed. But there was really nothing to fear at their campground during the night.

She'd never felt edgy before.

That night, she lay awake in her sleeping bag.

Through the canvas walls of the tent she could see the shapes of distant trees, making giant shadows that waved and moved in the breeze, looking like monsters that might reach into the tent and drag someone out. She told herself that was a childish fantasy, but couldn't quite dispel her nervousness. . . .

She was just staring at the trees when she became aware of something moving outside — coming toward the tent.

She bolted halfway up, glancing over at the other women.

Neither Sandra nor Mariah was in the tent. She hadn't heard them rise; maybe she'd dozed off, after all.

Whatever was coming toward her seemed to grow large with menace — as if a tree had uprooted itself and become a monster stretching its skeletal fingers toward her. . . .

She jumped to her feet, ready to rush out and scream an alarm. But even as she did, she heard someone speak sharply. She recognized Dustin's voice.

"Aaron!"

There were no monsters and trees didn't uproot themselves to attack.

She hurriedly left the tent to see what was happening.

Aaron was out there.

And Dustin was right behind him.

"What's wrong?" Dustin asked.

"Nothing — I think," Aaron said. He

looked at Olivia. "I heard something rustling over here. I wanted to see if you three were okay. We should've put the women in the middle tent."

Sandra came walking out of the woods. "Aaron Bentley! You employ extremely capable women. I had to make a dash to the powder room, so to speak."

"Where's Mariah?" Olivia asked.

"Well, she must have taken a bathroom break, too," Sandra said.

"I don't like this," Aaron muttered. "I want to make sure she's in her tent before I go back to sleep. I thought . . ."

"What?" Dustin demanded.

"I don't know. I thought I heard someone prowling around."

"You did! Us. So much for privacy," Sandra said, shaking her head.

"How long can a break in the bushes take?" Aaron asked.

He probably meant it as a rhetorical question, but Joey emerged from the tent, saying, "Um, it takes as long as it takes, doesn't it? Especially for women . . ."

Aaron ignored that and walked toward the bushes. "Mariah!"

She didn't answer.

"Mariah!" he shouted louder.

"Hey!"

They heard her call back to them. Her voice didn't come from the bushes. Olivia saw that she'd been down to the stream; she'd apparently filled her canteen. Her face was damp and she was smiling. "What's wrong?" she asked quickly, her smile fading.

"Nothing." Aaron let out a sigh. "I was just worried about you."

"Oh, Aaron, I'm sorry," Mariah said. "I went down to the stream for some more water. And it was so beautiful in the moonlight! I was looking across the water — hoping maybe I'd see the general on his horse on the other side."

Somewhere, far in the distance, a coyote howled at the moon. The sound was so forlorn, so chilling — and foreboding.

"Well, we're all here now," Sandra said with a shrug. "Let's get some sleep."

"Dustin, you're going back in the tent, right?" Joey asked. As he spoke, Brent, too, came out. He looked frightened. Brent was a joy to be around, always loving, but he was also easily frightened when things weren't precisely as they were supposed to be.

"Livia?" he said worriedly.

"I'm here, Brent. We're all here. Everything's fine," she assured him, going over to

253

give him a hug.

"Oh, for God's sake," Sandra said. "We've got to get some sleep!"

"Okay, okay, everyone back where they belong." Grinning, Aaron joined Olivia and put his arm around Brent. "It's all good, buddy."

Brent nodded solemnly. "The general is watching over us," he said.

"Yeah, that's right, Brent."

"He *is* watching us. I saw him. I saw him — he was on the other side of the stream. I saw him with Livia when we were washing the plates," Brent said.

Sandra shook her head. "I'm not so sure we should've brought him," she whispered.

"He's fine," Olivia said. "Half the world sees the general."

"He thinks he really saw him," Sandra snapped.

"Come on, buddy, back to bed," Aaron said.

"Yeah, come on, we're all going in," Joey added kindly.

"Good night, all," Aaron said, and, ducking through the entrance, escorted Brent back into the tent. Joey followed.

"I'm going to sit by the fire awhile," Dustin said. "You all go back to sleep. Sorry. I'm just restless. I like to watch the dying embers — helps me sleep."

Sandra went back in. Mariah waited for Olivia, then returned to the tent. Olivia fell into a deep sleep.

She awoke to early daylight — and the sound of a high-pitched scream. Bolting out of bed, she collided with Sandra as they both tried to get out at the same time.

Drew was already outside, looking around wildly, trying to ascertain where the scream had originated.

"Stay here!" Olivia ordered Sandra. "Watch the boys. Drew, come with me!"

It wasn't really her place to give instructions, but Olivia hadn't thought it out. She started running into the bushes, assuming the scream had come from the women's side of the "bathroom" area. But when she saw a glimmer of light through the trees, she realized it must have come from farther back. Olivia kept running, with Drew on her heels. They burst into a little clearing. The gray skies of dawn made it hard to see clearly.

To her astonishment, Olivia found Dustin there — bending over Mariah, who was crouched on the ground. His small flashlight didn't reveal much detail but did show her horrified expression.

"What's going on?" Olivia shouted.

Drew barely managed to stop himself before colliding with her; she felt his hands on her shoulders.

Mariah rose, shaking, clinging to Dustin. "Oh, Lord, I am sorry . . . again!"

Olivia frowned at Dustin.

He shrugged. "I wake easily and run fast," he said.

"What's going on?" Olivia demanded a second time.

"I — I thought I saw . . . oh, this is so stupid!" Mariah apologized. "I thought I saw the general when I went to use the, uh, bathroom, and I tried to follow him and I got here and . . ." She stepped aside, displaying what she'd stumbled on.

The torn remnants of cow's hindquarters lay there, blood trailing off into the bushes.

"A coyote got a cow," Olivia said calmly. "Unfortunately, it happens."

"I know, I know. I just wasn't expecting it!" Mariah groaned.

"Let's get the hell back now," Drew suggested. Olivia could feel him close behind her — and she could tell that he was shaking. "The others are going to be worried."

"Yes, let's go!" Mariah said. "Oh, Lord, I'm going to have to apologize to the kids and tell them what an idiot I am!"

They walked back. By then, the others

were milling around by the fire, waiting wide-eyed.

"What happened?" Sandra asked anxiously.

"Freakiest camping trip ever!" Mason said.

"Cool," Nick murmured.

Sean jabbed him with an elbow. Mariah went into her explanation, but before she'd finished Dustin interrupted.

"Where's Aaron?"

They looked around; Aaron wasn't among them.

"He must be . . . I don't know, in the bushes, too?" Mason asked.

"With this much commotion going on?" Dustin demanded.

"We'll all go look for him," Joey said.

"No, you boys stay here. Drew, you, Sandra and Mariah stay. Mason, check out the bushes. I'll try the stream. Liv . . ." His eyes were on hers.

He didn't want her alone with any of them, she realized.

"I'll go with you," she said. "We can cover most of the stream that way."

They headed off together.

When they reached the stream he stood dead still for a few seconds. Then he swore and ran straight in.

Olivia saw why.

They'd found Aaron.

He was floating facedown in the water.

10

Dustin was afraid that Deputy Sheriff Frank Vine simply didn't like him. Vine arrived with Jimmy Callahan, but Vine did most of the talking. Callahan was younger, more sympathetic, more concerned about those who'd witnessed the event, especially the boys.

Dustin knew damned well that he'd done everything right, performing artificial respiration competently and with determination.

And he'd gotten Aaron Bentley breathing again, although not conscious, before the rescue crew made it to the campsite via helicopter.

The med techs had commended him. Everyone around him had been in shock; they'd watched helplessly, holding one another while he brought Aaron out of the cold water. Olivia had run back for blankets, and the others had followed her to the stream. They'd carried him back to the campsite, where Drew had gotten the fire going again.

But Frank Vine . . . He and Callahan had arrived on the medevac helicopter, then stayed behind at the campsite.

Now Vine stared at him as if he were the Antichrist.

Dustin had watched as Frank tried to find out what had happened. The group had mostly talked at once, trying to explain where they'd been, how no one had any idea that Aaron was down at the stream. Mariah was nearly hysterical, certain that it all was her fault. If she hadn't been startled and screamed, they might have found Aaron earlier.

No one could say just how long he'd been in the water. The med techs didn't know if he'd live. If he did, they didn't know if he'd suffer brain damage. He was breathing; he was alive. That was all anyone knew. He might walk out of the hospital, perfectly fine, the next morning.

Or he might live for years in a vegetative state.

They'd find out when they got him to a hospital.

"So, no one saw Aaron get out of the tent and walk to the stream?" Frank demanded.

Sandra was sobbing. "No. We heard Mariah scream from the other direction. Some of us stayed right here . . . some of us went to look for her."

"It's all my fault!" Mariah said again and again. "All my fault. If I didn't want to see the general so much . . ."

"That's right. You were chasing a ghost," Vine said sarcastically.

That made Mariah cry harder. Olivia went to slip an arm around her. So did Deputy Callahan.

Olivia looked at Deputy Sheriff Frank Vine and spoke evenly and clearly. "None of us was anywhere near the stream. The fact that Mariah was in the bushes had nothing to do with Aaron. Even if we hadn't run after her and she hadn't screamed, Aaron was still at the stream. He probably thought nothing of being down there. We've all been camping here dozens of times." She turned to her friend and coworker and said, "Mariah, there's no reason you should feel guilty. What happened was *not* because of you. Aaron was already there when you screamed. And think of it this way — we were all up, and Dustin found him at the stream because of you. If it hadn't been for you, we might not have known he was missing. We might not have searched for him until it was too late."

"Really, Liv?" Mariah whispered. "You think so?"

"Definitely," Olivia said.

Frank Vine looked at them and shook his head. "There's something not right with you people. How can so many bad things happen in one group? Pretty careless if you ask me. First Danby and now this . . . How could Aaron have such a ridiculous accident?"

"Accident?" Dustin asked, entering the fray despite the look Vine had given him. "A grown man, Aaron's size, accidentally falls face-first into a stream, knocks himself out and nearly drowns?"

"If it wasn't an accident, what *did* happen, Agent Man?"

"I don't know. That's why law enforcement investigates such situations," Dustin said flatly.

Frank Vine scowled at him. Everyone was quiet. Dustin almost felt as if they were on some dusty street in the Old West — about to have a shoot-out.

"And you're going to investigate and figure out what happened, is that it? When *you're* under suspicion?"

"Of causing an accident?" Dustin raised his eyebrows.

"You found him, didn't you?"

"And saved his life. Before that, I was the first one to dash into the forest when I heard Mariah scream," Dustin told him.

Mason cleared his throat and said, "Hell, Dustin wasn't even around when Marcus Danby died."

Callahan stepped into their group, looking shy and young — and yet speaking with a soft calm that belied his years.

"We need to get these kids out of here."

Vine spun on him but held his temper. He let out a long breath and Dustin realized the man was frustrated.

"Fine. We'll get the kids out of here," Vine said. He looked at the boys again, his eyes narrowing. "And not one of you saw anything?"

Joey spoke up. "I saw Aaron get out of his bedroll, but I was still half-asleep. I didn't jump out myself until I heard Mariah scream. Then . . . we stood around with Mama Cheever — Sandra — waiting. . . . Drew, Olivia, Dustin and Mariah came back from the woods and that's when we noticed Aaron wasn't with us."

Frank Vine studied him suspiciously. "So everyone knew where everyone else was — except for Aaron?"

"Yeah," Drew said, gesturing around at all of them. "Sandra's not here now because she went in the helicopter with Aaron, but I was with her, so I know exactly where she was. I mean, all of us were here, except for Mason, who was searching in the bushes, and Dustin and Liv — who rescued Aaron."

"I'm not sure where everyone was when Mariah first screamed," Dustin explained. "But when we found Mariah and returned to camp with her, we did know. That's when we discovered that Aaron was missing. None of us necessarily knew where everyone else was before that," Dustin said.

"Nor do we know if anyone else was in the area," Olivia added.

Mariah suddenly started sobbing again. "Aaron!" she wailed. "Oh, my God, Aaron." She sank onto the ground and Olivia crouched down beside her. With everyone upset, Brent began to cry, as well. Dustin went to him, trying to offer some comfort. Brent was extremely susceptible to the emotions of others.

"It's all right," he said soothingly. "Aaron's gone to the hospital. They'll see what they can do for him there. He might be fine by tonight, Brent."

"I like Aaron," Brent told him between sobs. "I liked Marcus."

"I know," Dustin murmured.

"All right, let's move along," Frank said.

"Jimmy, get these people moving. Who's in charge now?" he demanded.

Drew cleared his throat. "Um — Olivia. If Aaron's out of action, Olivia is in charge."

"Liv," Frank ordered, "get your stuff packed and take these boys back to the Horse Farm. I'll get on the horn and see that someone from Parsonage House shows up and that Brent's mom knows to come for him."

"Have them ride back as they are — don't pack up. Leave the campsite as it is. There might be something here that can give us some explanation . . . or at least a hint," Dustin said.

"This is *my* jurisdiction," Frank Vine told him. "You're not going to find anything that might cause a man to walk to a stream and fall in. You want to investigate? Fine, walk down to the stream. Olivia, you get the others packed up and out of here!"

Short of doing something that would land him in jail or get him shot, Dustin was afraid his options were severely limited. So he took the risk of sharing the one piece of information he'd hoped to hold back — until he had the lab results, anyway.

"We need to look for a dart gun," he said bluntly.

"What?"

It wasn't just Frank who stared at him as if he'd lost his mind. Everyone did.

"Ask Joey. We heard something whizzing by us in the woods the other day. Later I was out here walking and found a dart." He decided this might be their only chance to discover the truth; he had to get Frank to at least consider the possibility. Coincidentally, he'd be able to observe the others' reactions. . . .

"I think Marcus Danby might have been hit by a dart, one that might have been tipped with horse tranquilizer. It would have knocked him out — and then heroin could've been administered. And down at the stream, Aaron could have been hit with a dart, causing him to nearly drown when he pitched forward. Someone could've put together a cocktail of acepromazine and barbiturates — just enough to knock someone out. Something that would dissolve quickly and not show up in the standard blood tests done at an autopsy."

They all looked at him incredulously. "That's kind of a stretch, Mr. Agent Man," Vine said. "You're kidding me, right? Someone's running around with a dart gun? This is twenty-first-century Tennessee! We're not in Africa or worrying about some ancient tribe on a Pacific island."

266

"I'm talking about drugs and tranquilizers readily available on any farm in the area," Dustin said.

"Still . . ." Frank protested.

"I found a dart in the woods."

"Why didn't you report it?"

"Was I supposed to report a dart?" Dustin asked with mock innocence. *To you? So you could say some kid simply got a new dart gun for his birthday?*

"You should report everything to local law enforcement — and that happens to be me," Vine growled. "Even if you are a federal agent."

"All right. I know that now. I know you're open to anything that might be out of the ordinary. So, Deputy Sheriff Vine, why *not* investigate?" Dustin demanded. "Are you trying to hinder an investigation or carry one out?"

For a moment, he thought he'd gone too far — that Frank Vine was going to order Callahan to put handcuffs on Dustin.

Maybe the man was even in on it. He'd been involved with the search the day Marcus was found dead; he'd been one of the first to arrive at the scene.

Why would a cop do such a thing? An old ax to grind? Maybe Marcus had refused to give him the dog he'd wanted. Murder over

a rescue pup? Seemed unlikely. He wondered what other reasons the deputy sheriff
might have to obstruct the inquiry.

But to his amazement, Vine seemed willing to listen to him. He looked at Dustin
for a long moment, his jaw tightening. Then
he looked down at the ground for an equally
long moment. Finally he raised his head.
"Believe me, I don't want to hinder an
investigation."

Dustin did believe him. Vine was trying to
be a good officer. He just had trouble accepting that something so absurd and devious could be going on.

"Olivia, you get everyone going," Vine
said. "The agent and I are —"

"Wait!" Matt broke in. "Is that legal?
Don't you need a search warrant? I mean,
what if you catch a killer, but your evidence
turns out to be tainted?" He looked around
worriedly. "My, uh, dad's an attorney," he
added. "Fruit of the poisonous tree, and all
that."

"You have my permission to search all
Horse Farm property," Olivia said. "There.
That handles the tents."

"You can search all our personal property,
as well. Does anyone have any objections?"
Drew asked. "Matt, I'm pretty sure that if
you say it's fine, it's fine. There are a lot of

witnesses who'll hear you give your permission."

"You can search anything of mine. Hell, we have our blood and urine tested all the time. What do I care about a backpack?" Matt said. "Guys?" he turned to the others.

They all murmured that they had no objections.

"Then, Olivia, if you'd please get everyone mounted up? We'll return everyone's property later," Vine said. "Deputy Callahan's going to ride with you."

"Wow. I finally got to use my iPod again," Matt moaned. "And you're taking it away."

"We'll get it back to you by tonight," Dustin promised.

Olivia helped Mariah to her feet. "We just leave everything?" she asked Dustin.

He nodded, speaking to her privately as the others went to get the horses saddled and ready for the ride back. It was decided that Callahan would be riding Aaron's horse.

"And stay with the deputy," Dustin emphasized. "Get the kids back where they belong, and you stay with Callahan. I don't like you being without me. I'd thought the answer might be here, but . . . no one reacted when I brought it up." He shrugged. "So, I just don't know."

"You didn't tell me anything about a dart gun," she accused him.

"It's a long shot." He grimaced. "If you'll pardon the bad pun."

She nodded distractedly. "But who could have struck him? We were all at the campsite together."

"None of us was at the stream when he went down there," he said. "We didn't realize Aaron was missing, there was so much commotion over Mariah."

"You suspected Aaron," she said. "You thought he killed Marcus."

"I never put that into words."

She took a deep breath. "Do you think he'll make it?"

"He's breathing, and they can keep him breathing. How long he was out, I don't know."

Drew had the kids saddling the horses. All the saddlebags — everything else — was left behind.

A dart could easily be hidden. And even though a dart gun was small, Dustin hoped he could see if anyone was carrying anything that looked suspect. He surveyed the riders and saw cell phones pressed against pockets, but nothing in the shape of a dart gun.

But, he figured, the dart gun could've been tossed in the forest somewhere.

When the riders were all mounted and ready to head back, he stood close to Olivia for a moment. She appeared to be calm and in control. She also looked drained and weary.

He wanted to rebuff the whole concept of searching for the dart gun — which he didn't think he was going to find, anyway. He wanted to head back with Olivia, take a steaming shower and fall into bed with her. He'd never in his life regretted trying to be noble as much as he did now. And he hated the idea that she was riding away while he stayed.

When they were gone, Vine turned to him. "Listen, we're not idiots or incompetent. Nor are we close-minded. We *are* a small department, though, and we don't get a lot of murders out here. When something bad happens, I'm afraid it's usually a domestic situation. So, G-man, what's your plan?"

"Methodical and boring," Dustin told him. "We search everything. And, to be honest, I don't think we're going to find what we're looking for."

"So why are we doing this?"

"In case we do find something."

He remained surprised — and impressed — by the turnabout in Frank Vine. But he figured the man was good at his job. He could probably maintain order, find the missing, collar rabble-rousers, and he no doubt ran a tight ship.

As he'd said, he wasn't accustomed to murder — or attempted murder. Especially when it appeared that no one had been in the vicinity to cause an "accident" that might lead to death.

"First, can you use your radio and get hold of someone to see that Aaron Bentley's kept under surveillance at the hospital?" Dustin asked.

"I can." He studied Dustin, then shook his head. "You really think someone might have murdered Marcus Danby — and attempted to kill Aaron Bentley?"

"I do," Dustin said.

"Okay, then. You call the shots."

"I'm not trying to take over."

"I'm not letting you take over. I'm giving you an order to call the shots."

Dustin grinned. "Thanks."

Using Dustin's light and the sheriff's more powerful one, they started at the stream. Daylight was upon them, but the water was murky and it was much easier to search ground, bushes and bracken with the extra light. Frank Vine was skilled at tracking; he found disruptions in the grass where Aaron had first walked. Vine also discovered exactly where he'd stepped into the stream and then fallen and nearly drowned. Dustin carefully searched the area where Aaron had fallen but to no avail. He'd been intent on saving a man's life, not on collecting evidence. If a tiny dart had gone whistling at the man, it was now lost in the stream.

"Needle in a haystack," Vine muttered.

"Doesn't mean it's not there," Dustin said.

He and Vine backtracked and starting going through the bags and equipment at the campsite. As Dustin had expected, they found nothing.

While they searched, he and Vine discussed the case. "Why?" Frank asked. "Why the hell murder Marcus Danby? I don't get it. Suppose someone had an old grudge. Something that festered in his mind for years. Okay, that might be a reason to kill. But we notice strangers and tourists out here. Say that had happened, anyway. Or, say, someone wanted the Horse Farm — but that someone would most likely have been Aaron Bentley, and now . . ."

His voice trailed off in confusion.

"I don't know. I wish I did," Dustin said. They'd gone through everything, every backpack and sleeping bag; they hadn't found a thing.

Not one of the boys had been carrying

"contraband," not so much as a magazine.

He looked around. That morning, when he'd heard Mariah scream, he'd dashed out of his tent into the woods, in the direction of her scream. Still, he could remember how he'd gone.

"Let's check the woods," he suggested.

"Which woods?" Vine asked dryly.

"This way." They started through the trees. There were a few trails — the woods in this area had long been the "washrooms" of the campground. But Dustin moved deeper, making his way to the exact spot where he'd found Mariah early that morning. Frank Vine walked ahead of him, while he searched the ground.

"What the frickin' hell?" Frank yelled.

Dustin looked up. Frank was staring at something stashed in the trees. Dustin walked over to join him.

Frank Vine hadn't found a dart gun.

What he'd found was even more perplexing.

The sun had fully risen now, but the wind was brisk and the ride back felt long. For the most part, everyone seemed subdued. But, of course, they were all worried about Aaron.

Olivia was numb. Cold and numb. She

hadn't wanted to believe that anyone at the Horse Farm could have wanted to kill Marcus, but now something had happened to Aaron, too. And it seemed highly unlikely that Aaron — with the most to gain from Marcus's death — would have attempted to drown himself. Especially when he wasn't in a position to believe that someone would be there to save him.

It all seemed crazy.

When they neared the Horse Farm, Olivia felt her phone buzz. She answered it. Sandra was on the other end, spewing furious words at her.

"Sandra, I can't understand you. Please, calm down."

"Is that idiot agent friend of yours around?"

"You mean Dustin?" Olivia was surprised by the way Sandra had voiced the question. Dustin was a guest at the Horse Farm. He shouldn't have been referred to as her "idiot agent friend."

"Obviously," Sandra spat. "I don't know what he's done, but they won't let me in with Aaron. There's a deputy watching him and they won't let anyone else in."

"Sandra, that would have been Frank Vine's call, not Dustin's."

"Your FBI man put him up to it," Sandra

said. "I want to talk to that man on the phone. I need to be with Aaron!"

"We're not with them. We're almost back at the Horse Farm."

"Well, then, you get down here as soon as you're back! You have to do something. This is ridiculous. And appalling!"

"Sandra, I'm not going to be able to do anything," Olivia told her. "I'm not law enforcement. Speak to the deputy. He can reach Frank."

Sandra swore. Olivia tried to tell her that, right now, Aaron really needed medical care more than he needed his hand held — even if he was having an affair with the person who wanted to hold his hand.

But as she tried to form the words, the phone went dead. Sandra had hung up on her.

"Who was that?" Mariah asked, riding up to her.

"Sandra. She's upset. They won't let her in with Aaron."

"What did she want you to do?"

"Make Dustin tell Frank that the hospital should let her in."

"She blames Dustin?"

Olivia just shrugged.

"It's getting kind of scary, huh? Two accidents, one deadly, the other one almost so. Well, I guess Marcus brought on his own accident, but Aaron's as straight as an arrow. Makes you wonder."

"Mariah," she said, irritated, "I still don't believe Marcus brought about his own death." She couldn't help sighing. "I guess we all need to be careful."

Mariah nodded. "Maybe we should close down for a while. Maybe —"

"What?"

"I'm not sure. Maybe the Horse Farm shouldn't be open for a while. Maybe that's what . . . someone wants."

Olivia turned to look at her. "Mariah, what's happened lately is bad. But the Horse Farm's done so much for so many people. Brent's a different person now. Lots of kids — and adults! — have developed their own sense of self-worth through the work we do."

"I know. The Horse Farm is my life — I wouldn't want it to close permanently, but . . . if there's another accident . . ." She shivered violently. "This morning . . . I was so excited. I thought I'd finally seen the general! And then, when I found the bloody remains of that cow . . . And who would've figured that Aaron would be drowning at the same time!"

"He's not dead," Olivia reminded her.

"Oh, Olivia! He has to make it!" she whimpered. "It's so horrible. We were all so close. We loved working together. We were a family."

"We're still a family," Olivia said firmly. "And, please, stop talking in the past tense. The kids can hear us."

"You don't think the kids aren't saying the same thing?"

Olivia turned in her saddle, looking back at the other riders. Matt and Joey were close together, deep in whispered conversation. At the end of the line, Drew was riding listlessly, as if he were in shock. Deputy Callahan was trying to be cheerful, riding beside Brent. Mason was with Sean.

"The work isn't what's wrong, that's for sure," Olivia said. "We'll get through this the best we can."

But Mariah's words were to prove prophetic. When they reached the Horse Farm, the van from the boys' rehab house was already there to get them; the driver and Sydney were out front, talking. Brent's mother was standing by the fence, her face pinched with worry.

When Olivia dismounted, Sydney hurried over to her. "This isn't good," he said. "The Parsonage is reconsidering. They're talking about withdrawing the boys because of everything going on."

"Oh, no," she murmured.

She saw Brent dismount from his horse. He ran to her, burying his face in her shoulder. "Liv . . ."

His mother hurried over. "Brent!"

She hugged her son, and Brent hugged her back. Brent gave others unconditional love, something Olivia truly appreciated. He loved his mother and he instinctively understood her concern. But he also understood that she'd come to take him away — and that he might not be coming back.

Olivia squared her shoulders. She spoke to Brent's mother, assuring her that the boys were never alone and nothing like this could happen to one of them; she didn't know why Aaron had been alone but he was an adult. Besides, she added, accidents did happen.

She didn't believe it for a minute.

"Olivia, we adore you — my husband, my other children — we all adore you. And this place. But . . . Well, Marcus is dead. And now this? It's a little frightening. No, it's *really* frightening. I . . . Well, I'll call before we come out for any more sessions."

"I understand," Olivia told her dully.

Accidents happened.

Well, they did, but in this case it was a lie.

But she gave the same lie to the boys' van driver from Parsonage House, saying that the Horse Farm premises and activities were safe. She said they were all devastated by Aaron's accident and that they prayed he'd make a speedy recovery.

When the boys were gone, she walked into the office and fell into one of the comfortable chairs, exhausted. Sydney followed her in.

"Where's Sammy?" she asked him. The dog should have been there when she arrived; he should've been around, wagging his tail and barking with excitement.

"He's in my room. I love that dog — and I know how much you love him — but he's been a pain in the ass! Howled last night, scratched at the door. I put him on a leash and took him out for a while. I guess he didn't want to be left behind. Or else . . ."

"Or else?"

"Maybe he sensed something was wrong. I don't know. I'll go get him for you, but . . . can you tell me more about Aaron?" His features were tense. "I've only spoken with Frank Vine and the info line at the hospital. Oh, and Sandra. They don't seem to know anything at all, except that apparently he wasn't breathing, the fed got him breathing again and . . . that's it."

"You know as much as we know. We haven't had phone service most of the way. I spoke with Sandra briefly and she was breathing fire. I was hoping *you* could tell *us* something," Olivia said.

Before he could answer her, Drew, Mason and Mariah trailed in, all looking weary and dejected. They perched on various seats about the room. Mariah started to say something but Deputy Callahan walked in behind her.

"Hey, Sydney, do you have coffee going by any chance?" he asked.

"I always have coffee going," Sydney retorted. "Or someone does, anyway." The stress he was feeling was apparent.

He poured the deputy a mug of coffee and handed it to him.

"So, at this moment," Sydney said, "no one knows anything. We could all go and sit at the hospital, but hell, Sandra's already doing that. I've been calling the hospital's patient-information line every thirty minutes," he went on. "They don't say anything except 'the patient is in stable condition.' "

"Stable is good," Mariah said.

"Yeah," Mason agreed. "Much better than . . ."

He didn't finish his sentence. They all knew what he *hadn't* said.

Dead. Stable was much better than dead.

"I've talked to Sandra a few times, too, and like you said, Liv, she's breathing fire."

"Well, of course. They've been seeing each other for ages — discreetly, or so they believed," Mariah said.

"I didn't know," Olivia murmured.

"That's because you aren't one for gossip."

"Nor, apparently, do I pay much attention to what's going on around me," Olivia said dryly.

"They did tell her this much," Sydney offered. "They're putting Aaron through a bunch of tests — brain scans — hoping he didn't do any permanent damage to himself. I guess right now . . . Well, he's breathing. They're doing all the things . . . that hospitals do." He looked at Olivia. "We can't lose Aaron."

"No, we can't," she said. "We have to go on faith and hope."

Sydney took a cup of coffee himself and sat on one of the sofas across from her. "You already know that the staff at Parsonage House don't think the boys should come back here, at least for now. They're afraid the parents will pull all the kids out of their program."

Olivia was quiet for a moment. "You

know," she began, "Marcus started this place with little more than one broken-down horse and an abused dog. He built it up, creating the wonderful facility that exists today. We'll hang in and wait this out."

"I believe in what we're doing. I kid all the time about wanting to be a movie star, but . . . I love what we do," Mason said. "The thing is . . . we've all still got to live."

"Eating is a good pastime," Mariah murmured.

"I've got savings," Drew said. "I'm fine, and I'll stick it out."

"Horses have to eat, too," Sydney reminded him.

Mariah stood up. "I'm going home, okay?"

"That's not a good idea right now."

"But I'm exhausted!"

"If you go home, you'll be doing so at your own risk," the deputy said.

Everyone in the room seemed to freeze.

At last Mariah repeated his words weakly. "At my own risk?"

"We don't believe these were accidents anymore," Callahan told her.

She sank back into her chair. "You think that someone . . . that something . . . that Aaron was . . . pushed into the water?"

"We don't know for sure. Not yet. We're hoping to learn the truth," Callahan said.

"We're hoping Aaron will wake up."

"And what if he doesn't?" Sydney asked sadly.

Drew managed a faint smile. "He *has* to wake up. I can't spend the rest of my life just looking at you guys! Not that I don't love you, but there are days Sydney and I can't wait for you to leave so we can head up to our apartments!"

The others tried to smile, too. It was then that Callahan's phone rang. He answered it and spoke briefly.

"Aaron Bentley is conscious," he announced.

11

"I don't care what Sandra Cheever does, she's not getting in to see Aaron," Dustin told Frank Vine. "And I'm thankful as can be that Aaron Bentley is alive. But he has to speak with us before he sees anyone else. It doesn't matter if they're a couple. For one thing, Sandra was out here in the woods. For another, I don't believe that Aaron going face-first into the stream was an accident."

"And you're still convinced he was struck with a dart?" Frank shook head grudgingly. "I've decided to go with you on all this, but you do know it still sounds crazy."

They were halfway back to the Horse Farm, Frank's discovery rolled up and draped over his saddle.

It was General Rufus Cunningham. Or rather, Frank had come upon a rendering of the general on cotton gauze. He'd stumbled across it in the trees, stretched between two branches. While the artwork was darned good, the cloth was the type often used by community theater groups — or colleges. Places without Broadway budgets for their backdrops. This particular piece seemed like the kind of thing frat guys might use to scare their dates.

But it was equally possible that someone in their group had put it up and done some vocal tricks to lure Mariah into the forest — just when Aaron was supposed to be dying.

With Frank Vine now grudgingly accepting the fact that things might not be what they seemed, Dustin had faith that the image would be investigated.

"Let's not mention the cheesecloth image of the general yet," Dustin suggested. "I think we should investigate and find out where it was produced and by whom."

Frank Vine glanced over at him. "Agent Blake, you must have a lot more resources at your fingertips than we have out here. I cover a pretty wide space and I do it with an eight-man team. Well, sorry, that includes two women. I'm not trying to be a sexist."

Dustin grinned. "I didn't take you for one, Vine."

"Or a yokel."

"Neither did I take you for a yokel, sir.

I'm grateful that you're giving me a chance — and that you're willing to look at this thing from all sides."

"Could still simply be accidents. Strange and sad accidents," Vine reminded him.

"Could be," he agreed. But they weren't. He couldn't explain to Frank Vine that a ghost had told them about his own murder.

They were almost back at the Horse Farm. Frank, who'd arrived via the rescue helicopter, had ridden back on Shebaan, Sandra's mount. The tents were folded up and the gear was being carried back on Gargantua, who was trailing behind them. Luckily the massive horse didn't seem to be overburdened.

As they closed in on the property, Frank's phone rang. At the same moment, Dustin felt his own pocket vibrate. He answered; Olivia was on the other end, speaking softly. "He's conscious! We got a call that Aaron is conscious."

"I guess that's the same information Frank's getting right now," Dustin said.

"Sandra's having a fit. They're giving her some information but not allowing her to see him."

"She can't see him. Not until I —" he glanced over at Vine "— not until we've had a chance to interview him."

"Where are you?" she asked, sounding a little desperate.

"Almost at the Horse Farm."

"Thank God. The natives are getting restless," she murmured.

"If you can get Drew and Sydney to meet us, that would be helpful," he told her.

"Will do," Olivia said, and hung up.

He glanced over at the deputy sheriff again.

"You don't want anyone in to see him?" Vine asked him. "They say Sandra's hollering up a storm."

"Like I said, she was there when it all happened."

"And you think she somehow got a dart into Aaron Bentley and ran back to the camp?" Despite his open mind on the matter, Frank sounded somewhat skeptical.

"Someone did," Dustin said.

"We don't really know that. Remember, you're talking to me about an investigation. We're going to need to deal with facts — not supposition."

"Okay. My *educated theory* — because of what I found in the woods when I was riding with Olivia — is that someone is knocking people out with a dart gun. Once they're unconscious, this person kills them and makes the deaths look like accidents.

Like they're caused by an overdose or a lack of coordination. Look, I know this still seems far-fetched to you, but I swear there's more to it, and if we don't find out the truth, there'll be another body. A dead one."

"I'll play along — best as I can," Frank told him.

"I can bring in help."

Vine was silent.

"You don't want me to invite in the FBI?" Dustin asked after a minute. "It doesn't have to be that official. If you prefer, I can just get a few people to drive over to Tennessee and do some legwork."

Vine shook his head. "Damn, I wish I could say I can manage this without help."

Dustin smiled. "Frank, we couldn't come in and manage anything — if *you* weren't giving *us* help."

"I see a couple of guys coming out to give us a hand with all this gear. I'm assuming you want to get right to the hospital?"

"I do. And I want Olivia Gordon with us."

Frank groaned. "Something else going on?"

"I think someone tried to break into her house the other night."

"You should've called. We could have done something."

Dustin didn't respond, and Frank sighed.

"Yeah, yeah, you're right. We would've walked around and seen nothing and probably thought she heard raccoons crawling around on her porch. But you don't think it was that."

"No."

Frank sighed again. "Things are weird around here, no matter how you look at it. I'm damned glad I've already taken my dog from that place! So, here's the deal. You bring in whoever you want — but you keep me apprised. You make me aware of everything."

"Agreed."

They didn't speak anymore; they'd reached the ranch and both Drew and Sydney were outside, waiting to take the horses as they dismounted. Sammy was out in the yard and he greeted Dustin as if he were his master, as if they'd been together ever since the big mutt had been a puppy. He could only give the dog his distracted attention because Drew was anxious to speak.

"He — he's conscious," he told Dustin. "That's got to be good, right?"

"Sounds good to me, Drew. Sounds good to me," Dustin assured him. He looked toward the office. Olivia was standing by the steps. Deputy Callahan came out behind her, presumably to see what his next orders were.

"Hang in here for a bit, Jimmy. Help these fellows keep an eye on things," Frank told him. "I'm going to the hospital with Agent Blake. Liv, you come on with us. You're in charge now, so if Aaron's up to speaking, he just might want to talk to you."

Dustin lowered his head, trying not to smile.

It was good to be in with the local law. That could make things so much easier. Frank knew he was worried about Olivia; he was helping him keep her close by.

"Sure. Okay. Thank you," Olivia said. She walked out to meet them. Sammy ran up to her, and she dropped down, petting the dog. "Sammy, I'm so sorry. You've got to stay here awhile longer. Okay? I'll be back for you, I promise."

Frank was already headed to his official car; he'd had a couple of his deputies drop it off. The dog was whining, as if afraid to see Olivia go.

"I've got him." Sydney grasped Sammy's collar. "What's gotten into you?" he demanded. "Olivia will be back!"

Sammy continued to whine as she joined Dustin, and the two of them followed Frank to his police car. Within minutes, they were halfway to the hospital.

Vine had decided to use his siren.

Aaron looked good. In fact, his appearance didn't even resemble the way he'd looked the last time Olivia had seen him — wet, a strange shade of pale ashen blue, his bones seeming to protrude everywhere.

He was in a semiupright position on his hospital bed. An IV was providing him with some kind of nourishment or medication, but his color was back and his eyes were bright.

"Aaron!" she whispered, entering. She ran to his bed and realized she was trembling. She'd almost lost another friend; she was suddenly weak at the knees, so grateful that she hadn't.

"Liv!"

She carefully hugged him. He hugged her back with a surprising and gratifying strength.

She stood at the side of his bed, gazing down at him. Dustin and Frank were behind her, while Sandra remained in the waiting room, fit to be tied. Dustin had told her they just needed a few minutes, and then she'd be able to see Aaron.

When Frank tried to explain that Olivia had to be first because of her position at the

Horse Farm, Sandra had looked at her resentfully. Olivia had been shocked by the venom in that stare.

But, in all honesty, she understood — in a way. Sandra was sleeping with Aaron. Something she'd apparently been the last to realize.

"Thank God you're here!" Aaron said, looking at Olivia and then Dustin and Frank. His voice seemed to tremble. "I understand I'm alive because of you, Dustin. Thank you."

"I did what anyone would have," Dustin said. "You're welcome. We're glad to see you."

"Why won't they let Sandra in?" Aaron asked.

"We needed to speak with you first," Frank said. "Aaron, what happened to you? You're not the kind of man who'd walk to the stream and just fall in."

"Yeah, I know. It was odd as hell, and dumb as hell!" Aaron told them. "I'd walked on over to the stream — didn't think anyone else was up yet — and I was getting ready to kneel down and wash my face. Then . . ."

He closed his eyes for a minute, puzzled. "Then I don't know," he admitted.

"What do you mean, you don't know?" Frank repeated, clearly annoyed.

"I was there, and then I was in the water," Aaron said.

"Okay, think, Aaron. Did you see anyone, hear anyone? Was there anything out of the ordinary?" Dustin asked, trying to encourage him.

Aaron was thoughtful. "No . . . Must have hit my head on a rock or something. I mean, the water isn't even deep. What, I was in about two feet of it?"

"Something like that," Dustin confirmed.

"Aaron, this just beats all," Frank said. "There must have been *something*."

"Nothing. It was just a regular morning," Aaron said. "Got up, looked over at the horses, felt the chill of the morning. I walked the fifty or so yards to the water . . . heard some birds chirp . . . the buzz of some insects and then . . . I woke up here. In some kind of brain machine! I'm fine now, honest to God, I'm fine now. If they'll just let me out."

"They'll keep you overnight for observation," Frank told him.

"Let's back up," Dustin said. "Frank — you heard insects? Like a buzzing in your ear?"

"Flies and mosquitos do seem to buzz in your ear, don't they?" Aaron asked, shaking his head and smiling.

"Which ear?" Dustin persisted.

"What?"

"Which ear?" Dustin repeated. "Never mind. May I look at your neck, at the side of your head?"

"Okay." Aaron shrugged. "They've pushed and prodded everything else."

Dustin walked over to Aaron and moved his head forward, studying it with intensity. He frowned suddenly, feeling something in his hair.

"Smarts there a little," Aaron said.

Dustin pulled out his penlight and inspected Aaron's scalp. He nodded at Frank, who walked over.

"Looks like an insect bite," Frank said.

"Except it isn't." Dustin stepped back. "Aaron, I believe someone shot you with a dart gun. There was enough of a drug cocktail on the arrow tip to knock you out. It wouldn't have killed you. But since you were standing by the water, you fell in and nearly died."

"What?" Aaron demanded incredulously.

"I believe Marcus Danby was murdered, struck with a like dart laced with a similar cocktail of drugs. When he was unconscious, he was injected with the heroin and 'helped' to fall into the ravine."

"Uh —" Aaron said, staring from one to

the other. "Why?"

"I don't know the answer to that yet," Dustin said.

Aaron turned to Frank Vine. "That's crazy," he said. "Why kill Marcus? Why kill me? All he had, really, was the Horse Farm and it's tied up in trusts and it's nonprofit, so . . ."

He broke off. His eyes fell on Olivia — not with accusation but with confusion. "Why?" he asked again.

"I don't know," Dustin said. "We were hoping you might've seen someone, heard someone . . . Been able to help."

"I — I'm sorry. The thing on my head must be a bite. Not a prick from a dart gun. Dart gun! Come on! Who the hell runs around the hills of Tennessee with a dart gun?"

"That's what we have to find out," Dustin said.

"And you're sure?" Aaron asked in a trembling voice.

Olivia glanced at Dustin, then turned back to Aaron. "I can't believe Marcus suddenly went mad in the woods and started shooting up. You knew him. Did you believe that when you heard it?"

Aaron swallowed. "No," he admitted. "But . . . dart guns?"

"Whatever the exact composition of the poison, it causes an instant knockout," Dustin said. "But it doesn't remain in the system. Or it's difficult to identify — and requires special tests at autopsy. The kind that aren't usually done unless poisoning is suspected. I think that same person tried to attack Olivia in the woods, and then went after you at the stream."

Aaron looked at Frank Vine. "This is crazy — crazy," he said.

Frank shrugged. "You wanna live, Aaron? Crazy or not, you might want to listen to him."

"So what do I do? How the hell do you hide from a dart gun?"

"You watch your step," Frank told him. "Stay with people at all times. It's hard for someone to pull off an 'accident' when you're in a group."

"How close are you to catching whoever is doing this?" Aaron asked.

"Not very close, I have to admit," Dustin said.

Aaron let his eyes drift shut. "May I please see Sandra? I figure most of you realize by now that we're seeing each other. Olivia, you know how to manage the Horse Farm. You take over. I'll do my twenty-four hours in here. After that, I'll rest at my place for another twenty-four. Then we'll see where we are."

Olivia inhaled and exhaled slowly. "Aaron, there may not be a lot to manage. We're starting to lose clients — guests." Aaron stared at her.

"What do we do?" he asked thickly.

"Find whoever is doing this," Dustin said.

"There had to be someone else in the woods with us," Aaron insisted.

"That is a possibility," Frank said.

"Will you let Sandra come in now? Please?"

"Yes, fine, we can do that," Frank told him.

Olivia gave Aaron a kiss on the forehead. He looked up at her and smiled. "You'll fix it, kid. I know you will."

I don't know, Aaron! I don't know.

She didn't say the words out loud. She offered him what she hoped was an encouraging smile and followed Dustin and Frank out of the room. As Frank spoke to the deputy who'd been assigned to watch the room, Dustin told Sandra she could go in.

She walked by Olivia, looking as if she'd like to scratch her eyes out. Olivia didn't believe Sandra would harm Aaron in any way. But, at that moment, she thought the woman would have gladly strangled *her.*

12

"We're going to reschedule all our weekend appointments," Olivia said.

They'd returned to the Horse Farm and she was speaking to Mason, Mariah, Sydney and Drew. Dustin leaned against the wall, watching as she spoke.

Sammy had taken up a position at her feet.

She'd announced that the police suspected the situation that plagued them might have nothing to do with a relapse and an accident.

The room had already buzzed with protests and disbelief. But now, the group was subdued and concerned.

"*If* they'll reschedule. If anyone even comes back," Mason said glumly.

"We'll hope for the best," Olivia responded. "If they don't reschedule, we'll be understanding, and we'll tell them we hope they'll come back in the future. We'll explain that we don't know what's going on, but

—" Olivia paused, looking over at Dustin "— but the authorities will discover the truth very soon."

"So, what do you want us to do, Olivia?" Drew asked.

"You and Sydney do what you always do — tend to the horses. And the cats and dogs and . . . I think that's all we have right now."

"If we close down, though," Mariah said, "don't we look like we're guilty of something?"

Olivia shook her head. "No. We look like we're concerned about all our guests and we want to make sure we're providing an entirely safe environment for them."

"Maybe we should start looking for work," Mariah said.

"If you feel you need to move on, everyone here will understand," Olivia told her.

"I'm not jumping ship! I'm just thinking about it," Mariah added quickly.

"The Horse Farm is all right for now. We can make it for a while with all the trusts and provisions in the will. I'll call the attorney and let him know where we are," Olivia said. "I'm expecting Aaron will be back in the office by Tuesday. We can try to reschedule our sessions for next week."

Mariah excused herself as her cell phone rang. She stepped into the games room to take the call.

"What should *we* be doing?" Mason asked Olivia. "I mean — no offense, guys — but this is easier for Sydney and Drew. They just keep looking after the place and the animals. But for you and me and Mariah . . ."

Olivia smiled at him. "Mason, why don't you get some new modeling shots done? See if there's any extra work in the area for the next few days."

Mason looked back at her and then laughed. "You know what I've never done? Visited the Hermitage. It's almost anti-American to be this close to Nashville and not have visited the Hermitage. Old Hickory's homestead! I think I'll do that tomorrow."

"Good plan!" Olivia said.

Mariah stepped back into the room, her eyes wide. "You're not going to believe this."

"What?" Olivia asked.

"I just got a call —"

"People want to support us, right?" Mason interrupted. "They're trying to book sessions, anyway!"

"Uh, no, I'm sorry," Mariah said, frowning. "That was the agency that sets up ghost tours for me. They say they're getting constant calls from tourists who want to

301

come out here and go on ghost tours!"

"Great," Mason said.

"No, not great," Sydney said, frowning. "Sounds like people just want to see where Marcus died, along with Civil War ghosts. That's ghoulish, not great."

"Oh, Sydney, I wouldn't tell stories about Marcus!"

"And you don't think it would come up? That people wouldn't ask you where Marcus Danby died?" Mason demanded.

"And where Aaron Bentley almost died?" Drew asked quietly.

Mariah stared at them all. "Hey, guys, I've always done ghost tours. History tours."

"I think it's fine, Mariah," Olivia said. "You give great history tours and you have for a long time. Just don't book anything until Aaron's back on Tuesday. Not tonight, though. We're all drained."

Mariah nodded. "Of course. I agree, tonight would be bad. And they're not my horses. They belong to the farm, and one of you guys usually comes with me and sometimes we camp. . . . But I'm definitely not camping again for a while! Anyway, it's all on hold."

Mason stood up. "I'm going home — at my own risk, mind you. Call me if there's anything new or if you need me. Oh, it's okay if we go see Aaron?"

"Yes, of course," Olivia said.

Mason started to walk out, but stopped and looked directly at Dustin. "What do you make of all this?"

"I don't know yet. That's why I suggest you all stay in public places, hang around in groups — and watch your backs," Dustin told him.

"Yeah, yeah, thanks," Mason muttered. When he reached the door, he paused and turned back. "Someone want to walk me to my car?" he asked.

Dustin smiled, pushed away from the wall and said, "Sure."

"Hey, I'll take off, too," Mariah said, rushing over. "Not that I think anyone would be after me. Or you, Mason. But then, I wouldn't have thought anyone would be after Aaron. . . ." She stared at Olivia. "You should be careful, Olivia. Really careful. I mean, if things go in order . . . Marcus, Aaron — you. Oh, Liv! I can't believe I just said that. Hey, you want to come and stay with me?"

Dustin stepped in. "Olivia will be all right. I'll be watching over her," he said.

Mariah started to smile. Her lips twitched as if she was about to make a sexual innuendo.

She didn't.

"Good." She waved at Drew and Sydney. "We won't just desert you two. I'll be here tomorrow."

"Thanks, Mariah," Drew said.

"Ditto," Sydney told her.

Mariah brightened. "Aaron is fine — and that's the main thing, right? By next week, we'll be back up to speed. I just know it!"

Her words seemed to fall into empty space.

Then Drew gave it a try. "Sure, Mariah."

Dustin walked Mariah and Mason out the door and toward the parking lot. Both hesitated as they stepped outside, looking out over the rolling pasture.

"This place is so beautiful," Mason said, his voice reverential.

Mariah nodded. "So, Dustin — even Deputy Vine thinks something odd is going on. But in a court of law, wouldn't we be looking at a bunch of circumstances? As opposed to solid evidence? Sorry, I guess I watch too much crime TV."

"I'm into being safe and if Frank wants us to be safe — well, I'm there," Mason said. "See you all. Thanks, Secret Agent Man."

Dustin didn't bother to protest. "Take care, Mason."

"Will do!" Mason promised. He walked

to his car. Mariah started walking to hers; by the end, she was running. She hopped in, revved the engine and lifted a hand to show that she was on her way.

He walked back into the office. Olivia, Drew and Sydney glanced up at him expectantly.

"What do we do now?" Drew asked him.

"Find a killer," Dustin said.

13

"That was pretty blunt," Olivia told Dustin as they drove away from the Horse Farm.

His rental car was staying there.

They were driving to her place. Together.

Sammy was with them, of course. The dog was in the backseat but his head appeared between them every few seconds, despite Olivia's suggestion that he stay in the back. Dustin had a feeling that she was usually a little more authoritative with the dog, but she was tired. Worn out. And she was feeling guilty about Sammy.

"Blunt? Perhaps. Not much else to say at this point, though." He turned to look at her. "Whoever is doing this has to be in your group. And you did the best thing you could have done — stopping all sessions until Aaron's back. If Aaron makes it back."

Olivia gripped the wheel and glanced his way quickly. "First of all, canceling our sessions wasn't entirely my choice. And what do you mean, *if* Aaron makes it back? He looked great. They're just keeping him for observation."

"He's keen to get out of the hospital. He almost died, Olivia. According to him, he heard a 'mosquito' buzz and went down immediately after that. He's not a stupid man. He listened to what Frank and I had to say, but he just wanted to see Sandra and get out. The sheriff's department doesn't have the manpower to put a guard on everyone at the Horse Farm, so I'm hoping he and Sandra stay together. For now, Aaron is fine. However, I don't know what'll happen when they release him — even if Sandra never lets him out of her sight."

"You're really scaring the hell out of me," Olivia muttered.

"There's more."

"What?"

"Someone had an image of the general on his horse out in the forest. I don't know much about art, but it's on some kind of cheesecloth, which, I assume, would make it look ghostly in the right light. Frank Vine was the one to find it. That's good, because it means he's bought into our suspicions about what's going on."

"I don't understand. An artist drew a picture on gauzy cloth — and put it in the forest? Why?"

"Because if you're stumbling around at night or in the early morning — when the light's hazy — you'd think you were seeing the general."

"But . . . wouldn't you check to see if it was real?" Olivia asked.

He grinned at her. "No, not most people. Most people would run like hell!"

Olivia nodded thoughtfully. "Okay, so what would the image of the general in the forest have to do with someone attacking Aaron at the stream? And are you *sure* Aaron was attacked?"

He shook his head impatiently. "No, I'm not one hundred percent sure, but anything else is unlikely. Aaron *might* just happen to have a little wound the size of an insect sting near the base of his neck. And I'll admit I'm not one hundred percent sure of the connection between those two events — Aaron's so-called accident and Mariah's discovery — either." He shrugged. "Maybe Mariah simply imagined that she heard the general speaking and then happened to wander into the woods where she found an image of him — and the torn-up carcass of a cow. Like I said, it's unlikely, but . . ."

"It *is* possible," Olivia said a little stiffly.

She pulled into her driveway and let out a

little cry of dismay. Dustin frowned, looking toward the entry.

There was a note on the door.

"The alarm company came and went," Olivia said. "I forgot all about them."

"So did I," he told her. "Don't worry. We'll just reschedule them."

"I'd have liked to get the alarm system in today. Funny, I've lived by myself for several years and I've never been afraid. But now . . ."

"Let's call them right away," Dustin suggested.

"And after that?"

"I have a few other calls to make. And for what it's worth — I won't be leaving. But we'll put some faith in Sammy, too. He does seem to be an excellent watchdog."

Sammy was apparently attempting to prove it by barking ferociously. As they got out of the car, the dog bolted past them and went dashing around the house.

"What is the matter with that dog?" Olivia asked, worried.

"Dogs are sensitive. He senses that something's going on," Dustin answered. He smiled at her. "Hey, come on. You know that. You're a therapist who works with animals."

"Yeah," she said huskily. "I know he's not

309

barking for nothing, and that scares me even more."

She hurried over to the house, taking the sticker the alarm company had left before opening the door. Sammy came rushing back and swept by their legs as they entered.

"Want me to call the alarm people?" he asked.

"I can do it."

"Of course you can — but I'm happy to do it. I thought maybe you'd forage through the kitchen and find food."

Olivia laughed at that. "Okay, you get on the phone. I'll look for food."

He sat in the living room and put a call through to the alarm company. They were exceptionally pleasant, completely understanding of an emergency and happy to reschedule for later that week.

He could hear pots and pans and cutlery being moved about in the kitchen, so he went ahead and called the office. He spoke to Jackson Crow first, filling him in, and then he was put through to Malachi, who was eager to hear what was going on.

"I told Jackson it's pretty much out in the open now," he explained to Malachi. "And the local lawman has been okay. I thought he was going to be difficult at first, but he came around. We're dealing with Deputy

Sheriff Frank Vine and Deputy Jimmy Callahan. Vine knows he doesn't have the manpower to work on this. Oh, the medical examiner is all right, too. I brought him the bits of dart and the pieces of tree bark I took from the woods, and I'm waiting on a report from him now."

Malachi put him on hold while he had a quick discussion in the office. A moment later, he was back on the line. "I'm heading out there with Abby, Sloan and Jane. We don't want to make an announcement or anything like that. We'll just show up. We should be in by tomorrow afternoon."

"Good," Dustin said. "Let us know when you're in the vicinity. I'll keep you posted on where we are."

As he ended the call, Olivia walked out of the kitchen. "There's a casserole in the oven. I'll be back down in ten. Oh, the guest room is across from mine upstairs. Make yourself at home."

He nodded, looking up at her. They were both the worse for wear, but even covered in trail dust with bedraggled hair, Olivia Gordon was . . . striking.

"Thanks." His voice sounded hoarse to his own ears. "Malachi and some of the Krewe will be here tomorrow," he told her.

"Really?" She seemed pleased. And yet,

he thought, not as pleased as she would've been a few days earlier.

Maybe he'd grown on her.

"That's great," she said. "I mean . . . considering all the variables."

"Yeah, it's good news."

"Not that you don't know what you're doing. You obviously do. You saved Aaron's life this morning," she said fervently.

"Anyone with a few courses in emergency medicine could've done what I did — and I'm sure that you would have acted if I hadn't been there."

"The thing is *you* found Aaron. *You* saved him. Will you excuse me? I'll be down in a bit."

She turned and ran up the stairs. He found his backpack by the door and hiked it onto his shoulders, then followed her up. The door to the left was hers, he knew. He pushed open the opposite door and went into the guest room, where he set his backpack on the bed. He headed into the shower, trying not to think about the fact that she was across the hall.

Naked.

While the heat of the water felt wonderful, he didn't want to tarry. And he didn't — the hot water lasted a few minutes, and then it went cold. He stepped out, swearing softly, and remembered that while the bathroom was probably fairly new and up-to-date, the house itself was very old. Hot water just wasn't going to last that long, not with two people showering at the same time.

He dressed, got his computer from his bag and left the room.

Sammy lay in the upstairs hallway between the two rooms, as if watching over both of them.

"You're a good old boy," Dustin said, bending to scratch behind the dog's ears.

As he made his way down the stairs and into the kitchen, Sammy followed him. Dustin saw a bag of dog treats on the counter and offered him one. "You tried hard, didn't you? You knew something wasn't right the day Marcus was killed. I think you went after the killer. But the killer wasn't really supplied with the customary murder weapons. No gun, no knife. So you were probably whacked with a good-size rock or maybe a branch. But you went up to the killer — close enough to get a walloping — because it was someone you trusted, huh?"

"Talking to yourself?" Olivia asked, sweeping into the kitchen. Her hair was still damp. She was wearing a casual cotton halter dress and sandals. There was something compelling about her — the naturalness of her movements, her lack of makeup, the tempting scent of her soap.

"Sammy is an excellent listener."

"And you were discussing . . . ?"

He smiled grimly. "Sammy and me? We were discussing my certainty that someone involved with the Horse Farm is doing this. I think Sammy trusted the person who hurt him."

"But if someone at the Horse Farm hurt him, wouldn't he be afraid of that person now?"

"Yes — unless the person threw something at him from a distance, maybe as Sammy approached. In that case, it's possible he never associated the person with the action and the pain it caused him."

She walked past him and into the kitchen, pulling a casserole from the oven. "It's just hamburger and potatoes, with a soup mix and crisp onion topping. Not very gourmet."

"I don't think I've ever smelled anything better," he said.

Not true. He'd never smelled anything as good as her.

"I'll bring it out. There's a dining table set up in the family room. You can eat *and* play on your computer at the same time," she told him.

314

She carried the casserole into the spacious back room. The table appeared to date from the early 1800s, and there were heat pads on it for protection. "Agent Blake, have a seat," she said, placing the casserole on one of the pads.

He was wondering how she'd managed anything other than the casserole, but she also put out a platter of raw vegetables and dip, along with glasses of sweet tea, plates and silverware.

He'd opened the computer while she set up.

She closed it as she joined him. "I'm starving, and I know you are, too."

"I am, and we can talk, which is almost as good as staring at a computer screen."

"Almost?"

He was pretty sure he actually flushed. "Sorry. I didn't mean it that way. It's just that the facts and figures I need are in the computer."

"Where do you think Marcus has been lately?" she asked.

"I assume he's off trying to solve his own murder — except that he could help a lot more by hanging around with us."

"He never did like camping," Olivia said. "Strange, because he loved nature so much. He loved a walk or a ride through the hills or along the stream." She looked away quickly and he realized she was close to tears. You could accept the death of a loved one, but it often took time to really remember the good times and be able to smile and laugh at a memory.

"Well, he's still with us," he reminded her softly. "Somewhere," he added. "But let's go back to that day. So Marcus was at the Horse Farm and we know he definitely went in to see Aaron. We know they talked. He probably talked to Andrew and Sydney, too, because they would've been working at the stables."

"Yes, and we know that because Frank spoke to them. They had casual conversations with Marcus fairly early in the day. I had a session in the morning. When I'm with my groups, I'm not paying attention to much else. As gentle as our horses are, they're still horses. I keep an eye on every interaction. Not to mention that I'm talking most of the time. So, the upshot is that I wasn't really watching."

"When did Sammy come back hurt?"

"During the lunch break. It's from twelve to one."

"Who was around during the break that day?"

"Hmm. You're not going to like this. I had

some paperwork to do so I was at my desk. I saw Drew when I brought in Trickster. He was cleaning Gargantua's hooves. I think he'd been checking all their shoes."

"Did you see Sydney?"

"Not until Aaron talked about how concerned he was once Sammy came limping back. I remember Sydney called the vet right away — and our vet is wonderful. He came out and made a house call, then took Sammy with him because he wanted to keep him still for the night. He was afraid Sammy might tear out his stitches. By the time the vet left, we were all worried about Marcus. We started calling him and looking for him, then we mounted up and headed out on a search. Everyone except Sandra. We needed someone to stay at the house. Oh — we'd called Frank Vine. He gave us a spiel about Marcus being a grown man, but Aaron insisted that something was wrong. Because of Sammy, you see. Sammy would never have left Marcus."

Dustin was glad to hear her memories of the day; for one, listening to her, he was able to eat. And he'd been famished. But now she was waiting for him to respond.

"As far as you know, any one of the others could have been out in the woods during the lunch break?"

317

"I suppose so. I wasn't keeping track. And we were focused on Sammy and on the fact that Marcus seemed to be missing."

"Someone could still have slipped through the cracks."

"Have you eliminated anyone?" she asked.

"No."

"Okay, but if you were going to eliminate someone, I'm assuming it would be Aaron."

"Not necessarily."

"Dustin! He almost died."

"Almost."

She shook her head and groaned. "Seriously?"

"If I were going to eliminate someone, I'd say Sydney and Drew."

"Why?"

"Because I like them."

"Now, there's a good reason for you. I like everyone I work with — most of the time. And you have to realize it might not be someone involved with the Horse Farm. You could be wrong."

"I could be — but I'm not."

"You're confident."

"Yes."

"Arrogant, really."

"No, let's be kind. Go back to confident."

She began to pick up their dishes, and he rose to help. As she moved into the kitchen she asked, "Who, then? Mason? His greatest flaw is his self-regard — but he's still a good therapist. Mariah loves history, is almost obsessed with it, but that doesn't seem like much of a flaw. Sandra — well, okay, she can be bitchy. I had my head in the clouds about her and Aaron. I mean, I had no idea there was an affair going on. But if they're in love, and I think they are, it sure doesn't make sense that she'd try to hurt him, does it? Anyway, Aaron is really a doll. He's always patient and never loses his temper. As you say, Sydney and Drew are great. They're both low-key. Drew works with the boys from Parsonage House a lot, while Sydney is more of a loner. He's the sweetest man on earth, but he does tend to like animals better than people. I don't really hold that against him. And . . . you did suspect Aaron."

He stood behind her at the sink. His arms were almost around her as he set down their glasses. He had to step away. He'd barely heard what she'd said; he'd been breathing in the scent of her hair.

He cleared his throat. "They all have clean backgrounds," he said. He paused. "None of them have any charges against them, no criminal history or official complaints."

"Does any of that matter?"

"I don't know, but finding out everything we can about all of them is important."

The dishes were done; the kitchen was clean.

"I've got to go outside with Sammy," she said. "Usually I'd just let him out, but to-night . . ."

"We'll go with him."

They walked to the front and unlocked the door, waiting for Sammy, who came running. Olivia stood on the porch, with Dustin just behind her.

"Sammy, stay in the front, please. Do what you need to do and come back in, okay?"

The dog barked as if he understood her every word.

Maybe he did.

When they were back inside, Dustin watched her lock the door.

"I wish we hadn't missed the alarm company," she said anxiously.

"It's okay. We have a dedicated watchdog — and I sleep with a big gun beside me."

She smiled at that, then yawned. "I . . . guess I'll go on up. Like I said before, make yourself at home."

She turned quickly and ran up the stairs.

Dustin double-checked the door. He walked through the house, checking all the windows but, of course, they remained bolted tight. The way the dog had behaved earlier disturbed him, though. He was pretty sure someone had been at the house — someone other than the mailman or the people from the alarm company.

Satisfied that no locks had been compromised, he returned to the back porch and his computer and tried to focus on the histories of the people involved. He needed to go deeper into their backgrounds, searching for motives, but he had a hard time concentrating. Restless, he stood and called the information line at the hospital; Aaron's condition was described as "good."

Next, he called Frank Vine, who seemed grumpy when he answered. Okay, it *was* nighttime, and it had been a long day. Yes, Frank had been in touch with the officers on duty at the hospital and everything was fine; Sandra Cheever was sleeping in a chair next to Aaron. Frank grumbled a little more about the overtime it was going to cost him and hung up.

He'd barely put his cell phone away when it rang. He could tell from his call display that it was Ellie, the young clerk at Willis House. "Hi, Agent Blake. I don't mean to bother you, but we were just a bit worried. We knew you were off on the camping trip, but then we hadn't heard from you. . . . It's pretty quiet out here, so we tend to worry about other people's business."

He smiled. "I'm fine, Ellie. But I won't be back tonight. Don't worry — and please don't let my room go, okay?"

"Oh, we wouldn't do that, Agent Blake."

"And I intend to pay for every night, whether I'm in the room or not."

She giggled. "Not to worry. We've got your credit card number. The management *definitely* intends to make you pay. I was just checking that you're all right. Because, of course, everyone knows what happened today!"

"Everyone knows . . . what?"

"You're a hero! You saved Aaron Bentley's life!"

He winced. "No, Ellie, that's kind of embarrassing. I'm not a hero. The real heroes are the nurses and doctors and paramedics who save lives every day. I've taken a few classes in emergency procedures, that's all. Pretty basic stuff. And it was more a matter of right time, right place."

"Yeah? Maybe I should take a class."

"Knowing first aid is always a good idea — for anyone."

"Yeah. Well, Coot says hello. He says he misses you and that you should go to the café for breakfast tomorrow."

"Tell him I'll try to make it."

He put his cell away and hesitated for a minute; instinct really did count for a lot in his field. His instincts told him it would be quiet tonight. Or maybe it was pure logic — if the killer didn't want to be caught, he or she would lie low for a while.

He walked to the stairs and paused there. "Marcus?" he said aloud. But he hadn't sensed the presence of the ghost. And Marcus didn't respond.

It was quiet on the second floor. He went into the bedroom and placed his Glock within easy reach on the nearby table. He prepared for bed, then prowled the room anxiously before he settled down to sleep. He was glad Malachi was coming with more Krewe members tomorrow. His concentration was at a low point, maybe because he'd figured out he was a fool. Everything wasn't forever; everything didn't need to mean something. Adults encountered one another in life, enjoyed physical relationships, moved on. . . .

Yes. Hell, yes, it happened all the time. Didn't make people enemies; didn't naturally make them lasting friends or lovers, but . . .

Sometimes the attraction was too strong,

too much was expected, he told himself. And in those situations, getting involved was a mistake.

Oh, bull. He'd been an idiot to turn her down.

As he lay there, he heard her door open and close. She was going downstairs. He waited for a few minutes and leaped to his feet. There was nothing that suggested a break-in; he was certain he would have heard.

He left the room and walked to the landing. Sammy was sleeping there. He raised his head, wagged his tail when he saw Dustin and went right back to sleep.

Nothing could be wrong if the dog was so sedate and unconcerned, but still . . .

Barefoot, he moved quickly and quietly down the stairs. As he rounded the staircase, he saw her in the kitchen, wearing a robe, something that clung to her body like silk, making a cup of tea.

"Uh, hello," he said, wishing he'd grabbed a robe himself rather than running down in his boxers.

"You all right?" she asked.

"Yeah," he said thickly. "I just heard you down here."

She stared at him. "Tea," she said. "I couldn't sleep."

"Me, neither."

She let the tea bag fall into the cup and, grinning, walked up to him. If a man could emit sexual desire like sweat, he'd have been drenched. He didn't move. He was afraid to — for several reasons. There was the way he felt. There was his lack of attire. She was so close he could breathe in her scent, and if he moved, he'd *have* to touch her.

"This is ridiculous," she said.

"This?"

"Us. Here. Not, um . . . not. You and me . . . *not*?"

"I know," he said.

"You do?"

"I agree."

"I mean, after all," she told him seriously, "I'm quite prepared. I'm on birth control. It doesn't make sense for two people to abstain when the desire is there. And, well, it's the age of *Fifty Shades of Grey* — and . . . I want to have sex."

"Hmm. Just sex?"

"Yes, just sex."

"Oh."

"Oh?"

"What kind of sex?" he asked, but he knew she saw the grin twisting his lips.

He thought she was about to say *normal sex.* But she stopped herself and moved a fraction of an inch closer, her presence touching him without touching him, the heat of her excitement reaching out to him.

"Mmm," she said softly, eyes alight. "Let's see. Hot, steamy, passionate, wet, sweaty sex? Energetic, explosive . . . sensual, vital, vibrant, amazing, incredible . . . The kind that makes you forget everything else in the world."

"Okay," he said. Still, he didn't touch her. Not yet. Then he asked, "Did you want that once — or twice? If you'd like it twice, I'll do my very best to oblige."

"Something tells me you're up for the job — and that you'll be pretty good."

"Just *pretty* good?"

"Possibly excellent. This is all still theory, you know?"

"Theories need to be tested," he said. "That's the only way to prove them." He didn't know which one of them moved first. She eased up on her toes; he crushed her into his arms. He found her mouth and kissed her, trembling in his effort to control the force of everything he wanted. She returned the kiss and it was passionate . . . and hot, wet, steamy. His hands were on her and the robe seemed to slide from her skin in slow motion. She was naked beneath; maybe she'd been dreaming of him, of this, before she felt the urge for tea. Maybe she'd even hoped he'd come down.

Maybe didn't matter. They were together. Everything in the kitchen — pots, pans appliances — seemed to evaporate. He slid down the length of her body where they stood, his kisses covering her flesh, his fingers sweeping along it. Desire stoked energy, and each time his lips touched a new inch of her, it seemed as though something gripped him and shook him and wouldn't let him go. He felt her hands on his shoulders, heard her sweet urgent whispers and sought her with ever greater intimacy. She trembled, crying out at last, as she slipped into his arms. Their mouths met in another kiss and he lifted her up, seating her on the counter. She was breathless and beautiful, lips parted softly, eyes intense with sensuality.

He moved against her, thinking about his boxers, but somehow he'd lost them; he couldn't recall when. Something on the counter crashed to the floor. Neither of them paid any heed. They just began to move, clinging to each other.

He'd wanted her. He denied himself, and now . . .

The excitement, the urgency, was almost unbearable. His muscles ached and trembled, and everything in him — muscle, flesh, blood — felt the building explosion.

It was inevitable; the moment of climax came and seemed to roar through him with the shattering force of a windstorm. He'd tried to hold out . . . and yet he felt her fall against him, heard the lyrical tone of her cry as she held him tight, shaking, all but melded to him.

And there they were, on the counter in her kitchen. Tremors continued to rack his body so that he almost feared he wouldn't be able to stand.

He smoothed back her damp hair, feeling awkward because, as he'd feared, somehow it wasn't just sex, although it had been incredible sex.

"I think we nailed the sweaty," he told her, trying to lighten the mood.

He felt her smile before she pulled away to look up at him. Her arms locked around his neck as she leaned her head back.

"Pretty good on the passionate, too," she said.

"And vital, I think."

"Oh, yes." Her smile deepened.

"Did you want to give our theory a second go-round?"

"There's nothing like checking and re-checking the facts," she agreed.

"Always important," he said.

She slid off the counter and into his arms. He ducked down to retrieve his boxers and her robe. They ran up the stairs.

Olivia stopped on the landing, and he nearly plowed into her. He looked over her shoulder.

Sammy had raised his head again. Once more, he wagged his tail — and promptly went back to sleep.

"Thank God!" he said. "I wonder where I'd be if the dog didn't approve."

She laughed, caught his hand and led him into her darkened room. The moon was almost full and its opaque glow seemed to shine like a strange and magical blessing.

He fell into bed beside her and felt her hands moving over him, felt the unrestrained passion of her kisses.

"Wow," he murmured.

"Hmm."

"Are you ready to try this again?"

"Hmm . . ."

"I know it's a cliché, but . . . I think the earth moved," she said solemnly. She rose up on her elbows. Her hair cascaded around her face. He marveled again at her stunning beauty, and he marveled that they were together.

He lay with his hands laced behind his head. He smiled. "Really? The earth moved?"

She shrugged. "Who knows? They might've been digging in a nearby mine."

"*Are* there nearby mines anymore?" he asked her.

"Oh. Maybe not. So the earth moved, and . . ."

He supported himself on one elbow, facing her. "And?"

"And it was even better than that," she told him.

"Oh?"

"I forgot the world," she whispered.

He pulled her back into his arms. The moon shined on.

They might forget the world when they were together like this, but reality always came back soon enough.

As if sensing his thoughts she sighed softly. "Nothing compares to a night like this." She smiled. "Our theory was a good one."

"Theories should always be thoroughly proven," he whispered. "Are you interested in some more fact-checking?"

Her eyes were absolutely hypnotic and dazzling in the moonlight. "I'll do my best to oblige," she said.

And she did.

14

When morning arrived, Olivia was glad they'd enjoyed such an incredible night. And glad that they'd slept in each other's arms.

In the morning, Dustin explained that he'd talked to Ellie over at Willis House and that she'd said Coot wanted him to show up for breakfast.

"Sounds like a plan," she told Dustin. "The café has a great Sunday brunch. But I wasn't aware you'd gotten to know old Coot so well."

"Can't say I know him *that* well," Dustin responded. "But I've spent some time talking to him and he seems like a savvy guy. He watches the people around him. He appears to be an elderly gentleman simply enjoying the beauty of the countryside as his later years slip by. People wouldn't expect him to be as observant as he really is."

"So, we'll meet Coot for breakfast," Olivia said.

Before they left, they let Sammy run around the yard for a while, and Olivia lavished some affection on the dog.

Delilah called out a greeting to them as they entered the café and indicated that Coot was sitting in a booth toward the rear. They waved to her and slid into the booth with Coot.

"Morning," he told them. "I'm just enjoying a 'Liv' here. Mighty good coffee. And I'm glad to see you two young people looking so healthy. That was something, what I heard about yesterday morning!"

"Far too much excitement for a camping trip," Dustin said.

Coot shook his head.

"Could've been much worse." Delilah served some tourists at the counter, then came bustling around to see them. "Why, honey, I am so proud of you!" she said to Dustin. "What you did was *amazing.*"

As he lowered his head, Olivia realized that she was loving more and more about the man; he was uncomfortable when people put him on a pedestal. He glanced at her and a little smile came to his lips. "I think we decided that the 'amazing' actually went to you," he whispered.

She blushed, hoping the others hadn't heard. Dustin looked up at Delilah. "Honestly, it was nothing more than simple first aid, but thank you, Delilah. I'd love to have a 'Liv' this morning."

"Me, too," Olivia said. "And I'd also love your Sunday-morning hash and — oh, Dustin! If you haven't had them yet, you have to try the cheese grits. They're the best in the South, I swear."

"Well, then, two 'Livs,' two orders of corned beef hash and two orders of cheese grits," Dustin said.

"Don't forget the biscuits," Coot added.

When Delilah was gone, Dustin turned to Coot and asked softly, "You know something?"

"Can't rightly say I *know* anything," he said. "But I just figured, what with everything that's going on, any small thing might be important."

Dustin nodded. "Yes, you're right."

Coot glanced at Olivia. "A bunch of those boys from Parsonage House were in here last night, with one of their monitors. I was sitting at a booth reading the paper." He shook his head sadly. "Aaron is great with those boys but I guess everyone over at the Horse Farm is kind of on the 'watch and wait' list."

Olivia cringed and stared down at the table. "The monitor was reading a book, not paying much mind to the boys. They were talking about the camping trip."

"And they said something," Dustin said, gently urging Coot to go on.

"Yeah, they were trying to reconstruct things for themselves," Coot told them.

"What did they talk about?"

"Who was where when. Seems Joey saw you go flying out of the tent when everyone heard the scream. He scrambled out himself. He saw Olivia — and she grabbed Drew and they ran off."

"That's pretty much what happened," Olivia said.

"They went on to talk about it, and they said there was one person they didn't notice until Dustin asked about Aaron. She must've been gone for a while, 'cause she came back to the group late," Coot said.

"Sandra?" Olivia asked.

Coot looked at her. "Yeah. How did you know?"

"She was the only other 'she' there."

"They didn't see her crawl out of the tent?" Dustin asked.

"They might have — they're not sure. But they're certain they didn't see her the *whole* time. They all mulled it over for a while, but then, of course, they started saying they couldn't be positive, so they'd best not say anything."

"Thanks, Coot." They all fell silent as Delilah came over with their food.

"There you go," she said, setting down the plates, which were garnished with melon and apple slices. "Now you two eat up. I'm glad you ordered big. This isn't a morning to be snacking on nothing but tomato juice and a few wedges of fruit. The body needs nourishment."

"It looks wonderful, and we're going to enjoy every fattening bite of it," Olivia assured her.

"You burn energy like a bird in flight, Liv," Delilah said. "Speaking of juice — want some?"

"Sure, juice sounds great," Olivia replied. "That will make it a bit healthier, right?"

"That's exactly what I told Sandra Cheever last night. She said she'd been sitting at the hospital for hours and was going back — but that she had to have something besides hospital food."

Coot frowned. "Sandra was here last night? I didn't see her."

"Oh, she came in before you and the boys." Delilah made a dismissive gesture. "First she says she has to have some good food — then she turns her nose up at my menu, saying I didn't have *healthy* choices. Why, I told her to have some juice and a salad and she said I needed fat-free dressings!"

As she spoke, the door to the café opened again.

Frank Vine came in. He nodded to the tourists at the counter and walked back to join them in the booth.

"Strong coffee, Delilah, please," Frank said as he slid in next to Coot. "Morning, everyone."

They all greeted him, and Delilah asked, "That's it, Frank, just coffee?"

Frank nodded. When she'd left, Frank looked at all of them.

He inhaled loudly and rubbed a hand over his eyes. "Aaron Bentley is dead," he told them.

Accident. Like hell.

Dustin stood in Aaron Bentley's bathroom, studying the scene.

Aaron had insisted he get out of the hospital that morning, and he'd been deemed well enough to go home. No problem; a cop had stayed outside his house.

Then, according to the police officer who'd been watching the house, there was a loud hissing sound and the house seemed to glow and then went dark.

He'd rushed in. Aaron had been alone in the bathtub, dead. Somehow, he hadn't had the sense *not* to place his iPod charger on the back of the commode — next to the tub. It was ridiculous. He'd been saved from drowning only to die in his bathtub — electrocuted.

Dustin still couldn't believe the man had died so stupidly. Or that such a death could have been an accident. According to the crime scene tech who'd first escorted him through, Aaron Bentley must have reached for the iPod to change it — but knocked the whole system into the tub. It had been plugged in. Electricity had raced through the water like wildfire.

There was nothing in the bathroom to suggest that anyone else had been with him. Dustin's first question, of course, had to do with Sandra Cheever. She'd been so determined that she was going to stay with Aaron. Where the hell had she been?

According to Sandra — and there were witnesses to verify that it was true — she'd dropped Aaron at home and gone, at his suggestion, to check on things at the Horse Farm. She'd promised to be right back. But by the time she'd returned, the officer on

duty had already flown into the house —
breaking the lock to get in.

So, the house had been locked, an officer
had been on duty, Sandra had been at the
Horse Farm — and Aaron had managed to
kill himself in his bathtub.

He remained in the tub.

Frank Vine had come to the diner to make
the announcement regarding Aaron's death,
then bring Dustin back with him to Aaron's
house.

Dustin hadn't left Olivia behind. But he
hadn't brought her in here, either. She and
Callahan were outside, waiting. There was
no reason for her to see a man she worked
with and cared about as he was now, naked
and scorched, his eyes still open as if they
were about to pop out of his skull, an
expression of horror on his face. The smell
of singed flesh hung all around them like a
musky haze.

"What do you say to this?" Frank asked
him.

"I say he didn't reach for anything — that
someone was here and tossed that charger
into the water and electrocuted him."

"There's absolutely no indication that
anyone was in here with him," Frank said.

"So I hear."

"You don't believe it?"

"Bring Sandra in for questioning. And, of course, the medical examiner may find something we're not seeing. Then again, he may not. Why the hell did the idiot have to take a bath?" Dustin muttered. "He made it so damned easy for whoever was here."

"He just got out of the hospital. After a camping trip. He was probably trying to relax — hell, why not?" Frank said disgustedly. "There was a sheriff's car right in front of his house. He must have felt safe and secure."

Dustin turned around and stalked out of the bathroom. The sheriff's department, crime scene people and medical personnel were all still at work. He paused in various rooms of the house, looking around, trying to stay out of everyone's way. He noticed that the medical examiner was Dr. Wilson.

Wilson walked straight over to him. He seemed to be glancing around to see if Frank Vine was anywhere near them and satisfied himself that he wasn't.

"Horrible business, this," he said. He lowered his voice. "I have results for you. That dart you brought me. There was a concoction of drugs — some had seeped into the bark. It was a cocktail of stuff, the kind that wouldn't be found in an autopsy unless specific tests were ordered. The kind that would do a swift number — a real doozy on someone — and then fade quickly away." He stopped speaking. Dustin turned to see that Frank had come out of the bathroom.

"It's all right, Robbie," he told Dr. Wilson. "You're not conspiring against me. Agent Blake is working this case with my permission and he's called in a few coworkers, I believe?"

Wilson — apparently "Robbie" to Frank Vine — let out a sigh of relief. "Frank, I haven't seen anything like this in all my years out here. Best to accept any and all help, I'd say."

"You might want to remove your corpse," Frank suggested.

"I'm going to get the body now," Wilson said. "At least we know the time of death," Frank pointed out. "The deputy made a note of it. Not to mention that all the clocks stopped at 10:23 a.m."

"I'll get Aaron down to the morgue and get right on this." Wilson shook his head wearily. "Hell, twice. Men I liked, men I admired. This is a sad day for all of us."

As he returned to the bathroom. Dustin looked at Frank Vine. "I still say you bring Sandra in."

"There were witnesses who saw her when this happened," Frank argued. "She was nowhere near the house."

"She still might know something. See if Aaron was talking about having anyone over, or if he said anything to her about what he planned to do," Dustin said. "We've got to shake this up, Frank. There could be other victims."

"You coming down to the station?" Frank asked him.

Dustin nodded.

"What about Olivia?"

"I'm not letting her out of my sight," Dustin replied.

Vine didn't protest; he just nodded. "All right. I'll have her brought in."

"Have your men checked whether there's any sign of forced entry?" Dustin asked. "Windows?"

"None."

"Is there a back door?"

"Yes."

Dustin walked toward it. He used a paper towel he grabbed from the kitchen to check it. There was no bolt, only a push lock, the kind you could depress as you were leaving and the door would lock behind you.

"Someone could have left this way," Dustin told Frank, who'd come with him.

"Yeah, they could have left this way, but how would they have gotten in?"

"With a key."

"Not Sandra. An officer followed them from the hospital. She let him off, waved to the deputy watching the house and drove away before Aaron even went inside."

"That doesn't mean someone else wasn't already in the house," Dustin said.

Disposing of the paper towel, Dustin walked outside. Olivia was leaning against the car; Deputy Jimmy Callahan stood next to her, arms crossed over his chest, looking vigilant. When he saw Dustin, he nodded and walked into the house to talk to Frank.

Olivia gazed mutely at Dustin, her eyes beseeching him to tell her it wasn't true.

She knew it was.

She didn't cry. Her face, though, was pinched and tight. She was in shock, he thought. Two men she'd worked closely with, two men she saw almost every day, were dead. He wanted to tell her to cry, that it was all right.

But she spoke before he could.

"Have they informed the others yet?" she asked.

"I think someone from the sheriff's department was calling — trying to reach the Horse Farm to let Sydney and Drew know what happened. I'm sure they'll try to contact Mason and Mariah, too. They're going to pick up Sandra now." He indicated a news van down the street, held back by an officer in uniform. "The media have picked up on it. The police always try to make the first notification."

"Of course. It's dreadful to hear that something horrible has happened to someone you know via the TV or radio or — They're going to pick up Sandra? Why? Sandra wasn't even with Aaron when he . . . died. . . ."

"They have to rattle some cages. They'll start interviewing everyone now, wanting to know where they were every second."

She nodded. "I'd like to go to the Horse Farm. I just want . . . I want to tell Sydney and Drew that we'll do everything in our power. . . . That we'll hang in there." She looked at him. "Dustin, if someone wanted the Horse Farm — I'm the next person in line."

"Yes," he agreed.

"So people can't be dying for the Horse Farm — I mean, there is no Horse Farm if we don't have any clients. Any guests."

"I know." Dustin looked straight ahead as he drove, hardly able to bear her stoicism, her emotional restraint. He knew she had to be suffering and understood that she wasn't ready to express her grief.

When they reached the Horse Farm, Olivia sighed audibly.

Drew and Sydney had dragged a couple of feed crates out front. They sat on them — both cradling shotguns as they squinted down the road.

Olivia hopped out of the car and approached them. "What the *hell* are you two doing?" she demanded.

"You heard, right?" Sydney asked her thickly. "Aaron — he's dead."

"In the bathtub," Drew said. "Electrocuted. They're saying it was an accident."

"Accident?" Sydney snorted. "Accident, my ass. We should've been listening to you a lot earlier, Olivia."

"You saved the poor bastard's life," Drew said, shaking his head at Dustin. "And then he goes and takes a bath!"

"Who knew bathing could be lethal?" Sydney said dully.

Olivia set a hand on his shoulder. "We're all so sorry," she said. "I'm going to miss him so much."

"What's going to happen now?" Sydney asked.

"We'll — we'll just go on. Somehow, we'll go on. I'm going to get out a press release saying that we're closed — in mourning. We'll reopen in a few weeks," Olivia said.

"Horses have to eat," Drew mumbled. "I can manage, though. And if you need financial help . . ."

"Thank you." She gave him a shaky smile. "But I think our operating sheets are pretty good. We can maintain the place for a few months without digging into anyone's personal funds and if it comes to that — well, we'll figure it out." Olivia cleared her throat. "I don't think the two of you need to sit here with shotguns."

"Yeah. We just need to stay out of bathtubs," Drew said.

"And out of the woods," Sydney added.

"Duck flying needles," Drew muttered.

"And darts," Sydney agreed.

"I have people coming in this afternoon," Dustin told him. "We'll get someone to stay here at the Horse Farm. I don't think either of you is a target, though."

"Maybe someone wanted to kill Marcus to get this place, except that doesn't make sense because of all the trusts and the nonprofit and . . ." Sydney's voice trailed off. He shook his head and began again. "If there *had* been someone who wanted Marcus dead, logically it would've been Aaron. But now Aaron's dead, and next in line is

Olivia . . . and . . ."

"Is Liv a target now?" Drew asked bluntly.

"Maybe. But you don't need to worry unduly. Some people will believe that what happened to Aaron was an accident. He was alone in his house — there was a deputy stationed outside it," Dustin explained.

"We had to go through this twice — thinking he died," Drew said. "That isn't fair." He glanced at Dustin with a look of resignation on his face. "He's really dead this time, huh?"

Dustin thought about Aaron's corpse in the bathtub. "He's really dead," he said. "I'm sorry. And I'm sure you're safe enough. You can go into your apartments. Just be aware of whoever's around. You have plenty of dogs here to bark if any cars drive in."

"Yeah," Sydney told Drew. "We've got all the dogs."

"We'll still keep the rifles handy," Drew insisted.

"Just don't shoot each other, okay?" Olivia said, trying to smile.

"We'll solve this thing. Really," Dustin promised.

Sydney looked at him skeptically. "How do you solve accidents, Dustin? How do you solve accidents that happen when no one else is around?"

"Someone else *was* around. And we'll figure out who. Liv, come on. We've got to get to the station."

"You two take care," Olivia told them.

Andrew nodded. "Yep. We'll take care. And you take care of Olivia, Dustin. Agent Blake. Don't you let anything happen to her!" he said fiercely.

"I'm going to be fine," Olivia vowed. She let Dustin lead her to the car. He could tell that she was trembling.

"You *are* going to be fine," he murmured.

He drove to the station. She sat beside him, pale and silent.

"Olivia?" he said quietly.

She turned to him. "I can't grasp it! I can't seem to grasp it. Aaron is really dead. I feel . . . numb. I should hurt more. A friend and a colleague is dead. I cared about Aaron. I just feel . . . numb."

"You'll cry in time," he said. "Being numb right now is probably good. It's a kind of emotional protection. We still have a ways to go until we get to the end of this case so being numb will help you get through it."

"If I do feel anything . . . I'm angry."

"Anger isn't a bad thing, either."

She was silent again until they arrived at the station. A deputy led them down a hall and into an observation area. It abutted an interrogation room with a one-way mirror. While Sandra could only see her own reflection, they could watch her sitting at a table. She looked lost and alone and she'd obviously been crying. For a moment, Dustin wondered if she *could* be involved in any way. She appeared to be stricken — with grief? Or remorse? She hadn't been the one to kill Aaron, but did she know who had? Was Sandra's *not* being at the house on purpose?

Frank Vine opened the door and came in to join them. "Hell, Dustin, do you really think this woman could've had anything to do with Aaron's death? She really looks like she's been through the wringer."

"Just go in and talk to her, Frank. Ask her if she can imagine why anyone would want to hurt Aaron," Dustin said.

"All right." He sighed heavily. "You do realize that to anyone else in law enforcement, I'd look like an idiot. An old addict's dead and a man — who was apparently alone in his house with a cop watching — electrocuted himself in a bathtub."

"But you know that someone's been running around with drugged darts. That's a fact," Dustin reminded him. "Frank, come on. First, Aaron pitches forward into a stream and nearly dies in two feet of water.

Then he's electrocuted in a bathtub?"

"The man should have stayed dirty," Frank muttered as he left them in the observation room and went in to sit across from Sandra.

Jimmy Callahan slipped into the room with Dustin and Olivia. He nodded to both of them. "Think this'll help?" he asked.

"We've got to try everything," Dustin told him.

Then he grew silent and they all watched Sandra as the interrogation began.

Sandra almost pounced on Frank. "Frank, what am I doing in here? This is one of the worst days of my life! It *is* the worst day of my life. The man I loved is dead, my work is in the toilet — no, it's already flushed away. Oh, that doesn't matter. Aaron is dead! And you have me here, treating me like . . . like some kind of suspect. I need to lie down. I need to be sedated. I want to sleep. I want to forget everything that's happened. I want to dream that it hasn't happened."

"Sandra, we believe you may be able to help us," Frank said.

"How?" Sandra dragged her fingers through her hair. "Frank, I wasn't there. I should've been there. But it might not have made any difference," she added in a low voice, "because I might not have been in the bathroom with him when he did whatever he did. And then you would *really* have suspected me. I loved Aaron. Oh, the others cared about him, too. We're a family. We all care about one another. But I *loved* him. We were going to officially announce that we were seeing each other. We were going to get married, Frank. I was going to be his wife!"

Sandra broke down in tears, sobbing hysterically. Frank pushed a box of tissues across the table to her.

"I'm sorry, Sandra. I'm very sorry for your loss. But if you loved him, you'll want to help us."

Sandra nodded, took a tissue and mopped her face. "How can I help in any way? I don't know what happened!"

"Why was Aaron so determined to leave the hospital so quickly?"

Sandra waved a hand in the air. "Because he was being *Aaron*! He'd recovered from his near-drowning, and there was no reason for him to be in the hospital. He didn't even have a headache, he told me. He was fine and he wanted to go home."

"Sandra, did you let anyone know when Aaron was going home?" Frank asked.

"Yes. No. Well, kind of," Sandra said.

"Who?"

"I called the Horse Farm to tell everyone that he was doing well and getting ready to check out."

"Who did you talk to?"

"I left a message," Sandra replied. "No one answered, but I know our group. They wouldn't have been able to stay away from the farm. Our therapists would've gone out to check on Sydney and Drew . . . who might well have gone into the office."

"Okay, Sandra. The morning you were all camping, where were you when Mariah screamed?"

"When Mariah screamed . . ." Sandra repeated dully.

Frank leaned forward. "Sandra, listen. First Aaron falls into the stream and nearly dies. Then he does die at home in the bathtub? Supposedly alone."

"Stop it! Stop it, Frank! I didn't kill him. I. Wasn't. There!" she said, enunciating clearly.

"You didn't answer my question. Where were you when Mariah screamed?"

"In my tent!"

"And right after?"

"Outside the tent — running around like an idiot. Watching the boys. Olivia grabbed Drew and went racing toward the sound."

"You loved Aaron, but you didn't notice he wasn't at the campsite with you?"

"Frank. We were asleep. Suddenly, there's this high-pitched scream. We jumped up. Aaron could have been peeing, for God's sake!"

"All right, Sandra," he said quietly. "I'm going to have a deputy take you home. I just have one more question. If you called the Horse Farm and left a message, why did you drop Aaron off and then go there?"

She sighed. "Aaron wanted me to. He asked if I'd reached anyone. I told him no, that I'd gotten voice mail. He asked if I'd go check in on Drew and Sydney, tell them he was feeling just fine and that he planned to be in the next morning. I was supposed to say we'd have a powwow so we could work on saving the Horse Farm. Not much hope of that now, huh?" she asked, and started to weep again.

When Frank rose, he placed a comforting hand on her shoulder. "Someone's going to take you home right now. Or would you prefer to go to the hospital? They can fix you up with something that'll help you sleep."

Sandra sniffled. "Home," she said. She looked tearfully at Frank. "Yeah, I know. I run the Horse Farm. Where we work with substance abusers. But I have a stash of sedatives at home for when I need them. I . . . occasionally have problems sleeping. Don't worry. I never abuse them. I know better than that."

Frank nodded. "Fine. Shall we go?"

As Frank rose to open the door for Sandra, Dustin felt his phone vibrate. He reached for it.

Both Olivia and Jimmy Callahan watched him.

"Sorry," he murmured. He glanced down at his phone and immediately saw a text message from Malachi.

"It's your cousin," he told Olivia. "I'm going to have him and the others meet us at your house."

She nodded in agreement.

Callahan stepped aside as Frank came in. "Okay, I questioned her like you wanted, but I'm not sure where that got us. Unless it's a massive conspiracy and both Sydney and Drew are in on it, Sandra *can't* have had anything to do with this. What she says is true. She dropped Aaron off and drove to the Horse Farm. He died before she ever got back to the house." He exhaled with frustration. "So. I questioned a grieving woman in tears. To what end?"

"I'm not sure yet, Frank. It might have

proven that she had an accomplice," Dustin said. "Someone could have been in that house — waiting for Aaron. Someone who knew when to be there, because Sandra had told that person when he was leaving the hospital and heading home. And she did make sure that both Drew and Sydney saw her."

"You're going to have to come up with a hell of a lot more than that."

"I know," Dustin assured him. "Can you make sure Dr. Wilson calls me when he's doing the autopsy?"

"He'll be on it this afternoon. I talked to him about thirty minutes ago."

"Thanks. I'll go over to the morgue in about an hour."

"You should catch him right in the middle of it," Frank said. "He only had one other body — an old-timer who keeled over eating his oatmeal. He'll be getting on to this one pretty fast."

Frank turned to Olivia. "Did you see Sandra when you got up yesterday morning at the campsite?"

"I practically collided with her when I burst out of the tent at the sound of the scream," Olivia said.

"Did you see her?" Frank asked Dustin.

"No. We'd been up during the night,"

Dustin said. "I woke up and found Aaron on his way to the women's tent. He was worried because he didn't see Mariah — who'd gone to the stream for water. When Mariah came back, half the campers were awake and Sandra was annoyed. She just wanted to get back to sleep. I stayed out by the campfire for a while, waiting to see if anyone got up again. I went back into my tent, and I heard Aaron stirring, but then Mariah screamed and I went chasing after her."

"Sandra was outside when I came out of the tent," Olivia said. "But Dustin *didn't* see her when he ran ahead, a few minutes before I stepped out."

"But she could have come out of the tent just before you did?" Frank asked.

"It's possible, yes," Olivia agreed.

"Sorry to interrupt, but we've got to get moving," Dustin said. "I do want to be there for that autopsy, and we've got friends coming to Olivia's."

"You're going to make sure I get to know your *friends,* right?" Frank's question wasn't really a question.

"You bet," Dustin promised.

Frank nodded. "Stay in close contact."

"We will."

Jimmy Callahan opened the door for

them, tipping his hat. "Liv, take care of yourself," he said quietly.

As they left the station and drove to Olivia's house, Dustin noted that she still looked shell-shocked. He wished he could do something to ease the pain and confusion she must be feeling — and he knew it was only going to get worse once she got over the sense of numbness. It protected her, to some extent, from the full reality of her losses. Still, her whole world had to be reeling.

When they pulled into the yard, she let out a yelp of joy, leaping out of the car before he'd turned off the motor.

Malachi Gordon stood on the porch. He was with the very tall cowboy agent Dustin had met at the office, Sloan Trent, and two women. He quickly realized that the women were Jane Everett and Abby Anderson. He hadn't had a chance to meet all his fellow Krewe unit members before he'd gone to Tennessee, but he'd studied some of the information on them. Jane Everett was an artist who had frequently worked with the Texas police before joining the Texas Krewe. Sloan Trent had joined after working with Jane on a situation in Lily, Arizona. Abby Anderson and Malachi were a couple; they'd met when Jackson Crow brought

Malachi in on serial killings that had occurred in Savannah.

Olivia wasn't bothering with formality at the moment. She ran over and was lifted into her cousin's arms to be greeted, hugged and swung around. Introductions were made, Olivia telling the others that she'd heard good things about them. She dug in her pocket for her keys, but even as she twisted the lock, they heard something behind the door, which appeared to move as if someone was trying to open it from within.

Inside the house, Sammy began to bark excitedly.

"I've got it," Dustin murmured, pushing her aside. The Krewe members instantly went into alert mode, drawing their weapons. Malachi pulled Olivia against the wall as Dustin drew his own weapon and threw open the door.

Sammy nearly knocked him over, jumping up with jubilation. Dustin holstered his weapon and stepped inside, greeting the dog and firmly ordering him down. But as he stepped into the entry, he heard excited words.

"I did it! I touched the door. I touched the door and it almost moved. I *am* getting some kind of . . . some kind of spiritual or ectoplasmic strength!"

Marcus Danby had finally decided to make himself known once again.

15

Olivia understood why Malachi had changed his life — why he'd stopped working for himself to become part of the Krewe.

She'd known plenty of people who would get excited and swear they'd seen General Rufus Cunningham seated atop his warhorse up on a hill.

She'd never believed that there were so many people who actually spoke with the dead and that she could sit in her own parlor serving tea to the living while the ghost of Marcus Danby was among them, repeating everything he'd told Olivia and then Dustin. It had been hard, he'd explained to her, to *be* somewhere. Long conversations wore him out. When he got too tired, he assumed he was in some kind of "ghost sleep" because he knew he faded, and he wasn't sure where he was. It seemed that he needed to rest in order to gain the strength to manifest himself again. He was thrilled that he'd managed to make it look as if there was someone on the other side of the door; he was heartbroken and disturbed to discover that Aaron Bentley had now joined his ranks. He went from deep sorrow to brightness in a whirl of emotions, astounded that he was facing six people who could see and hear him.

Dustin told the other Krewe members and Marcus everything that happened during the camping trip and what had occurred so far that day. Malachi listened gravely, then asked, "The deputy sheriff in charge, Frank Vine, he's really come around? He's ready to have us here?"

Dustin nodded. "He wants to meet you all and he's asked that we keep him in the loop. And the medical examiner is a great guy. He had the fragments of the dart I found analyzed, so they're all aware that these deaths aren't accidents at all. It's been impossible, of course, to have someone on guard everywhere. The deputy should've gone in with Aaron this morning. But despite the information about the dart and the fact that Aaron nearly died, I don't believe anyone thought the killer could possibly be in his house, ready to finish him off."

Malachi looked at Olivia. "So, you're in

charge of the Horse Farm now. It's fallen to you."

Abby Anderson said, "It seems that you might be the next target, then. What happens if you're . . . unable to run the Horse Farm?"

"The will is complicated," Olivia said, glancing at Marcus. "Marcus had it go to Aaron and then me. If the Horse Farm fails — even as nonprofit — the land is to be sold off and we're to see to it that every animal ends up in a good home. And then, we move on."

"There's no one after you to 'inherit' the leadership position?"

"Hey!" Marcus interrupted. "I never thought there was anyone who wanted to kill me, much less Aaron! I figured by the time Aaron and Liv were ready to retire, they'd know who should take over next."

"We can't be prepared for insanity or evil in those around us," Sloan Trent said. "You probably did an excellent job thinking it all out, Marcus. No one could have expected this."

Marcus seemed to sigh. "I didn't. I certainly didn't."

"But you haven't learned any more about what happened since we saw you?" Olivia asked.

"I'm dead, not omniscient," Marcus snapped. "I . . . just lost all energy. Like I already told you, it's not easy being dead."

"Maybe that's why the general doesn't talk to anyone," Olivia mused. The others, except for Dustin, gave her questioning looks. "As far as I know, he just watches," she explained. "He's always watching. I think he tries to warn people, tries to stop bad things from happening. Many people have seen him — or claim to have seen him — through the years. But no one's ever mentioned having a conversation with him."

Sloan cleared his throat and sat forward. "You have to remember that ghosts are the spirits of those who were alive. Some were shy, some were gregarious. Some were graceful or athletic — and some were clumsy as hell."

"The speaking thing wasn't difficult for me, at least when I was talking to Olivia," Marcus said. "Others . . . I don't know. I was aware of Olivia when she found me and passed out. Then everyone else came over and I tried . . . I tried to tell Vine and Callahan and the medical examiner what happened. I tried to talk to Aaron and Sydney and Drew. But no one heard me."

There was silence for a minute.

"Well," Dustin said, "we know for a fact

that someone was using drug-poisoned darts. So we can go into the backgrounds again and see if we can find anything that suggests someone might know about darts. We also need to find out who'd know enough about drugs to mix the right cocktail, in the right quantities. And who would have access to that kind of pharmaceutical. Then, there's the rendering of the general."

"Artwork," Jane Everett said. She smiled at Olivia. "My specialty. I'll find out. Where's the cheesecloth art, or whatever it is, now?"

"Frank Vine has it at the station," Dustin told her. "You could head over there. Oh, I promised Sydney and Drew that we'd have someone at the Horse Farm. Any volunteers? I want to get to the autopsy and I don't think Olivia should be alone."

"I can watch over the Horse Farm while Jane goes to the police station," Sloan said.

"Later, I'd like to ride back to the stream. I keep figuring there's something we missed somehow. A sign . . ."

Olivia assumed he meant an otherworldly sign, a message from the general, perhaps? Not the kind of hard evidence the sheriff would be looking for.

"The campsite by the stream," Malachi murmured. "I didn't grow up here, but my family often came out, so I've been to the stream. And the little cemetery in the woods."

Dustin nodded. "Then let's plan a ride for later. But . . ." He hesitated and looked at Sloan. "I don't want Sydney and Andrew left alone there," he said.

Trent nodded. "Don't worry. I won't take my eyes off them. Among all of us, we'll keep up a twenty-four-hour watch."

"What about the others — the therapists?" Abby asked.

Olivia already knew, of course, that Abby and Malachi were a couple as well as team members. Malachi had been eager for her to meet Abby before any of this had come up. She'd been just as eager. Malachi had been married to a wonderful woman who'd died. He hadn't been the same after that. Not until Abby. . . . She made him want to live again.

Olivia automatically liked her for that reason.

They seemed to fit; Abby Anderson was striking, with tremendous blue eyes and pitch-black hair. She managed to look like an agent, smart and savvy and agile. But Malachi had told Olivia that Abby's heritage included a many-times-great-uncle who'd been a famous — or infamous — pirate known as Blue. Whether that was because of the darkness of his hair or the blueness of his eyes, no one knew. The distinctive coloring had been passed down through the family.

"Mason is supposedly off seeing the Hermitage. He's never been there for some reason," Olivia said. "I'm not sure what Mariah's doing. She said she'd go by the Horse Farm today. And we heard Sandra say that she was going home to sedate herself."

"Sedate herself," Dustin repeated. "That did make me wonder . . ."

"I'm sure she's talking about Valium or something like that," Olivia said quickly.

"Who at the Horse Farm knows about drugs and sedatives?" Dustin asked. "All of you?"

"We all know the rudiments," Olivia told him. "We've had to tranquilize rescue horses now and then — and once a pit-bull mix that wanted to chow down on Drew when he was trying to help him. We all know what we're doing. Everyone there knows where we keep the tranquilizer gun and how to use it."

Dustin stared at her, frowning. "How can you know how much it's loaded with at any given time? Some of your horses are close to a thousand pounds, but a pit bull mix, you're looking at forty or fifty."

"It's always loaded for a seven-hundred-pound horse," she said. "But, in the tack room, we have different size . . . tranquilizer darts."

Dustin stood. "I'm on my way to the autopsy. "I can drop Sloan at the Horse Farm first and give him the keys to the rental, and then drop Jane at the station." He turned to the now-fading ghost of Marcus Danby. "Did you know about the affair, Marcus? Sandra and Aaron?"

"Sure," Marcus said. "But I didn't care. I don't know why they thought they had to be secretive about it."

"And Sandra really did love Aaron?" Dustin asked.

"As best I could tell," Marcus replied, his voice faint. "I never asked either one of them but I could tell from the way they talked to each other, looked at each other . . . but I figured it was their business. They'd say something when they felt like it. What does that have to do with anything?"

"I'm trying to figure out if she'd conspire with anyone to kill him," Dustin said. "Or you. . . ."

"We'll try to sort out motives later," Malachi said briskly. "Let's meet up at the

Horse Farm in a few hours."

"It'll be close to dusk," Abby pointed out.

"That's all right. It *will* be dusk," Malachi said. He smiled at Olivia and she returned his smile, so glad he was there. "The general always had a tendency to prefer dusk."

Despite the fact that he was at a morgue looking at the electrocuted body of a man he'd known and *tried* to save, Dustin felt confident that they were finally starting to get somewhere.

Sloan Trent had been an immediate hit with Sydney and Drew — because he knew horses. He talked about his own, and how the move from Arizona to northern Virginia had been interesting for him *and* his horses, and they were soon discussing feed, hay, saddles and tack. Sydney and Drew both seemed to forget, for a few minutes at least, that they'd lost two bosses in less than three weeks.

Jane Everett also did well at the station; she charmed Frank Vine, Jimmy Callahan and the other deputies milling around her. She described how researching the general's picture — determining who'd created it and how it had ended up in the woods — might help them uncover just what was going on.

At the morgue, Dr. Wilson had already

cut into Aaron Bentley. His assistants were sewing up the body when Dustin arrived, but Dr. Wilson showed him just what electrocution did to the body.

Blood samples had been sent to the lab and Wilson suspected they'd find trace elements of whatever medication Aaron had been given in the hospital — but nothing else. Too much time had passed. However, it appeared that he'd died because of his own carelessness in knocking the iPod charger into his bathwater.

"It's like a closed-door mystery," Wilson said, frustrated. "No way in, no way out." He shrugged, asking, "Do you think Aaron might've just been tired and sloppy? After all, there was no one else in the house."

"There was no one else that we *know* of," Dustin reminded him.

"I wish I could help you more — that the body was telling me more," Wilson said. "But in this case . . . it really does appear to be accidental."

He shook his head. "If only a corpse could talk . . ."

Dustin stared at the corpse, wondering if this one could. At the moment, he saw nothing, felt nothing, to suggest that Aaron Bentley could suddenly speak to him, tell him what happened.

"Naturally, when I get the lab results, I'll let you know immediately," Wilson said.

Dustin thanked him and drove to the police station to collect Jane. By the time he arrived, she was ready to leave, having taken dozens of photographs and done considerable research on the internet. She summarized what she'd discovered thus far.

"The cheesecloth is cheap and available in almost every art store in the United States. The rendering of the general was done in chalk and watercolor — and wouldn't withstand a rainstorm. The artist was fairly decent, so I'd say you're looking at the work of an art student, either someone who went to a good school or is still taking classes. That's what I have so far."

"So," Jimmy Callahan said, "we're looking for someone with access to the workers at the Horse Farm, someone who knows their hours and their habits. This someone also knows the campsite and the surrounding area. And he or she knows about tranquilizer drug concoctions that don't show up in blood tests at a customary autopsy. *And* this person happens to be a fairly decent artist."

"Except maybe our killer doesn't need to be an artist at all, decent or not."

"Yes," Jane agreed. "This person — the killer — could have bought the image."

Dustin nodded. "The murderer knew that Mariah would go snooping if she thought she was about to see the general. Although I don't think she ever got to see this picture of the general floating in the forest mist. She happened on the pieces of coyote-torn cow first."

Frank sat on the edge of his table and shook his head. "How did this person lure Mariah out — and hit Aaron Bentley with a dart at the same time?"

"It could've been done," Dustin said. "The plans would have had to be laid the night before. And then the killer had to count on luck, as well. But most people know that Mariah is the local historian and ghost-queen. An eerie sound would definitely have caught her attention. Not a rebel yell or anything like that — too loud. A whisper? A distant bugle? Whoever this was came prepared."

Frank shook his head again. "You still think Sandra?"

"At the very least, I think she knows something."

"What's your plan?" Frank asked.

"I'll take a group riding — retrace our steps again, see what we can discover," Dustin told him. "I particularly want to check out the stream."

"My partner and I will be at the Horse Farm," Jane told him quickly.

Frank looked at Jimmy. "Go pay Sandra Cheever a visit. Tell her you'll be watching over her so that she can get some rest. See if you can stay inside at her place, rather than out in the car."

"Yep, you got it." Tipping his hat to Jane, Jimmy left the room.

"Is this crazy, or what? Is everyone at that place supposed to die in some kind of presumed accident?" Frank asked.

"Could be. What's still eluding us is the reason," Dustin muttered.

"You'll be watching over Olivia, right?"

"A killer would have to get to her over my dead body," Dustin assured him. "And you know that Malachi Gordon — Olivia's cousin — is here, too."

Frank nodded. He walked around to his desk and rummaged in his bottom drawer, then handed Dustin an outdated walkie-talkie. "You can reach the station with this. Keep me apprised of your movements."

Dustin agreed to do that. As they drove back to the Horse Farm, he asked Jane, "There was nothing else you could get from that image of the general?"

She shrugged. "I've just spent a couple of hours with Frank Vine. We're working with the facts, sir, just the facts. Like I said, the artist was decent. The rendering seems relatively accurate, judging by some of the Civil War photographs I looked at online. And some of the shading was really nice. This artist probably does have a career in his or her future."

"So, you'd say a young artist?"

"I think so. Although art is — no pun intended — a sketchy field. It might be an older artist who's a better technician than he or she is at finding a personal style. That's my opinion. I work with reconstruction a lot. Or doing sketches from someone's description. This seems to be along those lines. There must be a portrait of the general like that somewhere. I didn't come across it in my online research but I'll keep looking. The artist almost certainly copied the painting — or maybe even a photograph. I asked Frank, but they weren't able to lift any fingerprints, nor did they find hairs or fibers or anything that might help."

"So, we have to locate the artist."

"We have to locate the artist," Jane agreed.

It wasn't that she'd been away for any length of time, but Olivia was glad to be at the Horse Farm. Everything was in good shape, just as it always was. Stalls were clean; horses were well fed and watered. Drew told her that Sydney had even gone on a cleaning binge in the office.

The two of them knew Malachi from other visits he'd made over the past several years, and they seemed to like Abby Anderson when they met her, as well. While they waited for Jane and Dustin to return, Drew and Sydney took them by the stalls, introducing them to each of the horses, the cats prowling around and the Horse Farm dogs. By the time Jane and Dustin returned, they were ready for their ride. Olivia, of course, would be on Shiloh. Dustin would take Chapparal. Malachi would ride Zeus, the big paint — a horse he'd ridden before — and Abby, who hadn't been on a horse all that often, would be on the palomino mare, Carina. Carina could move when needed; she was also extremely gentle.

But while Olivia rummaged around in the cupboards below the coffee machine in the office, gathering supplies, Jane told them about the rendering of the general she'd studied.

Olivia paused. "You think it was a copy of another work?" she asked.

"Yes. The general appeared to be posed — as if for a picture," Jane said.

"I think I might know the painting, then.

Of course, I haven't seen this particular rendering. But there's a Civil War picture of the general in the county archives. It was actually taken by Matthew Brady — according to local lore. And it's possible, since the general had been assigned to different fields of battle during the war, although legend has it that Brady did take the picture of him somewhere in Tennessee. Both he and the general were at Chattanooga. I'm sure there are copies of the picture here and there. I only know of one, but it's in a coffee shop near Vanderbilt University."

"So it's likely any art student might see it?" Jane asked. "And copy it . . ."

"Imitation being the sincerest form of flattery and all that. Plus, kids come out here to camp. A lot of this land is public access and public park. It's possible that some students recently decided to scare their friends — and left their artwork behind."

Dustin had entered the office. "And it's possible someone bought, borrowed or stole it. As you mentioned yourself back at the office," he said to Jane. "While you and Sloan are keeping watch here, can you get on the computer and look up the different universities in the area and the art departments? It's a long shot, but you might find something."

"Will do," Jane promised.

"We ready?" he asked Olivia. "We've got a tent packed, matches, lanterns, all the fixings. Did you find any food?"

"We'll be having hot dogs, canned grits and soup," she told him. "Oh, and some muffins for breakfast. They don't taste too bad when heated over a fire. And we have lots of coffee and water."

He grinned. "Then we're good to go."

"I just wanted to check in with Mariah and Mason before we leave. Is that an okay thing to do?"

"It's a very good thing to do," he said.

When she reached Mason, she wondered if it had been a mistake. He went on a rampage for what seemed like several minutes, horrified about Aaron, worried about their lives — and then worried about her. She managed to calm him down and ask him, "Mason, where are you now?"

"Still at the Hermitage," he told her.

"Oh?"

"Well, I'd planned to come, and when I heard about Aaron, I almost changed my mind, but I couldn't stay home. So I'm here. And I'm glad I came. Andrew Jackson was really an interesting guy. Yeah, he was a bastard as far as the Native Americans went, but he could be kind, too. And he loved Rachel — and Rachel was so reviled! But he didn't give a damn. He loved her. She didn't live long enough to go to the White House with him, but —"

"He was definitely an interesting man, Mason," Olivia broke in. "And I'm glad you're out and enjoying the day." Dustin made a motion indicating that he wanted her phone for a minute. She handed it to him.

"Mason, you should keep on doing what you're doing," he said. "Seeing Nashville. Can you stay in the city tonight?"

Olivia couldn't hear Mason's response, but he must have agreed because Dustin continued with, "Good. Just to be on the safe side. Do something else that includes a lot of people tomorrow. Visit the Country Music Hall of Fame, for instance." He said goodbye and gave the phone back to Olivia. "Mariah?"

She punched in Mariah's number. Mariah answered almost immediately. She was upset, as well; she was whispering, but she sounded calmer than Mason. "I'm fine. One of the deputies came in with me to see Sandra. She's sleeping now, so I'll hang here for a while. Maybe I'll just stay, since he's still here."

Olivia lowered her cell and told Dustin what Mariah had said.

He took the phone from her again. "Keep in touch, Mariah. And when you leave, see if they can send another deputy with you. Just call Frank Vine. He'll make sure it happens. Callahan's with you now, right?"

Mariah had obviously said yes, because Dustin nodded and handed the phone back to Olivia.

"Take care," she started to say. But Mariah had already rung off.

"We should get moving," Malachi said. "We'll keep Sammy at the Horse Farm."

It was nearing dusk; one of those beautiful evenings when the moon, although not quite full, rained down a glorious opaque and ivory light.

Dustin and Olivia led the way as the group set out on horseback. When she neared the ravine where Marcus had died, Olivia glanced over at Dustin and asked, "Do we stop?"

"Probably a good idea," he said. "Let Malachi and Abby take a look around — see who or what appears. If anyone does, of course."

Olivia dismounted and walked the few feet back to Malachi and Abby.

She didn't have to say anything. "This is

where Marcus died?" he asked.

She nodded.

Dustin, down from Chapparal, joined Malachi at the ravine's edge.

"It's obvious, even at night — and Marcus died during the day — that this ravine is here, that there's a drop. And," Malachi said, hunkering down at the edge, "if you did fall in, you'd roll and brace yourself and —"

"But Marcus had been knocked out and then shot up with heroin," Olivia reminded her cousin. "He wouldn't have been able to stop his fall."

Malachi nodded. "Someone *could* have died under those circumstances, even if he was trying to save himself, but . . ."

"The general came. He looked down at me when Marcus was in my arms and tapped me on the shoulder at the same time, and . . . and I passed out," Olivia said, embarrassed.

Dustin was glad that Abby laughed. "Trust me!" she said. "That kind of surprise would get to the most hardened of us."

"She's right," he concurred. "We learn that we see and hear what others don't. Doesn't mean we can't be startled as hell. That really never changes. Ghosts. Sometimes they show up when you least expect them — and hide when you're trying to reach them!"

"It's just the right time," Abby said quietly. And it was. The moon was rising; the sun had almost fallen below the horizon. The hills, the plains, the landscape — all had that magical quality of twilight.

They were still for a minute, until Dustin cleared his throat, and the sound roused them from their trance.

"Maybe the general's at the cemetery," Malachi suggested.

Olivia nodded. "Let's forge ahead."

They rode on and eventually came to the clearing that led to the small cemetery.

"This is one of Mariah's favorite places," Olivia told them. "The stories, of course, that go with the cemetery are tragic."

"Ghost stories often are," Malachi said

Dustin dismounted, lifting his lantern high. "Liv, do we leave the horses and walk along the trail?" he asked.

"No. There are coyotes in the area. We don't want spooked horses. If we had to walk back, it would be a *very* long walk."

"All right, this is your terrain, Liv. I'll stay with the horses," Dustin offered.

"No, I've been to the cemetery plenty of times," Malachi said. "Olivia's house belonged to our uncle when we were growing

up," he reminded Dustin. "I came out here
—" he paused, grinning "— to the frontier
often enough. You show Abby."

Dustin didn't argue. Olivia raised her own
lantern high and led the way along the trail.

They came to the graves, and the old
lichen-covered stones were haunting and
sad in the moonlight.

"I'm surprised the general has been allowed to rest here — that someone hasn't
decided to dig him up for a memorial,"
Abby said. She knelt down by the grave,
dusting it off. "It's nice here, though.
Lonely."

"Seems to be a Tennessee thing, respect-
ing his right to this place," Olivia said, getting down on her knees beside Abby.
"There's never even been any vandalism out
here, nor do we ever find beer cans or any
hint of frat kids fooling around. Not here,
not in the cemetery." She glanced up at
them. "There's an urban legend about the
place — that in the 1960s or '70s, some kids
came out here, but there was a coyote
prowling the area and they got scared and
started to run. One of the boys got tangled
in some vines. He was in a panic and he
swore afterward that the general came and
helped him. People believe that this cemetery is haunted — by more than coyotes. I

guess it's been tacitly accepted through the generations. The cemetery is maintained by local restoration groups, and no one interferes with it."

"It's a little forlorn," Abby said. "And definitely out of the way."

Olivia shrugged. "Maybe that's why the general keeps riding."

But the general wasn't riding.

He was leaning against a tree, arms crossed over his chest, watching them. Dustin watched him for several minutes without moving or speaking. He didn't warn the women. At last he spoke, very quietly. "General Cunningham, we could really use your help."

Neither Abby nor Olivia started. They looked over at him, where he stood by the trees. Olivia rose, wiping her hands on her jeans. "Sir," she said. "I know you tried to save Marcus. We desperately need your help now."

Abby rose slowly to her feet beside Olivia. The general stared back at all of them. He lifted his hand in a dignified greeting.

But then he disappeared.

Abby sighed. "I hope it wasn't me," she whispered.

"He just — he just isn't a talker," Olivia told her.

"Maybe he will be when he has something to say," Abby suggested.

"Let's get going. We have to pitch a tent for the night and then I want to go over everything that happened when Aaron fell into the stream," Dustin said. "Every single thing we can recall. . . ."

They returned to the horses, and Malachi instinctively seemed to know something had happened.

"We saw the general," Dustin explained.

"And?" Malachi asked.

Abby shook her head.

"Well, we know he's been here — watching," Malachi said.

They rode on. When they broke into the clearing by the rocky hills, the sheer beauty of the area made them pause in unison. "We should get the tent pitched," Malachi said once they'd reached the campsite. "Hey, Liv, this has been fixed up nicely over the years. The rocks around the fire pit — great! You can keep embers going at night without worrying that you'll start a forest fire."

"If it's windy, of course, we still douse it completely," Olivia said, dismounting. She untied the saddle pack she had on Shiloh. "Who has the tent supports?"

"I've got 'em," Malachi called out.

They went to work erecting the tent. Soon

it was done; Dustin was glad they'd chosen to bring one — it was getting too cold for sleeping bags alone. They'd take turns being on guard duty during the night.

They gathered firewood and got a blaze going. By then they were all famished and eating became the next order of business. Even the canned food tasted delicious at that point.

While they ate, Dustin and Olivia relayed everything that had occurred when Aaron had nearly drowned. Malachi and Abby nodded, asked questions and, after they'd finished eating, were shown the routes taken by the different players during the event.

"Tomorrow we should act it out. Count the seconds each movement takes, and so on." Abby yawned. "I wouldn't mind if I got to sleep first," she said.

"Everyone go ahead. I'll take this shift," Dustin told them.

Olivia rose with Abby, obviously feeling a little awkward. She turned to face Dustin; he gazed back at her, meeting her eyes.

It's up to you, he tried to tell her silently. *I'm not afraid of Malachi. He's sleeping with his partner — well, beside her, anyway. In separate sleeping bags. . . . So I think it's okay if we do the same thing!*

She didn't say anything, but joined Abby

and they entered the tent.

Malachi studied him across the fire. "Don't underestimate my cousin's strength," he finally said. "She may not carry a weapon, but she's a powerful personality."

"I never doubted that for a minute."

"And she's beautiful. She might be my cousin, but she's still one of the most beautiful people I've ever seen."

"I agree. I . . . Well. Hell. I care about her. A lot."

Malachi said nothing further, but he grinned. Maybe that was what he'd wanted to hear. "Okay. I'm going to get some sleep."

He got up and went into the tent. Dustin shifted, wrapping his arms around his chest. It was chilly. He didn't want a blanket, though; he wanted to stay awake.

The flames grew small. The embers barely burned anymore. There was still light above him from the moon, and in the distance, a coyote howled. A branch snapped on the fire.

He stared out into the dark woods, but saw nothing.

He could hear the trickle of the nearby stream.

And then, walking toward him out of the trees, came the general.

General Rufus Cunningham.

He stopped across the fire from Dustin, then sat down to join him.

His voice was gruff when he spoke. "I'd help you — God knows I'd help you. But I didn't see enough!"

"Thank you. I understand," Dustin told him. "But, please, tell me whatever you did see. Anything — anything at all might help."

The general sat back, gazing into the darkness.

And then he began.

16

Olivia wasn't sure what had awakened her.

At first she'd thought she'd never sleep, but she'd closed her eyes and drifted off with surprising ease. Maybe it had been a release of tension; so much had happened. Aaron had almost died and been saved — and now he was actually dead. The Horse Farm was falling apart. But two armed agents rested nearby and Dustin was just outside. She felt . . . safe.

But just as easily as she'd slept, she awoke.

She lay there for a minute, trying to ascertain what had wakened her, her heart beginning to beat too fast. Fear set in so quickly these days.

But then she realized she heard Dustin's voice and that it was calm and relaxed. She saw movement near her; Malachi had risen and crept to the opening of the tent. Abby was awake, as well, watching Malachi.

Olivia inched silently toward Malachi. He

turned to her in the darkness. She could barely see his features but he whispered, "Move slowly."

She nodded. Malachi eased himself out of the tent. She saw that he stood motionless for a few seconds and then moved toward the rock-circled fire, where the embers still burned with a soft glow.

Olivia glanced back at Abby, who rose carefully and together they stepped out of the tent. Malachi had just taken a seat near the fire by Dustin.

Across from them sat the general. He was in his cavalry uniform and appeared as he surely had in life. Olivia felt as if she'd stumbled upon a campfire meeting after a reenactment.

She hesitated, and then moved very slowly, coming around the fire to sit cross-legged on Dustin's other side, facing the general as the men were doing. A second later, Abby joined her. The general nodded to them each in turn. When he spoke, his voice seemed raspy, like a wind on leaves, and she thought again that he didn't speak often, that he saw his role in the afterlife as something that didn't require words.

"The dog cried out and I hurried to the sound," the general said. "A fine dog, a loyal animal. When I reached him, he was trapped. There was a large rock at his side. It must have been thrown at him and shoved him into a tangle of brush. It was all I could do to ease the tangle so he might run on. When I emerged from the trees, I saw someone wearing clothing in earth colors, greens and browns. In one of those short coats that covers the head."

"A hoodie," Dustin mused. "But you couldn't see a face."

"No. I first went down to the ravine where Marcus Danby lay. But to my great sorrow, the man was no longer living. Danby was a fine man. We spoke sometimes." The general was silent, reflective, for a moment. "And so I rose from the ravine and mounted Loki, and I went after that person. But as I rode, many people were out riding. I did not recognize anyone — and no one appeared in the clothing I had seen."

"Thank you, sir," Dustin said politely, but Olivia could hear disappointment in his voice.

"We'd suspected that Sammy, the dog, had been hit from a distance, which you've confirmed. If he knew who'd harmed him, he'd growl at that person. Thank you," Dustin said again. "Sammy is a good dog, and we're grateful he's alive."

The general nodded gravely, but a slight

smile curved his lip.

"I did see a horse," he told them. "When the hooded figure disappeared, I saw that he ran to a horse."

"Which horse?" Olivia asked. "What did it look like?"

"A large animal. One of the largest horses in the area."

"Gargantua!" Olivia whispered.

"That would be a fitting name," the general said.

Dustin turned to her; she could feel his tension. "Who was riding Gargantua that day?" he asked her.

Olivia let out a breath. "Aaron. Aaron Bentley," she said in a shaky voice.

Dustin frowned and looked back at the general. "Sir, were you in this area when we were camping? The night before last?"

The general nodded.

"Did . . . did you try to talk to one of the young women with us? Mariah?"

"I seldom try to speak," the general said. "No, I did not try to speak with anyone."

"Did you see anything that night — or early morning, as it was?" Dustin asked.

"I watched over the camp. I saw the man walk to the stream. I followed him at first. I saw him slap at his neck, as if he had been stung by a bee. Then he fell. There was nothing I could do." He raised his arms. "I have little strength. By will, if something . . . if something is light enough, perhaps my will can make it move. But he was a big man. I could not lift his face from the water."

His sorrow was evident.

"Did you see anything else?"

"I heard the scream and I followed. I saw you race into the woods. I wanted to try to bring you to the water, but you were gone before I could show myself to urge you toward the stream," the general said. He shook his head sadly. "I wish I could help more."

"You have helped incredibly," Dustin told him. "We are grateful, sir."

The general nodded and stood. "The truth must be discovered. Such a man as Marcus Danby must not be falsely remembered for living a lie. He salvaged his soul and his life and gave life to others, in quality and in years."

Dustin got to his feet; Olivia, Malachi and Abby quickly followed suit.

"We *will* find the truth," Dustin vowed.

"Yes, you are fine soldiers. You will carry on. I have spoken too long, but I will remain here. I will not leave, although I grow faint and weak," he said, pausing to offer them a grim smile. "I am but a ghost of the man I was. Still, I will watch, and I will do what is in my power."

Olivia smiled in return, thankful for his promise — and appreciating his unexpected humor.

He walked away from the fire, fading as he did. Just as he reached the heart of the forested shadows, Olivia saw his white horse, radiant in the moonlight. She thought she heard a whinny. Then the general mounted Loki, and they disappeared into the darkness as if they'd never been.

"Olivia, are you sure?" Dustin asked when the general had ridden away.

She stared at him, disoriented for a minute.

"Am I sure . . . about what?"

"That Aaron Bentley was riding Gargantua that day?"

She nodded. "He always rode Gargantua. And when they found me with Marcus, he'd definitely been riding Gargantua."

"Perhaps there was a switch-up with the horses?" Malachi suggested.

"I — I don't know how or when. When we all rode out from the Horse Farm that day, Aaron was on him. When I came to, Aaron was there, and he got back on Gargantua when we left."

Dustin looked at Malachi. "We'll have to ask at the Horse Farm. If someone else had taken the horse out first, Drew or Sydney would know."

"Hmm." Malachi frowned thoughtfully. "I'm not so sure about that. But it *is* possible that Aaron killed Marcus — and someone else killed Aaron."

"You mean, perhaps someone knew that Aaron had killed Marcus — and then killed Aaron *because* he killed Marcus?" Olivia asked.

"There are a few other possibilities," Abby pointed out. "Like Dustin said, someone else might have taken the horse."

Malachi shook his head. "I doubt it, since Liv seems convinced that Aaron was on Gargantua during the day."

"And here's something else," Dustin put in. "Aaron and someone else might have been working together — in which case his partner could have taken the horse. It could've been part of the plan. And then . . . this partner may have decided Aaron was too much of a risk, that he was going to blow it all somehow."

"But if someone knew that Aaron had killed Marcus — with or without that person as an accomplice — would he or she have gone to the police?" Olivia asked slowly.

Malachi draped an arm around her shoulders. "Hey, you know better than most how twisted and corrupt people can be, cousin."

Olivia sighed. "So, we're more or less nowhere."

"No," Dustin said. "We have more clues to follow now. Tomorrow we'll search this area again. And as soon as we get back, we'll find out what went on with the horses. And, with Jane's help, we'll track down that image of the general Frank found in the trees."

"I still think we should reenact what happened that morning," Abby suggested. "Try to understand the timing of what went on better."

"I agree. But for now, let's get some sleep," Dustin said.

"Yep, my turn to take over," Malachi announced. He sat back down by the fire.

"I'll never sleep now," Olivia muttered.

"I will," Dustin said. "Come on. Give it a try."

He set his hand on her back, pressing her toward the tent. To her surprise, once she'd climbed into her sleeping bag, with him beside her and Abby just feet away — and Malachi on guard duty by the fire — she did begin to drift off.

If it wasn't so serious, it would be amusing. It was the most asexual situation ever despite the fact that they were crammed together in such intimate quarters. And yet she was comfortable because she could feel his warmth.

The packaged muffins weren't very good, but they were edible and Dustin had to admit that the coffee they brewed with stream water was excellent. When they'd eaten, Abby did the directing.

"She used to play a pirate wench at her grandfather's tavern," Malachi told Dustin with a grin.

Abby pointedly ignored that. "Malachi, you'll be Aaron. I'll be Mariah, and Olivia and Dustin, you two will be yourselves. So . . ."

"Okay, I'm Aaron. I've woken up, stretched and I'm going to the stream."

He walked away.

"Okay, what next?" Abby asked.

"I hear the scream — I bolt up and run into the woods," Dustin answered.

"Go!" Abby said.

Dustin shook his head.

"What?" she asked.

"You're Mariah, so you're supposed to be in the woods already."

"All right, I'm going. How far?"

"Just past the 'powder room' bushes over there, past the first trees, and into the first clearing," Dustin told her.

"Okay, wait until I get there and scream."

Abby ran ahead. A few seconds later, she screamed. Dustin went flying after her; he heard Olivia coming after him. They met up with Abby in the woods.

"That was only about ten seconds," Dustin said.

Abby nodded. "What next?"

"We were here with Mariah for maybe two minutes and then we all went back to the site. Drew was with me," Olivia said.

"All right. We head back now." Abby led the way. When they returned to the campsite, she asked, "And everyone was here then, at the campsite. Everyone except Aaron."

"Everyone except Aaron," Dustin confirmed.

"How long until you realized he wasn't here?" she asked.

"Almost immediately."

"Okay, so now we go to the stream," Abby directed.

This time Dustin ran ahead of the others, just as he had that morning. Malachi, who was waiting by the water, looked at his watch. "The entire thing took place in under five minutes," he said.

Olivia gazed around her and then back at the campsite.

"What is it?" Dustin asked.

"This just keeps getting worse."

"Why? How?"

"Well, it really could have been anyone. Even Mariah," Olivia said. "Although that would never have occurred to me if we hadn't done our reenactment. . . . She could've been at the stream — and then looped around the campsite to get to the woods. And since we don't know if anyone else was out before Dustin went racing off, one of the others could've gone to the stream and come back." She paused. "I'm positive we can rule out the boys, but . . ."

"Don't worry. There are more of us working on this now," Malachi told her, slipping an arm around her shoulders.

"Let's finish searching through the trees again, see if we can find anything else," Abby said.

They returned to the woods; Dustin described what it had looked like where he'd found Mariah. "The, uh, cow pieces are gone now. I guess the coyotes came back and finished them off."

"Probably," Malachi agreed. "Let's split

the area into quadrants, start in the middle and we'll each work outward."

"What exactly are we searching for?" Olivia asked.

"Anything that doesn't belong here," Malachi said.

They explored in silence for a while, combing through the bushes, trying to identify anything out of place on the forest floor.

Suddenly Olivia let out a little cry.

"What is it?" Dustin asked, hurrying over to her.

"Maybe nothing, but . . ." She opened her hand. She was holding something red with a tiny needlelike point. The small object was in the shape of a horse. "This is one of the tacks we use to put notices up on the office bulletin board," she said. "Someone might just have had one in a pocket."

Dustin shook his head. "No, it wasn't a random find, Olivia. This is where Frank Vine discovered the image of the general. I'd say that means someone — most likely from the Horse Farm — hung it here."

"To lure Mariah out," Malachi said, approaching them from the other side.

"So Mariah is innocent. One down." Olivia raised a finger as though counting.

"Not necessarily." Dustin shook his head

again. "What if she put it here herself to make us believe her story?"

Olivia groaned in frustration. "How will we *ever* get anywhere?" she demanded.

"Well, Sydney was at the Horse Farm, watching over the place, right?" Malachi said. "Or . . ."

"Or was he?" Olivia finished for him.

"Maybe that's something we can prove one way or the other," Dustin suggested.

"We reach the solution by following every direction," Malachi told her. "It was a good find, cousin. Now we know it wasn't just left here by some college kid. That's important — and it narrows down the possibilities." They searched a while longer, with no further results, and started back.

En route, Dustin used his radio to call in; Frank Vine told him the night had been uneventful.

When they reached the Horse Farm, Drew and Sydney came out, hearing their arrival. Sammy came out, too, barking excitedly. Olivia immediately dismounted and captured the big dog in a hug, sternly ordering him not to jump.

"Anything?" Drew asked anxiously.

"Nope," Dustin said. "Anything here?"

"Quiet as a tomb all night."

"Drew, I heard people say that Aaron

always rode Gargantua," Dustin continued. "Is that right? The day Marcus died, was Aaron riding him?"

Drew raised his eyebrows in evident surprise. "Yeah, it's true. Aaron — when he went riding, which wasn't that often — always took Gargantua. He's a big horse but he's gentle. I once saw him let himself trip rather than step on Aaron when he'd fallen off. He'd gotten on him bareback, which was kind of foolish for Aaron. I wouldn't call him an incompetent rider, but he wasn't the best by far."

"Where was Gargantua before everyone saddled up to go looking for Marcus Danby that day?" Dustin asked.

"In his stall," Drew said. "I think."

Sydney had been listening, Dustin realized, because he walked up to the two of them. "Drew, no. Remember? We had all the horses out in the pasture."

"Sydney's right," Drew said. "I remember now. We had to round them all up to get saddled."

"Is it important?" Sydney asked.

"I don't know. Do you ever worry about the horses when they're out in the pasture? I'm sure you don't notice all of them all the time. Have you ever worried about one of them being stolen? *Could* one be stolen?"

"We've never had any horses stolen," Sydney replied. "I guess all the ones we have now are known by people in the area, but we've also brought in rescues. Some could be dangerous — unless you knew the horse, knew the problem and the animal's behavior. Like Shebaan. She was a kicker when we got her. But the first thing we teach anyone who comes here is that you don't stand in kicking distance behind a horse. Any horse."

"Should we be worried?" Drew asked.

"No, no," Dustin assured them. "I wasn't suggesting that. But could someone, say, use a horse and put it back in the pasture without anyone noticing?"

Drew looked at Sydney; Sydney looked back at Drew.

Then both men looked at Dustin and shrugged.

"What does all this mean? Does it matter?" Drew asked worriedly.

"I'm not sure. Maybe," Dustin said evasively. "Thanks, you guys." He left Chapparal with the men and made his way to the office.

Sloan was standing behind Jane Everett at the door, waiting for them. "Anything?" Sloan asked as they entered and shut the door behind them.

"More confusion," Olivia said, going straight to the coffeepot, Sammy following her every move.

"We spoke with the general," Olivia said. She poured her coffee and sipped it.

"And?"

"He didn't see a face, but he did see someone running from the ravine when Marcus was killed."

"And he saw a horse," Dustin filled in for her.

"Which horse?"

"Gargantua," Olivia said.

"Gargantua — the massive horse, I take it?" Jane asked.

Olivia nodded.

Dustin turned to Olivia. "Could he just have disappeared from a pasture and re-appeared? Drew and Sydney didn't seem certain."

"Well, I guess it's possible," she said. "You see and do things every day and you don't really pay much attention to your surroundings. We often keep the horses in the pastures, and we've never had to worry about them. Sometimes they hang around the fences. Sometimes they cluster in the corner by the trees. When I get here every morning, at least some of them are usually out in the pasture, unless they're being brushed for a session or saddled for a ride. They're always in their stalls at night, but during the day . . ." She shrugged. "Honestly, you'd have to ask me to count them. Otherwise, I'd assume they were all where they're supposed to be."

"So, it is possible someone took him without being seen," Dustin concluded.

"I guess so," Olivia said unhappily.

"Anything else?" Sloan asked.

"We found one of our horse-shaped thumbtacks out in the woods. We're assuming that means whoever tacked up the image of the general brought it from here — and probably came from here."

"I believe I've learned the source of the image," Jane said. She sat on the sofa with her laptop and opened it. "Five weekends ago, there was an art show at the Opryland Mall in Nashville. It was kind of a big deal. They had name bands playing there, as well as a contest for artists to create props for haunted houses." She turned her computer around. There was the gauze cloth, with the watercolor and chalk image of the general. A young man of perhaps twenty-two was standing next to it; a judge stood beside him, handing him an award. "The kid who won is a senior at Vanderbilt. His work will go into a haunted house being set up in an old farmhouse near Murfreesboro. His prize was a grant of five thousand."

"Have you contacted him?" Dustin asked.

Jane nodded. "His name is Simon Latinsky and you can visit him this afternoon. He rents a room on Capri Street. He's expecting you anytime before five. Oh, by the way — the original, the one we're seeing in this picture, is already in the haunted house. But he did a few practice runs, which he sold."

Dustin looked at Olivia, meeting her eyes. "Why don't we go talk to the budding artist?"

"Okay with me," she murmured.

"Meanwhile, I'll spend some time with Sydney and Drew," Malachi said. "See if I can find out anything else."

"Maybe one of you could drop by the café," Dustin suggested. "Delilah is a veritable fount of information and sometimes some of the kids from Parsonage House go there. Oh, if you run into Coot, say hi."

"I'm going to check up on the whereabouts of your fellow therapists, Mason and Mariah — and I'll stop by and introduce myself to Sandra Cheever," Sloan said with a grimace. "I've already talked to her on the phone a few times."

"Really? Why?" Olivia asked.

"According to the last will Aaron Bentley wrote, you're his executor. And Sandra wants to plan the funeral. Oh, by the way — she quits."

Olivia groaned. "Another funeral . . . and I'm not surprised she wants to handle it. All she had to do was talk to me. I'm happy to let her make the arrangements."

"I don't think she likes you a lot right now," Sloan told her.

Dustin nudged Olivia. "Finish your coffee and let's go," he said. "We have an art student to see."

"Sammy and I will hold down the fort here," Abby said. She yawned. "Maybe take a bit of a nap on that sofa."

Olivia set down her cup and took Dustin's hand. "Come on, let's go. Let's see what Simon Latinsky has to say." Sammy let out a mournful howl, as if he knew he was being left again.

"Ah, come here, boy. I'm going to cuddle you while we take a nap," Abby crooned, enticing him over.

"Just FYI, he's not supposed to be on the couch," Olivia said.

Abby grinned at her. "Okay, I'll be on the couch — and he can sleep on me!"

Olivia smiled. It was evident that she approved of the woman who'd become Malachi's partner in every possible way.

Simon Latinsky lived in a turn-of-the-century house on Capri Street near Vanderbilt. When they knocked on the door, the woman who opened it seemed to be expecting them; she welcomed them in and asked if they wanted coffee. They declined, and she directed them to Simon's room, explaining that she owned the house but rented four of her rooms to students.

The house reminded Dustin of his college days. The tenants seemed to be musicians and artists. He and Olivia could hear someone practicing a guitar as they walked up the stairs, and the hallway was lined with lithographs.

Simon let them into his room. He looked much as he had in the picture Jane had found online.

"Hi!" he greeted them. "Come on in. Sorry, it's such a mess." It *was* a mess. Simon dumped a pile of clothing from a chair and another from the foot of his bed so they could sit. "I heard you're with the FBI!" he told Dustin.

"I am," Dustin said, introducing himself and Olivia.

"Cool. But I'm not sure what I can do to help. The lady on the phone was asking me about my General Cunningham picture. She says the sheriff out by you found one — in some trees. The thing is, it can't be the one in the newspaper photo. That's owned by Hysterically Haunted Happenings — they're the guys who had the contest. I was really happy to win. Tuition is stiff, you know?"

"I remember," Olivia said. "And I sympathize."

"Hey, want to be a model? What a great face you've got."

"No, but thank you."

"I didn't mean a nude or anything. I have a little money now." He grinned. "I could even pay you."

"Maybe some other time." Olivia smiled at him. "If you're looking for models, we have gorgeous horses at the Horse Farm, not to mention adorable dogs and cats. You could come out and see them sometime."

"Yeah, a woman on a horse. A naked woman on a horse! Oh, no — sorry. You can tell I like historical images," Simon said.

"I'm no Lady Godiva."

Dustin brought the subject back to their original purpose. "My associate told me that you had a few other renderings of the general. Practice runs, she called them. But you sold them all?"

"Too bad I didn't know I was going to win!" Simon groused. "I'd have held out for more money. Yeah, I did two practice images. They weren't as well-shadowed or defined as the one I entered, but they were still pretty good. They probably wound up someplace where they won't really be appreciated."

"Oh, I think one of them is appreciated," Olivia murmured.

"So, you sold two. Who did you sell them to?" Dustin asked.

Simon screwed up his face. "We had an art sale right in the yard," he said. "We do them every few months. Mrs. B. — you met her, she owns this place — is really cool. Some of my friends play their own music, she makes lemonade and sangria and we have a great day. I sold a bunch of stuff, sketches, some watercolors — and the practice pieces."

"Yes, but who did you sell them to?" Olivia asked, repeating Dustin's question.

"Well, I'm trying to remember," Simon told them. " 'Cause I sold so much."

"Was it all cash?" Dustin asked.

Simon brightened. "No. No, I took several checks. . . . Oh, yeah! I took a check for one of the renderings."

"Who wrote it?" Dustin persisted.

"Um — a guy," Simon said vaguely.

"Old guy, young guy?"

"Sort of in the middle. He wasn't a kid, but he wasn't keeling over or anything, either."

"Was he dark- or light-skinned? What color were his eyes? Did he have a beard? How was he dressed? Is there *anything* you remember about him?"

"Well, he was wearing a baseball cap, I'm pretty sure. I don't remember his eyes. No, he didn't have a beard."

"Do you have the check he gave you?" Olivia asked.

"I already deposited it," he replied. "Everyone told me I was an idiot to take a check. But here's the good thing — it didn't bounce!"

"Simon, I swear we're not after your bank account, but you must have online banking," Olivia said. "If you pull up your account, you should be able to find a copy of the check."

He got up. His desk was piled high with pens and pencils, art sheets and school memos. He brushed them out of the way to get to his computer. A minute later, he'd drawn up his records and hit all the right keys. He swiveled in his desk chair to look at them proudly. "I found it!"

Olivia got up and walked over to stand behind the boy, studying the computer image of the check he'd been given.

She turned to look at Dustin with stricken eyes.

"Aaron," she said softly. "*Aaron* bought the general's image."

17

"I don't know how we'll ever get at the truth," Olivia said as they drove out of the city. She realized that although she'd discovered something she hadn't wanted to know, she'd been glad to get away — even if Nashville wasn't really "away." Any trip there, however brief, was a pleasure; the city was sophisticated and filled with music and charm and yet still had a smalltown feel.

But she loved the Horse Farm, too. She had adored Marcus; she'd cared about Aaron. But Aaron might have gone crazy before he'd died — or been killed. Every clue seemed to lead them in circles.

"We will," Dustin said in a reassuring voice. He was driving, and she sat in the passenger seat, gazing out the window, wishing she could roll back time.

"What now?" she asked him.

"I'll call Frank in a little while and find out if he's come across anything new." He reached over and squeezed her hand. "Hungry?"

"Yes, actually. We never did have lunch. We could turn around. I know some incredible restaurants on Elm Pike or back by Music Row."

He grinned at her. "I was thinking more of the café."

"I thought Jane was going."

"Maybe she hasn't gone yet. Maybe we should all meet up there."

"And to think I once really enjoyed that café!" she said.

"Grab my phone and call Jane. See if they want to meet us there for an early dinner. Someone should stay at the Horse Farm, though."

"All right." As directed, she got his phone. Jane hadn't been to the café yet; she and Abby had spent most of the afternoon on the computer, hacking into her coworkers' social network sites.

"You can do that?" she asked Jane.

"Sometimes. Pretty easy in this case. Your coworkers use their email addresses as their user names and the name of one of the horses as their passcodes. It wasn't terribly hard."

"And?"

"No red flags, but we'll talk at the café."

Olivia leaned back in the passenger seat.
"Tired?" he asked.

She glanced at him. "Well — I'm tired of being on edge," she said. "Uh, where are we sleeping tonight?" She meant the question to sound very casual.

"Your house," he told her. "Jane and Sloan will remain at the Horse Farm, and Malachi and Abby will go and stay at Marcus's house — or more accurately, your other house."

"Oh," she said. "Will everyone know that?" she asked carefully.

She thought he was smiling. "I don't think Malachi will mind."

"He's kind of protective. . . ."

"He just wanted to make sure I knew how extraordinary you are."

"He *is* my cousin."

"I assured him that I think you're completely extraordinary."

"Ah," she murmured.

He was quiet for a few minutes. "We've talked a little about what others see as our strange experiences. Do you remember the first time you had one of those experiences — when you saw a ghost?"

"It was the general," she said. "I saw him sitting proudly on his horse. He was so dignified. And I wasn't afraid. . . . And, of course, there was Malachi's resident ghost.

He lives in the family home in Virginia. I sometimes wondered when I was young if I really saw him or if it was just Malachi's way of teasing me. But . . . he was a good ghost. A family ghost. You'd never be afraid of him. I haven't spent my life having conversations with ghosts, though. Not the way it seems the rest of you have."

"Ghosts don't always have a reason to speak or make themselves known," Dustin said. "But once you've gotten accustomed to the fact that the dead can walk — and speak — you can seek them out. Not everyone, of course. But you definitely have the talent."

"Talent," she echoed. She closed her eyes. "If I didn't have the 'talent,' as you say, I would've been forced to accept — whether I really believed it or not — that Marcus had relapsed. And in that case . . . Aaron might still be alive. There might be hope for the Horse Farm."

"But Marcus Danby deserves justice. You know that."

"I do."

"But . . ." he began. He didn't finish. It was almost as if he regretted speaking at all.

"But?" she demanded. "Don't you dare give me a 'but' and then go silent!"

He looked over at her. For a moment she

wished she'd met him under better circumstances. She loved the line of his jaw, the strength of his conviction and inner resolve and, admittedly, she loved lying in bed with him. . . .

"Jackson would find a place for you," he murmured. "Jackson Crow. Working with one of the units. You could even be based in northern Virginia."

She laughed. "Dustin, I know how to fire a tranquilizer gun, but I've never held a real firearm in my life. I'm a coward!"

"If we didn't have the sense to be afraid, we'd be worthless. Fear can consume you — or it can make you wary and intelligent about what you do and how you do it. I'm just saying that if you were looking to move . . . on to something else . . ."

"If the Horse Farm goes under and we're forced to find homes for the animals and sell the land, I'll have to," she said.

"It hasn't happened."

"It *is* happening."

He squeezed her hand again. "We'll find the truth, and the truth could repair all the harm that's been done."

"So far it *looks* as if our founder died of an overdose and our first-in-command was so off his rocker that he nearly drowned and then managed to electrocute himself in his bathtub. The other alternative — to the average observer — is that one or more people who work at the Horse Farm is a devious, bloodthirsty murderer."

"The truth could still salvage the situation," he insisted. "Whatever that truth is."

They'd driven off I-40 and taken the back road. She could see the café ahead; the SUV in which Malachi and his team had arrived was parked in the lot.

Olivia braced herself to go in.

The Krewe agents already had the largest table at the café, the one at the far end, away from the door. As Olivia and Dustin walked through to join them, Delilah was serving a coffee refill to a lone tourist. She returned the pot to the burner and came toward them and, as Olivia had feared, she threw both arms around her in a huge hug. The last thing Olivia felt she could cope with right now was pity.

"Oh, honey, I am so sorry. I can't imagine how hard this is for you — all of you. But Sandra, well, she's a tough bird, and Mariah and Mason just aren't as invested . . . Oh, and poor Drew and Sydney! What will they do? They've both given their lives to that place!" Delilah said. "Anyway, I'm so sorry about Aaron! Now," she added briskly, "what can I get you, love?"

"Iced tea would be great, Delilah."

"Same for me," Dustin said.

"Well, this table is just one big group of tea drinkers!" Delilah chuckled. "I have chicken potpie tonight, and if I do say so myself, it's the best!"

"Chicken potpie?" Malachi asked, looking around the table to nods of assent. "We'll make it easy, Delilah. We'll all have potpie."

"Why, that *is* easy!" Beaming, Delilah bustled off to fill their order.

"I see you've gotten to know her," Olivia said to the others.

Jane smiled. "It's impossible *not* to get to know Delilah."

"What did you learn?" Malachi asked.

"Aaron bought the drawing of the general," Dustin said, getting right to the point.

"You're *sure*?"

"I know his handwriting — and I know Horse Farm checks," Olivia said.

"But," Abby argued, "his buying the art doesn't mean he put it in the forest during the camping trip. Or even if he did, it might have been a practical joke."

"We don't play practical jokes," Olivia said. "Not when we're dealing with kids who are struggling with addiction or other issues."

"He might have intended it for some other

purpose," Malachi said. "Maybe he bought the artwork and then someone else discovered it — and took it."

"And used his horse?" Olivia asked grimly. "I suppose that if anyone had a motive to kill Marcus, it would've been Aaron. And, of course, if anyone had a motive to kill Aaron . . . people would think it's me."

"Except," Dustin pointed out, "by the time it got to you, so much damage would be done to the Horse Farm's reputation that you really *wouldn't* have a motive to kill him — certainly not this quickly."

"Shh," Malachi warned.

Delilah came sweeping down on them with a massive tray. Chicken potpies were served with a large plate of biscuits. Delilah fluttered around the table, making sure they had butter, jam and honey for the biscuits, silverware and iced tea refills. When she was finished, she said, "Olivia, honey, have you heard from that lawyer fellow yet?"

Olivia shook her head, feeling a little guilty. "No, I haven't. I do need to call him."

"Well, I just wanted to let you know. One of my regulars — another attorney fellow who runs back and forth between Nashville and Memphis — was asking me about it. I just wanted you to know that if it comes to selling, which of course I hope it won't, he'll buy the place. He'll meet the price Marcus always wanted so the money could go to his charities. If you have to sell, you let me know."

Olivia forced a smile. "Thanks, Delilah."

"Who is this attorney, Delilah?" Dustin asked.

"Name is Henry Whittaker. His main office is in Nashville. I'm sure you can find him easy enough. If not, I've got his card somewhere."

She beamed at them again and swept off.

"We've been thinking about this all wrong," Dustin said.

Olivia gave him a puzzled look. "How do you mean?"

"Well, we suspected Aaron might have killed Marcus — because he'd get to be in charge of the Horse Farm. But Aaron's out of the picture. I don't think someone wants to kill everyone in order to run the Horse Farm. I think someone wants it to fail."

"But why?" Olivia asked.

"That's what we have to figure out. Sloan, anything on the women today?"

"Sandra Cheever never left her house. I followed Mariah to the Horse Farm and she saw both Sydney and Drew, hugged them a lot, cried a little — and then I followed her back to her place. She didn't leave again.

There's still a deputy watching over Sandra." He glanced at Olivia. "I called the office in Virginia and had a trace put on your boy Mason's credit cards. He's been in Nashville. Last uses were at the Country Music Hall of Fame and then a restaurant on Music Row."

"We can't solve anything tonight. I say we eat our potpies and get a good night's sleep," Malachi told them.

"I'm going to take Liv for a drive first," Dustin said. "I think we should stop in and see the Horse Farm guests who live at Parsonage House."

Olivia nodded. She wasn't sure what they'd get from the boys, but she agreed that it was a good idea for her, as one of their therapists, to see them. They must be in shock. None of them had been particularly close to Aaron, but they knew him.

And now he was dead.

As she and Dustin left the diner, Malachi requested the keys to Marcus Danby's house. Dustin must have discussed the plans with him while she was in the restroom. She found the keys in her bag; as she handed them to her cousin, she asked, "Do you think anyone's made any attempt to get in there? Is there something they could be looking for?"

"We'll go through whatever papers we can find. Sometimes even a greeting card can be a clue. Or he might have received some other correspondence that didn't seem significant to him at the time," Malachi replied.

"You don't think you're in any danger there, do you?"

He shrugged. "I doubt it, but it's not impossible. Marcus doesn't understand why anyone would kill him so there's definitely some unknown factor here. However, Abby and I are both well trained and," Malachi added with a grin, "we're armed."

When they'd all said good-night, Olivia and Dustin drove the short distance to Parsonage House. They were greeted by the director, Lance Osterly, a kindly, middle-aged man who still had the look of a pro wrestler — which he'd been at one point in his life.

"Liv, good to see you," he greeted her as he waved them both in. He nodded at Dustin. "And you're the FBI man, right? The boys talk a lot, you know," he said with a wink.

Dustin offered his hand to Osterly.

"I'm sorry about Aaron," Osterly told Olivia.

"I am, too. It's so strange — I don't even know how to handle this one," she said.

Osterly shook his head. "The poor guy survives what should've killed him, and he still dies in a ridiculous way. The kids have talked of nothing else for the past few days. Anyway, I appreciate that you're here. Come on — they're outside on the patio."

Osterly escorted them to a back door, which led to a pool and patio; the pool was covered until warmer weather returned but the patio was pretty with a rock wall fireplace and plenty of seating.

"Liv!" Joey was the first on his feet, rushing over to her. She thought of him as a boy, but he wasn't really; he was an adolescent, taller than her — and awkward, as many young men his age were. She greeted him with a hug. By then, Matt, Sean and Nick had joined them, and she realized that although they were once-upon-a-time tough-guy addicts, now they were scared.

"You're all doing okay?" Dustin asked them.

"We're — we're in an awful dilemma," Matt said. "We know we're okay and everything will be fine, but our parents are acting paranoid."

"Somebody killed Aaron, right?" Nick asked. "I mean, I can't forget that morning at the campsite. He almost drowned. And then he electrocuted himself in a *bathtub*? That's what they're saying — that's what we're supposed to believe. And changing our lives, going clean, is all about being honest, but there's no honesty going on here."

"And," Sean muttered, "our parents have all been on the phone with Mr. Osterly. They're questioning our safety."

"I have another six weeks here," Matt said. "They're talking about pulling me out. I don't want to go, Olivia. It's like this place saved my life and a lot of that's because of the horses. They taught me about boundaries and respect and they made me . . . they made me want a different life. A good life."

"Some of us want to become therapists," Joey told her. "Equine therapists."

Olivia glanced at Dustin, grateful that he'd decided they should come here.

"Listen to me, all of you," she said. "We *will* find out what happened. What they're telling you isn't a pack of lies — it's just all anyone knows. But wherever you go from here, whatever you do — nothing changes the incredible strides you've made or the wonderful young people you are. I'm so proud of every one of you, and I'd love to see you go forward and get into therapy or working with horses, or whatever you feel is best for you."

She felt Dustin's hands on her shoulders. "You know we don't believe Marcus Danby fell back into drugs," he said. "And despite the fact that it *appears* Aaron was alone when he died, it's just too ironic or coincidental — or *stupid* — to believe. Sometimes, though, it takes time to uncover the truth. If you *are* pulled out of this facility, don't forget what you had here — your friendships, everything you learned. And you can call on us anytime."

The boys nodded.

"Now, do any of you know anything?" Dustin asked.

They looked back at him wide-eyed.

"Like what?" Matt asked.

"Were you all around the day Marcus died?"

"Yeah — until Aaron called Mr. Osterly to have the van come and pick us up because they were all going off to look for Marcus," Matt said.

"Do you remember anything odd about that day?" Dustin asked.

"Poor Sammy, coming back looking like he'd met up with a bear," Sean said.

"Before that, did any of you notice if the horses were all there?" Olivia asked.

"I was playing Ping-Pong. I didn't even see Sammy until everyone started screaming," Nick said.

Joey frowned, then suddenly grew excited. "I didn't see the big guy — Gargantua. I like him a lot. Olivia used him now and then, I guess to show us that the biggest, toughest animals — and people — could be the kindest if that was the choice they made." He looked at Olivia.

"Something like that," Olivia agreed. "Did you ask anybody about him?"

"Yeah, I did. Sandra was there, and I saw her heading for Aaron's office. I asked her if they'd let somebody take Gangantua out. She said he was probably just hanging around by the trees and we couldn't see him. I don't think she was paying much attention to me. She seemed distracted," Joey said.

"She was distracted *before* Sammy came back injured?" Olivia asked.

Joey nodded.

"But she was there," Dustin said.

Joey nodded again.

"Who else do you remember being in the office right before you were sent back and everyone went riding off to find Marcus?" Dustin asked.

"I think Sandra's the only one. And then

Aaron, once Sammy showed up. And then everyone," Joey said.

"I saw Mason." Matt grinned. "He was fixing his hair in the mirror in back."

"Thanks," Dustin told them.

"You guys are great, and what you've accomplished is great," Olivia said. "No matter what happens."

They wished the boys a good night, thanking Lance Osterly.

"No, thank *you.* They really respect you, Liv. I'm praying that all this gets sorted out quickly. We offer the kids all kinds of stuff here — group therapy, individual therapy, art therapy, massage therapy — you name it. But there's nothing like the Horse Farm for most of our boys."

"We'll keep it afloat — and we'll get our reputation back, I promise," Olivia said fervently.

When they reached the car, she burst out with, "What a liar I am!"

"You're not a liar."

"An impossible dreamer, then."

"I keep telling you, when we discover the truth, the world will spin more smoothly on its axis." They stopped by the Horse Farm to pick up Sammy. The stables were quiet; evidently Drew and Sydney had gone to bed for the night.

Sloan and Jane Everett were still up, though. Of course, sleeping on couches couldn't have been conducive to going to bed early. Jane had been looking through Aaron's correspondence. "I found an offer from a firm, sent to Aaron. He must've ignored it and shoved it in his desk," Jane said.

"What kind of offer?" Olivia asked.

"An offer for the property. It's from the offices of that Nashville attorney Delilah mentioned. Henry Whittaker. And it came last week."

"He wanted to buy the Horse Farm — and went straight to Aaron?" Olivia asked, puzzled. "But an attorney would know, or could easily find out, just how tied up the place was! Why didn't he go directly to Fairchild?" When she saw Jane's puzzled look, she explained. "Fairchild was Marcus's attorney, and he's been dealing with everything concerning the Horse Farm."

"Well, this is a friendly letter. It just says that if the Horse Farm is ever in trouble, he's willing to pay a more-than-fair asking price for the property and buildings, and to see that the charities nearest and dearest to him received the greatest benefit," Jane said.

She showed them the letter.

Olivia said, "I can't imagine that an attorney from Nashville would be able to manage any of this without insider assistance."

"No, I don't think that's possible, either," Sloan agreed. "But it does speak to the theory that someone is trying to ruin the Horse Farm rather than take it over."

"Maybe we'll head back to Nashville in the morning," Dustin said. "But right now . . . we need to let Sammy search Liv's house before we go inside!"

They left the Horse Farm, with Sammy happily back in the car, sticking his nose between them. When they reached the house, Sammy showed no sign of fear or suspicion.

Olivia let Dustin and the dog search for evidence that there'd been any sign of invasion in their absence and went up to shower. She didn't bother dressing; she went straight into the bedroom and waited.

Twenty minutes later, Dustin came to her room.

She saw him in the doorframe for a moment, and the longing and anticipation she'd been feeling seemed to overwhelm her. She loved his analytical mind, his concern for others, his kindness. . . .

She also loved the way he looked, so tall and powerfully built. She loved the scent of him when he walked in, and she loved the feel of his naked flesh when he lay down beside her.

Their mouths met in a kiss that seemed desperate. But she had to touch him, all of him, taste him, feel his heat and passion rush through her. She felt his lips, his tongue, move over her breasts and down to her belly and below, felt his vibrant life and strength. The pulse of the world became that of her heart as she kissed and teased and stroked him in return. She crawled atop him and looked into his eyes, and he smiled and grasped her, and then he was in her. . . . The first time was frantic.

The second began slowly . . . and became frantic.

They lay together, panting, slick and sweaty and still entangled, and she breathed again.

"Hot enough?" he asked, his voice a teasing whisper in her ear.

"I feel like an inferno," she whispered back.

She felt her heart begin to slow. She touched him again. The third time their lovemaking remained slow for long enough that she kissed nearly every inch of his flesh, felt his fingers touch her everywhere, felt the passion in his kiss. They spiraled out of control and lay entwined together once again.

She nearly dozed and then realized he still lay awake, staring at the ceiling.

He sensed her movement.

"I was just thinking about what Jane and Sloan told us," he said. "I still can't believe a Nashville lawyer could have pulled any of this off without insider assistance. I somehow doubt he's really involved, except in a nominal way. Besides, there's other property available in the Tennessee hills. It has to be more personal and yet . . . that might well be the key."

"And I thought you were dreaming about hot and sweaty."

He grinned and pulled her close. "We're almost there," he said.

"Almost?"

"No, no, I meant *almost* as in discovering what's going on."

"How do you figure?"

"We know it's someone who has something to do with the Horse Farm —"

"You've said that from the beginning."

"But . . . now I'm positive that two people had to be involved." He rolled over to look at her. "Two people — that means each of the killers can have an alibi. For instance, we wouldn't think it was Sandra because

Joey saw her. We wouldn't think it was Sydney because he was watching over the Horse Farm while we were out camping. We wouldn't think it was Mariah — because she was screaming while Aaron was on the verge of drowning."

"So where does that get us? We wouldn't think it was Aaron — because he actually wound up dead?"

"There'll be a way to trip someone up," Dustin said. "Now . . ."

"We'll trip them up now?"

"No, I think we're ready to get hot and sweaty again now."

She laughed and curled into his arms as he kissed her. And she wished the night could go on forever.

Eventually, they both slept.

When Olivia woke the next morning, she saw that his eyes were still closed. She started to get out of bed, trying not to disturb him. But she saw him smile and realized he'd probably wake at the slightest sound.

"You look cute, cuddled there," she told him.

"Cute?" he asked indignantly.

"I'm going to go put coffee on."

Sliding from bed, she slipped into her

robe. She was surprised that Sammy wasn't sleeping at his usual post in the hallway.

"Sammy?" she called. His food and water bowl were in the kitchen, and she assumed he'd gotten tired of waiting for her.

Still, she walked cautiously down the stairs.

When she reached the landing, she paused, gasping.

There was Sammy. He was curled at the foot of the sofa, lying near the first of the three men in her parlor — Marcus Danby, who sat at one end.

General Rufus Cunningham sat in the wing-back chair, straight and dignified as ever in his uniform, his cavalry hat in his lap.

Aaron Bentley was at the other end of the sofa.

When he saw her, he rose.

"I did *not* kill Marcus!" he said, his words trembling with passion. "And I most certainly did not idiotically kill myself!"

18

Dustin practically flew out of bed, wrapping himself in the sheet and grabbing his Glock when he heard the voices downstairs. He raced to the first-floor landing — and then saw the strange trio in the house.

"Agent Blake," Aaron said, "nice of you to join us. I was just explaining to Olivia that, no, I didn't kill myself. Nor did I kill Marcus."

Dustin looked at Olivia. "I'll be right back," he muttered.

He headed back upstairs, still shaking. The sound of the voices in the house had scared the hell out of him; he was still afraid Olivia was at risk. He couldn't allow himself to get comfortable right now, he reminded himself harshly.

This time, the house was filled with ghosts — with the dead. Next time, it just might be the living.

The lethal living.

He had to move when she moved, hell, breathe when she breathed. And if he wasn't with her — in the same space — another agent had to be.

Dressed, he came back downstairs.

He was truly astonished to see the Civil War general — with the two very recent ghosts.

Aaron was wearing a handsome suit — and his cowboy boots. Dustin figured Sandra Cheever had brought the clothing to the funeral director.

"We're here to help," Marcus told him. "The general's been teaching me. With his help, I made it all the way to the mortuary. I was very proud of myself. Aaron was still reeling at the fact of his death. We were able to make him see more than himself in the present — that is, fried."

Aaron winced. "Marcus —"

"Gentlemen, you are beyond all earthly cares now, other than to help those who remain," the general said.

"So who the hell did it?" Dustin asked. "And don't tell me you don't know."

Aaron stared back at him. "I *don't* know," he said.

Dustin turned to Olivia and groaned.

"You have to know *something,*" he insisted.

"Tell him what you do know — what you believe, son," the general said. "You people were good for these hills, and now . . . I cannot bear this kind of treachery. Where has honor gone?" he declaimed.

Aaron looked from the general back to Dustin. "I'm dead — and I still can't bear the pain of it. *And* I'm being badgered by the past." He glanced significantly at Cunningham.

"Honor should not be in the past, sir!" the general said.

"I'm sorry, I didn't mean that," Aaron said. "I'm just . . ."

The ghost of Aaron Bentley faded. "He's really not very good at being dead yet," Marcus told them. "I think, perhaps, I was better adapted. . . . In my misspent youth, I came close to dying many times." He straightened. "We did learn something from Aaron — something that may be important, and something you would probably have discovered in your questioning. Aaron doesn't want to believe that Sandra could be involved in any way — he loved her, you see. But she was the only one besides him who had a key to his house. He's convinced that whoever killed him was in the house when he arrived. He says he came in, threw his mail on the table and decided that he smelled like antiseptic from the hospital. He went straight to the bathroom, decided to linger in the tub and listen to music. He turned on his iPod, crawled in and closed his eyes. Next thing he knew the iPod station came flying into the water and he was burning in agony."

"I'm calling Frank Vine," Dustin told Olivia. "He needs to bring Sandra Cheever back to the station. At the very least, he can grill her about her key to Aaron's house."

"I'll get dressed," Olivia said, and went upstairs.

Aaron was probably still among them, but couldn't be seen or heard. Dustin called Frank, who sounded tired. "I already questioned her. She couldn't have killed him."

"She was the only one with a key, Frank. She has to have given that key to someone."

"What the hell? You come down here, then. I'll bring her in — but you ask the questions."

"I'm on my way."

"Can't get much worse around here," Frank muttered.

Dustin sighed. "It can always get worse — that's why this has to be solved now." He hung up and turned back to the duo still in the parlor.

"He should've been more careful after

nearly dying at the stream," Marcus said sadly. "Aaron should've been . . . afraid."

As Dustin had assumed, Aaron was still there — just not visible. "Hey," he protested. "I was in my own house and there was a deputy posted outside. I should've had a dog," he said mournfully. "I should have taken one of those rescue mutts. A dog would have barked. Warned me. Oh, wait — that didn't help *you*, Marcus, did it?"

"Aaron, I have an important question. Why did you buy that artwork?" Dustin asked. "That rendering of the general?"

Aaron didn't answer. He seemed to have lost the energy to speak now, as well.

"He bought it because he wanted it for the Horse Farm. He thought Mariah would love it — that it would be great when she was telling her ghost stories," Marcus explained.

Olivia came back down the stairs, ready for the day in jeans and a denim shirt, her bag thrown over her shoulder.

"We're going to go through everything with Sandra one more time. And then we're going to tear the Horse Farm apart," Dustin said.

"We'll keep watch," Marcus said. "We'll split up and . . ." He sighed. "Thing is, we can't be everywhere."

"Sammy, look after the house," Olivia said.

They left. For once, Sammy didn't care. Marcus had risen, but Sammy was still at his feet.

Dustin tossed Olivia the keys. "You drive. I'll make calls." She nodded and slid behind the wheel.

First, he called Malachi, who said he and Abby were still going through Marcus's house, hoping to find *something*. Dustin told Malachi about the ghosts in Olivia's parlor — and that he was going down to the station to question Sandra again.

Then he called Sloan at the Horse Farm and gave him the latest information.

Sloan asked him, "Can Olivia hear me right now?"

Dustin glanced at her. She couldn't hear, he decided.

"No."

"You may want to bring her here first. Drew suggested it. He's called the vet because there's something wrong with her horse."

Dustin barely prevented himself from saying, *"Shiloh?"*

"Drew says it might be colic. He might have gotten hold of something bad for him out in the pasture."

"All right, you two —"

438

"Stay on that horse like flies. I know, Dustin. Don't worry. We'll watch over her or die in the attempt. You know that." He paused. "I guess you'd better tell her."

"Yeah," he said thickly.

Dustin ended the call and looked at Olivia. "Head over to the Horse Farm. I'm going to leave you there with Sloan and Jane."

"Oh?"

"They're getting the vet out. I'm afraid there's something wrong with Shiloh."

Her skin grew ashen but she concentrated on the road, carefully taking the next turn.

"People are dead," she said, her voice heavy. "And still . . . I love that horse."

"It's okay to love your horse."

They arrived at the ranch minutes later. Olivia had barely turned off the ignition when she was out of the car and racing for the stables. As he followed, he saw that Drew was there, coming toward her. Dustin heard Sloan call his name and turned to see him leaving the office.

Dustin slowed as he saw Drew give Olivia a hug and talk to her. Sloan reached Dustin's side.

"The vet's delayed. Apparently, there's only one guy in the immediate area and he was called to a dairy farm some distance away," Sloan explained. "Drew had just come to tell me this when you phoned. He gave me a few other numbers but it'll be at least half an hour before anyone can get out here."

"How bad is it? You know horses."

Sloan kept his own horses at a farm in Virginia, close to their base. "Looks to me like it's just a matter of very mild colic. Shiloh's down right now, but I believe he's going to be all right. Right after I talked to you, Drew and Sydney and I got a hose down his throat and did a decent job of pumping his stomach."

"Thanks, Sloan," Dustin said. He and Sloan hurried to the stables and over to Shiloh's stall. Olivia was in with the horse. Shiloh lay on the ground, but his head was up.

"His eyes are brighter," Drew remarked. "Sloan, you made the right call."

"I hope so," Sloan said.

"Thank you, Sloan," Olivia was kneeling on the ground by her horse. She looked up at Dustin, and there was anger in her eyes now. "Go to the station," she told him. "Go! I'm fine. I want you to find out who did this!"

"You . . . you think someone poisoned the horse?" Drew asked.

"I do — and I'll find out who did it!" Olivia said. "Or, rather, *we'll* find out."

Dustin nodded. "All right. I'm on my way. Don't make a move without Sloan or Jane, Olivia."

"I won't be making a move, period — not until the vet comes and we're sure Shiloh's okay," Olivia said. "Go. Sandra knows something — and I want to know what!"

Dustin looked at Sloan and turned back to the car. He drove fast. If a deputy stopped him now, he'd just say he was on his way to see Frank Vine.

It was wrong, Olivia told herself, to feel such intense anger and fear over Shiloh when people were dead. But the general, who'd kept his horse haunting the hills with him for a century and a half, and Marcus, who had loved all living creatures, would understand. Aaron . . . Maybe he wouldn't understand completely.

She was encouraged, though. Drew had described how the horse was at first — eyes rheumy, unable to stand, wobbling. Now, since they'd pumped his stomach, he seemed to be on the mend.

She hugged the horse's neck, just sitting with him. He nudged her and gave a little whinny. She stroked his big, beautiful head and curled his forelock with her fingers.

"You're going to be okay. It's not a bad thing to have a cowboy around, huh?"

"Liv, I'll go in and get you a cup of coffee," Drew told her. "Sloan's right here, and Sydney's in his room, within shouting distance. I'll be back in a minute."

"That sounds great, Drew." Olivia said gratefully. She glanced up. Sloan was on guard, smiling at her from the stall gate. "The horse is going to make it, Liv."

She nodded. "Thanks to you."

"It's also thanks to Drew and Sydney. They run a good stable here."

She nodded, but before Sloan could speak again, they heard a shout from the office.

"Hey!"

Sloan frowned and backed away from the stall, peering through the stable entrance to the office. Olivia jumped up to join him and together they started toward the office.

Drew was running in their direction.

"Jane! It's Jane. I don't know what the hell's wrong with her. She's down."

"Down?" Sloan shouted. "Stay with me!" he ordered Olivia, and tore for the house.

Olivia did stay with him — right on his heels. Sloan burst into the office and she ran in behind him.

Jane Everett was on the sofa; she'd been

there with her computer, a cup of coffee on the driftwood coffee table in front of her.

She had collapsed onto her side. Her computer lay haphazardly on the floor.

Sloan rushed to her.

"A dart! Look for a dart — a small dart somewhere!" Olivia told him. She fell onto her knees by Jane's left side as Sloan took the right.

Olivia saw the tiny dart that had struck Jane; she reached for it. "Sloan! I've got the dart."

But even as he turned to her, reaching for his gun, she heard a "zzzz" in the air.

The big cowboy fell onto his partner and beloved. Olivia ducked close to the couch, trying to see who was in the office shooting the darts.

She stared at the door, but the sunlight was streaming in. She couldn't see the man's face. And then . . .

"Drew!" she gasped.

"I just don't know what you're going to get out of the woman," Frank Vine muttered to Dustin. "She has an answer for everything — and I don't have a single thing to hold her on."

They were in the observation room. Jimmy Callahan stood watching Sandra while

Frank and Dustin talked.

"Hold her on suspicion of murder," Dustin said.

"With what proof? We have nothing! No district attorney would be able to take this case to court!"

"I doubt if Sandra knows that. Just tell her she's going to be booked for murder. Then I'll go in."

Dustin watched as Frank went to talk to Sandra. She immediately flew from her chair in a fury, telling him he was an idiot.

"Strange, huh, that they called her *Mama* Cheever? She's a real virago. I guess she ran a tight ship, though. But it seems like she did love Aaron. You really think she might have killed him?" Callahan asked.

"She didn't do the deed — but I think that, somehow or other, she was in on it."

Frank returned to the observation area. "She's all yours," he said.

Dustin nodded and walked into the interrogation room. Sandra watched him suspiciously, radiating pure tension. "You," she spat. "You are a despicable federal *ass!*"

"Sandra, you were the only one who had a key to Aaron's house — besides Aaron." Something in her manner changed slightly.

"That's ridiculous!"

"You loved him and you were having an

affair with him. Are you telling me you didn't have his key?"

"Of course I had his key! But how the hell would I know just how many keys Aaron had out there?"

"He didn't have any other keys out there, Sandra."

"How do you know that?"

"Aaron told me."

"Aaron? Aaron is dead."

"Yes. Yes, he is."

She stared at him, her lips twitching with derision. "You spoke to a dead man?"

"He spoke to me," Dustin said. He could well imagine Frank Vine and Jimmy Callahan frowning at each other in the observation room. Their lips would be twitching, as well.

Dustin leaned forward. "You had the only extra key, Sandra."

"I didn't kill Aaron! I loved him."

Dustin eased back in his chair. "You know," he said slowly, "I don't think you realized he was going to be killed."

"He wasn't killed. It was an accident."

"I just told you — I've talked to Aaron. Or, as I said, he talked to me. It wasn't an accident. He didn't reach for anything electrical, including his iPod charger, while he was in the bath. Someone was in his house. Someone who probably knew he liked baths." He shook his head. "I never took you for stupid, Sandra."

"Stupid! You bastard, I'm hardly stupid!"

"No? Then you did know what was going on. So, which is it? Are you stupid — or guilty?"

"Neither!" she yelled.

"Who had the key? Who did you tell about your affair? What was the *real* plan — if you didn't want Aaron dead? And, if you loved him so much, why did you leave his house when you knew your accomplice was in there, lying in wait for him?"

She didn't answer.

He stood up. "Frank? Frank, come and book her for murder. She's definitely involved. She didn't do the killing, but she was in on the conspiracy. She facilitated the killer." He turned back to Sandra. "But then the whole thing got away from you, didn't it? Then you started fearing for your own life, right? So you figured you had to keep quiet. Because unless we caught the killer —"

He broke off. He was pretty sure he had it figured out, but he needed to trip Sandra up just once.

He slammed his palms down on the table. "The Horse Farm was supposed to go under, right? But not so it could be sold to a Nashville lawyer. *Right?*"

Sandra glared at him. Then she jumped to her feet and pointed to the one-way mirror.

"It's his fault — all his fault! Jimmy Callahan! He was always talking about the countryside and how wonderful it is, but he said the Horse Farm was a nothing place. He's the one who talked about the land, and how someone who came from such a long line of Tennesseans should be the one to own it! Someone like that could turn it into a special destination, he said. It was him — he started it all!"

Dustin turned and stared at the mirror himself; that wasn't the direction he'd been going with this at all.

Before he could move, Jimmy Callahan burst into the room.

"What are you talking about?" he shrieked. "Oh, my God!"

Even as Olivia watched Drew, a dark silhouette in the doorframe with sunlight pouring in behind him, he pitched over. She hadn't heard the whizzing sound that time; she'd been watching Sloan fall before she turned to Drew.

Something told her she needed to get the dart out of Sloan's back.

She managed to rip out the tiny shaft and drop down by the sofa, ruining anyone's clear shot at her.

It wasn't Drew trying to kill her, though, because poor Drew was out on the floor. Sydney?

But Sydney was in the stables.

No, he wasn't.

"Drew? Hey, Drew! Liv? Sloan? Where the hell is everyone?" Sydney had left the stables; he sounded perplexed, and he was on his way to the office.

"Sydney, no! Go back, get on the phone! Call for help!" Olivia shouted, staying down, hoping she was protected by the sofa — and the drugged bodies of the two agents with her.

Too late.

This time she heard the strange "zzzz" sound.

And she heard Sydney's body hit the earth, a few feet from the door.

FBI agents are always armed!

Down in front of the sofa, she groped at Sloan's body until she found the holster at his side. She struggled to find the gun — and get it out without killing herself. She had no idea how to use it.

It was a gun, she told herself; you took the safety off, you pointed and fired.

But even as her fingers curled around it, she heard movement behind her.

"Come on out, Olivia. They're all down. And I don't want to hurt you. Not yet. We're going for a little ride. Don't you want to buy all the time you can? Come on, now, get up — slowly."

Olivia's fingers were curled around Sloan's gun. She straightened her back, which was toward the killer. Not allowing any other part of her body to move, she slipped the gun into her fingers.

"No more cutesy little dart guns, Olivia. I have a Smith & Wesson trained on you now."

Olivia stiffened, arching, trying to pretend she was giving up.

She managed to shove the gun under the waistband of her jeans. Then she rose slowly, just as she'd been ordered.

She was terrified. She was going to faint, her knees would give out. . . . Being afraid could make you smart; that was what Dustin had said.

She hoped the gun didn't protrude from her belly — or that she wouldn't shoot off the lower portion of her body.

A shot suddenly exploded over her head, and Olivia froze in shock.

"Just wanted you to know I have a real gun with real bullets."

She turned to face the killer she should have known.

"Where are we riding to? And which horse am I taking? You nearly killed Shiloh."

She was answered with a careless shrug. "I had to be sure you'd come here today. So . . . don't worry. We have a number of horses to choose from. Let's go."

Dustin drove in the sheriff's department car with Frank Vine and Jimmy Callahan.

Not one of his phone calls to the Horse Farm had been answered. Malachi and Abby were on their way and backup vehicles, including ambulances, were behind them.

"Explain this to me again," Frank said to Callahan. "Damn you, Jimmy, why the hell didn't you figure out what was going on?"

"How was I to know I was dating a maniac?" Callahan demanded. "Frank, we talked about family history. I thought it was really interesting that she could trace her history back so far, and I also suggested that maybe she should consider taking a job in Nashville when it was offered. She might have gotten one of those ghost tour shows — she might have gone really far. I had no idea that . . . that . . . whatever!"

They reached the Horse Farm; Dustin

paid no heed to the arguing officers.

He saw the prone body of Sydney Roux in front of the house and rushed to him, crouching down to check for a pulse. It was faint. On the porch, he found Drew. He, too, was still alive.

As he rushed into the house, he saw that Jane was trying to help Sloan stagger to his feet.

"Dustin, they used the darts. . . . We were down. . . . Olivia . . . I think Olivia pulled the darts out of us," Sloan said, and swore furiously.

"Whoever . . . came in from the back — none of the dogs barked," Jane told him.

"Where is she? Where's Olivia?"

"I don't know. But the attack came from inside the house," Sloan said. "And whoever it was took my gun . . ."

Dustin rushed out. Sloan and Jane came tearing after him, but as they arrived at the stables, Jane faltered.

Sloan stayed back to steady her. Dustin swung on both of them. "What's the matter with you? You're in no shape to be running around! Wait here — ambulances are on their way." As he spoke, Malachi came driving in with Abby.

Frank left the stables and headed for Dustin, while Malachi and Abby ran to meet them.

"Two of the horses are gone," Frank said breathlessly.

"Yeah, and we need to get going. Malachi, tell them — they've been hurt. They can't come."

Malachi pointed at Sloan and Jane. "You two — emergency attention," Malachi said.

"Come on," Dustin urged, "we've got to follow quickly. I can't imagine what she's planning for Olivia, but if she rode away with her, we've got a chance."

Jimmy Callahan hurried to the stables. As Dustin followed, he heard movement in one of the stalls. He pulled his gun and whirled around.

It was Shiloh. The horse was back on its feet.

"Wait!" Malachi shouted.

Dustin turned to stare at him. "Look, we're not talking about someone in her right mind here. And she's just about gone over the edge while being in a desperate situation at the same time."

"What are you saying?"

"I'm saying we have to be prepared to play mind games."

"And do you have a suggestion?" Malachi demanded.

"I do," Jimmy Callahan said, striding between them. "I do. Mariah is crazy about the history here — crazy about General Rufus Cunningham. She'll say everyone sees him except her, but that *she's* the one who deserves to know him. If you want —"

"Dammit, tell me what you're talking about!" Dustin snapped.

"It'll take another five minutes. Come with me. To Drew's room. He's involved with a reenactment group. Come on, I'll show you."

Dustin had no idea whether it was going to work or not; it might be his only chance. He was trying with all his might to think rationally, like an agent, and not like a man who felt he'd die if something happened to the woman he, yes, loved.

He looked at Malachi and remembered that he and Liv were cousins and that Malachi must be feeling as torn as he was.

"All right. I'll do it. I've done a lot of reading on the general," he said.

Five minutes later — as Jimmy had promised — he was ready.

Malachi and Abby were on their way out, while ambulances thronged the drive to the Horse Farm. Various deputies were mounted up and moving, and Chapparal had been saddled and bridled for him. He climbed on the horse and started to leave the stables.

"Whoa!" Malachi held up a hand. "Let's divide the area into sections. We've got a lot of property to cover."

Callahan was on Battle-ax. "The ravine?" he asked Dustin. "The ravine — where Marcus died?"

"Maybe. Frank, why don't you take the ravine with some deputies. Malachi, you and Abby stay with me, but give me some space. I'm going to follow the trail to the campground."

He galloped out of the stable on Chapparal and across the pastures.

If you were crazy and thought you had some kind of divine right to a piece of land — as well as the hereditary right to speak to a ghost — where would you go?

A cemetery.

"Here's what I don't understand," Olivia said. "You're a good therapist, Mariah. And I always thought you loved what you did."

"I'm an okay therapist," Mariah told her. "You're the great lover of the downtrodden, confused and drug-addicted. And, oh, yeah, they love you, too. You should see the disappointment on their faces when they find out they're with Mason or me for the day. Now,

454

what *I* am is a great historian. I can tell you everything about the occupation of Nashville. I can describe every Civil War battle in this state — oh, and I can tell you anything you want to know about Andrew Jackson."

"I grew up in Nashville," Olivia reminded her. She felt the gun inside her shirt and wondered if and when she'd get a chance to use it. During the ride they'd taken so far — running the horses hard most of the way — she'd had no opportunity.

Mariah was a good storyteller. She was also a skilled horsewoman. The entire way — gallop, trot, canter and walk — Mariah had kept the gun on her.

And Mariah knew a lot about marksmanship; she'd proven that.

"Yes, you grew up in Nashville. And your good-looking cousin is with the FBI. And you have a great house from your uncle, so naturally you just have to inherit another house from Marcus. And, of course, an agent comes out here with drop-dead looks and *of course* he immediately falls for you while . . . Never mind."

"What do you mean, never mind?"

"Don't pull any therapist bull on me, Olivia. You can't analyze an analyzer."

"Isn't it more like you can't con a con artist?" Olivia asked.

"Whatever. Give it up."

"Okay. I take it you plan on killing me, although that's pretty dumb. They'll know it's you."

"They arrested Sandra Cheever."

"And you think she'll go down alone?"

"I'll call her a liar. She had the motive. She was the one sleeping with Aaron."

"But she's in custody now, Mariah. She couldn't have done this. People will arrive at the Horse Farm. They'll find all the bodies you left strewn around — and they'll realize I'm missing."

"No one saw me. There are dozens of other people who might have done this," Mariah said.

"You're crazy. Aaron's dead. Drew and Sydney are half-dead. Sandra is in custody and —"

"Mason is out there somewhere and, God knows, I'd implicate that crazy old broad at the café."

"Key words, Mariah — crazy old broad *at the café.* She's always working, always surrounded by witnesses. When could she have done any of this? But the point is, if you're going to kill me . . . What started all this? Marcus was good to everyone. Why did you kill him?"

"I looked it up, Olivia. My great-great-

great-grandfather was born on this land. *I'm* entitled to it. The Horse Farm *had* to fail."

"So you could buy it?" Olivia asked incredulously.

"It's really my land. I have the right to it. I shouldn't even *have* to buy it — but I will."

"It was Marcus's family land — that's how he got it," Olivia said.

"Yeah, well, I went on one of those ancestry sites. And it led me back a bunch of generations. My great-great-whatever was Marcus's great-whatever's brother, which means I have just as much right to the land as he did. And then I wouldn't have to be a so-so therapist. I'd get to be a great hostess for a haunted bed-and-breakfast, and every night I'd give history and ghost tours."

"You're crazy."

"No." She shook her head. "It should have been so simple. Everyone should just have said, oh, how sad. Marcus Danby became a heroin-whore again and it proves that the whole therapy thing was a pile of bullshit. It would've been simple as hell."

Simple? The murder had been *simple?*

"But no . . . you wouldn't believe it. You dragged in the law, and then when the law here realized that yes, addicts do fall back, you just had to call your cousin. You know,

I was onto you — I knew as soon I saw Mr. Handsome Federal Agent walk in that you'd pulled some strings. Yeah, he needed therapy, my ass!"

"Sandra was in on it, though, right?" Olivia said. "I mean, you needed help, didn't you?"

"Sandra is an idiot!" Mariah snapped. "She wanted Marcus out of the way because she wanted Aaron running the place. She wanted Marcus's house, and she wanted Aaron in charge, and she wanted a raise. After that, she wanted the two of them to play house forever and ever. But then, when everything seemed to be coming together once Marcus was dead, it looked like the Horse Farm was going to survive! And Aaron was a jerk —"

"But Sandra just let you kill him?"

Mariah sighed. "Sandra might have been a bad choice as a helper — although she *should've* been good. She can be such a bitch, but she's really a total coward. And dumb! She actually thought what happened at the stream was an accident! I set up the image of the general so I could get all excited and create a diversion before Aaron was found. She didn't help me. She didn't even know. I didn't count on the ripped-up pieces of that cow being all over — they really did make me scream. And it meant I could leave the picture behind, which made everything that much more convincing."

Olivia stared at her. It was almost impossible to fathom the complexity of a deranged mind. The old cliché about method in madness occurred to her. "What . . . what about the darts?" she asked. "How did you come up with that?"

"Olivia, I have to tell you — the dart thing is just great. I make those little suckers myself. I add the tiny feathers and then they fly like a damn. They fall out at the slightest movement, which is another plus, and the concoction I put together is pretty impressive. You'd have to be looking for specific poisons to even hope to find them at autopsy. I learned all that from Drew and Sydney, by the way. They know how to mix stuff up because Marcus insisted they had to be prepared for animal emergencies at all times."

"Good to hear you're such a wonderful student," Olivia told her. "So, Sandra didn't know you were going to kill Aaron — but she gave you the key to his place, anyway?"

Mariah didn't answer.

"She didn't give you the key, did she? You took it and had a copy made."

"I did that months ago," Mariah said

proudly.

"So, Sandra's really innocent?" Olivia asked.

"No. Sandra innocent? Give me a break. She's totally conniving. She knew what I was going to do to Marcus. In fact, she told me that if I wanted to make it look like someone else was involved, I should take his horse — or hers. Depending on who I wanted to implicate." She giggled. "I would've taken Shiloh, but you were riding him that day. As far as Sandra's concerned — well, if this bit her in the butt, she deserved it."

Olivia reined in and turned around. "Where are we going?"

"Don't you know yet?"

"No, I don't."

Mariah smiled at her. "There's something I want from you — before you die, of course."

"What's that?"

"I want to see the general."

Olivia gaped at her.

"I know you've seen him. I should have that. And you can give it to me."

"Mariah, I'm trying to stay alive here, but —"

"Then don't lie."

"Ghosts were people, Mariah. They remain the real essence of the person they were."

"Spiritual crap, Olivia. Keep at it."

"Ghosts don't just appear on command!" Olivia felt the gun against her waist. There *had* to be a chance for her to use it. Maybe now . . .

By the time she drew it out, she'd be dead.

"Keep moving and quit stalling."

"Why? Because you know it's all over? That someone will come searching for the two of us."

"If they do, we'll go out together," Mariah promised her sweetly. She smiled. "You're always telling the kids to do their best — to reach for what they want and work hard to achieve it. I'm just listening to you, Olivia. So, keep moving. We're almost there."

They rode again and came to the point in the copse where they had to dismount so they could walk the trail to the cemetery.

"Do you think the general's going to hang around his grave?" Olivia asked.

"You'd better hope," Mariah muttered. "Now, get down."

Olivia dismounted. Mariah waved the gun she was carrying.

"Move."

Olivia followed the trail to the small cemetery where General Rufus Cunningham's mortal remains lay buried. It was still daylight, but the surrounding trees shaded them from the sun.

The cemetery, situated in the shadow of the forest, was touched by traces of sunlight. It was difficult to tell if anyone had used the trail leading to the cemetery in the past hour or so. Although there were a few signs of recent use, he couldn't be sure. Still, as they neared the small collection of graves, Dustin became convinced that he was right — and that Jimmy Callahan had been right, as well.

He reined in before they came to the clearing in the woods. Behind him, Malachi and Abby stopped, too.

He slid down from Chapparal and walked back to Malachi. "There are some broken branches here that seem fresh. I think they dismounted a short distance ahead and walked to the cemetery. There's really only one main trail. I'm going to crawl through some of the trees and bushes to approach from the other side." He hesitated. "If I get a clean shot at Mariah . . ."

"Take it," Malachi told him. "I intend to do the same. Abby and I will tether the horses and come up along the old trail."

Dustin tried to move as quietly as possible

— and as quickly as possible.

He thought of the different situations he'd faced in his life.

This was just one woman.

One crazy-ass woman with a gun — a gun she was pointing at Olivia.

He paused, stepping on bracken and expecting to hear the crack of a branch. But he heard nothing. Until, moving forward, he heard voices.

"Olivia, I'm from this land — don't you get it? This land right here. You're from the city."

"And don't *you* get it, Mariah? It's all connected. The city needs the country, the country needs the city. Look, if you want to see the general . . . you have to be open to him. And he has to be in the area."

Malachi finally came up on the cemetery. He hid behind one of the trees that grew around the little area, as if they were nature's homage to the dead.

They were at the general's grave site.

Mariah had Olivia by the arm. Her gun was wedged into Olivia's side. He could take a shot; he could kill her easily. But there was no guarantee she'd go down before she pulled her own trigger.

Mariah suddenly swung Olivia around. Dustin could see that she was sweating, agitated. The hand that held the gun against Olivia was jerky. The trigger might be pulled easily.

"Where is he?" Mariah demanded.

They were looking right at his position, right at where he stood. Dustin straightened his cavalry jacket and pulled the plumed hat he wore lower over his forehead.

"Mariah," Olivia said. "I told you — I've tried to explain. Ghosts don't appear on command. They exist, and if you're just open to them —"

"I've spent my life being open to the general!" Mariah shouted. "He's part of me, part of my soul, my existence! You've got ten seconds, Olivia — ten seconds!"

Olivia suddenly spun around, jerking something out from under her shirt. She fumbled with it; Mariah, thrown from her, fired.

Thankfully, the shot went wild.

Olivia fired, too. The recoil sent her falling back and she tripped, crashing into a tombstone, the gun flying from her grasp. Mariah stumbled to her feet and half walked, half crawled over to Olivia, rising with the gun aimed directly at her.

"Miss Mariah!" Dustin said in a hollow voice, stepping from the trees.

Tension knotted in him fiercely; he was

no actor.

"Miss Mariah!"

Mariah turned and looked at him. For a moment, she stared at him in awe. Then she smiled and slowly raised her gun. "You're not a ghost!" she said. "But good try, Agent Blake."

"I'm not alone, Mariah. If you fire that gun, you're going to go down in a hail of bullets."

She aimed at Olivia again. "She goes with me," Mariah said.

Dustin felt something touch him — or almost touch him. He closed his eyes, praying that the real general had come. A man seemed to rise from mist and take shape before him.

It wasn't the general. It was Marcus Danby.

"I am a ghost, Mariah. I'm a ghost because you killed me. And because you tried to ruin the good that honest, caring people were doing. You won't join me, Mariah, when you die. I'm not sure what lies beyond this — where I am now — but I know you won't be there. I can feel sun and light — and all you can feel is darkness."

Mariah's gun remained on Olivia. She frowned, as if trying to ascertain how they'd created the illusion she was seeing.

Someone else stepped forward, entering into the green shadows of the little cemetery.

Aaron.

"We tried to get the general to come, Mariah," Aaron said. "But he doesn't want to know you."

"This is bullshit!" Mariah cried. She turned to take aim at Olivia again.

Dustin moved as he'd never moved before. He was out of the trees as if he were propelled by a sudden spark of fire. He caught Mariah in a tackle and brought her down, rolling with her.

She was strong; they fought for the gun.

A shot went off and Mariah screamed in agony. Dustin tried to wrench her gun from her but it eluded them both and landed several feet away. But the woman had been shot — and he realized that Olivia had recovered her own gun and managed to fire off a round.

Despite the fact that she was bleeding, Mariah strained to reach her weapon. Yet she suddenly went still and Dustin struggled with her weight, trying to move around her. And then he saw what she saw.

The general had come. He stood with his foot on the gun.

"Not on this land!" he said. "Not on this land. Cruelty and murder will not happen, not on my land."

Dustin inched forward; his fingers grasped the weapon and he threw Mariah off him. She huddled in a ball, sobbing.

Malachi burst into the cemetery with Abby at his side.

"It's done," the general said.

And he faded away. The ghost of Marcus Danby grinned and saluted Dustin, then faded, too.

Aaron, also, was gone. Malachi had rushed to his cousin's side, while Abby assessed Mariah's injuries.

Dustin turned quickly to reach Olivia. She was hugging Malachi, but she pulled away and smiled tremulously at him.

"You'd make a horrible reenactor," she said.

"Yeah, I know. I'm sorry. You, uh, need to learn how to shoot," he told her.

She nodded. "I guess I do."

She was shaking, but she appeared to be all right. She didn't even seem traumatized. "The others?" she asked.

"Ambulances came pretty quickly to the Horse Farm. Sloan and Jane were already up. You managed to get the darts out of them?" he asked her.

She nodded. She started to take a step, but she wasn't walking very well. He stopped her, looked into her eyes and muttered, "Oh, the hell with it."

Then he swept her into his arms and headed out on the trail, leaving the shadows of the dead behind — and Malachi and Abby to deal with Mariah.

EPILOGUE

Mariah Naughton proved to be full of surprises — and her last surprise was especially dramatic.

She never reached a hospital, and she never explained her entire story. They had to piece together what they could from Jimmy Callahan, who'd been dating Mariah, and from Sandra Cheever, who was willing to do anything to get the D.A. to deal with her as leniently as possible.

What happened in the end was because Mariah had no intention of leaving "her" land. She had used a gun on Olivia, but she'd still had a supply of poisoned darts. Frank Vine arrived at the cemetery to arrest her, but before he could cuff her, she managed to use her poisons on herself — in a greater dose than she'd used on anyone else. Frank radioed for a helicopter; it came, but Mariah was pronounced dead on arrival.

Olivia tried to feel something for her. She

couldn't. She knew she should have sympathy for someone who'd lived with such a disturbed, tormented mind. She worked constantly with people who had issues and problems; she understood the addict and triggers and . . .

One day, she thought, she'd forgive Mariah. But it wouldn't be for a long time.

The Horse Farm was a shambles. Mariah had set out to destroy it and she'd done an effective job. It would be hard to convince others of the good that had existed, now that Marcus, Aaron and Mariah were dead and Sandra Cheever was busy working out a plea bargain.

But on Wednesday morning, when she sat with the Krewe members and her Horse Farm team in the office, she was determined.

"We're fired," Drew said dully. "I understand."

"Of course," Sydney said.

"No. We'll close our doors for about a week, but we're actually in a sound financial situation. Of course, we can't use our reserves forever or we'll be left with no choice but to move on."

"So what will we do?" Mason asked.

She pointed a finger at him. "Mason, you're gorgeous — yes, we all know that and you could probably have a future as an actor or model. But you're also a good therapist. You'll be our new director."

"*You're* director," he said.

"I'll be an absentee director," she told him. "You'll take over as acting director. Sydney and Drew, if you don't mind, you'll continue sharing responsibilities as stable managers and horse masters."

"But —" Drew began.

"I've already spoken with Mrs. Lockwood — Brent's mother. He's going to come back. Apparently he cries because he's afraid he won't be able to see us again. I spoke to Brent myself. He says he likes me best, but that's okay, he'll work with you."

"Well, um, thanks," Mason said, still confused.

"I've also spoken with Patty Sobles. Remember her? She's one of the local women we work with. Anyway, she's coming back. I've been on the phone with the parents of the kids at Parsonage House. They'll give us another chance. As I said, we won't open our doors for a week. Aaron deserves a good funeral with all of us at it, and Mariah . . . Well, we have to see that she's buried, too. I don't think she had any family left — maybe that's why the land meant so much to her. Mason, you're going to have to find a few more therapists. Oh, we're going to steal Ellie Villiers from Willis House to run the office. She was only part-time there and she's looking for full-time work. Mason, you'll move into Marcus's old house — that'll save you from paying rent. I'll just have you guys check on my place now and then, make sure everything's all right."

"So, you will come back?" Drew asked hopefully.

"I'll always come back," she replied. "Tennessee is my home. These hills are my home. We all have the right and even the responsibility to love the place that's our home, to love our heritage. Mariah just let it consume her. But, yes, I will come back as often as I can."

Sydney rose, rolling his hat in his hands as he did when he was a little nervous about what he was going to say. He looked at Dustin. "You treat her right, you understand? Your intentions had better be honorable!"

"The most honorable," Dustin promised him. "Don't worry — I work with her cousin."

Sydney smiled and sat down again.

"This will work," Olivia said. "The Horse Farm will survive. *We* will survive — all of us. Marcus Danby was an incredible man who did incredible things — and the Horse

Farm will continue to rescue animals and we'll continue to do our best to rescue people, as well. Just as Marcus always did."

She smiled as everyone in the room applauded. "Thank you," she said softly. "I —"

"I don't get it," Mason broke in. "Where will you be?"

"Virginia," she said. "I'm going to the FBI Academy and I'll take what I know in a different direction. But I'll just be a phone call away."

"What?" Mason said. "You — you . . . you don't even *like* guns!"

"And I never will. However, I'll learn how to use one," she told him.

The room was silent. Then Mason stood up and came over to hug her. "I realize you do have other talents," he murmured. "And we'd be selfish if we didn't think you should use them." He cleared his throat and stepped back, looking at the other agents in the room. He nodded shrewdly. "I read up on you people. And I know what your talents are. And . . . Well, I guess we have to let Olivia go."

Olivia hugged Mason again, and then Drew and Sydney. Abby announced that she had Delilah bringing over a feast — and that today they'd celebrate the lives of Marcus

Danby and Aaron Bentley and all they'd tried to do for others.

It was a nice afternoon. Olivia caught Dustin's eye across the room; he and Sloan had been talking horses, since she intended to bring Shiloh and Chapparal to Virginia, and Sloan had the land and the stables to house them until she and Dustin could make other arrangements.

Sammy ran around the room woofing happily.

There were so many people there to pet him and make a fuss over him. But Sammy, too, would be moving.

Malachi and the others had to get back the next day, but Olivia needed to stay behind to deal with various legal matters.

Dustin stayed with her.

And so, a week later, the day before the horse trailers were ready and before she let Mason take over, Olivia and Dustin rode out to the campground. The weather was growing a little brisk, but they still played in the stream and made love beneath the moon.

When they rode back, they stopped at the cemetery where the general was buried. There was a fresh bullet hole gouging his tombstone, and Dustin looked at it regretfully.

"I don't think he'll mind," Olivia said.

"Probably not. Do you think he's still here? What about Marcus and Aaron?" Dustin asked her.

"I think Marcus and Aaron have moved on," she said. "I've thought about it over the past few days. They did a lot of good while they were alive. All right, so Aaron wasn't terribly bright in his choice of love interest, but he was a decent guy. He didn't kill himself and we proved that. He and Marcus can both move on and I hope there is a heaven. They deserve to reach it."

Dustin gnawed on a piece of grass and smiled, gazing up at the beautiful green overhang. "The general deserves his piece of heaven, too, but . . . I think he sees these hills as his heaven."

"I think so, too," Olivia agreed. "Do *you* believe in heaven?" she asked him.

He pulled her into his arms. "Every time I see your face," he said.

He kissed her.

And Olivia was certain that whatever spirits roamed the hills, dales and forests of Tennessee, they looked on and approved.

ABOUT THE AUTHOR

New York Times bestselling author **Heather Graham** has written more than one hundred fifty novels and novellas, has been published in nearly twenty-five languages, and has over seventy-five million copies in print. An avid scuba diver, ballroom dancer, and mother of five, she still enjoys her south Florida home, but loves to travel as well. Reading, however, is the pastime she still loves best, and is a member of many writing groups. For more information, check out her Web site, theoriginalheathergraham .com.